THE KISS LIST

MAYA HUGHES

Cover Design: Najla Qamber

Cover Photographer: Aldrin Paul Del Carmen

For everyone who knows the family you find can be the family you keep

1

COLE

It wasn't even six a.m. yet and I was already dead meat. At my desk, I patted my coat pockets. "Shit." My whisper sounded like a shout in the quiet, but damnit. Being late for practice wasn't an option. I dug through a pile of clothes beside my closet, moving aside still sweat-soggy clothes, and crawled under my bed using my phone light. Nothing. Downstairs, I dug through my duffel by the front door before tossing the threadbare couch cushions. Not even the buzzing fridge was safe from my search.

No keys. What the hell? Coach would kill me and anyone in my vicinity if I wasn't suited up on time.

In the living room, I dragged my hands through my hair. Outside in the dawn dimness, streetlights flickered off. At the curb my headlights winked, steam billowed from the back of my car.

Irritation rocketed through me. "Damn." I snatched my bag off the floor, rushed out the door and down the porch steps.

The sleeping campus and rising sun screamed, "you're late." A few insane morning runners who couldn't help tempt the February ice-patch gods jogged down the center of the street.

Salty slush crunched under my shoes.

I slammed into my car, dumping my bag into the backseat. "Assholes, I spent the past fifteen minutes looking for my keys."

Next to me, Hollis rested against the passenger seat window. "We knew you'd figure it out eventually."

Ezra was spread out in the back with his hat tugged down low over his eyes. "We didn't think it would take this much time. Now we're almost late."

I wanted to call them assholes again, instead I revved my engine, pulled out of my spot, and headed down the deserted street. Approaching the light, my tires slid a bit, but not too bad.

"Just run it," Hollis grumbled.

"So the campus cops can write me a ticket?" I cruised to a stop, drummed my fingers, and yawned.

"Do you really think they'll write you a ticket?" He cracked an eye.

"They report infractions to Mikelson."

"We're going to be late."

"I'm not—"

"Just go." Ezra nudged at the back of my seat.

"Fine." I checked both directions, rolled ahead.

A bike darted into the crosswalk.

The rider grazed the bumper of my car.

I slammed on the brakes, the tires crunched and slid, and we all lurched forward.

The biker swerved and shouted a string of expletives fit for the locker room.

The steering wheel bit into my chest.

The almost flattened bike rider hopped off their bike,

leaving it in front of the car, ripped off his helmet—her helmet.

My stomach knotted and I slammed my eyes shut. The perfect start to another perfect day.

"Are you fucking kidding me?" Kennedy smacked her hands on the hood.

I sank lower in my seat.

"Cole." Her eyes narrowed, face flooded with fury. "I should've known it would be you."

"Oh shit." Ezra's knees jammed into my back. He shifted away from my side, and the car rocked.

"You almost hit her. She doesn't look happy."

"No shit."

Hollis snapped his eyes shut again. Ezra folded his arms over his chest with his hat tugged so low it almost touched the tip of his nose.

"You two are going to hang me out to dry?"

"No sense in us all dying today," Ezra grumbled from the back, keeping his lips still.

She braced her hands on the hood. "There's no one on the road and you try to mow me down."

I rolled down my window. "Like I'd go out of my way to hit you. I didn't mean to. Didn't even see you."

She stormed around to the driver's side. "Then maybe you've taken too many hits to the head."

My fingers tightened on the steering wheel. Sure, I'd almost killed her, but that didn't make Kennedy any less of a pain in the ass. The clock was still ticking to get to practice. "Sorry, okay? Now move your bike."

I swore fire glinted in her green eyes.

She leaned her head in my window. "You nearly kill me and all you have to say is move your bike?"

"I did throw a sorry in there. We've got to get to practice."

Her gaze ripped from mine, to Hollis, to Ezra. "Saving all the brain cells for the field?" She folded her arms.

I swallowed and snapped my gaze from her chest. Even under the black peacoat, she was more than a handful, not that I needed to leave that to my imagination. Six months back, I'd had a front row seat. Before I blew it—literally. "Wouldn't want to spare those brain cells in a conversation with you, that's for sure."

Seething, her gaze switched to piercing. Those daggers were sharp. "Do you have any idea how much I hate you?"

I smiled and leaned my arm out the window just to piss her off. "Not as much as I hate you."

Her eyes sparked like a fuse had been lit behind them.

My grin went real. Mission accomplished. She'd once looked at me with a much different type of heat in her eyes, but that felt like eons ago from where we were now. And where I really needed to be, which was practice.

Another car blew through the still unchanged light.

"Gotta go." I threw the car into reverse and back into drive, skirting around her downed bike.

Her curse-filled shouts punched through the still, dawn quiet and against every bit of reason rolling around in my head, I checked the rearview mirror.

She flipped me off, picked up her bike, hopped back on. Why the hell was she out this early in the morning?

Which could've run to more thoughts about her, could've had me stopping, going back, and asking. Instead, I pulled into the practice-field parking lot with time to spare. The relief was short-lived.

A dozen guys trudged through the practice-field gates. The lot was filled with cars and the zombie-like bodies of other players headed into what had to be the worst practice we'd have all season after our stunt making Mikelson look like the ass he truly was in front of the whole campus.

My stomach knotted, my leg bounced. My muscles were already tight waiting for the expectation of pain to take hold. Practice always meant pain. A lot of pain. The pain would be doubled, tripled, multiplied by a thousand.

The three of us followed the others into the silent locker room. Nobody high-fived, nobody spoke, nobody whispered.

A couple guys looked almost green, the weight of what we'd brought down on us hitting home now. A dozen guys waited for the guillotine drop. Standing up for Reid during his declaration of love to Leona, in front of everyone, including her dad, the university president, had felt good at the moment. The solidarity meant we were safe from all getting cut.

Now, retribution loomed.

The equipment team had everything out for us, ready to change. No sounds other than the rustling of cloth, snapping buttons, and the thwip of laces. But Mikelson didn't come in. Uneasiness rolled through me, churned my stomach, and soaked my hands in sweat.

As a group, we left the locker room headed for the practice field.

Mikelson waited. Clipboard in hand, he had an almost serene look on his face. Toward the back of the squad, a teammate puked. The retching and cold splatter of bile lightened Mikelson's expression even more. We were beyond screwed.

Ninety minutes of laps, drills, sprints, and burpees later my shoulders screamed and my stomach ejected what little was left into a trash can beside Reid and Hollis. I gripped the plastic rim. This was only the beginning. Then again, I was more conditioned to Coach Mikelson's "teaching" philosophy than anyone else.

Guys lifted themselves up off the ground, sat if they couldn't stand.

On the sidelines, Mikelson's air of self-satisfaction choked the oxygen from the wide-open practice field. "You all want to be smart-asses." He used his playbook to emphasize his point. "You don't get to be smart-asses if I don't have another trophy on my shelf." He whipped his arm out in the direction of his office. "When it's up there nice and shiny with its brand-new spotlight, then you get to think about besting me." He slammed the clipboard down over his knee. The thin particle board snapped, spraying brown shards all over the frosted grass. "Until then, I hope you liked me easing you into how things will go during the off-season."

A ripple of unrest rolled over the guys beside me. This was only the beginning. He'd make us pay for as long as he could before we broke.

He charged back inside, leaving the support staff to peel us off the field.

In the locker room, the equipment team took our gear and after showers the physio team directed guys to ice baths, deep tissue, teeth-gnashing massages, and doled out ice packs and ace bandages. They patched us up as best as they could.

Hollis sat on the padded bench in front of his locker with his head in his hands. "Did you ever think it would be like this?" Both his knees were wrapped up with ice.

Ezra straightened his leg. "Feeling like your joints are ready to give out just past twenty-one?"

"Or puking after every practice?" I rotated my shoulder, winced, and adjusted my bag of ice.

"Both." Hollis lifted his head and huffed.

Down the way, Reid rubbed his towel over his head. "Come on, guys." Remorse and exhaustion dulled his eyes. "Just think of how much we'll miss all this next year." He cracked a smile and tried to lift our spirits. "The rising seniors will be doing all this shit, and we'll be waiting for the draft." His smile spread dreamy-wide.

I wanted to slap him, but I was also happy he was happy. "A big, fat paycheck will make it all worth it." Freezing rivulets of water traveled down the front of my shoulder and tickled my ribs.

"The paycheck will be the cherry on top, but when we're not playing together"—Reid pulled on his shirt with a wince—"I'll miss you."

I closed my eyes, trying to keep my lungs inside my body. "Who said we won't be?"

Ezra kicked off his cleats. "The odds of that are astronomical."

"Maybe, but there's always hope." Reid took off, likely to meet Leona.

They were lucky they found each other and were willing to jump straight over the roadblocks being together created. I wasn't sure anything could be worth that risk.

I pulled on my jeans, and could barely lace my sneakers. Reid was right of course. This might be brutal, but this was our last off-season before heading into our final season next school year. The last time we'd all be together. It sucked. And it didn't suck. It was complicated. I had no clue how I really felt.

Except hungry. Punishment, pain, hunger. That was the combo we did after every practice.

"He's disgustingly in love with her." Back in the car,

Hollis traced a heart in the condensation in the back window.

I turned the nose of my trusty Civic. Reid was lucky. He'd found someone who made all the other horrible shit going on fade into the background. I'd never met anyone I'd been willing to put it all on the line for. I slid to a stop at the same red light I'd almost killed Kennedy at. I'd never been that lucky and probably never would be.

2

KENNEDY

After four hours of moving boxes, cleaning shelves, counting books, and a fifteen-minute bike ride home—not to mention almost getting killed this morning—all I wanted to do was sleep. Sleep. Sleep.

Extra shifts were always welcome, but I swear I was hallucinating. Like how I thought Cole looked cute in his car after, you know, almost mowing me down. My scholarship money was just enough to pay rent and buy my books for next year. I swear they both cost the same. If only I could create a shelter out of textbooks and save half the money.

One janky elevator ride up to the apartment, a quick shower, and a liquid breakfast, my eyes were cotton-ball dry. The apartment was freezing, but I was too tired to worry about that now and dragged myself into my room.

Next door, sound escalated. At first muffled, then full on screaming. Loud enough for me to hear the cadence, but not individual words.

My whole body tensed. The buzzing hit the tips of my fingertips.

Our neighbors—the roommates from hell, shouting at each other all hours of the day and night. It was how they communicated. Always at decibels never considered acceptable for a normal conversation. Why they continued to be roommates was nothing short of insanity. We'd tried to intervene for the first few months, pulling each of them aside to make sure everything was okay. That was when both launched into a shouting match with Melody. They say no good deed goes unpunished.

It was too early for this shit. I grabbed my headphones and popped them on to drown out the noise and loosen the knot forming in my stomach that made me want to jump from the bed and leave although I was dead tired. But eventually I drifted off.

Burritoed in my quilt, I closed my eyes.

Yes, sleep.

My door slammed open. "Kennedy?" Melody burst into my room after my eyelids felt like they'd barely touched. "I know you're tired, but I'm freaking out. It's a fashion emergency."

"Kennedy to the rescue." I closed my eyes for one more second and shimmied my arms out of my blanket cocoon, scrubbed my hands over my face and yawned so loudly my jaw popped. Another day closer to graduation, a real job, real money, and the real-world problems.

Melody fidgeted inside my room with her gym bag on her shoulder. She didn't know I'd only gotten home—I checked my phone—twenty minutes ago.

"You want me to help you pick out your outfit for your date tonight, don't you?" I rubbed my neck trying to massage out the sore muscles.

She rolled her shoulders forward and bit both of her thumbs nodding. "I know you had a shift this morning, and

I know you still need to get ready for class, but you'll be gone all day and then you have Taylor's party later, so this is my only chance."

I unrolled myself from the blanket, sad to be leaving the warm comfort behind when the freezing air slapped into me. "You know I normally charge $50 for this," I teased.

"But I'm your favorite roommate, so you'll let me have another freebie."

I propped my hands up on my hips. "No."

Her smile slid off her face.

"I'll let you have a freebie because you're my best friend."

She bounced on her heels. "You're the best."

I yawned and covered my mouth with both hands. "You get coffee and take out what you're thinking of and I'll come in and work my magic."

She nodded and rushed back out.

At my closet, I grabbed my black jeans and boots. From my drawer, I took out a gray cowl neck sweater. I threw everything on and put on a bracelet and earrings and headed over to Melody's room.

"Damnit, Kennedy."

I froze at her door. "What? What happened?"

"I left you like five minutes ago while you were still drooling in your bed and you walk in here looking ready for a photo shoot."

My body relaxed and I rolled my eyes. "Hardly. I'm not even wearing makeup." I jabbed my finger toward her. "And I don't drool."

She folded her arms over her chest with a smile. "You're

trying to make me hate you more. You look more pulled together without makeup five minutes after waking up from a nap than I do when I'm trying my best."

"It's called practice." I walked to her bed, shivering and pulling my sweater tighter around myself and scanned the pieces she'd laid out. Cold forced air blasted my face. "I think it's warmer outside." I shivered and ran my hands up and down my arms.

She sipped from her mug and handed me one. "The front desk said they'll knock $50 off our rent until they get it fixed."

"Wow, a whole $50. It should be free." I ran my hands over the steam wisps rising from the top.

"I nominate you to fight that battle." She air tapped her spoon against both my shoulders with a haughty queen's tone.

Frustration swamped me. "I'm sick of fighting battles. Just once I'd like someone to ride in and fight one for me. I'm a strong, independent badass, but maybe I'd like a half second where I didn't need to be."

She peeked through her mini blinds.

"What are you looking for?"

"A knight on horseback." She scanned the street below. "Nope, sorry. Fresh out of knights, so your damsel's going to have to take charge for a while longer."

"Or your damsel can take the lead." I blew on the dark roast coffee and sipped it.

Melody shuddered. "How can you drink it black? I put a pound of sugar and half a pint of creamer in mine."

I shrugged. "Those aren't always available, so I got used to drinking it this way. I notice how you totally evaded my suggestion you go talk to the property manager."

"Why would I when you're so good at winning them over? You walk into a room and everyone's all tongues hanging out of their head and ready to do your bidding. Why do you need a knight when you're a one-woman fairy godmother?"

I flinched. Sometimes fake it 'til you make it worked a little too well and without the actual making it part. "Fine, I'll go talk to him, but if he starts the puppy-dog routine, you'll be running interference for me in the lobby. Plus, you have to handle all the cooking for the next week. Now, show me what you've got. Which piece do you love most?"

She shrugged. "I like them all."

"But which one do you love. Or which one makes you feel best or most confident or most beautiful."

She stared at the bed. "None? They fit, they look fine, and I own them. That's how I feel about them."

"You're killing me, Mel. We've been roommates since August and you're just now telling me you don't own anything you love?" If I didn't love it, it didn't go into my closet. Why wear stuff you hated rather than clothes that made you smile? Sometimes it meant I didn't have much or I'd have to go thrifting or bargain hunting for longer than most people, but I'd rather mix and match the same ten pieces than shove myself into something I hated wearing.

Mentally, I flicked through her closet. "What about that plaid skirt you wore during classes in the first week of September?"

"You remember specific dates I wore my clothes?"

I tapped the side of my head. "It's a gift."

She rummaged through her closet, held it up and ran her hand down the side of it. "This one."

Perfect! I took it from her. "You love this skirt."

"But it's too cold to wear it. I'll be walking around with frost bite on my lips and I'm not talking about up here." She waved at her face.

A burst of air shot through my lips and I dissolved into full laughter at the look on her face. "Trust me, I'll make sure you're warm enough to keep the frostbite from taking you out."

Ten minutes later, her outfit of the skirt she loved, tights, boots, and a sweater were ready for her date tonight. "When's Taylor's party?"

"After my shift at the bookstore." My feet felt heavy thinking about it, but then I remembered the shimmery green top I'd found a few weeks ago and the gray boots that hadn't been worn nearly as much as they deserved. A killer outfit. Recharge ready.

We chatted accessories before I ducked into the bathroom to complete my makeup.

After a few brush strokes, I stood taller. Makeup and the clothes weren't to make me look better, but mainly to feel better. They were my armor against the world and I rarely went anywhere without it.

"Want to go early tonight?" Melody stood in the bathroom door behind me.

I swept my mascara wand over my lashes. "Can't. I go straight from class to the bookstore."

"Weren't you there this morning?"

"More shifts equals more money. Do you want to be stuck in the same place next year?"

"Good point." She twirled her keys on her finger. "See you later."

"Bye." I finished up and got my notebooks and laptop packed away.

After a not so quick stop down at the property manager's office where the guy kept trying to peek down my shirt, I headed to class with reassurances that the heat would be fixed by the end of the week.

Kennedy to the rescue—again.

3

KENNEDY

Yawning so widely I hoped my jaw didn't lock, I walked from the bus stop toward Taylor's party.

My body buzzed with nerves shooting off like misfiring fireworks. This is for Taylor. This is for Taylor. I repeated the mantra. Too bad I'd most likely run into Cole tonight. Going to his house made that possibility sky high although I'd been avoiding him successfully for months— until our run-in this morning.

On his street, competing music vibrated the air, drunken laughter, screams, and droves of students spilled out onto the sidewalks from all the three-floor apartment blocks and brick-and-wood multicolored townhouses for as far as I could see.

The housing here had been too expensive to swing this year. Maybe, if I got more styling clients, plus my bookstore shifts, next year Melody, Ashley, Taylor, Leona, and I could split one of these houses.

I hurried down the street although curling up on the roof of someone's car or porch steps weren't out of the question. The dry, freezing air at least helped me stay upright with the needles of cold stabbing me in the face.

The tip of my nose pulsed like a glowing beacon. Ice and slush crunched under each step. Riding the campus bus hadn't been my first choice, but Melody couldn't drive me, and I wasn't going to ride my bike drunk. And I planned on getting at least a little lit up tonight.

People leaned against the railings and sat on the steps. Some smoked, some shivered, some screamed the fight song to other party porches. Some just needed a bitingly cold escape from the heat of their house and basement parties. Each massive house was split in half with a porch at the front. The houses ranged from run-down to charming.

A guy I'd hung out with before, Mitchell, jumped off a porch. I sidestepped. A huge splash of his beer splattered the front of my boots.

"Ack." I gave him my best glare. "Are you fucking kidding me?"

I'd gone out with him once. Correction: I'd given him a chance to prove he was more than a pretty face. A please-don't-talk-to-me prayer running through my head, I hurried past.

"Sorry." He looked sheepish, but he wasn't. "Hey, Kennedy."

I sighed and squeezed my gloved hands in my pockets. Hook up with a guy once, and you're on the hook for a long time. "Hey, how've you been?" I didn't stop, but he hopped in front of me.

He'd been nice, but our night wasn't exactly memorable. "Better, now that you're here." His cheeks were flushed and he stood so close his breath cloud mingled with mine. "You coming in?"

"Going to Taylor's birthday party." I shrugged like I was

helpless against the birthday gods. I'd have had to be a lot drunker to even entertain a peck from him let alone kiss him again.

He glanced down the street. "At The Zoo?"

"You know how much she loves football. It seemed appropriate."

"Once you're done there, I wouldn't mind being a little inappropriate with you." He grabbed for my ass.

My vision narrowed and I spun on my heels. "Not tonight." Not ever. I walked away. On the porches and stairs, people watched like they'd never seen a guy get shot down before. Sorry, I wasn't hard up for attention and didn't need to settle for a blah make-out partner.

Mitchell marched up the steps like a lost puppy. It cooled little of my anger. At least he hadn't gone into aggressive, chase-me-down mode.

"Kennedy! We've got a beer pong table with your name on it," Josh shouted from his porch across the street.

"Not in this outfit." I waved. Maybe...but not tonight. Josh had at least put in a little effort, unlike Mitchell back there.

Leona, Ashley, and Taylor were the only reason I was out tonight. Taylor's birthday was a can't-miss. Too bad it's happening at The Zoo aka the Pigsty aka Cole's house, the location of my humiliation.

A tickle of treachery tightened in my stomach thinking about him. After everything, those hints of feelings were still there. Apparently, I was a glutton for punishment. Straightening my shoulders, I strolled down the street. I didn't care about Cole. I'd never cared about Cole.

He didn't want me. Good, I didn't want him either.

"ST!" someone shouted half a block away.

"FU!" someone else screamed back, but I wasn't sure if

they were completing the chant or just pissed that someone was bellowing. Drunken STFU chants were volleyed back and forth across and down the street.

It was at the green townhouse where the people screamed even louder and crowded the porch as well as the sidewalk and small patch of grass next to the curb.

I climbed the stairs to The Zoo, tension gripped my spine. The porch swayed under the weight of all the party-goers. This was my first time back here since *the* night. The night Cole had made it embarrassingly apparent how not interested he was in me the second I took off my clothes.

The driving music rumbled gently beneath my feet, but not deafening like in some of the houses I'd passed.

Straightening my shoulders, I caught a sliver of my reflection in the windows. A perfect college-party look. I armored up with more gloss, pushed open the already cracked door and stepped inside.

Driving pop melodies and rap lyrics flooded the air. From across the room, Ashley waved her hands above her head. In her STFU hoodie, sneakers, and jeans, she'd done her version of dressing up.

I moved away from the door and headed into the crowd and damn...

Cole stopped on the last step, midlaugh. He looked at me with surprise-wide eyes. "What are you doing here?"

I pointed at the pink glittery Happy Birthday Taylor! banner hanging from the ceiling. An excessive amount of glitter rained down on people dancing under it.

His jaw clenched.

My teeth gritted before I snapped back to pleasant, pasting on a shiny smile. "Thanks for welcoming me into your wonderful home, Cole." I poured my syrupy sweet sarcasm straight down his throat.

He stepped back and scanned the room over my head from the spot on the last step, like he didn't want to get too close. "Whatever."

"Where's—"

A body slammed into me and arms wrapped around my neck so tightly it was hard to breathe. "You're here," Leona drunk screamed, her long black hair stuck to my lips.

I jerked back, fishing her strands from my lipstick and shook with laughter. "I'm here. I said I'd be here."

She let go of my neck, but not her arm lock. Her semifocused eyes, flushed cheeks, and a molar-exposing grin were signs she'd started pre-gaming before the sun went down. "I was worried." She swallowed like she'd sprinted across the house to get to me and prevent a murder.

"No need."

From how far Reid trailed behind her, she probably had sprinted. He waved.

"Hey, Reid."

"Nice to see you." Reid took Leona's hand, unlocking her arms from around me.

"Thanks for the invite." They were a cute couple—if you were into that sort of thing. Dating, long-term relationships, putting your still beating heart out on your sleeve to be potentially crushed.

Cole finally joined us on the floor, not from his perch on the steps. "Like Taylor wouldn't fight to have you here, just like she fought to have her party in our house."

I rankled under the intensity of his gaze. "Decided to join the peasants down here?"

"Something like that." He gulped the rest of his drink and shook the empty. "Anyone need another drink?"

"Me!" I raised my hand high, straining and jumping up

and down. He could be my errand boy all night, although there was a chance he'd spit in my drink.

"Anyone except for Kennedy." He looked from face to face avoiding mine.

I smiled wider. "What's the matter, Cole? Can't get up the strength to carry that many drinks?" Maybe it wasn't only in the bedroom he was lacking. Maybe it carried over to other areas of his life and I hoped the look I gave him spelled out everything going on in my head right now. I let my gaze drift to his package and snap back up to his face just in case I'd been too subtle.

His jaw tightened.

I lowered my hand and batted my eyelashes. A snort of a laugh escaped. Target hit.

"Why don't I serve it to you out on the porch?" He stepped closer.

Flames licked at the edges of my vision. The fact that he thought he could intimidate me only made it that much more fun to piss him off.

"Hey, you two." Leona slipped between us and pushed us apart. "It's Taylor's party. Can we not have bloodshed and get it all over the cake?"

"What kind of cake?" I didn't take my eyes off him. He wouldn't win.

Cole scoffed and rolled his eyes.

A bolt of fury flowed through me. "Do you have a problem, Cole?" My pulse pounded in my ears.

"You know I do."

Fuck him. Did I like cake? Who the hell didn't? I wasn't going to let him make me feel bad about enjoying every damn bite.

Leona pressed her palms against both our chests, attempting to put some space between us and not get squashed. "Come on, you two. It's a few hours. You can play nice for a few hours," she pleaded. "Don't talk to each other. Don't look at each other. Just stay far away from each other and pretend the other isn't here."

"For you, Leona." I dragged my glare off Cole and inspected my home manicure. "I'll treat him like furniture. Droopy, soggy furniture no one would ever want to go near."

Two hundred ten pounds of muscle, a steel jaw, and blazing blue eyes, he lurched forward.

I swallowed, not scared in the least, but this was the closest we'd been since that night.

His looks were certainly not the letdown he'd been in the bedroom, but they were still killer.

I leaned in. "Did you have something to say?" I cupped my hand around my ear.

With a quick scan of my face, he whipped around and marched off.

Leona dropped her hands. "Do you have to tease him so much?"

I shrugged. "I wouldn't do it if it wasn't so easy to push all his buttons." Too bad he didn't want to find mine.

"Are you sure there's nothing between you two?" she asked, her tone skeptical and her eyebrows pinched together.

My heart rocketed into my throat and I scoffed. "No. Nothing. Of course not."

She eyed me, suspicion reverberating in each slow blink. "What?"

"Kennedy!" A woo-girl screeched through the crowd, and I spun away happy to be rescued from Leona's intense gaze. Taylor streaked across the packed room and plowed through people to get to me. "You're here!"

I swear, she took a running leap at me and Leona. Reid

served as our backstop and kept us from toppling to the floor.

"Hey, birthday girl." I hugged her tightly.

"You're the third person she's done that too." Ashley handed Taylor her cup back. "I think she's trying out for the WWE." More people flowed into the party jostling us.

I pressed my palm against my chest. "Now I don't feel special at all."

"Yeah, right." Taylor tipped her head back, finishing off her punch. "In that outfit, you're screaming special." She circled her finger. "I need a twirl."

A new keg was tapped, which invited even more traffic past us.

I spun on my toes giving her a 360 view.

Taylor stuck her two fingers in her mouth and whistled so loudly a few people clamped their hands over their ears. "Where'd you get that scarf?"

All sound was replaced by a high-pitch ringing. Slowly, the beat of the music returned and hopefully, most of my hearing. "A place in Pittsburgh."

Leona's eyebrows dipped. "You and your mysterious trips." More glitter rained down from her banner. We wandered closer to the cake table. The cake only had a few finger-poke holes.

"Yeah, Pittsburgh. The mystery capital of the world. How's it feel to be another year older, birthday girl?"

"Weird." She turned her empty cup upside down before stealing Ashley's and power chugged it.

"Hey." Ashley snatched it back and checked the now empty cup. "You're lucky it's your birthday."

"It was an emergency. I was having a moment. We'll all be expected to be full-grown adults in a little over a year."

I scanned the room filled with people. Beer pong. Keg

stands. Sloshing foam over the edges of red plastic cups. Outside someone had started up with the STFU fight song again.

Leona nibbled the rim of her Solo cup. "Imagine being wheeled into surgery and that guy over there is about to put you under."

I poured some of my drink into Ashley's cup. "Remember that the next time you have to go to the doctor. The doctor will be one of these guys to someone out there who went to school with him."

"Thanks, guys." Taylor threw up one hand. "I'll never be able to go to the doctor again."

I took her empty cup. "You know what'll make it better?"

"More drinks," Ashley, Taylor, Leona and I all responded at the same time.

We turned in unison toward the approaching Reid. As a pack, we looped our arms around each other's shoulders.

Reid backed up looking like he wanted to bolt. "Please for the love of god, never do that again. You four are creepy when you do that."

"Even me?" Leona stepped forward.

His scared look cracked and he smiled. "Nope, you're perfect."

My stomach lurched, but I swallowed. They were so adorable. They had each other. They were happy and hadn't had a single screaming match, so in my book they were a top-ten best couple.

The night sped by, complete with the STFU football jersey cake made by Ashley and Leona that Griff and Hollis topped off with fountain fireworks, which shot high into the air and scorched the ceiling.

"Whoops." Ezra's cheeks were red or maybe it was a

flame burn from the spraying fire that had been set off inches from his face.

Taylor touched her face, fingers running across her eyebrows. Only then did her look of concern become full-on beaming. "That was epic! Thanks guys!" She hugged them both.

With no plates or forks, the cake cutting devolved into Leona serving out slices onto paper towels or for some of the drunker partygoers, straight into open mouths.

"Guys! We have plates." Reid burst into the room with a stack of paper plates half his size, but it was too late.

Cake-and-icing-smeared faces multiplied. Ezra walked back inside before throwing his hands up and walking right back out.

I'd hate to be whoever had to clean this place up in the morning, but I was sure to eat my piece extra messy just in case it was Cole.

Someone toward the back cranked the music louder. Sugar-rush infused and on my third drink, I joined everyone in the living room dancing.

Hollis took my hand and spun me around like we were in a swing dancing class. His bright blue eyes twinkled in the low party light. "I was wondering when I'd get a chance to dance with you, Kennedy."

My head swam. I grabbed onto his shoulders, trying to ward off the dizziness. There was no spark, no tingling, no connection other than aww-adorable feelings.

His style was always infectiously friendly and flirty. No moves being made, which made it a lot easier to let him get close. He tried to spin me again. "I've already had a couple drinks. You trying to make me puke?"

He laughed. "Next time I'll be more careful. Plus, I'm just

doing this to piss Cole off." He tilted his head toward the kitchen where Cole glowered in the doorway.

I stole a glance.

His gaze collided with mine sending a flare blazing in my stomach.

His head snapped in the other direction. "There's nothing for him to be pissed off about. We're just dancing."

Hollis leaned in, whispering in my ear, "Don't think I didn't notice you two sneaking away during that party in August."

My breath stalled and shock rippled through me. "You're too observant for your own good."

"Not always." A sadness settled in his gaze. "But in this case, hell yeah. He's never acted with anyone else like he does with you."

"Like a petty, annoying pain in the ass baby."

"Looks like someone's gotten under your skin too." He grinned and I scowled.

"Nope. Sometimes people just can't stand each other and it's best they stay away. No harm, no foul."

Hollis nodded with a knowing expression.

Before I could ask him what exactly he knew about it, we were jostled by a tipsy Ashley balancing a chunk of cake on a knife. "Do you guys want more cake?"

I jumped back.

"Thanks, Ashley." Hollis grabbed her wrist and slid the knife away. "Why don't I take this for you? Kennedy and I will eat it."

"Awesome. Love you guys." She flung her arms around the both of us, nearly making us knock heads before wandering off.

Hollis laughed and kept the slab of cake centered on the knife. "Want some?"

"Sure." I held out my hand and he dropped half of the cake into it, palming the other half and biting into it.

"Let me hide this before she goes Michael Meyers on anyone else at the party." He rushed off with the knife raised high above his head like a tour guide wand.

"Can I have some of that, Kennedy?" A cute guy in a thermal whose name I couldn't remember stepped in front of me. And he was just that, cute.

"Go for it." I held out my hand to dump the vanilla cake with chocolate-iced-fondant-covered mess into his palm.

He looked younger although I swore we'd had a class together, but he had the kind of face that made you want to ruffle his hair. He took my hand in his and started eating out of my palm.

A shudder rolled through me, colliding with laughter at the weirdness of what was happening. I jerked on my hand, trying to release it, and finding it hard to catch my breath. "Gross, you have no idea where my hand's been."

He peered up at me, laughing with chocolate on his nose. "I know where I'd like them to be."

"You're an over-the-top flirt, you know that, right?"

"Takes one to know one." He took another bite.

"Am I at a petting zoo?"

He snorted.

"Can I have my hand back now, so I can go wash it?"

"Cake waster," he chided when I tugged my hand free.

The line to the bathroom made it all the way down the stairs, so I walked into the kitchen. A keg sat in an ice-filled bucket, bottles of beer and liquor were lined up on the counter, and there was a trash can of jungle juice with a red ring on the floor around it.

Beside the sink, Cole braced his hands on the counter, taking growling loud breaths. He'd probably been doing push-ups or pull-ups or some kind of "up" football players did. He'd leaned full tilt into the football player hype and persona.

I dumped the rest of the cake into an open trash can. The cake hit the bottles and cans stacked inside with a jingle.

His head snapped up and he scanned me. A moment of hesitation and then he grabbed the keg nozzle filling a cup from the stack beside him and a spray of beer missed his cup. "Shit." He seemed flustered. Off.

My skin warmed, even after entering into the cooler kitchen. "Hot out there." I let out a tinny laugh and walked to the sink, turning it on, wiping off the icing and cake coating my skin.

My elbow bumped into him. "Sorry."

"Don't worry about it." He waved an empty cup at me and I glanced over my shoulder. "Do you want a drink or not?"

My body tensed. "I can do it myself."

He exhaled like he was a dragon about to let loose. "I'm trying, Kennedy."

That bristled me and I shifted my weight to one leg and folded my arms over my chest. "Trying to..."

"Be nice," he snapped. He slammed the cup down.

I jumped at the bite in his tone. "Could've fooled me." But forcing him to get me my drink wasn't the worst thing. Maybe that girl he'd been dancing with earlier would find another less growly guy to hook up with tonight. She'd be better off. I was doing her a favor. I glanced down at the cup and held it out just as he turned away from me.

"It's fine, I can do it—" I started.

"No, let me take it—" he said at the same time.

An uncomfortable ripple of laughter passed between us.

"This tap sucks. I can do it."

"I prefer punch." I held out my cup and he took it from me.

His hand brushed over mine. The coarse pads of his fingers tickled my skin, shooting sparks straight to my elbow. It was the same way his fingers had skimmed my shoulder when he'd whispered in my ear inviting me up to his bedroom.

The memory turned sour, curdling in my stomach like two-week-old takeout.

Cole was great at playing his part out in public, but behind closed doors, I knew how he really felt.

Hadn't Leona asked us to play nice tonight? That was exactly what he was doing. I wouldn't make the same mistake twice. Cole Hauser and I were not going to be a thing no matter how much I'd thought that was what I wanted half a year ago.

4

COLE

I was in hell. My body ached and my brain felt like it was stuffed full of pissed-off bees. The buzzing hadn't stopped for days now.

Another practice. Another day sitting in the same class as Kennedy. Another day wishing someone had a pill to selectively delete memories from my brain. Like the night Kennedy had come up to my room. Or watching that guy eat cake out of her hand.

"It's been so long, I almost forgot what a party felt like." Griff walked beside me.

Why didn't she just walk in with that knife Hollis had and ram it into my chest? I swear she did it on purpose. And no matter how nicely our conversations started they always veered offtrack straight to Biting Snark-Ville.

"The party was okay."

Ezra was on my other side keeping quiet like he always did.

"Okay?" Griff's voice spiked. "Only okay? There was booze. There was cake. There was a piñata."

Ezra skidded to a stop. "There was a piñata?"

Kennedy had been the one to burst it open. Her bow with flair after smashing it to bits had given me a straight look down the front of her shirt. *None of those thoughts. Currently purging visions of her cleavage from my mind.* The last thing I needed was wood walking into class.

"It was filled with mini alcohol bottles and chocolate." Griff looked up at the sky with faraway happiness. "That chocolate was damn good."

Ezra jogged to catch up. "When did that happen?"

"Oh, I don't know Mr. I Love to Leave a Party without Telling Anyone."

Ezra ducked his head and tugged on the brim of his hat.

"That's what happens. You miss the alcohol piñata." Griff checked his phone and his shoulders dropped. "See you guys later. Are we meeting at the east dining hall for dinner?"

It was Griff's turn to cook.

"Unless *someone* wants to cook."

He scoffed and rushed off.

Ezra marched beside me—silently.

I shoved open the door to the Commons. It was one of the bigger student centers on campus, but today wasn't bursting with people like it usually was. It was deader than normal in the quarter of a football field–sized open space that was overlooked by a three-story atrium. The upper floors had game rooms with pool and ping pong tables and air hockey. A food court in the lower level was between breakfast and lunch service, so most people hung back not wanting to be stuck eating stale pancakes or waste a dining hall credit on salad and a sandwich.

At an empty table, I stopped and set my backpack down.

Ezra did the same and unzipped his, taking out a ratty notebook.

I peered over at him. "Where did you go last night?"

He shrugged.

"Seriously? You're trying to shrug your way out of this."

"Works with most people." A smile darted across his lips.

"And I'm not most people." I grabbed his shoulder. "You never told us about your mystery friend after the play-off game. The one who you let into our house to get the food ready. Now you're leaving parties. That's not like you. You're usually Mr. Sentry trying to make sure no one gets out of hand, especially when you're on clean-up duty."

"I had somewhere to be." He kept his head down, shadowing his eyes. "Sorry I bailed."

I squeezed his shoulder and steeled myself, stomach diving for my throat. "You sure nothing's wrong?" I needed to at least know this. Worry wrapped cold fingers of dread around my chest. Was he in trouble? Was he sick? My mom was secretive with me about her sickness for a long time. I stared at Ezra, looking for anything off. "You'd tell me if you needed help?"

His head snapped back and he stared at me. "Of course. If something was wrong, I'd let you know."

Relief loosened my muscles and I patted his shoulder. "That's all I needed to know. You know you can talk to me, if you need to."

"It's all good. I don't need to. Just figuring some stuff out." His gaze bolted from mine like he'd caught something over my shoulder. "I gotta go." He scooped up his bag and rammed the notebook inside, tearing the cover, but didn't stop his exit. He darted around a stage set up in the middle of the space, which meant although it was winter, the spring fling and prank war season would be here soon.

I squinted to see who he was going after, but all I saw

was the doors on the far side swinging shut before he all but jump-kicked them open to rush out.

A few other people turned to see what the noise was. Almost like my eyes were giant magnets and she was a goal post, my gaze snapped to Kennedy opposite me on the other side of the stage. Not that she's easy to miss. She stood out amongst all the other sleepy, dreary students huddled at their tables. While most people were happy to roll out of bed in whatever they'd had on the night before, she always looked like a magazine version of college students on the go.

I couldn't help it. I went into defensive overdrive every time she was near me. Other than the one attempt back in high school to be a wide receiver that ended up with my facemask filled with grass and dirt and literal cleat marks on my back, I'd never been more embarrassed than my night with her. I overreacted, but I didn't know how to not overreact.

The whole reason we'd gone up to my room in the first place was because I was into her. Too into her.

A mic squealed. People didn't tend to stay on the ground floor for long. Mainly because it was where all the student groups came to shill for whatever their newest event or fundraising drive might be. Couldn't they stick to flyers only?

But the guy and girl who hopped up on stage spent at least eight minutes going back and forth with the student worker running the tech. First, feedback on the mic, then it went dead.

I kept myself from looking at Kennedy, but I could still picture her annoyed, shrewdly sharp glare.

Slumping back in my seat, I flipped my notebook closed and grabbed my phone. Twenty more minutes until I needed to leave for class. Exactly enough time to not be able to do anything else other than fuck around on my phone.

The mic squealed again. I winced and rammed my finger in my ear, whipping my head away from the skull-slicing sound.

On the other side of the stage, my gaze darted to Kennedy. Her face was exactly as I'd pictured it, only even more pinched with pain from the ear-splitting feedback. For a second, I was happy to endure the pain. She was closer to the speakers, so it had to hurt her even more than me.

Was it an asshole thing to think? Sure, but after being the focus of her limp-dick jokes for the past semester, she deserved it.

We locked eyes.

Up on stage the couple chattered on about the Puppy Love competition kicking off on Valentine's Day. Just when I thought what was happening up on stage couldn't get worse than the brain scrambling sounds, they had.

Kennedy's scowl deepened and she flicked her gaze up to the stage with a sneer before returning her disdainful stare to mine.

Well, I wasn't about to look away now. Losing wasn't in my DNA, and I hadn't planned on being in a staring contest, but here we were.

"Last year's prizes of a night in Pittsburgh and romantic dinner have been blown out of the water by two very generous and gracious alumni."

Kill me now. What a bunch of bull. Students like Kennedy thought football was annoying, but how about the people racing all over campus creating three-person flash mobs or interrupting classes to hand their boyfriend or girlfriend wilted grocery store flowers?

"They won this competition back when they were here

for three years in a row and wanted to return the favor to two deserving STFU lovebirds."

Or the truly embarrassing one where they'd dressed up as cupid, complete with a diaper.

"There will be two prizes up for grabs that the couple gets to decide between."

Half the couples didn't even make it to graduation. True life if I'd ever seen it.

"One is an all-expenses-paid trip to a golf Pro-Am that will culminate in a private dinner with football legends and Hall of Famers as well as an autographed 1998 Liberty Bowl trophy."

Shock floored me. Holy shit, that was when my dad had played football. He'd idolized every player on the list she'd read out. And golf had to be the only thing he didn't hate in life. He had his number-one love—everything else, he hated —then golf hung in the middle null zone filled only with food and sleep.

Kennedy's head tilted as she stared at me, probably trying to figure out what was racing through my head right now.

"The other prize these two sweethearts have a chance at is an all-inclusive week in Paris this June that'll include a five-star hotel experience complete with meals and spa treatments, a shopping tour, and tickets to Couture Fashion Week."

Kennedy jerked so hard her arms flew forward and knocked her bag off the table. She lunged to catch it, but half ended up spilling onto the floor.

Staring contest won. It was petty bullshit, but right now I'd take the small wins. And maybe a big win with this prize.

"Tickets and costumes for the Versailles Masquerade

Ball, and a behind-the-scenes look at the upcoming fall fashion week designs are also included."

Kennedy gasped so loudly it echoed in the massive room.

I glanced around the Commons and noticed there were more than a few interested gazes, but none as extreme as Kennedy.

But the golf and trophy package was more than enough to get the wheels turning in my head. A weekend away from normal life. A weekend surrounded by all the things that might break through the prickly exterior and maybe give me a chance to finally connect with my dad.

"The competing couples will need to register by Valentine's Day. The Puppy Love competition will last for five weeks where the best couple will be crowned the Puppy Love Champions and choose between the insane prizes. Sort of wished we'd known what they'd be before we took on coordinating duties since we're not eligible to win." She grumbled that last bit into the mic.

They ended their announcement and hopped off stage. Other than a couple people who walked up to them, no one else seemed to believe how big a deal this was. And I hoped to hell they wouldn't realize it. That meant less competition. Only one small problem. I wasn't dating anyone. I'd made a point not to date anyone.

The sparsely populated tables were even emptier. I checked the time and grabbed my bag heading toward the Exeter Business Building. Glancing behind me, I saw Kennedy trailing a couple steps back, distracted.

What was she thinking? Her major had to do with clothes, so maybe she was coveting the Paris portion of the trip. Just as well. It wasn't like we'd be able to team up to pull this off. Winning her over between now and Valentine's Day also wasn't an option.

Not that I wanted to win her over. Not when she'd been witness to the most humiliating moment of my life and was happy to dance on that awkward grave every chance she got.

I sat in my unassigned seat in Strategic Brand Management.

Kennedy arrived just before the door closed at the start of class.

She trudged forward and rammed into one of the desks just inside the door. Her head snapped up and she locked eyes with me.

Her thoughtful expression turned to a frown and she hurried to her seat in the back corner of the class as far as she could get from me. Good, because if she'd tried to sit closer, I'd have moved. The last thing I needed was a Kennedy barb or snipe when I needed to figure out the next play for that prize.

The professor droned on and my head buzzed with the possibilities of the trip. I promised my mom I'd work on connecting with my dad, that I'd do whatever I could to finally see the good in him like she had. So far the opportunities for a true conversation had been few and far between —let alone a heart-to-heart. I had to believe given the chance I might finally get my shot.

"Mr. Hauser."

Startled, I knocked my notebook off the desk. "Yes?" Scrambling to pick it up, I grimaced. The back of my neck burned.

He was only a desk away from me and the whole class was staring—all except for Kennedy. So much for not letting anything get past me, apparently it only applied to when I was on the field.

"I don't suppose you might have an answer for the class about the ladder-up versus waterfall-down measurements for the interplay of product and corporate brands."

I kept my head down. "Sorry, sir. No, I don't." My fingers clenched my pen hard, leaving indents in my skin.

"Ms. Finch. How about you?"

Kennedy's head shot up. "Sorry, I missed the question."

At least I wasn't the only one.

The professor flapped his arms like a wounded bird. "Honestly, I don't even know why you two came to class if you don't plan on paying attention." He spun and walked back to the front of the class. "Anyone else want to try their hand at the question?"

I peered over at Kennedy, who sat straighter in her seat but kept dropping her gaze to the notebook.

An idea *tink*ed in my brain like a slow accumulation of marbles, but I quickly swept them aside. There had to be a better way to get what I wanted. One that didn't include putting myself back into the frying pan with Kennedy.

The hairs raised on the back of my head and I glanced up.

Kennedy's head snapped straight ahead.

Or maybe she was having the same thoughts as me. I'd rack my brain for every option, and I'm sure she'd work just as hard, but what if we were the only best option each other had? In that case, we were both screwed.

5

KENNEDY

"I knew you couldn't get enough." Tristan grabbed my ass and tugged me against him.

I shoved him backward and crossed my arms over my chest. There was a lot I couldn't get enough of, but Tristan's lackluster seduction wasn't one of them. "I'm talking about going for the Puppy Love prize."

His face scrunched up. "Why the hell would I want to do that? It's a hell of a lot of work for some bullshit prize."

Word hadn't gotten out about the prizes yet. And I couldn't exactly tell him what I had planned because he'd probably blab without even realizing it. And he wouldn't be going with me on the trip anyway. My little sister and I would have the time of our lives exploring Paris.

Tristan was a beautiful specimen of a man, but he was also dumber than a box of rocks. It was why he was good for one thing. If it weren't for his stamina and pleasing enthusiasm that wouldn't even be all that impressive. It also meant finding a way to swipe the prize from under him wouldn't be too hard.

I pinched the bridge of my nose. "What's the most romantic thing you've ever done for someone?"

He sidled back up to me and tried to grab my ass again. "Why don't I show you?"

"Ugh." I snatched my bag off his chair and marched out of his room. This was a mistake.

Tristan was the third guy I'd attempted to feel out for a possible Puppy Love partner-in-crime. All I'd ended up getting was felt up. It was telling that this had gone better than the others, which told me how well and truly screwed I was. It was what I got for always being the one to kick a guy out of bed or being fully dressed by the time they took care of the condom.

Attachments weren't my strong suit, so it made sense when I showed up at a guy's house, dropping hints about getting closer, they all jumped straight to the sex conclusion.

New tactic. Back in my room, I grabbed my notebook and scribbled down the names of every guy I knew on campus. It was how I worked through my merchandising selections for the bookstore and it hadn't lead me astray so far. Start with every available option and scratch out the duds one at a time.

My mission was locked in. I would be part of the winning couple who won Puppy Love. I'd get exclusive access to the top fashion minds and Miranda Priestly my way into retail fashion. A fashion buyer was only as strong as their research, and I'd be getting face time and first-look insight into what would be coming down the industry pipeline.

My phone lit up beside me on the bed. Grinning, I answered.

"Hey, Pickle."

"Ugh." She sounded just like me. "You know I hate that name."

"Which is exactly why I keep calling you that. What's up?"

"Kenny, our parents are driving me nuts." She sounded ready to yank her hair out in clumps.

"What did they do now?" Dealing with them alone hit her hard. At least when we'd both been there, we had each other. Now she was on her own. "What's going on?"

"It's getting worse. They're fighting all the time. Mom wants Dad to leave the house and he wants her to leave. They're shouting over each other whenever they're in the same room together. I can only stay at my friends' houses for so long."

Guilt panged inside my chest. "I wish I could be there."

"I wish you could too." She sounded much younger than sixteen. At five years apart, it would've been a prime gap between us for me to be annoyed by my much younger sister, but we'd always been close.

"Can I come stay with you this summer?"

My heart ached. "I don't think you can. I'm hoping to be in a better place next year. My current apartment is a dump." This lit another fire under my ass to make it happen. Leases would need to be signed in the next few months and I didn't want Melody and I trapped because I couldn't get the money together in time. "But I hope I'll find a better one, and if I do, then you can totally come stay with me. Are you even sure Mom and Dad would be okay with you staying here?"

"They won't even notice I'm gone. I wish I could be this invisible at school."

"You're the one who wants your name up in lights. That's the opposite of invisible. How'd the musical tryouts go?"

She'd been ecstatic when *Footloose* had been announced as the spring musical and finally ready to step out of the costuming shadows to try her hand at the big singing role after sticking to the chorus and smaller parts in years past.

A soul-shaking sob erupted from her end of the line.

I shot up from the bed, my heart bolting for my throat. "Hannah, what happened?"

"Mrs. Mason said I was too fat to play Rusty."

"She what?" My screech rattled the windows.

"Not in those words, but that's what she meant. She made me the mom. I'm always the mom." Her sniffles transported me back to the same feelings I'd had back in high school. Those moments of intense, cutting self-doubt where I wanted to fade into the background. How I'd been so worried about what everyone else thought.

"I'm sorry. I know you wanted that role."

"The girl who got it can't even sing. She can't hit the high notes, but Mrs. Mason said she's got the look." Her watery laugh made me want to fly to Washington, take her out for ice cream and watch crappy movies all night.

"Hannah, I know this is when I should talk about there's no small part and say you'll make your part shine and I know you will, but it still freaking sucks."

A relieved sigh. "Thanks, Kennedy. Everyone keeps trying to say it's okay, I still have two years left to try, but all I needed was someone to tell me it was okay to feel this way. Mrs. Mason did offer to let me sing the part from the wings so the other girl could lip-sync to it."

My teeth clicked together. "Good to see she's still every bit as horrible as I remember." Seething, I squeezed my phone, happy to note my former drama teacher—who'd somehow managed to not be fired yet—was her same lovely self.

"She really is."

"What did Mom and Dad say when you told them?" I braced myself. It couldn't be good. It was never good.

"That's what they're fighting about." Misery saturated every word. "Dad's all about how Mom builds me up only to watch me get kicked down when she should be more realistic about what we can achieve. Thanks, Dad. And Mom's screaming at him about how he can never even for a moment entertain things not going to shit."

"Hey, language."

She snorted, no longer sounding like she was about to burst into tears again. "That's nothing on what they're shouting at each other. I wish I was a senior, then I'd only have to put up with this for a few more months. Maybe I can ask for my own place in the divorce."

"I don't think that's how that works. Plus, you're only sixteen."

"It'll be good practice for when I finally go away to college like you." A dreamy faraway-ness seeped into her voice. "Are you having fun? Please tell me you're having so much fun you can't even keep up."

I laughed and sat on the edge of my desk. "It's fun, but also a lot of hard work. Long nights studying, my part-time job, challenging classes—"

"Blah, blah, blah, tell me about the good stuff." Were those her hands rubbing together diabolically on the other end of the line? "The freedom, the parties, the guys..." Her eyebrows were totally waggling.

"The guy situation is the same as always." Never too close for anything serious, never too close for the feelings to get deeper than the fun of a hookup.

"Chewing them up and spitting them out."

My lips pinched together. If I were a guy, would anyone

have a thing to say about my dating life? No, now my own sister thought I was a maneater. It's never been my intention, but I'm not exactly into empty romantic gestures or dates, not that I let anyone close enough to make them less hollow. "I'm having fun. I don't need to justify myself to a preteen."

"Sixteen is not a preteen thank you very much."

"What about you?"

She sucked her teeth. "You first. Give me some juicy news that'll tide me over for a while."

PG details were all she needed about my life. "There's a contest on campus for couples. They have to be obnoxiously lovey-dovey and shove it in everyone's faces for a month, so they can win their pick of two amazing prizes. It's nauseating."

"You're totally trying to find a guy to team up with to win, aren't you?"

The phone nearly fell out of my hand. "How the hell did you know that?"

"You think I don't know you by now? I could hear the plan forming in your head. The prize must be pretty amazing."

I paused. Did I even want to put this in her mind? I wasn't even sure I could find a guy willing to go along with the fake out. "It's a trip to Paris Couture Fashion Week, and the Versailles Masquerade Ball, costumes included."

She must've dropped the phone because her scream didn't burst my eardrum, but came through loud and clear. "Are you kidding me?!"

"It's a crazy contest and the odds are long, so incredibly long."

"You can do it. I know you can win." I could hear her hopping around the room.

"Hannah, I'm not making promises." My pulse spiked. "I don't even have a guy to work with."

"I know. You never make promises you can't keep."

"Good, I'm just letting you know. If I won, and the guy was cool with it, we'd go, but I haven't even found a partner yet."

"You're a magician, Kennedy. If there's anyone who can do it, it's you."

"Thanks for the vote of confidence."

"It's what little sisters are for."

"I thought it was for being bratty, annoying clothes stealers."

"Unfortunately, you took all yours with you." The volume on her end kicked up. "I'm going to my friend's. I'll see you later, and keep me updated about this love thing."

"You know I will. Bye, Pickle."

"Bye, Kenny."

Hannah's excitement for the trip drove me back to the notebook with the list of names. There had to be a way to make this work. At this point, I'd do whatever it took for a chance to give her a once in a lifetime trip that just so happened to be mine as well. Scanning the list, I went back to the drawing board. First order of business, find a sucker to win this thing with me.

6

COLE

"He's got a good heart." My mom had repeated those words to me so many times over the years. Every missed pickup for visitation. Every time he came to visit her and left without so much as patting me on my head. Every birthday or Christmas that passed without a word from him.

"Why do we have to go, if we're passing?" Griff mumbled beside me. "It's not like they don't get weekly reports from all our professors." He ducked his head lower like he could hide inside his jacket collar.

"It's a chicken or egg situation. They don't want to be proven wrong and then some of us aren't eligible to play."

"Stupid when we could take summer classes to get our GPA up if we needed to."

"Why don't you make that suggestion to Coach? You know how receptive he is to feedback about how the team is run." My breath lingered in front of my face on the way to study hall required for all football players. A shiver raced through me that had nothing to do with the oppressive cold.

She'd dragged the oxygen mask down from her face and

asked me to try. Her hands had been freezing, like frail ice cubes. How could I say no? Only now, I was trapped without a single way to make an inroad with the man who'd been a black hole in my life since before I could remember.

Until now. It felt like a Hail Mary. A trip like this could change things.

Griff shouldered the door open like it had personally offended him.

The dry, heated blast of air inside the athletics building chapped my lips instantly. "At least we can get most of our work done here."

The tip of my nose thawed and seared the further into the building I walked.

My idea felt dumber and dumber to even try, but it would always linger in the back of my head if I didn't. I couldn't let my mom down, even if she wasn't here to see it.

But the list of problems multiplied. The most important one loomed overhead like a quarterback sack. Who would I even try this fake out with?

I hadn't even touched anyone since that disastrous night with Kennedy. I hadn't even wanted to hook up with anyone since she stormed out of my bedroom. If I randomly showed up at someone's door and tried to get them in on this they'd either laugh in my face or, worse, drop a tip in STFU Dirt about Cole Hauser being hard up for a date.

A giant mental block stood in my way and it felt like a correction to the universe needed to be made. A do-over. Then I'd be over this hump and could stop obsessing over her.

That settled it. Kennedy was my target. Her face had lit up when they announced the prize. She didn't seem the type to like golf, so it must be the Paris trip she was after.

Maybe winning her over wouldn't be so hard. The next

hurdle was figuring out who got the prize. But first things first, I had to convince her to fake loving me. Sure felt a hell of a lot safer than going for the real thing. Fake love, I could try because real love lead to nothing more than heartbreak.

7

COLE

It was Valentine's Day. The campus was covered in red and pink hearts. Washed-out chalk declarations of love were scrawled all over the brick walls surrounding the main quad and on the slate paths crossing the space.

I'd debated with myself all night trying to talk myself out of this, but there was only one solution. She was it.

If it worked out as planned, I'd win and no longer be neutered.

I walked past her desk. One page had writing all over it. It took me a second to recognize names. Guys' names. My name. A note crossed out about me.

My heart stuttered and I looked again to be sure I hadn't been hallucinating. It was there. I reversed and sat in the seat beside her.

She stiffened and slid her book over the notebook, but I saw the names.

"I'm surprised I was fourth down the list."

She moved the book and flipped the notebook closed. "I don't know what you're talking about." She knew exactly what I was talking about. My name written there meant she'd thought about me for at least a second, even if she'd been ungenerous of her assessment of how it would pan out.

The professor stood up front and got to work, digging into the brand recognition trifecta.

Throughout the lecture, I couldn't stop glancing over at Kennedy—and her now open notebook where she was sketching. But it was what she was sketching that told me this might actually work. An Eiffel tower. She had Paris on the brain, which meant she wanted the prize, which meant I had a shot. Kill two birds with one stone although she might kill me if I came out victorious at the end, but a fifty-fifty shot was better than no shot.

The professor droned on about our next assignments, reiterating that we'd be sticking to the syllabus, and then we were all dismissed.

Kennedy shot up and yanked her bag along with her without putting it on her shoulder.

I caught up to her in the hallway and hooked her arm to keep her from rushing off. "Kennedy."

"What?" She shook off my hold and glanced over her shoulder. "What do you want?"

"I want what you want."

Her eyebrow shot up and her gaze dipped to my crotch before sliding back up, a bored slant to her lips. "Not even if you paid me."

"Same," I barked out and kicked myself for letting her goad me. This was the exact opposite of what I was supposed to be doing. "Listen, I have a way for us both to get a shot at the prizes."

She folded her arms over her chest. "I don't know what you're talking about."

I checked over her shoulder at the people filing out of their classrooms and dragged her toward an empty hallway. "I know you want to enter Puppy Love."

Her body straightened. "Who said that?"

I yanked her notebook out of her hands and evaded her grasping hands until I found the page. "This said that." I held the notebook overhead and waved it from above.

Should've known she wouldn't take that laying down. Her elbow rammed into my stomach, trying to snatch it back. "Don't touch my stuff."

Damn, she had strong muscles behind that elbow. The wind was half knocked out of me.

"Liar. You were only going to make it more difficult if I didn't have my proof."

She shot me a withering glare. "How do you know it wasn't a hit list? Or how do you know this isn't another Cole I know?"

"I'm sure campus police might've brought it to everyone's attention if this many bodies had shown up around here. And I know it's my name because you literally wrote..." I checked the words to make sure I had them right. "'Football fuckboy' beside it. As far as I know, I'm the only Cole on the whole team." Holding out the notebook, I couldn't help but gloat a little.

Her full lips thinned. "It's nothing to be proud of, although now I know the rumors were greatly exaggerated. Did you pay off all the girls to shout about your bedroom skills?"

I gritted my teeth and shoved all the simmering feelings down with a deep breath. "Let's refocus on what's important. You want a shot at one of the prizes and I want one too. Right now, we've both got no shot."

"And what do you propose? That we pretend to be in a

relationship. Enter Puppy Love. Evaluate all the past winners, one-up whatever they did in a strategic plan to escalate the gestures into a grand finale."

I was stunned silent, then folded my arms and leaned against the wall, letting my smug smile get to her. "No, you haven't been thinking about this at all."

"I might've been thinking about it a little." Her lips pursed. "So why me? Why not one of your many adoring fans all over campus?"

My heart leapt.

She hadn't stormed away. She was considering it.

"This isn't about getting involved with someone. It's about winning. It needs to be unemotional and tactical. We both have a goal. We work toward that goal without all the problems that come along with a real relationship."

Her gaze narrowed, never wavering from my face.

Each second of silence felt like she was trying to peel back the layers of my soul to get to the gooey center. She'd better get a backhoe for that dig. It would take a long damn time.

She shifted and her stance softened, slightly. "Who would even believe we were together? We haven't exactly been known to be even friendly with each other." She rolled her eyes at "friendly." "Everyone knows we hate each other."

I jumped in to head her off. "We can just say we were fighting our attraction and masking it with animosity." Thinking about this for far too long was finally paying off.

Her frown deepened. "There's got to be an easier way."

A clock at the end of the hall ticked a minute closer to one. My palms were sweaty. The chance was so close to slipping though my fingers. "Thirty minutes. That's how long we have until registration closes. If you'd had another way, you'd have already entered."

Her shoulders sank. "We're going to have to be disgustingly loved up on each other in public."

It wouldn't be a chore. It would be less than a chore, which was part of how this whole problem started in the first place. But I hoped being around her might immunize me to the feelings she stirred in me when she touched me. "I'm willing to make the sacrifice if you are."

A flare burned in her gaze. "You are a dick."

"What? You're so excited to make out with me in public?"

"There was a time I wouldn't have minded, but that's now buried under a glacier. It's practically a prehistoric feeling." She adjusted the strap on the bag slung over her shoulder. "But if you're serious, I'm game."

The crowd cheered in my head and I stopped myself from doing an end-zone dance. "Do you want to give this a trial run?" The words stalled and my heart raced. A pounding gallop thudded in my chest. I wiped my sweaty palms on my jeans.

She paused, then nodded like she'd been told her frostbitten arm would be amputated. "Fine, let's do this." Her feet were toe to toe with mine.

The first time we'd been this close since August. The first chance to touch her since then. I swallowed past the ball of sawdust lodged in my throat and reached for her cheek.

She jerked back, slapping my hand. "What, are we supposed to press our lips together and that's it? If it's going to be a real kiss, then it needs to be a real kiss."

Her gaze hardened. "Fine." She closed her eyes, shook out her body, and took a deep breath.

Annoyance pinched at the tingle of anticipation rushing

down my spine. "We're not entering into the uneven bars gymnastics final. It's a kiss."

"I just need to mentally prepare." She glared at me. "So I don't puke all over you."

"It's not like we haven't kissed before." Her soft lips. Her tongue. Her taste. My brain still sizzled with the brand.

"Don't remind me."

Irritation scratched at the base of my skull although my body hummed being this close to her. "Five weeks is all it will take."

"How do we decide who gets the prize at the end?"

I scrambled to figure out a way to decide once we won this thing. "Each person in the couple is given a point score. We'll go by that, so it's fair." Once I let the guys know the deal, they'd vote for me and the win would be an easy lock.

"But anyone on campus who wants to can vote on each gesture."

"So..."

"So, if anyone else finds out we're faking this or that you're trying to win this for yourself, they'll vote for you, even if I'm kicking your ass. It's an unfair advantage. You'll just have the whole team stuff the ballots for you."

Shit! Back to scrambling. The countdown clock continued to tick. "What do you propose then?" Seconds slipped away. "We've got like twenty minutes to get over there."

"We don't tell anyone." She glanced over her shoulder at the empty hallway and leaned in closer. "We don't tell anyone we're faking it."

It never occurred to me the guys wouldn't be in on this big joke. I figured she'd want to at least tell the girls. "You think the guys or Leona, Taylor, and Ashley are going to believe it?"

"I don't care. Between that and STFU Dirt reporting on the couples like they did last year, it's just us who know or I'm out. The last thing I need is anyone thinking you're only going out with me for a prize." The wound to her pride bled through each word.

I checked the time again. Fifteen minutes. Sweaty palms leaked like faucets. "Fine, we can figure out the rest of the details later, but it's a deal." I raised my hand for a shake.

Instead of taking my hand, she tugged me forward and kissed me.

Her taste exploded in my mouth. Her tongue teased mine and our noses brushed against each other. She smelled like scented fruity lotion.

My body revved, shifting into high gear. I grabbed the sides of her neck.

Her pulse jumped beneath my touch.

I spun us around and pressed her against the wall. One hand braced my body over hers, trying to keep myself upright.

Her fingers tightened around my jacket, keeping me close.

I free-fell and forgot anything else existed other than this moment with her lips on mine.

A door slammed down the hallway and she shoved me back.

"There, was that good enough for you?" She ducked from under my arm.

I stared at the space in front of me she'd deserted, frozen and trying to get my growing erection back under control. "Yeah, that was serviceable." I cleared my throat and grabbed my backpack off the floor.

"Service my..." Her grumbles were lost beneath the click of her boots against the tile floor.

I rushed to catch up and slung my arm over her shoulder.

Her head whipped around, gaze piercing.

"Might as well get started now, right?" I pushed the door open and a wall of freezing air blasted us back.

Her lips flattened and she stared through the open door, but she didn't shrug my arm off. Then she shifted, looking into my eyes with a smile like I'd given her the world's best gift. "You're right, babe. We need to hurry up, so we're not late."

My heart flipped. Confusion clouded my brain. I blinked twice and jerked to a stop.

She almost walked out from under my arm. "Come on, Cole. I thought football players were good on their feet. We've got twelve minutes. Let's go." Her fingers wrapped around the hand draped over her shoulder and she switched her hold, threading our fingers and taking off in an almost sprint.

The heat from her hand seeped into mine. Blistering winds chafed my cheeks as we wove our way through the brick-paved quad to the Commons. We're really doing this. She'd actually agreed. And right now her fingers twined with mine. Could she feel my pulse pounding in my hand?

We got to the Commons and I wrenched the door open. We both looked around for the Puppy Love table.

"There!" Kennedy pointed and tugged me to the row of tables with printed and handmade posters hanging off the front.

She brushed her hair back from her face. Her cheeks glowed and her chest rose and fell. "We're here to sign up."

A guy chewing on a pen looked up from his notebook and his eyes widened and bounced back and forth between the two of us.

"Kennedy?" The pen fell out of his mouth.

"Hey, Mark." She waved at him, her neck flushed a deep crimson. "I didn't know you were helping out today."

My heart stomped its way up my throat with cleats. Who was he to her? Had his name been one she'd crossed off her list?

"I'm sitting in to close things out. They didn't think anyone else would show up. Most people signed up on the first day."

"You know me." She shrugged.

My stomach clenched curdling like spoiled milk. They had history.

"I do." His gaze lingered on her and darted to me. He straightened a little, recognition lighting in his eyes.

Satisfaction sped through me.

"Cole?"

The feeling was swept away like an ice bucket to the face. I turned to the blonde whose name escaped me and smiled.

"Hey..."

"Chelsea." Her eyebrows arched like an arrow trying to burrow straight through my forehead.

"I was just going to say that."

"You're entering?" She sat beside the guy. "I thought you weren't a relationship guy?"

Kennedy stared at me with alarmed eyes.

I shifted to lift my hand, but it was still tangled up with hers. "Things change. Sometimes when you know, you know."

Kennedy held up our still interlocked hands. "Kennedy Finch and Cole Hauser entering the competition."

"You're dating Cole?" Mark stared at her with a look bordering on disapproval.

My adrenaline spiked. I didn't like the way he looked at her and I sure as hell didn't like the way he looked at me. "Is there a problem?"

"No problem. Surprised is all. Kennedy, didn't you mention eating raw three-day-old roadkill before ever wanting to speak to him again?"

Her stiff and overly loud laugh drew the attention of the ten nearest tables. "Sometimes you're fighting against feelings so hard you overreact." She hugged my arm to the center of her chest and leaned her head on my shoulder looking up at me with adoring eyes.

My heart shuddered, stuttering through the closeness and the way she looked up at me. A flood of heat entered my bloodstream.

"If you say so." Mark typed out a few things on the laptop and motioned us toward the heart-shaped balloon arch behind the stairs. "I'll need to take a picture of you two for the site and social media."

"Great," Kennedy said, overly brightly. "Come on, babe." She tugged me along with her.

We stood under the pink, red, and white balloon construction, facing each other, trying to pull this off. A part of me had thought she'd back out at some point and then I'd be screwed, but she'd surprised me. Now the prospect of the next five weeks trying to convince everyone that we cared about each other—hell, loved each other—felt scarier than anything I'd done before.

"Can we have one second?" She held up her finger and smiled at Mark, who held his phone to take the picture.

She leaned in, so close her lips almost brushed against mine.

A jolt shot through me and blood pounded in my veins. I

needed to get myself under control if I didn't want to embarrass myself again.

"Make this good. You're not selling this hard enough."

"You seem to know how."

"That's six years of theater for you. Now, we're going to make this look believable. Grab my ass in the pic."

"Are you serious?"

"Like it's not a grabbable ass. You know it is."

It was.

"Fine."

"Don't make it sound like you're about to be waterboarded." Her smile brightened and she turned back to our photographer without taking her eyes off me.

I cupped her ass, the soft curve of it fitting perfectly in my palm, and thought about every botched play of the season. Every dropped snap in practice. Every lap I'd been forced to run.

"We're ready."

8

KENNEDY

My hands trembled as I walked out of the Commons.

Mark eyed the two of us the whole time.

I kept a straight face and tried to exude calm and breathe evenly through my rapidly closing throat.

Cole slipped his hand into mine. "Calm down. You having second thoughts?"

Damn, had my theater skills left me that quickly? I wasn't sure how I felt about him being so in tune with me.

He held open the door and the jet engine blast of cold air helped snap me out of the spiral I'd been riding.

"No, are you?" I whispered, scanning the people walking by us.

"No. I want to win."

"So do I."

"Then it looks like we'll both have to do our best to outdo each other."

"And the other couples." My cheeks stung from the whipping wind. I licked my chapped lips, which had sucked up all the moisturizer I'd put on earlier.

"Them too." He looked around and leaned in. "What now?"

"You don't have a plan?"

"Honestly? I never thought you'd go for it."

I wasn't sure how to take that. "Glad I surprised you." I fished my gloves out of my bag and shoved them on. "We need to go over the game plan. Is there anyone at your house right now?"

He shook his head. "Not for a few more hours."

"Good." I grabbed the front of his jacket.

"We're going to my house?"

"And you're driving."

We hustled to Cole's car. I reached for the door handle at the same time he did and his elbow plowed into my stomach. I doubled over and wheezed. "What the hell are you doing?" My eyes watered.

"Sorry." He grabbed my shoulders trying to steady me.

I glared at him. "What was that?"

"I was opening your door for you."

Grimacing, I sucked in a deep breath, no longer feeling like I was about to puke. "Warn a girl next time."

He nodded and opened the door.

I jumped inside and waited for him to turn on the car. Once the engine was running, I held my hands up to the vent pumping out heat. A blast of warmth smacked me in the face.

Cole's hand dropped off the heat controls.

"Thanks." I rubbed my hands together and sat back in the seat.

"What did you have in mind once we got to my house?"

I rolled my eyes. "Not that."

"Who said I was thinking that? Maybe you're the one thinking that," he snapped defensively.

My stomach soured. Of course, he wouldn't want that. "We need our initial game plan, which will include places to be seen, a social media campaign, and costumes for the dance-a-thon at the end."

He glanced over at me. "You've been thinking about this a lot."

"I plan for a lot of things, whether they pan out is another story." If all my plans worked out, I'd have been a fashion merchandising major in New York or RIT or studying abroad in London. Instead, I was stuck making do with what I had to work with.

"Why do you want to go to Paris?"

I blinked at him, caught off guard by him wanting to know. What would my career plans or plans with my little sister mean to him? That was too deep for a guy who'd rejected me once already. "What does it matter? Why do you want to go play golf with a bunch of old retired guys?"

His lips pinched so hard they turned white.

"Exactly, you have your reasons and I have mine. Let's get one thing straight."

He parked in front of his house. "Lay it on me."

"We're not really in a relationship. We don't have to share our deep dark secrets. We don't have to hang out with each other outside of the plan we make. It's part of why I agreed to do this with you in the first place, so there's no confusion."

He popped open his door. "Trust me, Kennedy. I know."

Bile churned in my stomach. He dismissed me like it hadn't even entered his mind. Maybe he was a better actor than I thought. I ran my fingers over my lips.

"Let's get this over with." He slammed his door.

I picked up my bag off the floor and my door swung open. I shivered at the rapidly escaping heat.

Cole's body blocked the sunlight.

"What are you doing?"

"What does it look like I'm doing?" He held out his hand. "I'm opening the door for my girlfriend."

My heart raced like I'd floored the accelerator. His girlfriend. "We—I—"

"Might as well start now, right? Plus, if anyone sees us it'll seem less weird once we make this officially official. I'm guessing you have a plan for that too?" His gaze dropped down to his extended hand.

Shaking off my muscle lock, I looped my bag onto my shoulder and took his hand.

Warmth spread throughout my body until it was licking at my cheeks. I was not blushing from a freaking handhold from Cole. I wasn't. Absolutely not.

The wind picked up even more and was speckled with flecks of sleet. I followed him to the porch, locking my eyes on him so that I wouldn't scan the neighborhood and make this all seem more suspicious.

He let me into the house and my chest loosened, no longer feeling like I was inhaling ice shards.

"What first?"

"Let's go to your room. I need to see your closet."

His head tilted to the side like a confused labradoodle. "Why?"

"So I can lock you in and steal all your stuff." I tilted my head imitating him. "To figure out how much of a makeover you're going to require."

He folded his arms over his chest. "I don't need a makeover."

I looked him up and down.

Worn-in sneakers. Dark jeans that did nothing to show off his assets. A faded STFU T-shirt with a thermal underneath, and the same coat he'd worn for years. What had I ever seen in him?

He shrugged off his coat and tossed it over the banister. His forearms flexed, sinew and veins popping.

A hummingbird took flight in my chest. Ah, there it was.

"Listen, I won't go crazy, but no one's going to believe we're dating if I don't at least shave some of the rough edges off you."

"Then doesn't that mean I should grunge you up a bit?"

I stood at the top of the two steps at the bottom landing. "You can try. Lead the way."

He brushed past me and took me up to his room, the first door on the right.

Like I needed the reminder. I'd replayed that night in my head so many times until I decided that every time I did, I had to throw out an article of clothing. That quickly ended the horror-show replay.

Inside his room, clothes were piled and dumped all over the place. Every surface, flat or not, had clothes on them just like it had been before. But, before, I'd been distracted by the prospect of hooking up. This time I had no such luxury. "How do you live like this?"

"It works for me. That's all that matters, right?" He sat in his clothing-covered chair and braced his arms on the back of his head, spinning in a circle.

I swept up the first armful of clothes from the top of his closed, empty hamper and dumped them on his bed. "This needs to be cleaned up so I can tell what we're working with."

"What are you even looking for?"

"We're doing a photo shoot."

"We are?"

I shook out a thermal and braced myself before leaning

in and sniffing it. A detergent-breezy smell filled my nose. I breathed with relief that I hadn't been plowed into with a wall of funk.

"We are." I folded the clothes and grouped them by type, leaving the boxers in their own untouched pile. "You could help, you know." I called over my shoulder.

He got up, full of grumbles, and gathered clothes from all over the room, piling them on his bed.

I moved to another bundle and sniffed it. The pungent one-two punch of old sweat and musty feet smacked me in the face. My eyes watered and I got woozy.

Cole snatched the shirt from my hands and swept away half the clothes beside me. "Sorry about that. Those were in my gym bag for a while." He threw them into the empty hamper.

"You could've warned me."

"I was gathering clothes. I didn't think you were going to sniff all my stuff."

"How else am I supposed to know what's clean and what's dirty?"

"You haven't figured out the system yet?"

I dropped the socks in my hand after checking the bottoms, which were filthy. "Enlighten me."

He stepped closer, putting both hands on my shoulders and turned me toward the rest of his room. "Clean." He pointed at one pile. "Dirty." Another equally large pile of clothes. "Clean." Clothes draped the rail in his closet. "Dirty." The heap below the window. "Clean." The pile on his windowsill.

"You divide them by elevation."

"I'm not an animal. I wouldn't put my clean clothes on the floor."

"What do you call that?"

I pointed at the mound by the foot of his bed.

He let go of me and walked over, lifting the clothes up along with a patch of cardboard.

"That's considered not on the floor?"

"Technically, yes."

"You sort. I don't want to end up picking up a pair of your boxers with skid marks in them."

"Don't worry. I throw those out."

Revulsion coursed through me. "I'm sorry I asked. Get to work. We don't have much time before your roommates get back and we're not ready yet." If his roommates showed up before we had gone over the plan, we'd have to wing it and that could spell disaster. We need to lay the groundwork first.

We worked in silence with the mound of clothes growing in front of me. "At least most are clean."

"I do my laundry regularly," he said, defensiveness punctuating every word, and dragged a sweater out of the pile. "Oh wow, I don't even remember getting this."

"You do laundry, then just throw it around. What's the point of having clothes if you're not going to take care of them? Organize them and know what you have."

"Sorry, we can't all have a new outfit for every occasion."

"I don't either."

"Please, I've never seen you wear the same thing twice." He finished sorting and moved onto folding.

"My closet gets plenty of recycling." I tucked in the long sleeves of a heather gray thermal and flipped it up into a neat rectangle. "I didn't know you were watching what I wear so closely."

"When you're peacocking around all the time, it's hard to miss."

"Peacocks are dudes." I repeated my folding on another thermal.

"Same difference." He dropped his folded shirt on top of my stack. "How the hell do you fold so neatly?"

"Retail experience. I've spent a lot of time folding and refolding clothes to stick back on shelves."

"You work at the bookstore, don't you?"

"Yeah."

He *hmm*ed and went back to folding.

"No snarky comeback?"

"Why would I? We're supposed to be getting to know each other, right?"

I wasn't prepared for this blunted Cole. Biting and caustic I was prepared for, it was the pattern we'd fallen into, but this version reminded me of a time before we hated each other. It was dangerous. "Right?" We finished the folding, this time going over our schedules.

"I didn't realize you still had so much football stuff to do even with the season being over."

"Football is life. Haven't you learned that around here?"

"You're not wrong. You should see the football section of the store during home games. You'd think we were running a Black Friday sale with the way people tear through the displays."

"That's got to suck."

"Comes with the territory. There are worse jobs to have. At least I don't have to deal with anything food related." I smoothed my hands over the six stacks of clothes on his bed. "There, let's figure out your wardrobe."

"Why can't I pick my own clothes?"

"It's not like I'll be dressing you for school every day and sending you off on the bus with a nice packed lunch, but we need to make it look like you at least put in a little effort in these pictures."

I sifted through the piles and pulled out eight options. "These will work. Do you have a suit?"

"In the closet." He motioned toward the open empty closet.

Curious, I peeked inside and sure enough, rammed against the wall was the hint of promise. Camouflaged against the dark interior, a garment bag called to me and got my Fashion Sense tingling.

I dragged the zipper down. "I can work with this. Why don't you ever wear this?"

His face contorted in disgust. "The only time I wear it is when we're forced to for football stuff. Booster events, awards, stuff like that. Why would I choose to put this thing on?"

"Because a suit can make you feel good. Confident. Powerful." I shoved the bag aside and pulled out the suit, running my fingers over the fabric. The fabric blend wouldn't be forgiving against his body. His shoulders and chest weren't standard measure. I picked up the pants and sure enough, they were way bigger than they should be for him.

"Sorry, I don't have the same love affair with clothes as you do. Wearing this thing makes me feel like an idiot."

"Then you're wearing it wrong." I shook it out and held it up to him.

"I've been wearing clothes for as long as I can remember. I know where my arms and legs go."

"If they're not making you feel good, then you're wearing them wrong. Change." I held up the clothes.

"Right now?"

"No, next week. Now. We don't have much time left.

They'll announce the couples in a few days. Our friends will find out. People will start getting suspicious, so we need to be locked and loaded with our answers and proof of our undying love and devotion. But first, I need you to try on the damn suit." I shook the hanger at him.

"Drama Club makes total sense." He dropped the suit and whipped his shirts off in one way-too-smooth motion.

All the air shot from my lungs and a yelp escaped my throat. "What are you doing?" I whipped around, turning my back to him. My heart jackhammered against my ribs.

"Getting changed like you told me to." Rustling and jangling increased behind me. "I'm decent," he grumbled.

"Now who's being dramatic?" I turned and stifled a laugh.

"What did I tell you?" He flapped his arms, slapping them against the sides of his legs. The cuffs were too long hitting at his knuckles. Across the chest, it was tight, but everywhere else, it was loose and hung oddly.

I ran my fingers over my chin. "This won't work."

"Why do I have to wear a suit anyway?"

I shook my head. "We'll figure something else out. I've got to get to my shift at the bookstore. Meet me tomorrow with these eight outfits and we'll get to work." I cracked my knuckles.

"That's only slightly terrifying."

"Don't worry." I picked up my bag off the floor. "It'll only hurt a little."

"Let me give you a ride to the bookstore."

"You don't have to."

"It's what a boyfriend would do, isn't it?" He said it matter-of-factly, not a hint of patronizing to it.

I opened my mouth and snapped it shut. If we wanted to

win this, I had to commit. "You're right. Lead the way, shnookums."

His face twisted and he walked down the stairs.

"Not your favorite?" I followed behind him.

He opened the front door. "Not even close."

A blast of cold air sent a shiver stabbing through me. "Fine, but we need to come up with an annoying, sickeningly sweet nickname for each other."

"Do we have to?"

"Only if we want to win."

We drove to the bookstore, both rattling off the most horrendous nicknames we could think of. Idling at the curb, he looked to me. "If you call me Poopsie, I'm out."

"It was only a suggestion." I reached for the door handle.

"Wait!"

My heart leapt into my throat and I gripped the front of my jacket. "What? You scared the shit out of me."

"Then stop opening your door. Wait for me, remember?" He hopped out and rushed to my side. "We've got to make it look good."

I stepped out and leaned in close, so our noses were almost touching. The door was the only thing separating us. "Tomorrow at two. My roommate will be out and we can get to work."

"Quite a proposition, Schmoopie."

My face contorted. "No. Bring the clothes and don't be late. We have a lot to get done and not a lot of time."

He saluted me. "Aye, aye, Captain." He leaned in closer until our noses did touch. "Hurry up and get out of here, you're letting all the heat out of my car." With a peck on the tip of my nose, he jogged back to his side of the car and hopped inside.

With gritted teeth, I waved at him and headed in through the sliding doors.

He wouldn't get under my skin. We were playing a part to win a prize, that was all. Every romantic gesture was just to up his chances of being the one who came out on top. I'd scribble that into my brain, if I needed the reminder. We were both on the same page, but my heart needed to be clued in to it because the damn thing was having a hard time separating fact from fiction, and the truth was it was all lies. And it would never be anything more.

"It looks like you're trying not to puke." I clicked through the pictures on her phone.

It was heating up under the blanket, but we were doing our best to recreate every staple couple photo from cheesy to classic, including the one where she straddled me with a sheet over her head and I took a picture while staring up at her.

We were both sweaty and it had taken at least twenty minutes to get the lighting right. Spur of the moment picture, my ass.

She flipped the sheet back, blinding me with the full blast of lights turned on in her room and exposing us to freezing fresh air after being trapped in our blanket tent. "I sneezed."

"All over my chest." I brushed my hands over the T-shirt, checking for signs of wetness.

"You're the one who hit me with the pillow." She jumped off the bed and glared down at me.

Outrage streamed through me and I shot up. "You're the one who kneed me in the balls."

"I was trying to catch my phone from falling off the bed." Both hands were propped up on her hips. Her shoulders were out in the tank top and short set she'd changed into. The shorts that hit her midthigh had ridden up some and showed off way too much leg for me to keep myself under control. When they'd been straddled over my thighs, I hadn't had a choice other than to improvise with the pillow. Or she was going to get an unexpected nudge from my dick and I'd probably come in my boxers—again.

I wasn't ready for another round of humiliation. These pictures were more than enough.

"How about we be done with the bed shots right now? How many couples are actually taking pictures of themselves in bed?"

"We only needed a few anyway." She brushed her fingers along her hairline, freeing a few strands from her floppy ponytail. "Let's swap into the formal look."

"You didn't tell me to bring my suit." Now she was going to lose it on me, and I'd spend the next couple hours dealing with Grumpy Kennedy.

"I know. Yours is over there." She pointed to the garment bag hooked on the top of her open closet door.

My body snapped straight, stunned at the innocuous-looking black bag on the other side of the room. "You bought me a suit?"

"No, I found you a suit. This one should fit better. If it doesn't, we can stick with the suit jacket only." She tapped her finger against her chin. "Actually, we'll go with the suit and these jeans." She bent at the waist to pick up the jeans from the stack of clothes on her beanbag chair. The shorts rose up even higher, showing off a hint of the curve of her ass.

Blood shot straight to my already straining erection and

I bolted across the room, picking up the garment bag and holding it in front of me. "I'll go get changed in the bathroom."

"Sure." She drew out the word and looked at me like I'd gone insane. Maybe a little. "I'll change in here. You'll need these." She tossed the jeans to me.

I caught them in midair and rushed out of the room and into the bathroom I'd gotten familiar with over the past few hours of wardrobe changes.

My other clothes were in a pile beside the toilet. Four pairs of pants and four shirts. I hooked the garment bag on the shower rod and stared down at the tent in my boxers.

"Can you cooperate please? I'm begging you." I flicked the lock on the door. The throbbing wasn't going down and I couldn't go back out there like this.

Shoving my hand inside my boxers, I wrapped my hand around my dick. A tremor of pleasure traveled down my spine. Cool air breezed across the sensitive head.

"Let me know about the fit."

I gripped myself tighter and bit back a strangled cry. "Will do."

"It might be too tight. But I think I got the size right. It should fit like a glove."

The pounding was impossible to ignore. Every syllable from her lips sent flashing images straight to my brain of what she'd feel like. None of this was helping. I stared down at my angry, ruddy dick against my palm, tempted to finish what he started. Wrenching the faucet handles, I cranked on the water.

"I'll be out in a few minutes. There's another pair of jeans I'll try with it too and see how they look."

"Take your time. Let me know if you need any help." Her voice trailed off and her footsteps retreated.

My mind wandered to the mental image I'd tried to lock away, but would forever be blistered into my brain.

Kennedy naked in my bedroom watching me with hungry eyes.

With a single pump of my cock, I came all over my hand at the thought of her. Excruciating bliss paralyzed me and nearly took me to the floor. I braced my hand against the wall and tried to catch my breath. Once blood returned to my brain from the now overly sensitive appendage dangling between my legs, I listened for Kennedy in her bedroom.

Panic seized me. I glanced around and washed myself off using the still running sink and grabbed one of hand towels —god bless girls and their considerate bathroom linens. Faster than I've ever moved, I cleaned myself off, dried up and threw on the clothes. With the towel stuffed in my pocket, I bolted out of the bathroom and back into Kennedy's bedroom. I tossed the dirty towel in my duffel. I'd clean it and bring it back, no harm no foul.

I turned, and my breath was stolen away. Like she'd reached in and scooped the air out with one look. A red lace overlay with shoulder bows. The knee-length dress accentuated Kennedy's curves and hinted at what was beneath to unwrap. Unfortunately for me, I knew that what she was hiding was better than what she was showing off.

She turned with the zipper to her dress halfway down her back.

"Sorry." I whipped around and faced the door, not wanting a repeat tented-pants incident. What the hell was wrong with me around her?

"It's okay. You can help me out with the zipper. I think it's jammed."

With deep breaths, I walked to her and tugged on the

zipper, not wanting to yank the damn thing apart. "It's stuck."

"Thanks for the update. Can you see what it's stuck on?" She looked over her shoulder.

"Let me get a closer look." I knelt behind her and steadied myself with my hands on her hips.

If I hadn't already taken care of myself earlier this would be a big problem. Eye level with the jammed zipper, I picked at the fabric stuck between the teeth. "I'll have to pull it down to fix it."

"Whatever it takes."

My throat was drought dry. I jerked the zipper down, pulling the fabric free, but the freed pull moved much easier and slid almost to the bottom of the zipper. The lace ruffle top of her underwear peeked out from the gaping fabric. Fuck, I was in trouble.

Swallowing, I kept the lace free from the teeth, but the move shifted my hand, so it skimmed along her spine all the way up. My heart sprinted like I was headed for the end zone.

Her body shuddered and her head snapped straight ahead.

"Sorry. My hands are cold." Dread at her wondering why my hands were this cold and slightly damp, sped me through the final zip.

"Don't worry about it." Her voice was hoarse and stilted.

Don't make this weird, Cole. I did the eye hook at the top of the dress and ran my hands over her shoulders. The curve of her neck was inviting. I wanted to bury my nose in her skin and inhale the scent that had enveloped me from our first pictures snuggled up on the couch.

Kennedy Finch was dangerous to my health. Bundled up

in a neat, entirely too-tempting package, she was a walking wet dream and a captivating disaster.

She sat on the edge of her bed. The neckline of her dress showcased her breasts, which swelled from her position deepening the cleavage that my mouth wanted to dive face-first into.

I cleared my throat and looked anywhere but at her.

Bent over, she laced up her heels. The red strands criss-crossed her skin.

"What are we doing now?"

"Date night, couple shots."

"But it's three p.m."

"They won't know that. Turn around. Let me look at you."

I took the scenic route and kept my hands in my pockets in case there was an erectile appearance.

"Looks good." She dragged her fingers through her hair while staring into the mirror attached to her desk. Using hair pins pinched between her lips, she flipped her hair around her hand a few times, braided a few pieces, and wedged the bobby pins in to transform it into an intricate hair knot with a couple braids wrapped around it.

"How'd you learn to do that?"

"What?" She mumbled around the bobby pins.

"The thing with your hair."

She caught my eye in the mirror and smiled.

My heart stampeded in my chest.

"A lot of practice. Costume changes in our musicals were mostly clothes, but sometimes hair. It forced me to be fast. Plus, a hair style can transform an outfit. Backstage, it was a trial by fire." Her gentle laugh spread warmth through my chest. She flicked one last bobby pin open with her teeth.

Every movement mesmerizing. "You should see what real professionals can do."

I'd been staring. She thought I was entranced by her hair handiwork, and it was better that way.

I ripped my gaze away from the mirror and focused anywhere else. "Where do you want me?"

"Let's go into the hall. Melody's got a mirror there." She paused and looked at me. "Your cuffs aren't done."

I held up my arm and looked at the undone sleeves. "I don't have cuff links."

"Shit, I didn't think of that." She scrounged around her desk. "Here, we can use these. Take off your jacket."

I shrugged it off and Kennedy stuck small-knotted fabric through either side of the cuff link holes. "You're good at improvising when it comes to all this."

"Being resourceful comes with the territory. It's not a big deal."

She'd always come off as someone who went through outfits and clothes because she could. I figured there was a daddy's credit card being maxed out weekly from the way she dressed, but seeing her room, it all felt more lived in and less perfect than I expected.

She finished up the second cuff. "There. Let me get your coat."

She walked behind me, and I let her slip it onto me. Her hands traveled up my arms to my shoulders. Standing behind me, she looked at me in the mirror. Our gazes collided and a pulse of electricity roared through me.

Her breath skated across the back of my neck. She reached around me and buttoned the jacket, never taking her eyes off me in the mirror. With her chin resting on my shoulder, she stood there and her gaze broke the lock on mine, shattering the connection.

"This is a perfect pose. But I need to figure out where we can put the camera to get the shot."

Everything came into focus once more. Why we were here. What we were doing. When it would all end.

I cleared my throat. "What about on that shelf?"

"Perfect." Her arms dropped from around me and I longed for her touch again. She set up her phone and set it for the delayed timer. Back in position, she wrapped her arms around me, but it didn't feel the same as before. It felt wooden and fake. It was wooden and fake.

After two more outfit changes, we crashed on her couch with a beer for me, swiped from her roommate's shelf, and a hard cider for her.

"I can't believe you don't like beer."

She scrunched up her nose. "I'd rather drink nothing than drink beer. I'll stick to cider or hard liquor." Her legs were stretched out with her toes less than an inch away from my leg.

My body hummed in anticipation of her touch. Not for a staged picture, but for real. "How'd you make it through party season?"

She waggled her eyebrows and took a sip. "I have my ways. There's always a stash of good stuff at every party, you've just got to know where to look and who to ask."

"I'm sure guys throw the good stuff at you at any party you go to."

"You did." Her smile faded like a dying star, and she tucked her feet under her on the couch.

My chest tightened. "What's the plan for posting these?"

"I'll split them up to make sure we're not double posting. I set up a scheduler, so if you give me your password, I can have them posted without you needing to do anything." She took another gulp from her cider. "Now the big question everyone's going to want to know..."

"How'd this all start?"

She nodded. "We could tell them we ran into each other over Christmas break."

"After the playoff loss, your roommate was gone and you consoled me."

"Consoled you." She picked at the label on her bottle.

"Campus was mostly empty. We played tag to kill some time, so we were all avoiding each other. I could just say I was avoiding by being here. That's what Reid did with Leona."

Her head cocked to the side. "You guys play tag?"

"A few times a year."

"How old are you?"

"I remember a certain someone"—I directed a pointed look at her—"heading up the toilet-paper brigade during the prank war last year complete with perfectly coordinated face paint."

She sunk a little deeper into the couch. "That's different. It's tradition." A mumble and another sip of her drink.

"Ours is too. It's not like we're standing in the back yard playing. There are serious rules. Last year, Ezra jumped through a window."

"A closed window?" Her fingers slipped off the condensation-covered bottle.

"Shattered it into a million pieces. There went our security deposit."

She jerked forward, shocked concern radiating through her voice. "Was he hurt?"

"Somehow no. The force of his stuntman jump left him unscathed. He was lucky."

"Beyond lucky." Her eyebrows furrowed. "Then that'll work. Melody was gone for the break, so she wouldn't have been around. What about once classes started? Why didn't we go shouting from the rooftops about being in love?" She drew out the last word and made it sound like a school yard taunt.

"Embarrassment?"

Her gaze turned molten. "What did you say?" Her words simmered.

"Everyone's been telling us we were into each other for a long time. We were embarrassed they were right and didn't want to give them the satisfaction."

The harsh glare lessened and the furrowed brow smoothed. Her death grip on the bottle loosened. After a few strained seconds, she nodded. "Yeah, that'll work. And we'll have the last laugh when it's all over and we tell them it was all fake."

"After we win." I held up my drink. Once they knew the truth, they were going to bust my balls from now until graduation, and that'd be after the ball busting when we convince them we're together.

She clinked hers against mine. "After we win, then I win."

"You seriously think you can out-romance me?"

Her gaze traveled up and down my body. "With my eyes closed." She took a smug sip of her drink and glanced at her phone. Cider spurted out of her lips. "Melody will be back any minute. We've got to get you out of here."

Back in her room, she scrambled to gather up all my clothes that weren't shoved in my duffel, but not before folding them first. The woman couldn't not treat clothes well. I jumped in, so she didn't see the dirty towel I'd lifted from her bathroom.

"It would be easier if you let me shove them into my duffel."

"Shut up and help me and it'll go a lot faster."

With my neatly packed bag, I was pushed out into the hallway.

The elevator door opened the second I pushed the button. Kennedy's roommate, who I recognized from pictures of the two of them, stopped coming out of the elevator.

"Hey, Melody." I stepped inside, scooting beside her.

"Cole Hauser?" She staggered out wide-eyed and turned to face me with her keys gripped in her hand.

I flicked my wrist. "Catch you later. Tell Kennedy I miss her already." The doors closed before she could say anything.

Hitting the lobby, I laughed. Let Kennedy deal with that one. It was only a matter of time before everyone else knew. Might as well start selling it now.

10

KENNEDY

"Why don't we start with a smaller intro?" Cole sat in the driver's seat of his car in front of The Zoo like he'd pull away at any second.

"Because it's a minor miracle no one has figured this out already. The Puppy Love announcement went out yesterday. This will get everyone out of the way all at once."

"They're going to know we're bullshitting them."

"Better make it convincing then." I grabbed his hand in a death grip. "Are you seriously losing your nerve? I'll drag your rotting, decaying, unromantic corpse across the finish line if I need to."

His face scrunched in disgust. "Nice visual."

"Use it as acting fuel." I flicked down the visor and checked myself in the mirror. "The longer we're in the car, the weirder it'll be."

"Maybe they'll think we're hooking up."

"In a car. Not my style."

"Not enough room."

The barb pierced through the civility we'd settled into

over the past couple days. "Get out of the freaking car, Cole."
I flung my door open.

"What did I say—" He shot out of his side of the car,
slamming his door so hard it shook the chassis, and rushed
around to my side. "About opening the door before I could?"
He flung the door closed with a glower.

I jerked my leg up barely escaping having it crunched.

He tugged it open and scowled.

Pasting on a self-satisfied grin, I stepped out, avoiding
his outstretched hand. "Got your ass out of the car though.
Let's go before people start wondering what we're doing out
here."

He closed the door behind me, and I reached for his
hand.

My stomach lurched. The oddness of how easy it was to
do after months of repelling one another like two magnets
unsettled me.

"Let's get this over with."

"Don't sound so happy about it."

"There's no going back now."

"There wasn't much going back once we signed up for
this, had our pictures taken, and had them posted all over
social media."

"You're right."

"Of course, I am." I straightened my shoulders and fell in
step beside him. With a deep breath, I exhaled. It lingered in
the air and was sucked inside the second he opened the
door.

The party was in full swing like it had been for Taylor's.
There were colored lights dancing along the walls. No keg
stands, but other drinking games were taking place on every
available surface. Flip Cup, beer pong, Asshole.

Leona finished her run of Flip Cup and double-high-fived Reid. Her gaze landed on me and she smiled, waving, but her arm stalled mid-wave.

I smiled wide, feeling a little shaky. We might not pull this off.

Ezra and Hollis popped in through the kitchen door at the same time, while Taylor and Ashley came down the stairs. A triangulation of confusion surrounded us.

They all stared like we'd walked in with bloody heads in our hands. My fingers tingled. If they didn't believe us, we were toast.

Cole leaned in and whispered. "Give them a real show. Let me take your coat." He kissed the back of our inter-twined hands and unlocked our fingers.

My face burned, not from rapidly heating after coming inside, but the ever-increasing number of eyes on both of us. I slipped my coat off and let him take it. Gotta go for the gold. "Thanks, babe." I turned and kissed him, trying not to make it look like a panic move, which it was.

He stiffened for a fraction of a second before kissing me back.

"What the fuck?" Taylor screeched from the bottom of the stairs, eyes wide, her head whipping back and forth from Cole to me.

"What?" I shrugged like this was the most normal entrance to a party ever. "Who's winning at Flip Cup?"

Their positions slowly encroached us.

Ashley stepped forward with a bewildered look on her face. She raised her hands and touched both our foreheads. "Are you two okay?"

"Of course we are. Why? What's wrong?" Cole laid my coat over the banister joining the twenty others.

She gripped both of my cheeks and turned my head, so I was facing Cole. "Do you know who this is?"

I laughed through my squashed cheeks. "That's Cole."

She repeated the process with Cole, squeezing his cheeks and turning his head.

"That's Kennedy, my girlfriend."

Taylor fell down the last two steps, catching herself on the banister. "We've got to get out of here. There's a gas leak." She bolted for the front door.

I snagged her hand and pulled her to me. "No gas leak. Cole and I are together." Looking at her, I smiled like this was a secret I could finally let her in on.

Her forehead creased. "Why? I know you had a thing for him last year, but you've both been in the 'I'd rather have my face gnawed off by a coyote camp rather than even talk to each other mode.'"

Cole draped his arm over my shoulder. "Things change."

"It's not a big deal, guys." My smile felt brittle enough to crack.

They all eyed us skeptically.

Ezra stepped forward with two cups. "After all these months, it's great you two finally got your heads out of your asses and are ready to own up to your feelings."

My stomach tangled, twisting into a gnarly knot. I clamped my lips together to not refute what he'd said and ruin all our plans.

Cole and I weren't fighting feelings all this time. After this was all over, we'd go our separate ways and maybe be friends, but nothing more than that. A means to an end, that's all we were to each other.

Ezra wasn't a big talker, but when he spoke, most people listened. That seemed to be enough to get everyone to calm down a little. Hollis raised his red cup. "To Cole and Kennedy."

The suspicious glances didn't die, but at least they let us

loose from the six-person microscope we'd been trapped under.

Taking our chance to exit the spotlight, we headed to the beer pong table. Cole grabbed the ball and a pitcher, refilling the cups. "Who's ready to go up against us?"

Reid and Leona walked over to us cautiously, like they were afraid at any minute we might go for each other's throats.

"We'll play you." Leona slid the cups to their side of the table.

"Reid, do we have any cider? Schmoopsy hates beer."

I gritted my teeth. Needles of annoyance rushed across my skin.

A hush fell between them both and Reid stared at me. "Who's Schmoopsy?"

"You know." He looped his arm around my shoulder.

Instead of punching him in the ribs, I leaned my head against his shoulder and patted his chest. "Thanks for thinking of me, Softie." I grinned extra wide and looked up at him.

His arm tightened around me and his eyes shot daggers.

Aww, poor baby.

Reid and Cole walked off to get my ciders and Leona sidled up beside me and close-talked. "Is this a joke?"

I breathed through the panic and laughed. "No, why would you think that?" I arranged and rearranged the cups into a triangle.

"This is Cole."

"I know."

"Cole."

"The heart wants what the heart wants, and it wants him." I waited for the rush of bile straight up my throat, but none came.

"Okay." She drew the word out like she didn't believe it one bit.

Shit, if they didn't buy it, how would anyone else?

Cole returned and I plastered a kiss on him and whispered in his ear, nuzzling his neck. "We've got to amp this shit up. We've put in too much work already, let's not fail now."

He cupped my ass and whispered against my lips. "How's that?"

My heart leapt, adrenaline pumping with each almost brush. Not to be outdone. I kissed his neck. "Way to take initiative."

His fingers moved in a maddening cadence on my butt. "Just doing what needs to be done."

Reid cleared his throat. "Come on you two. Break it up. Let's play."

Cole took his first shot and sank it into a cup on the far end of the table.

Reid picked it up and downed it in one gulp.

Leona tossed hers and it swirled around the rim of a cup before bouncing onto the table.

Not wanting to be shown up, I took my spot and hooked my shot, sinking it cleanly into a cup in front of Leona.

Her eyes narrowed with a huff. "You two are dangerous."

We ran the table, clearing out all their cups before either of us had to drink more than two cups. High-fiving overhead, we laughed after another game won.

Griff and Ezra grumbled and downed the beers they hadn't been able to finish after going double or nothing with us, which meant doubling up the amount of beer in their cups as well as the number of cups.

"Next victim." I cupped my hands around my mouth calling for another taker.

"I'll go." A hand raised behind the heads of everyone else. A head bobbed through the crowd assembled to watch our twelve-game streak.

The syrupy brown eyes collided with mine and my stomach clenched, bile roiling inside. "Josh." My laugh was like rocks dropping into a glass vase.

Cole's head snapped in my direction with irritation flashing in his eyes.

"You need a partner to play."

Ashley hopped off her perch on the windowsill beside the table. "I'll play with him."

"Thanks so much, Ash." I gritted my teeth.

Josh nodded to her and picked up a ball, practicing his shot without releasing it.

"Kind of crazy you two are dating, isn't it, Kennedy?" He let go and it sank straight into the cup in front of me.

"Not really." I picked it up and downed the now flat cider.

"Really. You don't even like a guy to stay over at your place or spend the night at his but you're here with Cole, shouting to the whole campus that you're together." He folded his arms over his chest. If this asshole ruined this for us, I'd find a way to make his life miserable. Hooking up didn't mean he owned me or I owed him a damn thing.

Beside me, Cole tensed. "She just needed to find the right guy she didn't want to kick out of bed." He threw his ball and it splashed into the beer pong cup on the table in front of Josh.

"Or maybe there's something you both want more than you hate each other."

Cole looked to me for confirmation and took my hand.

A tingle traveled up my arm at his touch, settling the hurricane brewing in my stomach. "We don't hate each other. Never have. Maybe for a time, we didn't see eye to eye, but we do now."

Ashley tossed her ball and it landed in a cup. "Nothing but net."

I picked up the cup and downed it, wanting this game over as quickly as possible.

"You're trying to convince me and everyone else here that this"—he gestured to the two of us and looked pointedly at our hands—"has nothing to do with Puppy Love." He held up his phone waving it around like a smoking gun.

Other people pulled out their phones, finding the social media post. I glanced at everyone ready to document this like we were on a freaking movie set. It was time to take this act up a notch.

I licked my parched lips, emboldened by Cole standing beside me. "No, we've been into each other for a long time."

"Since when?"

I mined for a deep memory I'd tried to repress. "Not that it's any of your business, but sophomore year."

Cole jerked and stared at me. "Sophomore year."

If I looked at him, I'd lose my nerve. "Sophomore year during the prank war, he jumped in front of a bunch of paintballs for me. That was when I started falling for him and I've been fighting it ever since."

Cole's gaze heated the side of my face.

I peeked over at him.

His jaw was clenched. Determination settled over his expression before melting into a half smile.

"And I've been crushing on her since freshman year when she loaned me one of her chewed-up pens in Business Marketing when mine burst in my mouth on the way to class."

My breath deadlocked in my chest. The memory plowed

into me. He'd had blue ink spread all over his lips without even realizing it. I'd given him a makeup remover wipe and a spare pen.

With hands on my shoulders, Cole turned me to face him. His gaze was filled with the kinds of feelings that made me remember every time I'd flirted with him before things fell apart. "Whatever you thought you were to Kennedy's got nothing on what I am to her." He was selling the hell out of this, and knowing it was all bull didn't stop the warmth from spreading from my chest to the rest of my body.

"And what I am to him."

Cole wrapped his arms around me and trailed his finger along my chin. His lips were like blistering heat against mine.

The people around us faded away and I forgot what was real and what wasn't. His kiss was a straight shot of adrenaline. My head swam and pulse drummed in my ears.

"Fuck the game. You win." Cole tossed the ball, which landed straight into a cup.

The crowd went wild and he grabbed my hand, plowing through people and dragging me behind him.

I scurried to keep up and followed him straight upstairs and into his room.

He closed the door and turned to me with a wide smile, not the heated one he'd served up downstairs.

"Holy shit! You're a master bullshitter. Prank-war paintball. How'd you even come up with that on the fly?"

My brain stuttered. Fact and fiction collided. He hadn't remembered. The way he'd held out his hand after holding up a Plexiglas shield blocking the paintball onslaught had been lost to a sea of other smiling women. Like the fans cheering for him in the stands.

"You know me. Acting," I choked out. "What about you with the pen? You made it up?"

"Sort of. But I just remember getting that chewed-up pen. I forget who gave it to me. Let's hope whatever girl it was isn't downstairs telling everyone how it was really her." He laughed and I joined in, feeling like I was gargling jagged glass.

He didn't even remember it was me. Not with droves of other women vying for his attention.

I'd been less confident back then. Less take-charge and only one of many women who wanted him. And now I had him, only not for real. Never for real.

11

COLE

I stood upright with my hands jammed into my sides to keep me from pitching over. The icy fingers of winter gripped my chest as my sweat turned to frost under my pads.

Coach stood directly in front of me with a sneer. "Some team solidarity. That was the most pitiful practice we've had since the beginning of this program."

A trickle of despondency rolled down my back.

"You all think you're so great at pulling off stunts, but none of you have been good enough to get this team where it needs to be. I want greatness, but you're fighting me at every turn with your insubordination and lack of hustle."

Helmets thudded against each other from how tightly we were packed in for yet another reaming.

"I thought you were finally the team that would get me there, but once again..." His gaze locked onto me. "Disappointment."

Bile tickled at my tonsils and I bit back the burning churning in my gut.

"I will not be disappointed again. If the transfer window wasn't closed and letters hadn't already been signed, I'd have replaced all of you with players who gave a damn and would get the job done. Instead, I'm stuck with you, so I'll keep pushing until you give me what I want or you quit." He handed off his tablet to an assistant coach and surveyed us all, looking at us like the dirty shower drains after a practice.

My pulse careened against my eardrums and pounded in my neck. My fingers tingled and I steeled myself to contain my fury. What he wanted was to break us down. He wanted complete control over every aspect of our lives until we couldn't even think without his say-so.

"Hit the showers."

Muted and defeated, we marched off the field and into the locker room.

My hands and feet stung with the sudden change in temperature. I cupped them around my mouth and blew into them.

Griff knelt with a groan and unlaced his cleats. "He really knows how to get everyone pumped up and excited for the next season."

I jerked my pads off and dumped them on the floor feeling like I was suffocating in the wide-open locker room. "He doesn't know another way to communicate."

Ezra wrapped a towel around his waist, already out of his gear like a quick-change magician. "Maybe he should learn."

I grabbed a towel. "Why don't you make that suggestion?" I shucked off the rest of my soaking frosty clothes until I was down to my boxers. With my towel wrapped around me, I grabbed my shower gear.

A shadow fell over me. "Hauser."

My only recently settled heart rate picked up pace.

I turned to face one of the assistant coaches and I sagged like I'd been forced to run a marathon through mud.

"He wants to see you." His lips twisted, set to a grim expression.

Unfortunately, I knew exactly who he meant.

"No time for a shower."

The eyes of everyone in the locker room were locked onto me. It wasn't the first time I'd been called back for my own private flaying and I feared it wouldn't be the last.

His slow, regretful head shake fired up the thunder-clouds in my head.

Tightening the fold on my towel, I slipped on my shower shoes and followed him.

My rubber soles squeaked against the polished concrete floor. The freezing air shoved its way under my skin with goosebumps erupting all over me. Gritting my teeth, I continued my march.

Outside Coach's office, the assistant coach knocked once and left me to my fate.

I stood in nothing but my towel, knowing he knew I was out here. The bitterness welled inside me.

"Get in here." That was as polite as he got.

I stepped inside his office and stood with my hands at my sides. These meetings always seemed timed to extract maximum embarrassment and I'd gotten better at knotting my towel, so it didn't end up pooled around my feet like the first time.

"Have you changed your mind?" He dragged a cloth over the crystal-and-brass trophy on the second highest shelf.

"No, sir."

He didn't stop polishing. "You've got more resolve than I expected given your background."

I clenched my hands at my sides and exhaled. My background. I wanted to shatter every trophy on his shelves. I wanted to scream and rage, but I kept quiet and locked my muscles against a tremor that rolled through me.

"Can't say I'm not surprised you've made it this far." His half laugh sounded more like a Brillo pad caught in a garbage disposal.

"I've always wanted to win."

"I guess I rubbed off on you at least a little after all this time." He turned and tossed the rag on the desk. "The question is do you have what it takes to win? Wanting it and getting it are two different things. You have to be willing to put the win above everything else—everyone else."

My vision clouded in a wave of fury, blistering memories trying to shred me where I stood. "I understand."

He made a gruff noise of dismissal.

I spun on my heels and marched out of his office. My body close to convulsions. I hated him. I hated myself that I cared what he thought. I hated that I needed his approval and wanted to win his respect. Deep down I wondered if I'd ever get it, and if I did, if it would be worth it.

"Fuck." A perfect slice in my skin seeped a thin line of red. I shoved my finger into my mouth. "Did you give me the razor-tipped paper?" I shook out my hand and inspected the cut. My back leaned against the wall beside my bed and she sat cross-legged to my right. Every crossing and uncrossing of her legs brought us a little closer.

Kennedy laughed and shook her head, going back to her flawless folding. "It was too expensive. I got the cyanide-laced instead. Once you lose all feeling in your arms and legs then I'll know my plan has finally worked." She dropped her paper, steepled her fingers, and released a super-villain laugh.

"What's the big plan? Slicing me to death and dunking me in a vat of lemon juice?" Folding hundreds of paper hearts in my room for hours on end with Kennedy hadn't been how I'd planned on spending my afternoon. I needed to review plays for our next practice and finish up an assignment I hadn't gotten done in study hall, but I wasn't going to incur Kennedy's wrath if I told her I had other shit to do. Actually, these hearts were more of a pain in the ass than she was.

She looked up, grinning. "You already know me so well." She created a bridge with her fingers and stretched them. "My fingers are cramping." Her body arched, cracking her spine up the entire length and pushing her chest out farther.

It wasn't the worst way to get through the time—not by far. "How many more of these do we have to do?" A smear of blood marred the perfectly symmetrical pink origami heart.

She dropped one more into the second laundry basket filled nearly to the top. "Only a hundred more."

"Only..." I dropped back onto my bed. My muscles screamed at the sudden movement.

Kennedy patted my thigh. "Don't even think of bailing on me now. We'll race. Winner buys drinks for the rest of the week." Her hand landed with her fingertips grazing way too close to my crotch.

My stomach clenched, blood hammering in my veins. I shot back up, cueing more screaming muscles and shifted myself in my jeans. "Rest of the week? What else are you plotting?"

"We're plotting, remember? Wasn't this your plan in the first place? I'd have thought you'd have a kiss list a mile long."

"What's a kiss list?"

"A name I've given to our list of over-the-top romantic gestures that'll make girls all over campus swoon and have guys kicking themselves that they won't be able to live up to it."

"I guess that's as good a name as any."

"After feeding me chicken fingers in the dining hall, pasting pictures of us around the Commons, and picking me up after class with flowers you stole from the botanical garden, your contributions are already running out. We need more ideas."

Inside my head tumbleweeds rolled across the backs of my eyes.

"Fine, how about we do a horse-drawn—"

"No, hell no." My heart rammed against my ribcage and I whipped my head back and forth, neck muscles screaming. "Nope, never."

Her face scrunched into a bewildered expression. "Why not?"

"You want to be dragged behind a thousand-pound hell beast that'll be shitting a couple feet from your face? Does that sound like a good idea?"

She stared at me in a wide-eyed stupor and a hint of skepticism. "Overreaction of the decade."

After a dare to run across the edge of a pasture when I was seven, I'd nearly been kicked by a horse in the field near my house. If I hadn't sprinted like my life depended on it to the other side of the fence the damn thing would've killed me. "Horses are out. Next."

"Fine, I'll think of something, but you're not scamming me for my best ideas to get ahead of me. You can slack all you want, and I'll skate to a victory."

"I'll think of something," I said, equally pissed she'd called me out and that I was drawing blanks on more gestures.

"If we're done before four, we should make an appearance at The Speakeasy before my shift at the bookstore."

"Why?" I forgot we were even allowed in there. But I usually avoided the place. It was where students brought their parents when they visited. Couples hung out once they were all loved up. Definitely not my kind of place.

"The couple's wall?" She stared at me like it meant anything to me.

"What the hell is that?"

"Where couples since the sixties have been putting Polaroids up on the wall..." She stared at me like I should know about every insane tradition on campus. "They say more than seventy percent of the people who've done it are still together to this day."

"Polaroids are still around?"

She snatched the finished heart from my hand. "Yes, they have them behind the bar. An alumnus donated a carton of them after celebrating their fiftieth anniversary with their STFU sweetheart."

"Not hearing any incentives for why the hell I'd want my picture up on that wall. I want to know where it is, so I can make sure I don't even sit near it." If we tried to put our picture up there, the whole thing might burst into flames like a vampire touching holy water. Relationships were a dead end, if you were lucky. Decades of torture if you weren't.

Her body stiffened and she went back to folding, putting extra force into the next heart. "It would help us look legit." Diligently, she creased each fold with her nail like it had spilled a drink on her favorite dress.

"How about hell no?" Kennedy was cool now and we were barely not at each other's throats, but the last thing I wanted to do was step into some circle of hell by linking us together through some screwed up STFU love mojo.

"We can rip it down once this is all over."

Before I could say anything, her phone buzzed on the bed beside her. "I need to take this. It's my sister." She tapped the unlock button. "Hey, Pickle. I've got you on speaker and I'm working on a project right now, so I can't talk long."

"What kind of project?" Intrigue filled the younger girl's voice. A high schooler? At least a teenager.

"A marketing project."

"Marketing?" I mumbled and kept folding. She never mentioned a sister. Not that she knew all the gory details about my life either. Sharing them was at the top of my "not going to happen list," along with dining hall tray sledding and crossing the team line in prank wars again.

A gasp. "Are you with a boy?" An overly loud whisper shot from the speaker.

Kennedy grimaced. "Do you have bat ears able to pick up a baritone from a football field away?"

"Maybe. Now answer my question."

Someone who rivaled Kennedy in not taking shit. She'd obviously learned from a master. I laughed, loving Kennedy getting a taste of her own medicine and impressed she'd rubbed off on her sister so well. Or maybe it was the whole family that was into ball busting.

"I'm with someone. He happens to be male." The words

sounded like they were being pried from her throat. Male. Not exactly the most flattering description. Not like the ones screamed to me from the stands when I was on the side-lines. What about my gorgeous eyes and the way my thighs looked in my jeans?

"What about my ass?" I whispered in mock outrage.

The caller made an "ooo" noise that would've been a perfect fit for any elementary school classroom.

Kennedy glanced up with her lips pinched together. Her reflexes were lighting fast and she whacked me with a pillow.

I laughed, liking the caller's ability to fluster Kennedy.

"Hi, Kennedy's boyfriend. I'm Kennedy's sister, Hannah. Nice to meet you."

"Hi—"

"He's not—" She raised her voice cutting me off, then stopped, glancing at my closed door. "What's up, Hannah?"

So she wasn't playing along with the fake relationship with her sister. Interesting. I didn't know anyone outside of this campus who'd care if I lived or died let alone who I was or wasn't dating.

Hannah cleared her throat. "I'm not talking to you. I'm talking to your boyfriend." She stretched out the word like it had twenty-two syllables.

A tangle of nerves knotted in my chest. The word hit differently this time. Boyfriend. The lie to our friends felt different than this lie. It was her sister. Family.

"You didn't even know I had a boyfriend"—she seemed to swallow that word—"before you called."

"And now, I do. So 'hi' Kennedy's boyfriend."

I looked to Kennedy who rolled her eyes and motioned toward the phone. "Hi, Hannah."

"Be still my heart. That voice."

I laughed at her character of a little sister doing what little siblings seemed to do best from everyone else I knew who had them. Growing up an only child, these types of embarrassing moments had been spared, but also missing. "How are you doing?"

"Just fine and so are you. Oh my god, you're all over her social media accounts and I can't believe I haven't been checking. She's been hiding you from me for all this time."

I liked her. She seemed different from Kennedy, but still take-charge in her own way.

"Stop scrolling, Pickle." Kennedy leaned in closer to her phone.

Not even my muscle control honed over the years could contain my smile. I risked receiving a Kennedy death glare. Even as a pile of charred ash I'd whisper "worth it."

Hannah gasped. "How dare you use my goof name in front of your hottie boyfriend."

"He's not that hot."

I slammed my finished heart into the basket of completed origami and glared at Kennedy.

She huffed and avoided my gaze.

Liar.

"You're a damn liar. I can see the flames from here, Kennedy."

I knew I liked Hannah.

Kennedy dropped her half-folded heart. "Was there a reason you called?"

"I'm thinking about summer plans and maybe visiting you for a few weeks or months. There are some good high schools around St. Francis."

"You can't come live with me, Pickle." Regret swamped each word.

Had her parents been on her about finishing her homework? Or maybe she'd gotten a bad grade and wanted to hide out from being grounded. Kennedy's version of family problems was probably needing to rewear the same outfit in the same season.

"I can't live here." A thread of pleading ran through the words. It didn't seem like normal teenager whining.

I strained to make out where she was. Maybe this wasn't what I'd thought.

"Sorry, Kennedy's boyfriend, but if you're part of the family you were going to hear all about this anyway."

"He's not—" She pinched the bridge of her nose. "It's hard. I know it's hard. In two more years you'll be free. You can go away to college and leave them behind."

"I'm not as smart as you are." The teasing tone left her voice, replaced with distress.

"Don't you dare talk about my sister like that." Kennedy was no-nonsense as always, but there wasn't a sliver of her usual sarcasm.

The center of my chest tightened like someone pressing their knuckles against it at how fiercely Kennedy stuck up for her sister, even against her sister.

"My odds of making it into a good school for costume design are almost nil. The tuition is so high for most and you have to know people to get in. That means internships —unpaid internships. Even if I get scholarships, I can't work for months or years without getting paid."

Kennedy's eyebrows knit together. Frustration? Concern? I couldn't tell.

"Stop catastrophizing." She picked up another stack of papers and set them on her lap. "You've got years to make a plan." Her voice was soft, like this was a conversation they'd had before.

"You did too and you're a lot better at making them than

me, and even you didn't get into any of your dream schools. You haven't gotten any internships, and you've told me how hard it is to get your foot in the door when you don't have connections to get you in."

"There are a lot of other—" She cradled the phone and closed her eyes.

A bolt of longing flooded through me. This was the most unshielded she'd been since I'd met her. The soft spot her little sister had in her heart was undeniable. It made me want to brush the hair away from her face and tuck it behind her ear for an unobstructed view of her.

I knew all about wanting to leave a shitty home situation. Poor kid. It couldn't be easy to be stuck at home with her big sister gone.

"And I can't get stuck in regional theater or a job that pays next to nothing. I refuse to have to move back home."

Some of the hard-ass layers Kennedy showed were peeled away throughout the conversation with her little sister. It was easy to see how much she cared about her. How much she worried about her. Her sister looked to her for comfort and guidance.

No wonder it was easy for her to walk into a room and take over. She wasn't only about running things, but also spoiling people close to her. Like the doughnuts and coffee during all-night builds on the dragon float last semester or any other time she went out of the way to help Leona, Taylor or Ashley. Another piece of who Kennedy was clicked into place. Each new discovery only made it harder to remember we'd hated each other for months, but made it easier to fall into the place we'd been back in August.

"Me too. I know—"

There was a bang in the background of the other line. Loud muffled voices.

"I can't think when I'm here."

Kennedy picked up the phone and hopped off the bed, taking it off speaker. "Can you go to a friend's house?"

Concern crept over me. Not just the change in subject, but how loud it got on the other end and how Kennedy snapped to attention with a sliver of panic running through her words.

She paced. "They won't care." The quick circle she marched in made me dizzy.

"Get your headphones. Crank up your music." She dragged her trembling fingers through her hair. "Do not get on a bus, Hannah. Don't you dare do it." Her voice was frantic.

I stopped folding and slid to the edge of the bed hating how helpless I was to do anything to help. There was a problem. A big enough problem that Kennedy's little sister wanted to escape. Maybe not dangerous since Kennedy hadn't yet stolen the keys to my car to go get Hannah herself, but enough to upset her. Upset them both.

She stopped and stared at the ceiling. "What about the play? What will they do without you?" Her shoulders rounded, folding in like she wanted to collapse. "Please don't cry. They'll get sick of screaming after a few hours. You'll be okay."

Was she saying that because she'd made it out too? Warring parents, it seemed like. The total opposite of mine. Mine were barely ever together. I'd always imagined families with both parents and felt they'd had to have been happier than my own, but maybe that was only wishful thinking. Shitty families came in all shapes and sizes.

"You have tons to look forward to. Graduation will be here before you know it."

"It's not that far—"

Her head shot up so fast, her hair was still tangled in her fingers. "It's a trip to Paris. We're going to Paris this summer. I wanted to surprise you. Use *that* as motivation." Her words were vehement.

And the room tilted, realization crystalizing in my mind. That had been what she planned on doing with her prize, if she won. A fun trip with her little sister. Laughter, joy, and bonding. My stomach plunged. It would be a hell of a lot different than my trip. If I even won, if he'd even go.

"The Champs Elysees, the Louvre, croissants and wine. There's no drinking age there. I'm serious. Deep breaths."

She turned and her eyes widened like she'd just realized what she promised with me right in the room. Her gaze skittered away from mine and she ducked her head.

"Go to your friend's and try not to think about them. Love you too. Bye." She ended the call and flipped her phone in her hand before peeking up at me. "I'm working extra shifts at the bookstore to be able to take her anyway, even if I—we don't win." Crossing the room, she tapped the phone against her palm. Her gaze evaded mine. Guilt? Embarrassment?

It wasn't only Paris. There was a lot of tempting extras with each prize.

"But this kind of trip would get you into a lot of other places you can't pay to get into."

Her mouth twisted. "I'm not trying to guilt you into giving this to me. She doesn't know about all the perks. She'd just be happy to get on a plane. I'm sure you've got big plans for the prize too."

The knot in my stomach tightened. Mine didn't feel as rooted in love and joy as hers. My plans felt more like a bare-knuckle brawl with the demons of my past. "You're right. I do."

"The plan still stands." She sat on my bed, but against the headboard and away from my spot at the foot of the bed. "We had a deal and I don't break my promises."

My final one to my mom rang in my ears. "Neither do I."

12

KENNEDY

I stood outside Cole's class a few doors down from mine five minutes after I'd been let out, for reasons I didn't want to dig deeper into. A nap in a cubicle in the library called my name, but for some reason I was still here. Waiting for Cole.

With both of us being business majors, it made sense that our classes were in such close proximity.

The presentation high rushed through my veins. In class, we'd had to make a fake product along with our product market–testing methodology for the group to rank. Mine had won by a landslide. The packaging and mock ads had been the bleary-eyed creations I'd worked on for a week, but for the win, it was worth it.

I tapped the box of chocolates against my hand and double-checked the time. The chocolate truffles were calling my name, but I planned on splitting them with Leona, Taylor, and Ashley. They were beyond rich, and while normally out of my price range, I'd grabbed them from the discounted section in the bookstore before my shift.

The door to his class opened and students started filing out.

Cole scrolled on his phone with a look of absolute concentration, even bumping into two people who stopped a couple steps away from the door.

"Hey..." What was so important? I faltered in my rush over to him. "Cole..."

A few people turned to look at us.

Then it hit me, I couldn't just stop and walk beside him. The world was our stage.

I flung my arms around him and kissed his cheek. "I thought I'd surprise you, Softie."

He grumbled at my nickname.

Cole's arms wrapped around me and he spun us around. "Showing up outside my class wasn't on the plan for today."

I buried my face against his neck and nipped him.

He jerked.

I threw my head back and grinned. "What's the matter?" I batted my eyelashes and bit my bottom lip.

His grip on me tightened and he stared at me with a mixture of shock and confusion.

I deflated a little and leaned in. "I'm improvising. The more obnoxiously all over each other we are, the better."

His eyes cleared, realization setting in. "Right." A frown creased his lips before he smiled, which slid from innocent to sly and he dipped me.

I clung to him, at my size I'd never thought of myself as a dippable person. Come to think of it, I'd never even had anyone attempt it before. But here was Cole, trying to drop me into a bridge in the middle of the hallway.

He snapped me back up so quickly spots danced in front of my eyes as the blood rushed from my head.

"Are these for me?" He pulled the box of chocolates from my hand and tore it open.

"They—"

He plucked one out and stuffed it straight into my mouth.

I coughed, nearly inhaling the rounded, rich chocolate. My lungs worked overtime to avoid death by chocolate.

The hallway cleared and I shoved at him. "What the hell?"

He popped one of the truffles into his mouth. "Trying to win bonus points? This wasn't on the agenda for today."

My body simmered with indignation. "Those aren't for you." I lunged for the box.

"Maybe you should've thought about that before your little stunt. Picking me up from my class with chocolates, please." He strolled away and popped another chocolate into his mouth.

I yanked his arm back, forcing him to face me. Cautious of the other classes in session, I got in his face and kept my voice low. "I wasn't pulling a stunt. I remembered you had a class near mine and I wanted to talk to you."

The smug look slid straight off his face. "Why?"

Why was right? Like he'd even care about how I did in class. "Right now, I'm asking myself the same question." I yanked the box of chocolates away and slapped the lid back into place.

A classroom door opened and students spilled out into the hallway.

Cole pulled me toward him. "Be good."

Like I was a damn dog. As much as I wanted to pull away, I plastered a dopey smile on my face and hugged him close.

Students bumped into us, forcing me closer against him.

I slid my arms around him under his coat, but only so no one else could see me pinching the shit out of him. "Fuck you."

He flinched and hissed, but stared at me like I was the most adorable person he'd ever seen with flashes of promised retribution in his eyes. "If you want to renegotiate our bargain, I'm game."

I stabbed him one more time in his side, so hard he jumped and yelped.

Letting my arms loose, I laughed and patted his chest. "You're so sweet. Of course, I'd love to read some of your poetry."

A couple people turned toward us and I winked. "He's so romantic, sometimes it's hard to believe he's all mine. Wouldn't you love to have an awesome guy like him?"

The girls glanced back at Cole and their eyes flashed with a flirty covetous look.

Seriously? Right in front of me. I grabbed the front of his coat and held him close. "It's why I brought him these chocolates. I'm just trying to keep up with all the romance he's showering me in."

"You're very lucky." The one girl tapped her pen against her bottom lip and devoured Cole with her eyes.

His heated breath fanned across my cheek. "You know you really are."

I clenched my teeth, but kept my smile in place. "It's hard to imagine he's really real. When he suggested we enter Puppy Love I didn't even want to. It felt unfair when he's like this every day anyway." After I dropped the PL bomb, Cole dragged me toward the exit using his arm around my shoulder as the tether.

We burst out into the freezing walkway leading to the parking lot.

"It's got to be hard having a boyfriend this amazing."

I slipped his hold and spun on him. "Smug much? God, I show up to talk to you and you're acting like I'm plotting some Machiavellian revenge."

"Why did you come to my class?" He crossed his arms, leaning against the ramp railing beside the entrance, suspicion in his murky blue eyes. "Trying to score extra points."

Suddenly wanting to share how I'd killed it in my class seemed dumb. Why did I want to share it with him at all? My mouth opened and snapped shut.

"Exactly."

"You're infuriating." This was what I got for forgetting we weren't friends. "I've got a shift. I don't have time to stand around arguing with you."

"Could've fooled me." He jerked his head toward the parking lot. "Let's go."

"Go where?"

"To the bookstore."

"Why?"

"Why not? It's on my way home and it's a thing boyfriends do."

I narrowed my gaze. "No—"

"It'll take you at least twenty-five minutes to catch a shuttle and walk. Or you can let me drive. Your choice." He shrugged and looked up in the sky like he didn't have a care in the world. Just enjoying the fresh air.

The bus would probably be pulling away just as I got to the stop. Irritation traced under my skin. "Fine."

He grinned and held out his arm for me to loop mine through his.

The anger building in my stomach cooled against the driving wind pushing us back when we rounded the corner.

And the way he switched from needling annoyance to dream boyfriend made it hard to find my groove.

Cole maneuvered in front of me to block the wind. At the car, he opened my door again, this time managing not to elbow me, but no one was around.

Standing in front of him, I braced my arms on the top of the open door. "You're annoyingly hard to read sometimes. I don't know whether you're actually being sweet or screwing with my head and setting me up for some massive rug pull that's going to take me out and knock out my two front teeth."

"That was an oddly specific visual. Now who's dreaming up insane Machiavellian revenge plots?"

I tapped my teeth. "Junior year theater production of Aladdin."

"Had to hurt." He sucked in a breath through clenched teeth, then looked at me. Really looked at me. His gaze roamed my face from the top of my head to my chin before settling back on my eyes.

The way he stared fluttered my stomach and made my heart race even as my cheeks froze.

"We're both playing the game, right? But I'm not trying to hurt you." He lifted his hand before dropping it. "It's a friendly competition and I swear, I'm not hatching some evil plan behind the scenes. I want to win fairly and I don't cheat —ever." His voice was resolute, gaze unflinching.

"Fair enough." I ducked into the car and shivered, huffing into my hands to warm them up.

He popped open his door. "Unlike you."

"I don't cheat."

"What do you call showing up outside my class today?" He looped his arm around my seat and stared out the back window, reversing. His eyelashes were so full and long. His Cupid's bow well defined. His stubble lickable.

Dragging my eyes from his jaw, they clashed with his. I'd been staring—hard—based on the amused smile he flashed.

"I don't have an insanely well-plotted trap for you either."

"Then why did you show up?"

Dodging his suspicions, I scrambled for a reason. "I'm going to Pittsburgh next week and I thought you might want to tag along. We could get great pictures there. Night out on the town. Who wouldn't love that?"

Someone honked. Cole had been sitting almost fully reversed out of his spot and blocking the lane. "Sure, why not?"

He drove me to the bookstore and I cursed myself for throwing out Pittsburgh. That was the last thing I needed. Even more alone time with Cole. Pittsburgh was my alone time. It was where I got to pretend I was in a different city, out on assignment, scouting for up-and-coming trends or styling a big client.

"When you came out of class, you were staring hard at your phone." As much as I didn't want to ask, I couldn't help myself. "Is everything okay?"

"Yeah, it was from Ezra. We were supposed to work out after study hall, but he bailed. He's been off lately."

"Anything I can do?" Ezra had always been nice. Quiet and intense, but nice.

He shrugged with a sigh coated in disappointment. "No. I don't even know if there's anything I can do."

At the curb in front of the bookstore, he parked and walked around to let me out.

Students, tour groups, and campus visitors pushed in

and out of the triple sets of double doors stretched along the front of the building. "About Pittsburgh, it was a stupid idea. You don't have to go. We can come up with something better."

He tapped his cheek and looked at me expectantly.

My pulse jumped. I pecked him, letting myself linger against the warmth of his skin.

Overhead, a rumbling noise came from the sky. I turned with my lips still planted against his hint-of-stubble cheek.

It was a plane.

Standing side by side, we both shielded our eyes.

I grabbed his arm. "You've got to be fucking kidding me."

He let out a low whistle. "Impressive."

A small plane dragged a massive banner behind it. "Nicola, you're my one."

"Who the hell has plane-banner money?" I dropped my hand, only to raise it again, when the engine noise returned.

It wasn't the same plane. It was a different kind, not dragging the banner behind it. Instead, it flitted through the sky releasing a trail of smoke to create a giant heart.

He grabbed his phone and checked the Puppy Love site. "They're in second place, which means we're bumped down to three."

"If people are willing to throw out skywriting money, we're toast. I don't have that kind of money. Do you have that kind of money?"

"No, but just like the prizes, people want stuff money can't buy." His brows drew together and he rubbed the back of his thumb across his lips before snapping and pointing at me. "When did you want to go to Pittsburgh?"

"This weekend?" I blurted out the date, half hoping maybe he'd forgotten a weekend practice and he'd have to bail.

"Perfect."

No such luck. "What's perfect?"

He slammed my door shut and jogged around his car. "You'll see."

Before I could ask more questions, he was gone. His car darted in-between two passing cars, drawing horn blares from one.

I walked into the bookstore not entirely sure of what he had planned and how my trendspotting and thrifting trip was about to be taken over by whatever tricks he had shoved up his sleeves. Then again, that seemed to be how everything was going today.

After clocking in, I clipped on my name tag and got to work. Three hours into my shift and my fingertips felt like they'd been ripped off after I'd had to label over three hundred items with yellow discounted labels.

"Those scarves you recommended we buy sold out so quickly, we're ordering a thousand more." My boss, Gretchen, set a stack of neatly folded T-shirts on a three-tiered display.

"That quickly?" I hefted another armload onto the rolling folding station.

"I've never had as many calls and emails about an item that wasn't football related."

Pride radiated through me. This was exactly the kind of recommendation that could be worth a check with multiple zeroes at the end, if I snagged one of the coveted buyer positions for a major chain after graduation.

"Do you think I could get actual numbers?"

She moved to the other side of the display and tilted her head with confusion in her eyes.

"I can use it for my business marketing classes and for my resume."

"How's that work?"

"If I can show an item I recommended was purchased three or four times higher than in previous years or previous items, it could help boost my applications once I start sending them out."

"I don't see why not," she said with a hint of pride. "You made a great pick, celebrate it for sure."

"Thanks, Gretch."

After folding, stacking, and reorganizing the third display, I was on cash-register duty.

My first customer, an older woman, set a rose on the counter along with a mug, a couple keychains, and a football jersey.

I picked the flower up and looked for a tag. "Can you tell me where you got this? I didn't know we had fresh flowers."

"It's for you." She grinned.

"Thanks? Any particular reason?" Alumni did strange things around here. Who knows, maybe she worked in the campus bookstore when she went here and it brought back fond memories. Stranger things had happened. I eyed it while ringing up the rest of her items. Or maybe she'd decided she wanted to attend STFU while wandering the bookstore aisles.

"No reason." She handed over her credit card and took her receipt.

I glanced around and nudged the rose with my finger. We weren't in a fairy tale. Could you even poison flowers? I picked it up and twirled the dethorned flower between my fingers. The deep red petals were a little wrinkly on the edges, but the smell was fresh and bright.

The next customer also set a rose beside my scanning gun. And the next. Some customers didn't even have anything for me to ring up.

I leaned over the counter, trying to see where they were all coming from. We didn't even sell roses. Where was the closest flower shop? Roses weren't cheap. Who was just showing up, handing them out?

It wasn't until the sixth that I spotted him in the security mirror pointed at the area around the corner from the register. Cole loitered by the postcards, grabbing anyone who passed by as they headed out or to the register and handed them a rose from the three dozen in his arms.

Warm, fuzzy feelings tingled across my skin. I sniffed one of the long-stem roses.

Waiting for the rest of the twenty-four flowers drew a crowd. People walking by from the food court were pulled into the display by others who'd handed over the flowers earlier.

Women stared and whispered with wide grins of approval and even sappier expressions once they saw Cole. Yes, he was hot. Yes, he was being super romantic right now. Yes, he was getting looks of longing from half the women who passed him.

Then it hit me. The shine lost a little of its glow. Don't get caught up in these warm fuzzy feelings. This wasn't a "sorry for eating your chocolates and being an ass earlier." This was him balancing the scales.

13

KENNEDY

I stood in the freezing quad blowing into my hands. Squinting, I peered up at the roof of the Commons. Cole was supposed to unfurl the banners from the roof four minutes ago. But it was cold as hell and his fingers were probably frozen, I know mine were.

Had he gotten someone to make the banners or did he do them himself? After my paper-linked-heart scavenger hunt through campus, I felt for him. Handmaking sucked, but it was also cost effective.

Students strolled or rushed past depending on how late they were to class.

I checked my phone again. My screen lit up.

Cole: Sorry, I can't make it. Let's reschedule.

Gritting my teeth, I shoved it back in my pocket. I had switched shifts at the bookstore to be here for this. I'd rearranged my schedule for him and now he wasn't going to show.

Me: You picked this time.

Cole: I know, but I don't have time for this right now. We'll reschedule

My fingers tightened around the phone. Marching out of the quad, I went to the closest bus stop to take me to the far end of campus, racing after the departing bus as it pulled away from the curb.

Cole loved to piss me off. I swear, it was a secret kink because it definitely wasn't him getting me naked. No, we'd been there and he couldn't even get it up.

After six stops, I hopped off the bus and walked the two blocks to his house.

Only the light from the kitchen and flickering light from the TV shined through the living room windows. Did he blow me off to watch freaking TV? I stomped up the stairs and knocked so hard my iced knuckles ached.

Ezra answered with a guitar in his hand, eyes unreadable under the brim of his hat.

"Where is he?"

He glanced over his shoulder. "Now's not a great time." What the hell was he hiding? Flares of anger shot down my spine. Had Cole ditched me to sneak around with someone else? Not that I cared. It wasn't cheating, but any misstep and we'd both be out of the contest.

"I don't care if now's a good time. Where is he?"

"It's not a great time."

"What the hell, Ezra? Where is—"

The door was pulled open wider and Cole stood at the threshold with wary eyes. "I've got it, Ez."

Snake.

Ezra wandered off into the darkened living room. The faint, low guitar strumming was a muted soundtrack to my boiling anger.

"What the hell, Cole?" I whispered and punctuated his name with a poke to the chest.

He grimaced and sucked in a sharp breath between clenched teeth.

My anger faltered and deflated at the look on his face. "Are you okay?"

"Fine, I just needed some rest after practice." He tried to sound nonchalant, but there was a struggle in his voice.

Now taking him in, he looked like hell. He was pale and leaning heavily into the door.

"Isn't that in the mornings? You don't look okay."

He straightened with some effort and folded his arms over his chest, but not touching his body.

Everything stopped and I scanned every inch of him. "What happened?"

"It's nothing." His attempt at a carefree smile sent the alarm bells blaring.

I latched onto the bottom of his T-shirt and pull it up baring the scrunched waistband of his sweats.

His hand covered mine, stopping my tug. "Really, it's nothing." His voice bordered on panic and he angled his body away.

"If it's nothing, then why can't I look? Just checking up on my boyfriend in the doorway of his townhouse. Nothing weird here."

With a resigned sigh, his hand fell off mine.

I raised the fabric. The happy trail of hair ended just above his waistband, next were the abs he'd put in the work for over hours on the field, and next was a color that didn't belong. Dark red speckles intensified to a deep red covering half of his upper chest. There were purple and blue under-tones already.

"Oh my god, Cole!"

His shoulder moved in what would be a shrug, but

without pulling his chest muscles. "It's an occupational hazard."

I dropped his shirt and snapped my head up to meet his gaze.

"Why don't you have ice on this?"

"Already iced it."

"Not enough." I marched past him and tugged on his shirt, not giving him a choice about following or not. Weren't you supposed to ice injuries? Or was it a warm compress?

He probably knew better, but I couldn't just say "okay" and walk off.

The door slammed behind me and I kept going.

Inside the kitchen, I rummaged through the drawers for a plastic bag. After settling for a grocery bag, I yanked open the freezer and poured in a whole tray of ice. Knotting the bag, I gingerly pushed him down in a kitchen chair and knelt holding the bag against his chest.

He flinched.

"Sorry." I gentled my touch. A panicky flush overtook me at my helplessness.

"I've got it." His hand came up to take the bag, but covered mine.

Pulses of electricity skated across my skin. The warmth of his touch against the freeze of the bag made the feelings even stronger.

"Kennedy, I've got it." He stared down at me with a tender look that sent my stomach fluttering to an earthquake setting.

"Of course, I—" I shot up and grabbed the empty ice cube tray, refilling it before sticking it back in the freezer. "Do—"

The roar of his stomach broke through the silence in the kitchen.

"You're hungry?"

"Don't worry about it." His attempts at reassuring me only made me more determined to do something he couldn't do for himself right now—take care of him.

I peered around him to where the music was still coming from the living room. "What kind of girlfriend would I be if I let my fake boyfriend starve?" I whispered. "We've got to keep you healthy, so we can win this thing."

His lips parted like he was going to say something before he closed his mouth and nodded.

"Let's see what I can make." I opened the cabinets, which weren't barren like I'd have expected from a bunch of dudes living together. The music from the living room stopped and Ezra called out that he'd be back in a bit and the door closed behind him.

Cole and I were alone now. If Cole would've told me he was hurt, of course I wouldn't have been pissed at him for standing me up. I gathered up ingredients and placed an order for campus delivery for a pie crust and a few essentials that were missing. It's his fault I'm feeling guilty for being angry. But a glance over my shoulder at how he was working so hard to hold it together once again evaporated all my anger.

What the hell were they doing to him at practice? How'd you field a team if you were trampling your players?

I started on the filling while waiting. The delivery didn't take too long, and Cole kept me company while I worked.

His answers were tight, but not terse, like he was trying. He sidestepped my attempts to get him to rest.

Rolling out the crust for the chicken pot pie, I checked over my shoulder.

He stared at me like he couldn't take his eyes off me.

Heat rose in my body like a match thrown on kindling.

Why'd he have to make me feel like that? It was unfair knowing how he felt once I took my clothes off. "Seriously, Cole. You don't have to babysit me. Go rest." I nodded toward the stairs.

"I like being here." He shifted, leaning back further in the chair, trying to keep his face neutral, but his nostrils flared and his lips pinched.

I went back to the dough, trying to shake the tingling from my hands and tore the crust. Growling, I tried to mend the gap with left over pieces. "You're making me nervous."

"Maybe I like that too."

A rush of desire flooded my body, but I locked it down. Grabbed it tight and tried to shove it away. We'd flirted before and I knew how that ended. There wasn't anyone else we were pretending for, which made this dangerous. I might start thinking this was real.

We were friendly at least and I didn't want to lose that.

"Then I guess you don't want what I'm making because it'll taste like shit if I'm distracted." I stirred the pot of creamy chicken and veggies.

The chair scraped across the floor. Each reverberation traveled through my body.

I braced myself against the counter, not glancing behind me. I was unaffected by him. It was no big deal.

His shadow blanketed my own, swallowing it up against the kitchen cabinets.

My breath stalled.

His body heat radiated against my back.

My grip tightened on the wooden spoon and I swallowed reflexively. Anticipation tingled through my skin.

"I can't wait for my chance to have a taste." His breath tickled the nape of my neck.

My body shuddered and I locked my knees. It was all part of the game. I cleared my throat. "Then get out of here and let me work."

"Have it your way." The ghost of his touch brushed against the small of my back and then he was gone. His measured steps thumped on the stairs.

Whirling around, I caught myself against the counter. Staring up at the ceiling, I wasn't sure which game he was playing anymore, and I was scared what happened if I lost.

The rest of the chicken pot pie–making went smoother with Cole no longer watching my every move and making me forget what I was doing.

Hollis, Ezra, and Griff returned and dumped their backpacks on the floor right inside the front door. Griff bounded into the kitchen. "Hey, pretty lady. What's that?"

Ezra hung back with his hat tugged down as always. Sometimes it seemed like he kept it on just so no one knew how much he was actually paying attention to everything around him.

"Chicken pot pie." I placed the mini pie pan into a bowl and picked it up with a few folded paper towels.

Griff's shoulders sagged. "You only made one."

I laughed.

The sad puppy look complete with big eyes and quivering lip was ridiculous on him.

I leaned in and whispered, "There are two big ones and a few more individual ones in the oven. They're probably done."

Ezra shot off the wall and grabbed an oven mitt. "How's Cole doing?"

I stifled my smile. Little sneak. "I'm going to go up and find out. Save some extra for Cole in case he's still hungry."

The utensil drawer rattled and the three of them dove into the big pie with forks, shouting about how hot it was through their open food-filled steaming mouths.

Shaking my head, I took the stairs two at a time. I knocked on Cole's door and opened it without waiting for a response. His desk light was the only one on in the room, which no longer looked like a disaster area. It was still messy, but there were only a few piles now and some clothes were in a laundry basket. Progress.

He was covered in shadow, under the blankets. Sleeping, the stark lines of his face were more relaxed. His arm and shoulder muscles were defined, but not like they might be from someone trying to show off. More from putting in intensive work toward a goal other than the look.

Shirtless, he sent my stomach into a somersault, until I saw the deep colors of the bruise peeking out from under the blanket draped over him. Suddenly, I felt like an ass for thinking about him being naked under there. The whole reason I was here was because he was hurt.

I closed the door and set the pie down on his desk. "Cole?" I gently shook his shoulder. "The food is ready."

He was curled up with his arms folded over his chest— over most of his giant bruise.

I crouched down and rocked him again. "Cole, eat something and you can go back to sleep."

His eyes opened slowly like a garage door rolling up. His gaze was unfocused before snapping to clarity on me. "Hey." A sleepy smile spread across his lips and he dragged his fingers along the hair framing my face.

My pulse drummed so hard, I felt it in my palms. "The

food is ready. If you want seconds you'll have to hurry up before Hollis, Griff, and Ezra devour it all."

He sat up and winced, holding his side. The blanket slipped down and the soggy bandage and ice pack wrapped around him slid lower.

"Let me take care of that while you eat." I touched the damp stretchy fabric.

His hand covered mine. "You don't have to."

"I know, but the faster you eat, the faster you can have more and get back to sleep."

He stared down at me with his lips parted and his other hand still holding his ribs.

I waited, breath stalling in my throat. Tension building, coiling, tightening.

Steps thundered up the stairs.

"Ezra, you can't take the big one. Get back here." Griff shouted on the other side of the door.

Cole cleared his throat. "Let me get myself together."

"Do you need some pain killers?"

His single head nod with a wince told me how much he was hurting.

My chest ached for him. "I'll get some, and water."

"That would be great."

I bolted from the room and ducked into the kitchen. Hollis made a grumbling sound of approval through his stuffed mouth eating over the full pan of pot pie.

"Use a plate, Hollis."

"Then I'd have to clean it."

"No one else wants your germs contaminating the whole thing."

"That's why I cordoned off my piece of this side of the pan." He pointed to the giant chunk of creamy meat, vegetables, and crust slid to the edge of the glass baking pan.

I shook my head. "Ibuprofen?"

"The cabinet closest to the back door." At least he covered his mouth when he spoke with it full of food.

I grabbed a couple pills from the industrial-sized bottle that was more than half empty. How many of these did the guys go through?

After filling a glass, I was back upstairs.

Cole was tugging his shirt over his head as I reopened the door. A testament to how slowly he was moving with his injury. The collar caught on his hair, tousling it.

"Are you sure nothing's broken?" Worry rose in me.

"Nah, it's just a shitty spot to get hit. I'll be okay." He flashed me a smile that flooded my body with tingling throbs.

I blinked, finally snapping out of the daze. "If you're sure." I held out the pills and glass for him.

"Thanks, Kennedy." He took both from me, his hands brushing against mine cranking that heat up higher.

I picked up the pot pie. The bowl was warm, but not too hot to touch now. I grabbed the fork and held both out to him.

"Did you eat already?" He lifted the bowl sniffing the contents with curls of steam rising from the pastry. His deep groan was knee-bucklingly smooth.

His desk, serving as my butt perch, was the only thing keeping me upright after that.

My lips twitched. "I like your hair."

His eyes darted up like he'd be able to look at his own hair before he smoothed it down with his hands. "Better."

"It'll do."

He shuffled across the room to me. "Have you—"

"I can—"

I chuckled and tucked my hair behind my ear. "You go first." I sat on my hands to keep from fidgeting.

"Have you eaten already?"

"No, I mean I taste tested as I went to make sure it wasn't terrible, but I brought this up as soon as it was finished."

"Have some of this." He lifted his bowl. A low hiss escaped his lips.

I resisted the urge to take the dish from him and force him back to bed. The quicker he ate, the quicker he could sleep. "There's only one fork."

A flare lit behind his eyes. "I know. It's what people who are dating do, right?"

My lips parted, shock at how easily we'd fallen into this rocking me. "But no one else is here." My feeble grasp at recovering some emotional distance.

"I know." His gaze dropped to the food.

The distance between us was now microscopic.

He used his fork to slice into the pot pie, getting a heaping helping of the creamy sauce and veggies before spearing some crust and chicken. His hand faltered as he lifted it to my mouth.

I steadied his hand, wrapping mine around his, and took the bite. The familiar creamy flavor coated my tongue. "Thanks," I mumbled trying to keep my mouth closed.

"You made it. It's only fair you get some." He smiled through the grimace and took a giant forkful and his eyes drifted shut. "Damn, that's good."

His praise washed over me like a warm sunrise.

"You finish the rest." I motioned to the chair, no longer covered in clothes. "Sit down."

He glanced at it before scrunching his face up. "I might be better in the bed right now." His steps were stilted on the way back to his bed. With inhaling bites, he finished the pot pie in minutes, using the bottom crust as a spoon to scoop up every last bit.

His contented sigh sent my heart soaring only for it to come crashing back down. The question had been weighing on me for longer than I'd like to admit. Every time I felt the pull toward him, it grabbed me like a giant rubber band keeping me from getting closer.

I glanced over at him. My heart beat so quickly it felt like a hum in my chest and my lungs seized, but I fought through the building dread. "What happened that night, Cole?"

The fork dropped into the empty pie tin. He stared at me, but didn't say a word.

I ducked my head, swallowing to relieve my parched mouth. "You know. That night back in August. I took my clothes off and you just shut down." I cleared the gravel clogged in my throat. I squared my shoulders. "I think I have a right to know. I deserve to know." I flinched at the pleading in my tone. Getting to know him better made it easier and harder to ask all at once.

"You're going to make me say it, aren't you?"

I lifted my head.

He stared up at me, breathing like he was winded.

My stomach knotted and I stared at the floor. It hurt me to say these words. To ask. All the work I'd done to be comfortable in my own body and I hated that I cared what he thought. "That you don't think I'm attractive when I take my clothes off?"

He shot up and winced, biting out a curse and gripping his side. "Is that what you think?"

I glared. "Come on, Cole. It's what I know."

Crossing the room, he stared at me with wide eyes still holding on to his bruised body. "You think I don't think you're hot as fuck. That I haven't dreamt about getting you naked again. That I haven't wanted to touch you like I did that night."

My gaze bored into his and he didn't shy away. There wasn't a laugh or joke in it. The revelation stunned me. I stared at him, looking for the lie. My body hummed. "But—"

He placed his hands on either side of me. "Do you want to know why that night went to shit?"

Not knowing wasn't an option. I nodded, throat tightening, and stared at the hollow of his throat.

His breath skimmed across the tip of my nose. "I came." The words were strangled and tight.

I jolted and jerked my head back. "Right now?"

He didn't joke or move away.

Our lips were less than an inch apart. The butterflies in my stomach flapped with a renewed intensity.

"That night." His Adam's apple bobbed. "The night I brought you up here. I'd been watching you at the party. Watching you dance, laugh, flirt." The corners of his mouth dipped. "And I wanted you. So I worked up the nerve and we danced." His fingers beside mine brushed against the sides of my hands. "You told me you were wondering when I'd finally come over."

Heat spread across my skin like a spiderweb of seduction. "You said you'd been waiting for the right time."

"I'd been waiting, trying to get myself under control, but I was barely hanging on, so I invited you upstairs."

I nodded. We'd climbed the steps, rushing into his bedroom and my stomach had buzzed with anticipation. The music from the party had made his room our own private club. "I danced for you here."

"So well. Too well." He scrubbed his hands over his face,

pinching his lips and nodding. "I wasn't expecting that. I wasn't prepared for you. I had plans."

My throat narrowed making it hard to squeak out the words. "And when I got naked?"

"The plans were toast. I came in my pants before I could even touch you like I wanted. Like you deserved."

There was a long silence where I watched him. The vulnerability and embarrassment shined brightly in his eyes. Everything I'd told myself about that night—everything I'd told myself about him. Everything had been wrong.

Completely flipped on its head, I ran back through the night I'd promised myself I wouldn't think about again. Keeping that promise I'd made about sacrificing clothes when I thought about that night again, I'd have to get rid of those brown ankle boots I hadn't worn since November.

"I tried to touch you." I flinched at the memory torching my insides. "You'd been hard when I danced and then I got undressed and you weren't. I tried to touch you."

"And I caught your wrist." His jaw clenched. "I didn't want you to know."

"You just threw my clothes at me and said I should go." Humiliation had burned through me so fast I thought they'd find me like a charred statue outside his door.

"What was I supposed to say? 'Listen, Kennedy, apparently I never learned self-control and came in my pants because you're so fucking hot. Give me a few minutes, I'll go clean myself up, and I'll try not to be a two-pump chump with you.' I was embarrassed. Face-meltingly embarrassed. I needed you to go."

I swallowed and it took me a few seconds to get out the words. "I thought you didn't want me." I hated how small I sounded. I hated how weak saying it out loud made me feel.

I shouldn't have given a shit what he thought. I was awesome and I knew it, but it didn't mean I didn't want other people to know it too. To show me.

He caressed my cheek, his palm resting against it and his thumb brushing under my chin. "How could I not?"

The zaps turned to sparks and streaked down the back of my neck. But those old feelings from right after I'd left his room were like tiny slices in the rapidly inflating balloon in my chest. "You were an asshole to me after."

"You kept making limp-dick jokes. The first time we saw each other after that night you called out across the Commons that the campus pharmacy carried Viagra, if I needed it."

"I—I was trying to embarrass you like you'd embarrassed me." Now, I replayed all the harsh things I'd said to him. All the times I'd tried to make him feel as terrible as he'd made me feel and regretted every one. I slid my hands up to his shoulders.

"Kennedy..." He leaned in, but he didn't kiss me. His arms wrapped around my back and he held me close.

I breathed him in, my heart skipping a beat. He smelled like fresh laundry and liniment.

"Doesn't your chest still hurt?" My arms were trapped between us.

"It's worth it."

Gently, I tried to push him back, not wanting him in pain.

His arms tightened so I couldn't move without possibly hurting him. "I never—" His lips brushed against my neck below my ear.

My heart galloped wildly in my chest.

"I'm sorry I made you feel that way. I—"

"I'm sorry I started teasing you about not being able to

get it up." My heart pounded like I'd finished a sprint. I held on to him, wanting to feel his lips again. I wanted a taste, but fear wedged its way in. This wasn't part of the plan.

Strained laughter shook his body. "Now I understand." His armlock loosened and he pulled away far enough to look at me again. "And I want you to know..." His gaze dipped to my lips.

A tremble of anticipation flowed across my skin. "Know what?"

The gap between us evaporated. Exploded in the heat of our bodies colliding. His tongue demanded entrance to my mouth.

I released control and sagged against him.

This seemed to galvanize him and his hands were on me. Against the back of my neck, not letting me pull away, not that I wanted to.

I craved it as confirmation of his attraction to me. For real this time. Not for show. Not for our plotting, but for me.

14

COLE

Napalm had been detonated in my veins. The fire tearing through my chest eclipsed the throb of my bruises.

Perched on my desk, she wrapped her legs around me and my dick strained against my boxers.

My heart hammered against my ribs. I gently tugged on her hair, tilting her head back further.

A mewl escaped her lips. Her hips ground against me. The friction of her body against mine sent me careening toward unstoppable pleasure. Raw and fierce, it crested toward the point of no return.

Jerking back, I broke the kiss and stared at the rise and fall of her chest.

"Too much?" Her chest heaved with each drag of breath, lips and cheeks rosy.

Tremors shook my body. I swallowed and nodded, trying to get myself under control.

She reached for me and I caught her hand midair with only her fingertips brushing my skin. Tendrils of pleasure tried to overshadow the giant throb in my chest.

"If you touch me, it's all over."

Her lips parted and her eyebrows pulled together. "Is this a regular problem for you?" She wasn't teasing or taunting me, genuine concern filled her eyes.

"Only with you," I croaked out. Tremors turned to trembling until I willed my body back under control.

"Now that's how you make a girl feel awesome." She kicked her feet against my desk.

"Seriously." I slowly lowered myself onto my bed. "You're happy about this."

"When the alternative was me thinking the sight of my naked body sent your cock retreating back into your body, of course." Her feet continued their happy drumming against my desk.

"If I'd known that's what you thought I'd have told you a lot sooner."

"If you'd told me a lot sooner—"

"Continue."

She brushed at her hairline. "Forget about it."

"I'm your boyfriend. You're supposed to tell me all your deepest darkest secrets."

"Pretend boyfriend."

A nail was driven into my heart. "Was that a pretend kiss?"

Her eyes widened. "N-no. Not for me, but we can't..." She stared back at me with flustered panic. "The whole point of this was to choose someone we wouldn't get attached to."

I was freaking her out. The barricade shot back up between us. "You're right."

She sucked her bottom lip into her mouth and chewed on it a bit, her jaw moving.

Swampy, sticky silence clung to the air.

"I'm glad you liked the food."

I dove for the subject change. "You're a great cook."

"The skills came in handy growing up. My little sister will be super jealous I made it for you. It's her favorite meal."

"Is she fifteen? Sixteen?"

"Sixteen. High school sophomore."

"That's a rough time."

"What would you know about a rough high school experience? I'm sure you were a big football player in school. You were top of the food chain. You went to all the parties, didn't you?" I hated how easily she'd dialed into what my school life was like, but it didn't begin to scratch the surface of how things had been at home. Rough was a good day where my family—well, my dad—was involved.

"Some. You never went to parties?"

"Theater parties are a bit different than football parties."

"In what way?"

She laughed. "Probably a lot more singing. Overacting and overreacting and a lot more hooking up. I swear by the end of each season ninety percent of the cast and crew had made out with each other."

"Damn, I should've been hanging out with the theater kids."

"We all have that wild side." She raised her eyebrow leveling a challenge.

"I can tell." I picked up the bandage and re-rolled it trying to imagine what Kennedy had been like back then. Had she joined in on the backstage hookups? She had never seemed afraid to go after what or who she wanted. And for a brief moment in the sun, she'd wanted me.

"Are you hungry for more?"

In more ways than one. I nodded.

She hopped down from my desk and gathered up the bowl and fork I'd fed her with. "Let me take these downstairs and see if there's anything left for you."

She opened my door.

"Kennedy—" The words stalled in my suddenly dry throat.

A whirl and she stared back at me.

The awkwardness had rolled off like a fast-moving fog. I didn't want to screw this up again. "Thanks for coming by and for cooking for me."

"Thanks for being my partner in crime, but know I'm still going to kick your ass when it comes to winning this whole thing. I can't help it, I'm just too irresistible." She slipped out of the door and I had no doubts that she was and that she might.

A war waged inside my head. It felt like the grains of time were slipping away to forge some kind of connection with my dad, but Kennedy's glowing smile became a drug I craved.

The air was cleared between us and for some reason that was scarier than falling into the easy old pattern of hating each other. Before, it all was fake, but this—this felt real and more terrifying.

She came back with the last bits of food rescued from downstairs and handed it over to me. "It was all I could salvage short of yanking it out of one of their mouths. There's only one mini pie left."

"Don't worry about it."

She refused my offer to share and I scarfed the food down, barely keeping myself from licking the bowl.

I picked up the bandage, placed the beginning at the center of my chest, and stretched to wrap it around myself.

"Let me do that." The mattress shifted behind me.

I sucked in a breath and drove my fists into my legs in anticipation of her touch. I couldn't lose it every time she came near me.

Kennedy was on her knees on my bed. Her body pressed against my back and her arms wrapped around my chest with her breath lingering against my neck. "All your wincing and groaning. Just ask me to help next time."

Goosebumps rose on my arms and I squeezed my legs tighter, running through the season's losing plays in my head.

"Let me know if it's too tight."

I looked over my shoulder.

Her mouth was too far from mine for my liking. She finished wrapping my chest and secured the small metal clips to keep the bandage in place. "I wish I could do more."

I turned and bit back my grimace. "You've done a lot. More than I deserved for standing you up."

Her eyes widened and she shook her head. "No, I'm sorry for snapping at you. If you'd told me you were hurt, I wouldn't have flipped out on you."

"It's our thing."

"I guess it is." She nibbled on her bottom lip and her eyes darted to the door. "I should go."

"What? Why?"

"I've got an early shift in the morning and I haven't even worked on my homework for tomorrow."

But she'd chosen to make me food from scratch for something we hadn't even planned on posting about. It almost felt like this was real. A hopeful flare warmed my chest. "Sorry for wasting your time and making you take care of me."

"You didn't. I wanted to. It was the least I could do." She slid off the bed and the space felt empty without her. "For nearly biting your head off the second you came to the door."

"I'm used to it. We should've taken a picture of the food and us eating a bite to post later."

She froze, slipping her shoes back on, and looked up at me. "You're right. That's a great idea. There might still be some left. No use wasting a chance to add extra points." There was an off lilt to her voice.

Had she wanted to keep this between us?

We went downstairs, fought Griff for the last piece of pot pie, and forced him to take a picture for us.

Back in my room, she sent the pictures to me and we posted them. "Wow, STFU Dirt just posted pics of one of the guys making out with another girl at The Speakeasy. Comments are not kind."

I found the picture and scrolled through the biting snark and quips. "That won't be us."

Kennedy spun her phone between her fingers. "No, it won't. How long until your next practice? You can't play hurt." Her concern continued to play my heartstrings like an orchestra.

"Playing when you're not hurt is a unicorn scenario. We're all playing a bit knocked around."

"Your coach doesn't give you a break when you're hurt?" Her outrage was so thick I could taste it.

Her worry over me like this, for no reason other than me, not for how I'd play in the next game or next season, was new. It shouldn't feel as good as it did.

Who did she think was orchestrating the hurt? "No, it helps us toughen up." At least I had to believe he believed it or else he was just an asshole sadist.

"You seem plenty tough to me."

This whole afternoon into evening had been unexpected. It made it hard to forget why we were doing this in the first place.

"Was that a compliment?"

"If you want to take it that way." Her smile widened. Each time it was breathtaking. "Okay, enough stalling, I've got to go." She clasped her hands in front of her looking nothing at all like the confident ballbuster she normally was. "We're good, right? The kiss and stuff." She gestured in the vague vicinity of my crotch.

"Don't worry. We needed to get it out of our system. We'll think of it as another practice for all those times we kiss in public."

"You're right."

I couldn't tell if she wanted me to be right or she wanted me to be lying.

She was unreadable although it seemed she wasn't unflappable. "We'll talk tomorrow and go over our plan for next week. Meet at my place?"

"I'll be there."

She ducked out of the door with a wave and strolled down the stairs.

The front door had barely closed before Griff slinked into my room with a bowl close to overflowing with pot pie.

"What the hell, man. Where were you hiding that? She made that for me."

"She told us we could have some." He spoke around the spoon shoved deep in his mouth. "And I might've stashed some since I knew you animals would be devouring every last bit."

"Some, not all. There was none left when we were down there. Where were you hiding it?"

Ezra leaned against the other side of the door jamb. "In his room."

I grabbed my pillow and chucked it at Griff although my side screamed.

He dodged it, holding his bowl close to his chest. "Asshole, you almost made me spill my food."

"*My* food."

"Have your girlfriend make you more."

"Not so your sorry ass can steal it all again."

Ezra shoved Griff's shoulder and stepped further into my room. "How's your chest?"

"Not so bad now. I'll be good next time we have practice."

"He's riding you harder than normal."

"Like that's anything new. You know how he gets."

Ezra's frown deepened. "We'll do what we can next time."

"I don't need anyone fighting battles for me or getting their asses handed to them on my behalf. I've got it handled." Guilt already gnawed at me that I hadn't stepped in to help Reid more than I did. The team had come to his rescue, but I could've done it single-handed. It made me a shitty friend. I wasn't going to put anyone else's neck on the line to deflect what I had coming to me.

Griff's spoon tinked against the side of his bowl. "Just think of those big checks a year from now."

Ezra ran his fingers over his hat brim. "As long as none of us get injured or, worse, benched."

We all made a noise of agreement.

"I'll see you guys later." Ezra took to the stairs.

"Tell her we said hi."

Ezra's steps fumbled, but he recovered and kept going like nothing had been said.

Griff stepped inside and glanced down the hallway.

"You should've seen his face. Any idea who it is?"

"None. You know how he is. He whispers to that guitar more than he talks to us."

I yawned. My stomach now full and mind racing through how to disentangle myself from this mess. It was easier when Kennedy and I were enemies. She was my sparring partner, now the situation was stickier. Stepping back from the prize would mean losing a chance to repair an old, broken relationship or starting a new one with infinite possibilities.

"God, this was good." Griff licked the bowl.

"You're really doing that in front of me with my food."

"Not just for you." His head was still firmly planted in the bowl.

"You're going to lick the paint off. Since you had so much of it, you're on dish duty. Grab that bowl."

"Fuck you." He pushed off the wall and ducked out into the bathroom.

"If you don't, I'll make sure Kennedy doesn't cook here again."

I had no idea if she'd even cook here again. I had no idea what the kiss really meant. I had no idea how to keep myself from falling for her even harder.

He stormed back in and glared, snatching the bowl off my desk, and marched back out. The dishes and plates clanked downstairs in the sink. A sink filled with dishes from Kennedy's unexpected visit.

When she'd shown up, I'd been prepared for the worst like another stomp to my ribs, but then everything changed. She'd thrown me off kilter and I wasn't sure I wanted to regain my footing.

Back in my bed, I closed my eyes against the aches and pains happy to not be going to sleep on an empty stomach or a choked-down bowl of cereal. Kennedy had done that for me, so I wanted to do something even better for her.

Pittsburgh was this weekend and the plans I'd made were coming together. My stomach clenched like I'd been punted with a cleat. This weekend was bigger than my plans. Bigger than our big con. Our big fake was the closest I'd come to anything real.

15

KENNEDY

I'd shown up to the practice field with my Cole Hauser jersey on over my coat. The cold was no less biting than it had been at the beginning of February and with the freeze bone-numbingly deep, I wasn't sure spring would ever come.

For open football practices, most people tended to watch in the fall, less so for the off-season according to Taylor. Ominous clouds also gathered overhead making it an even more uncomfortable cold dampness.

I scooted closer to Taylor with my hands clutching the spiked warm cider in an insulated cup. The heat seeped through my gloves, which meant it was too hot to drink. Instead, I inhaled the fragrant mix of spices to try to thaw out my nose. "I thought these were supposed to be spring practices."

Taylor snorted. "Any time in the spring semester." She had her binoculars out and focused on the far end of the field. She looked more like a scout than a fan. "He's got to lift his knees. I swear, it's like he loves getting tackled from behind."

I inhaled steam from my cup. "Maybe he does. Maybe he wants you to do that to him."

"Please, I've learned that I much prefer most of these guys on the field than off." She dropped her binoculars and took a gulp from her cup.

"How are you not burning the crap out of your mouth?"

"Years of practice to numb my mouth to keep my whole body from freezing during games."

"Not mad you're prepared though. These seat warmers are amazing." I shifted my butt and felt the driving cold freeze half an ass cheek.

"Hand warmers too." She shook one at me.

"You've been holding out on me." I took the innocuous looking packet from her, snapped it in half, and slipped it into my glove. Warmth spread along my skin. A blissful sigh escaped my lips.

"They're my secret weapon."

"That and this hat." I tugged the edges of the borrowed thick, woolen hat with a satin interior, perfect so it wouldn't destroy my hair.

"Just because it's functional doesn't mean it has to be ugly." She knocked into my shoulder.

"Preaching to the choir over here."

"Where's Cole?" I raised my voice and made sure the sprinkling of people around us heard me. My breath was a quarter of a degree from turning to icicles on my lips. If I was going to be out here for my fake relationship, I could at least go all out.

She picked up her binoculars and scanned the field. "He's over with Mikelson. That's never a good thing."

"What's the deal with the Coach? Cole had a massive bruise a few days ago from practice."

"Mikelson is the perfect balance of almost wins and past

championship runs to give people enough hope and keep him in a job. He's also got enough bowl wins to make people happy, even if they haven't won the championship. He's a hardass, but not in a way where you believe he's just pushing you because he knows you can do better."

My stomach sank at her description. "And the guys just put up with it?"

She pointed to a spot on the field where a bunch of guys were huddled together and handed me the binoculars.

"What other choice do they have? Once you're in a program, it's hard to transfer and not lose eligibility for at least a year. No one wants to have to start all over and prove themselves at another team. Even if they don't think they'll make it in the pros, and a lot of guys at this level *do* think they'll make it, they also don't want to lose their scholarships. So options are limited once you sign."

"That sucks." Cole hadn't let me in on his aspirations.

Reid had always shouted about how he wanted to go pro. But Cole's motivations felt different. Was there another reason he wanted to win? To make connections, if he couldn't go pro? Asking him about the future felt like a loaded topic. What if he didn't want to share?

"When football is all you've got or your one shot at making your life better, you'll put up with a lot. Plus, for so many of them they've been playing the game their whole lives. From the time they were five or six they've played the game and they love it. It's hard to leave something you love. And you're more likely to weather the shitty times to get to the great times."

"Like the games." I watched Cole.

He repeated his drills, getting faster with each repetition. But during every bit of downtime, he found me in the stands. Under all the gear, I could still see him looking for me and it made me happier that I'd come at all. Had anyone else watched him from the stands before? Probably whatever girl he'd been hooking up with at the time. I took a steeling breath against the jealousy trying to knot my stomach. He had a past and so did I, but I was here now. "It's got to be hard to put in all this work when you don't even have games to look forward to."

"It can be. It's why I like to show up to practices. Give them a small cheering section when shit's hard."

"Do you know you're annoyingly awesome?"

She laughed and shot cider out her nose. "Thanks for that." She used handfuls of napkins to dab her face and wipe her nose.

"It looks like they're finishing up." Droves of guys jogged off the field.

"Good, they're already at least an hour over how long they're technically allowed to practice." Taylor gathered her setup as did the smattering of other people in the stands.

But Cole's practice wasn't over. I tried to get a better look before stealing Taylor's binoculars. I'd been ready to wave to him like a good girlfriend when he jogged off the field with almost everyone else.

He and ten other guys were all on the field looking dead on their feet.

"What's going on?"

Taylor shielded her eyes from the sun setting over the back of the bleachers, simmering disgust etched on her face. "They must've done something Mikelson didn't like, or nothing at all. Who knows. Sometimes it's hard for me to watch."

Their group moved closer to the sidelines.

My heart pounded in my throat. A thundering urge to

rush down the stands to launch myself onto the sidelines overwhelmed me.

Cole braced his hands on the field. Bile shot through his facemask. The horrible retching sound traveled all the way up to me in the stands. Even with the hand warmers shoved inside my gloves they went ice cold.

He wasn't the only one hurting, but watching him try to pick himself up off the ground made my chest ache.

Ezra went over to him and offered him a hand.

Cole shook his head and pushed himself up, standing straight when I knew all he wanted to do was keel over. My heart ached for him. Why wouldn't he take the help? Ezra was his friend. I wanted to run out onto the field and tell everyone to hit the showers. Somehow, I didn't think it would go over well.

Mikelson's blustering drifted up to the stands, but I couldn't make out the words.

Finally, he left.

I rushed down the rows to the metal railing, slamming into it so hard it bit into my hips. I gripped the railing and called out to him. "Cole."

His head jerked up and I met his gaze. It was clouded with fatigue and defeat. But for a moment, there was a flicker of a smile. "I didn't know you were still here."

"I thought I'd surprise you."

He glanced over his shoulder at the spot in the grass where someone hosed down his sick. "Sorry you had to see that."

"We can talk later. I'll wait for you outside."

He shook his head. "Don't wait. This might take a while." Defeat saturated every word.

My hands clenched harder around the railing. "I don't

mind. I don't have a shift tonight. Cause for celebration." My attempt at lightening the mood fell flat.

His head didn't lift and his whole body sagged. "Let me call you once I get home and we can go out to dinner or something." He walked alone into the tunnel leading to the locker rooms.

I turned and yelped.

Taylor was right behind me, all her gear tucked into perfectly coordinated bags. "Need a ride?"

"I'm going to wait for Cole."

She looped her arm through mine and we walked up the concrete stairs to the exit. "When you two first showed up together, I was sure it was bullshit."

A nervous knot twisted in my belly.

"But now seeing you two together, it seems like the most natural thing in the world. I don't know how you two resisted each other for so long." She shot me a sly sidelong glance.

I bit back the words I wanted to say, not because they were lies, but more because the denial would've been hollow.

It was easier to pretend, and sometimes it didn't feel like pretending at all.

Taylor left me outside the practice field, and I waited by the entrance wishing I had a car to sit inside. The temperature dropped even lower now that the sun was setting.

The hand warmers had long since died, so now I was left with body heat only. My hands were shoved deep in my pockets and I bounced around to get myself warm. In the elongating shadow of the massive wall of concrete, I waited.

Tiny pelts of icy rain spat at me every few minutes. I glanced up at the sky and prayed for a few minutes more where I was only cold, not cold and wet. Players walked out and nodded in my direction, followed by familiar faces.

Ezra exited first, lifting his chin in acknowledgment.

I waved back.

Hollis, Reid, and Griff came out next. They were all dragging with a mixture of exhaustion and relief. I couldn't blame them after watching that practice. Even I was thankful it was over.

"Where's Cole?"

They exchanged looks that sent my stomach into a knot spiral.

Reid stepped forward. "Coach grabbed him in the hallway when we were leaving."

"And you guys just left him?" I peered through the narrow rectangular window of one of the doors, hoping he was right behind them.

Reid glanced at the metal door behind him. "It happens. Cole said he'd meet us back at the house."

"Is he okay?"

Hollis nodded, his sparkling blue eyes clouded with concern. "He'll be okay. This happens a lot. Don't worry. He always makes it out." His stiff laughter hit me along with another blast of cold air.

"Want to ride back with us?"

I shook my head. "No, I'll wait for Cole." I wrapped my arms around myself.

The trio got into Reid's car. Headlights swept over me and the parking lot lights flicked on. There were only two cars left. I checked the time again and sent a message to Cole.

The ping sounded on the other side of the door.

Cole rounded the corner, charging toward the exit. His coach grabbed his shoulder.

I jumped back, stepping into the shadow.

"This can all go away, Hauser."

"Now's not the time, Coach." Cole tried to shake off his grip.

"You give me what I want and maybe I'll give you what you want."

"The second I do, you'll cut me." Cole spun, voice full of desperation.

Confusion ricocheted through me. This felt like it was about so much more than football.

"Maybe. It all depends on how useful you are." They burst through the door.

"That's all I am to you, isn't it?" Cole's face twisted into a mask of disgust unlike any I'd seen from him before, not even when he was pretending he hated me.

Their raised voices set me on edge. The tips of my fingers tingled. I wanted to go, but I didn't want to leave Cole on his own like everyone else seemed to have. That pissed me off on his behalf.

"It's nothing more than I said it would be. Now give me the box or get the hell out of my way." The coach shouldered past Cole and marched over to his car.

Cole stood looking after him like he'd been punched.

I faltered. Normally, I had no problems jumping in, but this all unsettled me deep in my bones. Ultimately, it was Cole's wounded expression that forced me to step forward and whisper his name. The rain picked up from a spritz to a drizzle. Each drop felt like an icy marble.

The coach turned, his severe face shadowed by the overhead lights. His gaze scanned from me to Cole and back to me. His scrutiny so sharp it felt like he was slicing me in half. "I thought you'd have better taste, Hauser." He sneered.

I gasped as freezing, stinging air shot needle pricks straight to my lungs.

His car door slammed.

Cole made a choking noise and stood staring after the retreating car like he'd have torn it apart with his bare hands. His body shook with waves of tremors making him look like a tree swaying in a hurricane.

I broke the freeze on my muscles and touched him. My hand on his shoulder did nothing to stop his staring contest with the retreating taillights.

His nostrils flared like a bull preparing to charge.

"Cole."

He didn't respond. A vein bulged in his neck, even as moisture gathered in his eyes. It was like he didn't even know I was there.

I pressed my hand against his cheek and then the other, forcing him to look at me. "Cole."

His jaw clenched, muscles popped and jumped under his skin. He rammed his hands against his eyes. "I told you not to wait." The words blistered with serrated, slicing edges.

The force of it reverberated through me. My hands shook and my heart leapt wildly in my chest. "I didn't mind." I struggled to keep my tone level.

"I minded!" He hitched his bag higher and stalked toward his car.

My blood pounded in my ears just like it did all those times my parents would start screaming at each other. "Don't shout at me!"

His step faltered, but he didn't turn around. "You're always so bossy. You just do whatever you want and it doesn't matter what anyone else wants. I have enough of that in my life."

His accusations charged through my head, stalling me before unlocking my muscles. I rushed after him and grabbed his shoulder. "You have a shitty practice and it's my fault? Your Coach is a piece of shit."

His back was pressed against the side of his car and he looked everywhere, except at me. His nostrils flared, but at least he heard me. "Leave."

My fury built. He'd leave me here in an empty parking lot while it was sleeting. "No, you don't get to tell me to leave." I jammed my finger into his chest, hitting a coat button with my ungloved finger.

"Then have fun standing out here until the shuttle comes." He flipped around and flung open his door.

I jumped back and bolted, sliding over the hood of his car and wrenching open the passenger door.

The rain fell in sheets. Sleet, mixed with freezing rain, pelted the windows creating an unsettling drum on the roof of the car.

"Get out of my car!"

The tingle rushed up my arms and my heart beat faster than the water smacking into the windshield. I choked out a breath.

"Don't tell me what to do. I get that you're angry. I get that you're dealing with some heavy football shit and an asshole coach, but I don't get why you're taking it out on me."

"Isn't that what everyone else does? Aren't we all that fucking selfish that all we do is take whatever the hell we want?" His voice boomed inside of the car. The enclosed space amplified every searing word.

My hands shook. My throat thickened. My blood hammered in my ears.

"Isn't that what we're both doing? The only reason we're

working together is so we can stab each other in the back at the last minute and run off with the prize."

My throat tightened and the back of my nose heated with hurt. "Maybe it started that way..."

He jerked, turning toward me. "And what? Now you like me? You're falling for me? It's all pretend, Kennedy." Each red-hot word blistered.

My stomach plummeted and I felt like I'd been dragged down into a dark pit. Tears welled in my eyes, stung by the freezing air trapped inside the car like it was mocking me for caring this much—too much. "You think I don't know that?" Anger roiled inside of me, firing its way throughout my body. "I also know your Coach treats you like shit and you think you can take it out on me. But I don't care, you don't get to treat other people like shit who've done nothing but try to be your friend, Cole."

"I don't need a friend. I don't need anything." He got up close in my face, livid, but he wasn't yelling.

"Or anyone." Finishing the sentence, I narrowed my gaze, focusing the bull brunt of my anger at him. It was every argument between my parents. Any chance to take a dig at one another and they got the shovels ready. It made more sense now. The anger. It was a lot easier than feeling the hurt. Than letting his words slice me deep. Their pattern fell over me like a worn-in pair of jeans. And it scared me, deep in my bones. To the depths of my soul. I refused to be like them. I'd walk away before I let that happen—ever. I reached for the handle. "Then I hope you love being alone because that's what you'll always be."

He sucked in a breath like his lungs were being yanked out of his body. His nostrils flared, moisture built in his eyes. He yanked on the steering wheel and slammed his hand into it over and over, so hard and fast his knuckles split.

"Cole!" I grabbed his hands to stop him from hitting the wheel again. My anger and hurt, which had been coursing through me and felt like they might burn me up from the inside, switched like the floodlights in the stadium had been turned on. I could leave, I should leave, but I couldn't. "What is going on?" My pulse pounded in my hands gripping his. My voice was frantic.

His Adam's apple bobbed. His chest trembled. His tears fell. "He's my dad."

It came out like a broken whisper. Like a secret long buried and finally dredged up from a shallow grave.

"Who?"

His gaze swung to mine, filled with unending misery. "Mikelson."

16

COLE

Kennedy gasped, body jolting, but she didn't let go of my hands.

They ached like the rest of my body. Bruised and damaged.

"No," she whispered. Tears swam in her eyes and crested down her cheeks.

My ribs felt like they were bursting outward. Everything hurt, but nothing as much as my heart as I replayed the biting words I'd shouted at Kennedy and the words she'd hurled back at me that hammered at the one hope I had—the one reason I kept trying too hard.

"He's your father?"

I nodded, blinking back the tears pooling in my eyes.

"But..." Her eyes searched mine looking for answers.

"No one knows."

An exhalation accompanied the driving rain pattering against the roof of my car. The car I'd tried to kick her out of, but she'd refused to leave. My chest felt like it was being wrenched open by a crowbar.

She hadn't left me alone.

"How...how can he treat you that way? How does no one know you're his kid?" Bewildered and stunned, she squeezed my hands harder.

I hissed.

Her hold loosened, but she didn't let go.

Blood pooled along my knuckles, but the cuts weren't deep enough for it to pour down my hands.

This was one of the secrets I'd been hiding. At this point, it felt like second nature. As easy as breathing. "We have different names. It's not like I grew up with him around much. I lived with my mom. He only came around sometimes." To see her. Only to ever see her.

"And he wanted you to come here—to play for him?"

My laugh sounded colder than the freezing rain splattering against my windshield. "Absolutely not. He probably wouldn't have ever seen me again after my mom died."

"Your mom died?" She launched herself at me and wrapped her arms around me.

I shuddered and buried my nose in her neck. With her body pressed against mine I didn't feel like I was drowning. The unmoored dingy being tossed between skyscraper-sized waves didn't feel so hopeless or out of control when I breathed her in and held on tight. "During the summer before my senior year of high school."

"I'm so sorry, Cole. Do you have any brothers or sisters?" She leaned back to stare at me.

Normally, sympathy was poured down my throat like a three-pound bag of sugar, but hers didn't feel sickening or suffocating.

"No, it's just me—alone." Saying the word out loud made it hard to breathe.

She gave a horrified look, and all the color drained from her face. "I didn't mean it." Her eyes widened in abject horror at the kernel of truth she'd dropped on me before about ending up all alone just like I knew I would. "I shouldn't have said that. I'm sorry." Her voice cracked.

Inside, I wanted to kick my ass all over again. Guilt gnawed a gnarly hole in my chest. "You're right. I deserve it." I brushed the tears from her cheeks.

"No, you don't." Her chin trembled and she sniffled. "You don't have to tell me, if you don't want to."

The words caught in my throat like I'd been clothes-lined, but I cleared it and let the words spill out. "I've always known he was my dad. But he was a vague figure that showed up in my life from time to time."

"Your parents weren't married or together?"

"Before I was born, they were together, but then my dad got a coaching gig in Alabama and that was a long way from Seattle."

"He left."

"Me and my mom." The lump lodged in my throat. The barb-covered lump I'd long been used to choking down.

"Was he around when you were growing up?"

"For a few days every year. He'd come by. Not to see me, but to see my mom. But when I was five, he brought me a football." An easy smile tugged at my lips. That dumb kid had been so excited for the ball. "Thought it was the best present ever. And I made my mom sign me up for peewee football. Money was tight, but she made it happen. I remember her mailing him a copy of my stupid player card with me grinning in my uniform." I thought he'd be proud. I thought he'd care.

"Did he ever watch you play?"

"Never." I'd stare into the stands hoping each game would be the game he showed up to, so I always pushed myself harder, faster, farther than anyone else to not miss my shot to impress him.

"What happened with your mom?" Her tone gentled even more and her fingers brushed small circles over my hands.

"The summer before my senior year of high school. Bone cancer. Her back was hurting her for so long and she didn't get it checked out." I sucked in a shuddering breath. "By the time she did, it was everywhere and she was gone within five months." I blinked back against the burning in my eyes.

"Where did you go? Was your dad there to help?"

I flinched at her calling him my "dad." That word was forbidden. Even back then I had to call him Coach. "I was eighteen, so I was on my own. He didn't even come to the funeral." My caustic laugh burned my lips. So much for my mom's one true love.

She stared at me with a haunted, bewildered expression. "Then why would you come here? Why would you want to play for him? Or ever speak to him again?"

My throat felt like it was on fire. I struggled to swallow, struggled to breathe. Struggled to let her in on a promise I'd never shared with anyone. "My mom told me he was different with her. He had a good heart. He truly cared for us. She wanted me to reach out to him. To finally see that side of him."

"That's not your job. That's not right." The anger bristling in her tone smoothed out some of the rough edges of my clawing sadness.

"He's all I have, right? My mom's gone. The guys will be

gone in another season. Then I'll have no one." If I went pro, maybe I'd jump to another team. If I didn't, then I'd be out there floating on my own with no family, and friends who'd moved onto bigger and better things. The loneliness was like staring into a black, yawning abyss. The same I'd had standing graveside after my mom's funeral where it felt like it might swallow me whole.

"Cole...." She climbed over on top of me. The horn blared and she shifted with her knees on either side of my legs and hugged me tight. Her arms kept a crushing hold around me and her breath flowed across my neck. "You're not alone. You have so many people who care about you and love you. I know we're pretending, but I'm here for you too. Whenever you need me. Wherever you need me. Whatever you need from me."

A shudder ripped through my chest. Comfort I didn't know possible in her arms cascaded over me. Because I believed her. I believed I'd made it into the circle of people she'd move heaven and earth for.

"Kennedy." I was staggered by her. My arms tightened around her back and held her close to me. The loneliness wasn't pressing in on me anymore, not when she held me close and I clung to her.

"How'd you end up here? If he was never around and you didn't even see him much, how'd you end up being recruited?"

"I wasn't."

Her back stiffened and she leaned back to look at me.

I licked my lips. The secrets I'd never shared with anyone came spilling out when I was this close to her. "I blackmailed him." Without even realizing it. Some mastermind I was.

She shot up and her head hit the roof of the car. "You what?"

"It's a long story."

"I've got all the time in the world, if you want to tell it. But first, can you scoot your seat all the way back? The steering wheel needs to be extracted from my spine." She grimaced.

I laughed, a brittle ridiculous laugh after how I'd felt when I got in the car. After how the day and practice had gone. And it was all because of Kennedy.

"Glad my discomfort could bring you joy." Her lips twitched in an almost smile, but her eyes laughed along with me. She made me feel like I wasn't alone, wasn't unwanted, wasn't going to collapse under the weight bearing down on me.

"Let's go to my place. Melody's staying at her boyfriend's this weekend." The invitation would be one I'd have taken a totally different way, if I hadn't blown up at her. She was probably worried I was still on the edge. Maybe I was, but it was easier to back away when she was with me.

We drove to her place holding hands. Her fingers skimmed over the cuts on my knuckles. Neither of us seemed to want to let go, and I wasn't going to be the one to pull away from her.

Inside her apartment, I shook off my damp jacket and she did the same.

"Do you want some soup? I can heat up some chicken noodle I made yesterday."

"You're the queen of the comfort food."

"Couldn't you tell?" She smacked her butt, which jiggled in a way that made me forget to breathe.

"You're perfect, Kennedy."

She'd cared about me even when I hadn't wanted it, even

when I'd been an ass to her. This side of her continued to surprise me and made it harder to stop my fall.

Her cheeks flushed and she ducked inside the kitchen. "The soup and the pies freeze well. I can batch cook and then it's easy to heat it up when needed. Prepackaged stuff is too expensive and the dining hall is too far. This is more convenient."

The gentle stirring of a spoon against metal came from the kitchen. I walked to the counter on the other side of the postage stamp–sized kitchen. She handed me the first aid kit and I cleaned up my hands.

Her back was to me. Tiny droplets of water still clung to a few stands of hair. She set out two bowls beside the small pot of soup. "About the blackmail..."

"You remembered that? I'd thought maybe that had been lost in everything else I'd dumped on you." I threw away the pink-tinged gauze and snapped the box closed.

"It's hard to forget."

I dragged out the two stools tucked under the breakfast bar feeling like a hundred-pound weight had been dropped onto my chest. The whoosh of my blood filled my ears. My stomach twisted in a nauseous knot. No one knew. "When my mom was sick, I took over everything in the house. I went to the hospital every day, then summer league practice, then back to the hospital. She relied on me, but she knew how things were going. She wanted to make sure I knew where everything was, could pay the bills and take care of the rent. I had her phone and her computer. Because I have no self-control, I looked up my dad's name in her email and on her phone."

She set a spoon in front of me on top of a folded paper towel.

I was so freaking stupid, I'd been searching for any

message where he asked about me. "In her email, there were messages going back a long time." I took a fortifying breath. "Including ones where Mikelson talked about my mom stealing playbooks from the football program she'd been working for when I was a newborn."

Kennedy gasped. Soup splashed onto the counter, falling from her ladle that hovered over the two bright blue bowls. "He had her stealing for him?"

I nodded. "In her bedroom closet, I found the playbooks with his writing all over them in her things. She'd told him she'd gotten rid of them. He convinced her that if she did it for him, he'd get a better job and not have to move around so much. That they could finally be together." Bitterness churned in my stomach at the lies he'd poured down her throat for years and how my mom had turned a blind eye to how little he cared.

Kennedy grabbed a box of Saltines from the cabinet and dumped a bunch onto a paper towel. "But they weren't."

"They weren't. He used those plays to get an even better job. It started his meteoric rise in the football world."

Kennedy stared hard at her soup.

"Ask me." It was a question I'd rumbled with in my head since I made the decision.

She peered up at me. "Why would you want to be anywhere near him? Why not tell everyone what a garbage person he was and is and clean your hands of ever knowing him?"

Tightness gripped my throat like a fist. "I promised. Toward the end, my mom made me promise I'd try to connect with him. I'd refused from the time I was twelve, once I got a true picture of who he was. Once I'd been left out in the cold one too many times and I wasn't a starry-eyed kid just happy if he'd speak to me for a few minutes before going into the bedroom with my mom or brought me a Happy Meal to keep me occupied."

"She made me promise, and swore he wasn't all bad. I called and emailed him after the funeral and there wasn't a single response. I told him I knew how things had started between them and had some of his old stuff and playbooks. He asked for me to meet him. I thought maybe he hadn't known she was gone. Maybe he wanted to talk."

Her fingers brushed against the back of my hand. "But he didn't?"

"I hadn't brought the stuff with me. Once he saw that, he offered me a spot on the team. It wasn't until later I realized he thought I was using it for leverage. Recruiters were all over me from other D1 schools across the country. If he wasn't the coach here, I'd have probably gotten a letter too, so it's not like I took someone's place." Guilt rode me hard for years over that choice. I chanced a look over at her, waiting for the disappointment in her eyes.

She was frozen with a stunned expression. "You honestly think that's what I'm worried about?"

"All this has been like shattered glass inside my head for a long time."

"Do they guys know?"

I shook my head, bile charging for the back of my throat. "No. I didn't want them to think it was favoritism that I got my spot and, later, I didn't want them to know because he was such a bastard. I didn't want them to think they couldn't talk to me or be around me because of him." They were all I had left, even if it was only for the next year and a half. I wouldn't have had them at all if they knew.

She covered my hand with hers. "They'd understand."

"Even after I didn't use my blackmail to bail Reid out last year?" My throat tightened. The guilt tightened its grip and cut off my air. Breaths were harder to draw in after saying the words out loud.

Her stool screeched across the floor and she jerked me to the side and stood between my legs. "Look at me. You're not to blame for who he is. You can't blame yourself for anything he does." A flash flickered over her face. "Why didn't you...why didn't you use what you had for Reid?"

"Once I give him those books...once I turn it all over, that's it. The door will slam shut."

The intensity in her gaze softened, understanding dawning. "What is it you want from him?"

"A conversation." It sounds so simple. So easy. So stupid.

"You've never had a conversation with him before?"

"He's not exactly a conversationalist. If it's not on the field or in his office pressuring me into giving him what he wants. Now part of why I put up with everything he's put me through is about proving he can't take me down. That I won't break under his rule. Football is all he cares about." And a small, sad part of me hoped that maybe I'd see some glimmer of the man my mom swore he was. The man she'd pined for years over. The man who deep down might actually care about me. "But the other part is about finally getting him somewhere where there's only me and him. Where he's not in the game."

"That's why you wanted the prize. The golf trip. It would be irresistible to a guy like that. A brand-new trophy for his shelf." Her fingertips brushed along my cheeks. She stared at my lips, hers flattening with determination. "It's yours."

I rocked back, catching myself on the front of the stool. "What?"

"When we win, it's yours. As much as I hate the idea of him getting anything he wants, you deserve the chance for closure."

My back snapped straight. I bristled at her just handing the win over. "I'm not asking for your pity."

"Good, because I'm not giving you any."

I shot my stool backward and stood in front of her. "I didn't tell you this so you'd just give it all over to me."

Her gaze was defiant and fiery. "Doesn't change the outcome. It's yours."

"You're willing to walk away from Paris." The trip meant a lot to her. Access she couldn't buy her way into, not to mention the promise to Hannah. The one she'd thrown out to give the kid a lifeline. One that I'd never been thrown.

"I can go to Paris any time. I'm saving to go there now."

"What about the fashion show thing, you can't get tickets to that. You love clothes and style. You live and breathe it." It should be hers. What did offering up a trophy and a trip to Mikelson get me? Most likely more disappointment, if he didn't flat out laugh in my face. My stupidity at even thinking it could work mocked me. She deserved this. A trip of a lifetime with her little sister.

She picked up her empty bowl. "It's my choice."

"No, you're not giving it up."

"Are you seriously going to fight me on wanting to do a nice thing for you?" Her voice sparked with anger, which was lighter fluid to mine.

"We had a deal."

"The deal's off. How about that?" She reached for my bowl and I stepped in front of her.

"No, it's not off. We're going through with everything, including deciding who wins. What about your sister? You're going to flush this down the drain for her too?"

Her body trembled. "Yes! Happy now?"

Overwhelmed and unable to stop myself I lurched forward and kissed her.

With her hands trapped between us, they went from shoving me away to pulling me closer.

I spun around and trapped her between the breakfast bar and my body. Hunger and desire rocked my body after baring my soul to her. Our hands were everywhere.

But there was too much between us and not enough of my skin touching hers. The trip from the breakfast area to the couch was strides short.

Clothes were sprinkled all over the living room floor and we were half on, half off the couch frantic to get one more inch of bare skin revealed.

My cock pounded in time to my heartbeat feeling so close to the finish line when we'd only gotten started. I tried to calm myself down. I clung to a sliver of control.

Standing, I looked down at her spread out in front of me. Her lips were wet and soft, parted as she panted. Her breasts heaved, no longer contained by the bra flung over the coffee table. Both stiff-peaked nipples called to me.

My mouth watered and the control was harder to grasp onto.

In my shadow, her gaze cooled for a second and she moved her arms across her chest, doubt in her eyes.

"Don't deprive me, Kennedy. This time, I won't fuck it up."

The heat was back. She huffed with a smirk. "Then get over here."

She fumbled for her purse, which was draped over the couch, at the same time I grabbed my wallet from my discarded jeans.

I took the shiny square from her grasp and rolled on the condom.

She beckoned me forward with a curled finger. The insides of her parted thighs glistened with her wetness.

The stranglehold I had on my cock was the only thing stopping me from exploding just by looking at her. Once I touched her, all bets were off. But I'd make this the best she'd ever had. I'd walk on broken glass for this woman.

I wanted her. I craved her. I needed her.

17

KENNEDY

Cole covered me, blanketing my body. The hard, toned lines of his muscles felt even sharper against my plushness. Curves had never been an issue for me, and they weren't an issue for him.

The explosive revelations of the night were eclipsed by how crazy he had me feeling when he looked down at me like he'd never won a better prize.

I wasn't supposed to care about all that, but it didn't hurt to be reminded.

He braced his arms on either side of my head. "You're beautiful, Kennedy."

"So are you." Flutters overwhelmed me and I traced my fingers along his chest.

His throaty chuckle dropped to a moan as his cock brushed against the heated entrance to my core.

The throbbing that had started in my chest traveled lower the second his lips were on mine.

Each shift of his hips wrenched a gasp from my lips. Electric pulses of desire traced up my spine. Every tease hitched my breath inside of my chest.

Leaning closer, he rested his forehead against mine. "I'm not going to last. I've wanted you too long—so long." A shudder ripped through his body.

The thick, blunt head of his cock nudged against my slick heat.

My heart fluttered, speeding like a hummingbird.

I rolled my hips. "We can take it slow next time, okay?" Anticipation lit up every nerve ending. From the weight of him on me to the heat of his breath against my lips, I was ready to crawl out of my skin with raw, aching need.

He thrust forward. One long, smooth, toe-curling thrust to steal my breath and set my body humming.

Reaching between us, he found my clit. His fingers rolled and squeezed the bundle of nerves.

My legs shook, sweat broke out on my forehead. I clenched around him and his whole body jerked.

Inside me, he stretched me and hissed through gritted teeth, filling the condom. Ragged groans were ripped from his lips, which found mine. His kiss scorched with hunger. Every muscle locked in the still heightening pleasure.

Perspiration dotted his skin. As he came down, worry invaded his gaze.

I locked my legs around him, not wanting him to freak out. Slowly cooling down, I touched his cheek. "You good?"

"Better than good." His eyes dropped away from mine. "I'll be even better in a few minutes and I've got something special for you while we wait. Sorry."

"Don't be. I'm insanely hot, you just couldn't help yourself."

His gruff laugh wreaked havoc on me, especially with him still inside me.

He shifted, pulled out and raised off me. "Stay right there." Quickly, he disposed of the condom and grabbed a washcloth. He returned on his knees, staring at me with hunger like we hadn't just had a hearty bowl of soup.

"While we wait for my recovery, there's one thing I've been waiting for." His fingers wrapped around my knee, spreading my legs. Keeping his gaze locked on to me, he dragged the warm cloth between my folds.

"Only one?" I lifted an eyebrow.

"It's an ever-growing list. We can add a few more items to that kiss list."

"Not for public exhibition." I might've been more comfortable with my body than I'd ever been before, but I didn't ever think I'd be ready for pressed ham against a library window or some other forms of extreme PDA.

"Not unless you're into that," he hedged.

"The rumors of my previous sexual exploits have been greatly exaggerated. Plus, for now, I want you all to myself."

"I was going to say the same thing." With both hands on my knees, he dropped to the floor in front of me. His hands slipped under me, palming my ass and dragging me forward.

A thrill flushed my skin at the hunger in his eyes.

My full thighs were on either side of his head. Over the curve of my stomach, I watched him watch me. Tingles tiptoed their way from my heels to my head.

"Fuck. I've never seen a prettier pussy." He whispered it almost like he hadn't meant to say it out loud.

His tongue worked its magic painting my pussy and teasing my clit, never touching it straight on. Damn he was good at this. Some guys had no control or direction, no finesse, or gave up after a couple licks. But Cole was hitting all the right spots and settled in like he could do this all night. As if I'd survive. Releasing a shuddering breath, he slipped two fingers inside and massaged, brushing against the spot to unlock all inhibitions.

Adrenaline surged through my veins, like fiery bliss flooding my system and strapping me into a rollercoaster where there wasn't a crest in sight.

I gasped, trying to drag air into my lungs when it felt like all had been sucked out of the room. My hands were in his hair, on the couch, trying to grab onto anything to keep me from the free fall.

His unrelenting tongue and fingers drove me higher and higher.

When I felt like I might black out, he sucked my clit and the explosion burned its way through my body. Spots danced in my eyes and my body was racked with tremors so hard, I felt like I'd fall to the floor in a puddle, if he weren't there holding me up.

My chest heaved and I tried to catch my breath. Each inhale sent a little more oxygen to my brain, which felt like it had been fried. "Don't ever worry about lasting that long, if that's how you make it up to me." My trembling was more like aftershocks. The pounding of my heart was more of an afterglow.

"I could do that every day." His fingers ran over my chest, rolling my nipples between his fingers.

"Don't tempt me." I laughed and relaxed deeper into the couch.

"I hope you're not ready for a nap just yet."

He tapped the inside of my thigh with his latex covered length.

"When the hell did you put that on?" I pushed up on my elbows.

"Magic." He squeezed my nipples, revving me up again.

"I'm up for a show."

"I'll need an assistant."

I reached for him. "Then I'm all yours."

His eyes flared and he covered me with his body and sank into me with one solid thrust and made my back shoot up off the couch.

Still sensitive, the grind of his body against my clit sent me on a pleasure spiral I wasn't sure I wanted to escape.

An hour later, I rode Cole in my bed. On top, I clenched around his hard length.

His fingers sunk deep into my hips, anchoring me to him. He stared at me with wonder in his eyes and I couldn't imagine I wasn't looking at him the exact same way.

His hips shot off the bed and we both tumbled over the edge of a keening bliss, clinging to each other.

Our thrusts were sloppy and uncoordinated, losing the rhythm we'd perfected, but the dissonance only drew out the swell of pleasure.

Cole fell back against the pillows and I collapsed on top of him. "Kennedy, you're too good to me."

My hair was plastered to my face. Perspiration coated my entire body. And I'd never felt more alive. "I could say the same to you. Three times over."

He huffed and held me tight when I tried to roll off.

"We're a mess. Let me up." I peeled off a sweaty strand of hair stuck to my forehead. So sexy.

He brushed his hand along the side of my face. "Just give me a second."

My heart rate, which had only just slowed, sped up again in a totally different way.

His gaze held a tenderness that almost brought tears to my eyes.

"Kennedy..."

"Yeah."

He broke off the connection and kissed the tip of my nose. "Sorry for holding you hostage." His hold loosened and cold air invaded the space, prickling my skin.

"I didn't mind." I crawled off the bed and he followed me. The connection between us had been so strong, stronger than I could've imagined. Sex had never been like that for me. What was he going to say? The question bounced around in my head.

We both went into the bathroom to clean up and I hopped into the shower for a quick cleanup.

His shadow closed in on the curtain, which I pulled back. "No, you can't join me. I don't feel like getting rushed to the ER after the wall caves in or we slip and have the shower curtain rod impaled through the both of us."

"Once again, a very vivid picture."

"I try." I slid the curtain back in place.

"I'll go clean up while you're in there."

I washed up quickly and wrapped a towel around myself when I'd finished. Cole and I had had sex. More than once. And it was the best I'd ever had. It wasn't where I thought we'd end up after meeting him outside of the practice field, but I'd leave the second-guessing for the morning.

Cole had put my clothes in the hamper, and my heart tripped when I saw my favorite pajama set sitting on the edge of the bed.

His body blocked the light behind me. The closeness of him made my skin tingle, not just from the drying wetness against the force-heated air.

"I'll jump in now that you're finished." His breath

caressed my ear. After changing into my pajamas and remaking the bed, I sat on the edge with my hands wedged between my knees. Legs bouncing, nerves tickled my stomach. Sleeping together went beyond *sleeping* together. But this was Cole. The truth of it stunned me. How he'd come to be someone I wanted in my life. He'd dipped me. He'd brought me roses, even if it was for a game. He'd made me feel like maybe I didn't have to do everything on my own—alone. The flutters of my heart smoothed out the nervousness running through me.

The bathroom door opened and a nervous flop of my stomach pounded in my throat.

Cole came out fully dressed.

Lead stones dropped right on top of the tingly feeling spreading in my stomach. "You're dressed."

He dumped the towel in the hamper and evaded my eyes. "I know you're not big into sleepovers, so I—" His uncertainty was even more endearing.

"Can you come here for a sec?"

He crossed the room with stilted steps and stood in front of me.

I grabbed the hem of his shirt and lifted. "I'd love for you to stay over." Then, my hands stilled and a thought struck me. "If you want. Don't feel like you have to." Now it was my turn to feel like I was on a swaying ship.

He brushed his fingers along my chin and kissed my lips. "I'd love to stay over." After pulling back the blankets, I climbed into bed and he stripped down to his boxers.

We both laid on our sides and faced each other.

"If I snore during the night, you can't tell me."

He smiled. "Same."

"If you snore, I'm pushing you out onto the floor."

"No fair," he said with mock outrage.

"My bed. My rules."

"Then I guess I'd better play by those rules because I do like being in this bed."

No longer in the sex haze and with a dimmer post-orgasm glow, all that Cole had shared with me came flooding back. I pressed my palm to the center of his chest. "Whatever happens, I want you to know I'm here for you, okay?"

The muscles in his neck strained and he nodded. "Thanks." He cleared his throat. "It means a lot to me."

"And I know the guys, Taylor, Ashley, and Leona would feel the same. You don't have to deal with any of this alone."

"I know. I don't have to anymore. I've got you." He kissed my open palm and scooted closer.

With my head against his chest, I tried to keep the worry at bay. This was supposed to be about a stupid game. My competitive drive and pride were on the line, but there was so much more at stake for Cole. He might not want me to give him the prize, and as much as I hated how disappointed he'd probably be once he had a chance to truly spend time with his dad, I couldn't stand in his way. I'd do whatever it took to win this for him.

18

___

COLE

I was up and idling at the curb outside of Kennedy's apartment for our road trip earlier than I'd be awake on a practice day. But there was no looming dread about what the day would hold. Only intrigue and excitement to spend time with her.

She hopped in and bounced in her seat, trying to ward off the March chill.

"Where are we going once we get there?" I cranked up the heat.

"Don't worry about it." She opened the maps app on my phone.

"You're afraid if you tell me I'll back out."

"Maybe a little." She typed in the destination with her hand covering my screen and only set it in the dashboard holder once we started moving. Once we were on the highway, she fiddled with her phone and found a station.

"Do you want to choose the music or do I get the honors?"

"Go ahead." I wanted to know more about her. More about her tastes, her likes, her joys.

Kennedy sang along to the music at the top of her lungs. Every high note. Every chance to belt it out. Every melodic journey was sung like her favorite.

Her smile was infectious, and she held out an imaginary mic to me for the songs I knew to get me to sing along.

With anyone else, it would've annoyed the hell out of me, but I loved her voice and her smile. Each hammed-up act to go along with the music showed me a side of her I hadn't gotten to experience before and made me want more.

"Two hours into our drive and I don't think there's a song you haven't known."

"I love music."

"Music, fashion, beer pong, making plans. Is there anything you don't love?"

"Football." She laughed as she said it and scrunched herself up against the passenger side door.

"You'll pay for that." At a red light, I dropped it into park and tickled her.

Her hands flew in a blur and she swatted at me.

"It's not a good idea to hit the driver."

"Then stop tickling me." She gasped and jerked on her seatbelt.

I let up and smiled at the half-in, half-out ponytail now messy from her tickle evasion maneuvers.

"Why are you looking at me like that? Keep your eyes on the road." I couldn't stop looking at her. I wanted to turn the car back around and stay in bed for a week watching movies, ordering in food and wrapping her in my arms.

She grasped my chin and turned it back toward the road.

"It's a red light."

She motioned toward the windshield. "And now it's not, but you'd know that if you were looking at where we were going." She pushed harder and I let her.

But I didn't let go of her hand.

Our fingers were twined together and mine were probably a little sweaty, but Kennedy hadn't complained.

After our night, I felt freer than I had in a long time. The weight that usually settled on my chest had lightened.

Kennedy knew. She knew a secret I'd been hiding so deeply, sometimes it felt like I'd been trying to keep it hidden from myself.

She'd been there for me. And despite what she thought, I'd be there for her. Determination stoked the fires of my competition. We'd win. I'd win this for her.

"What's the super-secret you've got planned for this trip?"

"It won't be a secret if I tell you."

She peered over at me with a playful pout. Her lips were kissably soft and full. It had been hard to leave her apartment the morning after our first night together.

"I'll have to buy an apology gift for Melody."

Kennedy's laugh caught in her throat. "I've never heard her scream like that before."

"It was impressive."

She snorted. "If my pajama shorts hadn't been around my ankles at the time, I could've saved you from the first hit."

"The couch pillows were thankfully soft." I shrugged, kind of loving how unexpected it was that Kennedy would have a guy sleeping over. Somehow I'd made my way into a coveted spot and I wasn't giving it up. "She's got a hell of an arm though. The throw knocked me clean off my feet."

"You and Melody can exchange apology gifts. She was mortified once she realized who you were and that you'd actually slept over."

"Did she think I was breaking in wearing only boxers?"

"Weirder things have happened." She stared out the window.

"Have they?"

"I'll never tell." The look over her shoulder sent my blood thrumming through my veins.

The final directions for our destination popped up on my phone and I parked outside the brick building beside a yellow and gray painted wall. "This is what you do when you come into the city?"

A bright sign hung over the door that read Case Clothes.

"Was there ever a doubt? Door, please." She grinned and slipped her bag over her arm.

"Finally learned." I turned off the car and jogged around to her side, careful of passing cars.

She got out and her breast brushed against my chest. "It depends on how much I like the lesson. And this is one I could get used to." She winked and grabbed my hand.

"Let's go. We have a stop before they open."

Tartan flags waved along the light poles on the streets in all directions.

"Enemy territory," I whispered, keeping close to her.

"Hardly. You're not even in the same division."

I looped my arm around her waist. "Is some football knowledge rubbing off on you?" Enjoying her squirming, I blew raspberries against her neck.

She yelped and pushed me away. "Being around Taylor, it was inevitable. Come on, this is my favorite breakfast place."

Pots of coffee brewed behind the counter with black scuff marks along the base. The walls seemed soaked in the caffeine and fried food smells bombarding us the second the door opened.

Inside, the diner's third-shift workers looked dead tired,

and there were weekend warriors in suits grabbing coffee or a light breakfast before starting their day. Although there were empty tables, Kennedy found two spots at the window. I plunked down beside her and rested my feet on the bar stool.

"What makes this place so special?" I glanced at the menu. Diner standard.

"This." She nodded out the window.

The massive intersection where four roads all criss-crossed was a mishmash of all types of people. College students, high school students, business people, tourists, and more.

Kennedy stared out the window like it was opening night at the best theater in town.

"A lot of people think fashion is about clothes, but really it's about people."

"Explain."

"It's about what they wear and what they're trying to say to the world. There are times, I'll see one or two people wearing a new color or a new way of styling their clothes or a pattern or the way they wear two pieces together. Then I'll come back six months later and there are tens of people wearing that, then hundreds. Picking up on who's wearing what and trying to figure out what they're trying to say can help guide me in what will be next."

"You can tell all that just by people watching?"

"You can't?" She peered over at me. "How about when you're on the field? I bet you can tell who's going to try to go for a big play or in a split second you can read your opponent and anticipate where they're going to be and stop them from getting there. It's a lot of the same, just less instantaneous. You get to find out if you're right within minutes or seconds. If I'm lucky it's a couple months, and if I'm really unlucky a year or more."

"Why not go for something with more instant gratification?"

Her gaze cut sidelong with a twinkle of mischief in her eyes. "Don't think I haven't entertained it."

The server came over and we placed our orders.

"Why'd you pick fashion merchandising? Why clothes?"

"It's one of those things everyone notices, even if they don't realize it. Two people can wear the exact same thing, but it can look completely different and make them feel the exact opposite." Her eyes tracked people on the other side of the glass. They followed flashes of color in a sea of drab.

"How can you even tell what they're wearing with the heavy coats and scarves on?"

"I can tell. Even the coats are a clue. For me, clothes are a way to express myself. They can tell a story not just to other people, but also to me. Finding the perfect shirt or pants or dress makes me feel confident or special or sexy."

"You're all three."

Her look poured lighter fluid on embers that had no business building this early in the morning.

I brushed my nose against her cheek.

The server cleared her throat and set our drinks in front of us.

She wrapped her hands around the mug and took a sip. "It took me a long time to believe any of that."

My body stilled and I looked at *this* Kennedy trying to imagine her any other way. Picturing her as anything other than the strong, hot as hell woman in front of me was impossible.

Her gaze darted to mine and I was walloped by the flash of vulnerability. She let me see that. She was letting me in close. Closer than she'd ever let anyone before, and I was humbled by that.

"Your clothes are your gear like when I suit up for football. They keep you protected like armor."

"They are my ultimate fake it 'til you make it." She buzzed with excitement that I understood what clothes meant to her.

Our food arrived and I tried my hand at pointing out interesting clothing choices although it was more colors or shapes that stood out. At first, she humored me, but I kept trying and listened when she explained what she liked.

Her smile widened with each attempt, which made me want to try even more. She probed for why a certain coat or shade had caught my eye. What I thought it meant. If I saw patterns or methods to the madness. I'd never understand clothes like she did, but I loved sitting shoulder to shoulder with her giving the thing she lived and breathed my full attention with her.

With the morning-hunger edge off, we walked back to Case Clothes. The woman behind the counter smiled at Kennedy. "Hey, Kennedy. There are a lot of new arrivals in the usual spot. Have fun."

"Your favorite place to visit?"

"How could you tell?"

"That clued me in." I pointed to the marker on a poster board sign taped up on the wall, which read "Kennedy's Korner."

Her laugh and excitement spurred me forward, following her.

The clothes in front of her had her complete focus. She ran her fingers over the fabrics, checked sizes, and pulled out one or two things, looking them up and down before holding on to them or placing them back on the rack.

"What exactly are you looking for?"

"Something exceptional. Or interesting. Or exciting. There are a few people who've reached out to me about helping them dress for interviews, dates, special occasions. I want to make sure they're getting their money's worth." She tugged open her purse, which had four white envelopes tucked inside.

"These aren't for you?"

"If I saw a skirt or shirt I liked, I'd take it, but the main plan is personal-shopper shopping." She held up a shirt and stared at it before putting it back.

"They're paying you to buy clothes for them?" People couldn't pick out their own stuff? How hard could it be? Pants. Shirts. Shoes.

"Couldn't ask for a better job."

After watching Kennedy in action, I saw how hard it could be. Her attention to detail and the way she saw clothes were like dissecting the play-by-play of an opposing team. Watching the tapes to break down every move to play your best. Only her best was out on the streets or in the quad and she wanted that for the people paying her.

She wandered through the store flicking through every rack and sorting through every stack of clothes. There wasn't an article of clothing bypassed. In her element, Kennedy spotted a bargain or a find in a flash. No indecision or waffling. She found what she wanted and grabbed it.

I respected the hell out of it. Like a fashion wide receiver, she was there to get across that fashion goal line. But it wasn't points on the scoreboard that lit her up, it was walking into a room and having every eye on her or the person she dressed. The personal limelight.

Making myself useful, I was her human closet rail. My

arms were filled with at least twenty pounds of clothes already.

"All this for four people?"

"I'm getting more serious about the whole styling thing. There are also a few things that'll be for me and a couple I can have on hand to use for anyone who might want to work with me next." She ducked her head and scrutinized a top on the other end of the circular rack.

"Why are you going so hard with this now?"

She shrugged. "It's extra cash. That never hurts." Her laugh was light, but she wouldn't meet my eyes.

Frustration surged through me. "You're still trying to save up the money for Paris."

"Of course."

"I told you the prize was yours."

"We're in second place, it's not guaranteed we'll win. And I told you that I didn't want it." A sharp flick of her wrist sent the hangers scraping along the metal rod.

"And I—"

"Do you want to spend the rest of the day fighting or do you want to have a good time?"

I dropped back, feeling like a sullen high schooler. "If you let me get something for you, then I'll feel better."

"I don't need anything." She gave a wave of her hand and a laugh to distract me, as if to paint what she wanted as unimportant.

It wasn't. It mattered to me. "But I want to do this for you."

She spun and stared at me like I'd crack under the scrutiny. "Why?"

"Why are you determined to give the prize up for me?"

"That's different."

"It's an even bigger deal. All I want to do is buy you

something. Do you want to spend the rest of the day fighting or do you want to have a good time?" The slam dunk of the Kennedy quote reversal.

She looked at me like she couldn't imagine why I'd want to. "You seriously want to do this."

Why wouldn't I? She'd shared a part of herself many people didn't get to see. They saw the outcome, but not the process. I've been given a behind-the-scenes look at a thing she loved, the least I could do was show her I'd been paying attention. Plus, there were some clothes in here I was dying to see her try on. "Completely and totally."

"Sure, give it your best shot."

19

KENNEDY

After I finished picking out the clothes for clients, Cole finally badgered me into letting him to choose some outfits for me, but he had one condition.

"Do you know how hard it is getting dressed without looking?"

"Like you've never thrown on your clothes in the dead of night with no light."

He wasn't saying it as a slight. There was no bite behind his words, which I appreciated. No judgment. I'd been with people before him and he'd been with other people too. "That's not the point. I was never trying to look presentable then, just trying to get home."

Three outfit changes later, I zipped up the pants. "Does the shirt go in or out?"

"Definitely in." So confident after one day of shopping.

I tugged the shirt down and tucked it in. Even through my barely parted lids, I couldn't see anything with the mirrors covered in scarves.

"No peeking." He reminded me from the other side of the curtain.

I snapped my eyes shut. Giving him my size hadn't been easy. Even after he'd seen me naked, we'd had sex, and he'd never even breathed a whiff of being dissatisfied with how I looked, for some reason that size number and my weight felt like closely guarded secrets.

I felt for the curtain and took a deep breath before flinging both sides open and stepping out for maximum dramatic effect.

"That's the one."

"You said that about the other three." I folded my arms and squinted at his smug expression.

"This jacket will finish it off." He held up a black and white puffy shouldered half coat that would end not too far under my breasts.

"That?"

"Trust me." He helped me slip it on, then knelt in front of me to button it properly.

"I could do that myself." Stopping myself from massaging his shoulders while I pretended I needed them for balance was a minor miracle. Normally, I was the one doing the dressing for other people or dressing myself. I wasn't much for being anyone's dress-up Barbie, hell not much of a Barbie at all, but this was the most fun I'd had clothes shopping in a long time. That was saying a lot, since I was willing to ride a bus for two and a half hours once a month just for the fun of these shopping trips.

"Then you'd have to look." He looked up at me, way too handsome and intense.

Now I did need to steady myself on his shoulders because my knees were seconds from giving out.

"I found these too." Standing, he let his body rub against mine. Freaking tease.

He grabbed two items off the small cushion outside the dressing room. A scarf and necklace.

"Both?" I looked at the scarf, eyeing him suspiciously.

"Not both." His eyebrows furrowed together and he held up both weighing the options. "Definitely the necklace." Closer, he reached behind me and clasped the necklace, running a finger under the chunky statement necklace and along my collarbones.

A tremor of anticipation crashed into me. "You think you're a pro already?

Amusement filled his eyes, which were intently on mine. "I've learned from the master."

"Tell that to the first outfit with the clown collar."

"This time it's true." He walked over to me and put both hands on my shoulders to spin me around.

His skills had gotten better with each outfit, but I wasn't expecting this.

The blue high-waisted, wide-legged satin pants with a black-and-white accent down the sides flattered me. Other than being a little wrinkly, they fit perfectly. I'd never thought I could wear a pair like this, and the lining made them comfortable. The white shirt added more negative space to the outfit that the black-and-white belted jacket brought back around. The pattern was similar to the pants, but not too matchy-matchy. And the blue statement necklace that looked like joined bubbles tied the whole thing together.

I stared at myself, staggered by not just how the whole thing looked, but how it made me feel. It felt like an outfit someone would stop me on the street in New York or Barcelona and ask to take a picture of it.

"Did I do good?" Cole stepped behind me, his gaze locked on to my face in our reflection. Where there had once been confidence, now flickered uncertainty.

"You did great. How...just how?"

From behind, he wrapped his arms around me and rested his chin on my shoulder. "I tried to pick things I thought you'd like and maybe not choose for yourself. Things I'd like to see you in that were bright and fun, like you."

Turning my head, I met his lips and yelped when he squeezed me tighter.

"Please don't do that when you're pressed up against me like that." The weighty length of his erection pressed between the cleft of my butt. "I don't want to have to buy new pants."

"I could pick them out for you." Rocking my hips, I upped the tease.

He nipped my shoulder and stepped away, smacking my ass. "Behave, before you get us kicked out."

"You started it."

"Go get changed. We've got somewhere to be."

Catching the color in my reflection, I ran my hands down my front and turned, taking another look at myself in the mirror. I felt comfortable, beautiful, and doted on with Cole's attention to detail and what he thought I might like. This just became my new favorite outfit. "I'm going to wear this out."

He dropped the scarf in his hand, shock scrawled across his face. "Seriously?"

"Did you think I was lying when I said I liked it?"

"Maybe a little."

I crossed to him and laid a lip-nipping kiss on him. "I wasn't."

"Good, but I'll need the tags so I can pay for it."

Checking the tags, I gulped. They were way too expensive. "No, never mind. Let's not get this now." I tugged at the jacket button.

He stilled my hands. "I said I'd buy it."

"It's too expensive." I hated the pleading tone in my voice. Why hadn't I checked the prices before gushing about how much I liked it?

"You're worth it." He rubbed his nose against mine and marched off before I could stop him. The whole thing was rung up and I was the proud new owner of the gorgeous outfit, mainly because of who'd picked it out for me and how that made me feel.

Dinner was window-front at a beautiful restaurant where I got at least two compliments on my outfit while walking to the table after I'd shed my coat. The rush of attention lengthened my strides and straightened my back. All the better was how happy it made Cole. These clothes had made the night for both of us in two completely different ways.

He practically knocked the server over in a race to hold my chair for me.

I reminded myself not to get used to this.

He'd shared things with me no one else knew about him and we'd slept together, but we hadn't talked about anything beyond this month, which was rapidly ending.

I'd almost finalized our outfits for the dance-a-thon. Ten days left until the winners would be selected. And I wanted him to win. Giving up Paris hurt. It hit like an anvil in my chest thinking about all the shows I'd miss and elbows that would go unrubbed.

Things never came to me the easy way, so I'd stick Paris Fashion Week up on my list of goals and get there in a more roundabout route, but I'd make it there—eventually. On my trip, Hannah and I might be staying in hostels and eating street food for a week, but I could get her there. Cole, he needed this for something more than an escape or career aspirations. He needed it for closure, no matter which way it went. If I could help him get there, I wasn't going to give up the chance.

A woman leaned over while I scanned the menu.

"I had to say, I love your outfit. The colors are amazing."

Under the table, Cole tapped my leg basking in the flattery.

"Thank you. My boyfriend did an amazing job putting it together."

Her mouth widened so fast, her jaw clicked. "He picked it out."

"He's not just a pretty face."

"Lucky girl." She spun back around in her chair and asked the man with her why he'd never picked out clothes for her.

Leaning over the table, I swatted my menu against his. "Look at what you're doing. Breaking up happy couples."

"I can't help it if my fashion skills are that kickass." He blew his breath on his nails and buffed them against his shirt. "Who knew. Maybe I'll go on that Paris trip with you instead."

The comment landed between us with a thud. "You're going on your trip."

A vein in his neck stood out before he took a deep breath, relaxing, and his gaze dropped back to the menu. "Let's argue about this later."

Swallowing back my words, I scanned the menu and tried not to wince at the prices. This was supposed to be a trip about making money, not spending money.

"Don't worry about the price."

"How can I not worry about the price?"

He leaned in closer with a self-satisfied smirk. "I promised the manager a quarter of my athlete tickets for next season."

"What about the rest? What will you do with them?"

"Find someone else to give them to?" The spark of sadness in his eyes was a knife to my heart.

He didn't have anyone else. All his friends were on the team.

"Sorry. But there's not someone else you'd like to have them?"

"They've gone unused for three years. At least I can finally get something out of them. Some of the others are going for what I have planned for later."

"You're crypticness isn't helping with my anxiety right now."

"Have a little faith, Kennedy."

There were more outfit compliments when I walked across the restaurant to go to the bathroom. Cole's head almost scraped the ceiling with each bit of glorious praise, which was only doubled once I let them know he'd dressed me.

"Proud of yourself, huh?"

"You have no idea."

His smile was contagious. The kind I didn't mind catching.

Food arrived at our table without us needing to place an order. Scallops for Cole and a crab cake with lobster cream sauce for me.

"You'd better get used to this. Restaurants will be fawning all over you once you go pro."

He raised his glass to mine, tapping the edge. "If."

"You think your odds aren't great?" I covered my mouth with my hand. What did I know? Maybe he didn't want to talk about it. But it surprised me. From the way Taylor talked about the team, she had high expectations for most of their draft prospects.

"They're above average, but nothing is a lock. Better to plan for the worst and be surprised if shit just so happens to work out the way you like. Hope can be a killer." He downed the glass of wine in one gulp.

"I get not wanting to set yourself up for disappointment, but you also can't talk yourself out of a great experience right around the corner."

"Since when are you my own personal motivational speaker?" There was an edge to his voice. We weren't just talking about football anymore. And as much as I hated his coach, and couldn't even think of him as his dad, I didn't want Cole to be robbed of finally getting his chance for connection.

I picked up my fork and sliced through the crab cake, getting extra sauce on the large lumps of crab meat. "Since you take me out to free meals like this." The second the food hit my tongue, every taste bud exploded in appreciation. My eyes fluttered closed. Creamy, salty, rich and beyond delicious.

Cole's eyes locked onto mine once I could see straight.

Heat crept up the center of my spine. I covered my mouth with my hand. "Did I make a noise?"

His nostrils glared and he gripped his knife. "Yeah." He cleared his throat and sucked in a long, loud breath. "The kind that means I'm not getting up from this table for at least another ten minutes." He hunched forward and speared one of his scallops.

A rumble of deep satisfaction came from him. At least I wasn't the only one truly enjoying the food.

He held a pan-seared scallop out to me on his fork. "This is the best seafood I've ever had."

"Only if you have some of mine too." I scooped up a forkful of mine and held it out with one hand cupped underneath to catch any sauce drips that I'd totally lick if there were any.

We shared our appetizers and Cole vowed he wouldn't be able to stand for at least an hour. Two wagyu filets, the fanciest mac and cheese, truffle fries and a few glasses of wine later, Cole pulled my chair out and we headed out to dessert.

Bundled up, we walked down the street to a donut shop. The yeasty, sugary smell filled my lungs before we even opened the door.

Once again, we grabbed counter seats in front of the window and shared our donuts. Birthday cake for Cole and salted caramel macchiato for me. Indulgent in totally different ways. They were the perfect pillowy-soft-and-fluffy, melt-in-my-mouth sugary goodness. My cheeks hurt from smiling so much.

"Are we heading back now?" I popped a chocolate curl off the now empty paper where my donut had once been.

"Not without your surprise." He balled up our papers and tossed them, wrapping his hand around mine.

A spark lit its way up my arm, spreading warmth in my chest. I kept waiting for this feeling to fade, but so far it seemed like it was going to stick around for a while. I followed Cole's lead two blocks away, happy I had on boots and not heels.

He checked his phone and hustled us along a little

faster, stepping through the revolving door of an office building.

"What is this place?"

"Right where we're supposed to be." He checked for the elevator before tugging me along.

The mystery was killing me. We'd already had dessert, so he wasn't stealing me away for some elaborate chocolate cake. I'd never been to this part of the city before, although it wasn't far from where the STFU shuttle dropped off.

Silence reigned in the office building, abandoned over the weekend. Darkened glass-walled offices and even emptier hallways.

It wasn't until we were on a totally empty floor that he let up on the race. The lights didn't come on, but the floors and ceiling were intact. New car smell versus abandoned murder spot was a better description for the place.

"They finished the office renovations a few days ago. It'll look different by the end of next week."

"No clues on why we're here?"

"All will soon be revealed. May I take your coat?"

My heart galloped in my chest. I'd have never pegged him for the most chivalrous guy before we started all this, and time and time again he continued to surprise me with his gentlemanly ways. I didn't want to be the girl who got all giddy by small gestures, but I couldn't help how they made me feel. "Yes, you may." Before I had it all the way unbuttoned, he helped it off my shoulders and neatly hung it over his arm.

He gestured toward the floor-to-ceiling windows and kept his hand on the small of my back.

In front of the perfect city view windows was a bucket of ice and a champagne bottle. A damp note was taped to the neck. "Thanks for the tickets, kid. Good luck next season."

"These tickets are like a fairy godmother's magic wand."

"And I'm waving it over both of us tonight."

The flutters in my stomach felt like they'd lift my feet off the industrial-carpeted floor.

"You opening that?"

He eyed it. "Have you ever opened one before?"

"Nope."

"Maybe we just let it chill out a little longer."

"Scaredy cat."

"Damn right. One of the guys on the team popped one in the locker room my freshman year and nailed our wide receiver right in the eye. Broken orbital socket."

I sucked in a sharp breath. "Seriously?"

His ominous nod sent a chill down my spine.

"I don't need to drink."

"Now who's scared?"

He set our coats down on a lone filing cabinet and directed me toward the windows.

His phone screen reflected in the glass, lighting up behind me.

"We ready yet?" Ready for whatever he had planned in this abandoned office. If he were a different kind of guy, I'd have never even gotten out of the elevator on the dimly lit floor, but instead anticipation buzzed under my skin.

"Just wait." He stepped in behind me and wrapped his arms around my waist. His chin rested against my shoulder. The tips of his fingers brushed against my stomach tapping out a rhythm we swayed to.

I relaxed against him, not trying to guess or control the situation. As content as I felt, my heart soared with each brush of his lips against my skin. The deep inhales like he was trying to imprint my scent on his memory.

No matter what he had planned for tonight, I'd never forget today.

This was all supposed to be pretend, but no one had reminded my heart about that.

"What—" I gasped as the colors in front of me changed, and took a step forward. Cole moved with me. Slowly, at first, the image focused, coming together like a connect-the-dots picture. "Cole, are you serious?"

He held tight and wouldn't let me turn to him, only walking me a little closer to the window.

From our vantage point on the twelfth floor, through the perfect alignment of the buildings, a message scrolled along the top of the building in front of us on an electric sign that ran along the observation deck spelling out our names. "Cole and Kennedy." A small STFU bulldog scrolled across as well along with our class year. The windows below were lit up in a giant red heart.

"They did all that for football tickets?"

His resources when it came to pulling this off weren't anywhere close to what I could get done. Had he been pulling his punches all along? With the promise of saying their name on camera after a win or in an after-game conference he could probably get anyone in a hundred-mile radius of campus to do whatever he wanted. My gestures felt sillier in comparison.

"Once again, you underestimate the fanaticism of a rabid sports fan."

"Apparently..." The electric tingles turned to full-on sparks as the message scrolled. My chest tightened, making it hard to breathe. Just staring in awe of the entire city seeing our names up there and thinking all their thoughts about who Cole and Kennedy were. But we weren't those two lovey-dovey people who couldn't get enough of each other, at least not for real.

While I wanted to bask in it and live in this moment, there was a reason we'd done all this. A reason we'd taken pictures at Case Clothes and during our breakfast and early dinner. A reason why everything we did was always a reminder of why we were doing this.

I hated needing to shatter the moment. Pretending I was on a whirlwind date complete with a makeover and delicious dinner only to be surprised with an over-the-top romantic gesture. It was the thing fairy tales were made of, which was why it wasn't actually happening to me. It was all for show. "We need to take a picture of this."

"Already posted."

"How—"

"The guy took one, since it wouldn't show up right for us from here. We'd need a long exposure, so he took some shots." He held up his blindingly bright phone glowing in the dark space.

"How'd you post them?" Letting my eyes adjust, a picture of what shone outside the window was already up and attracting likes.

"Auto forwarded it straight to our account."

"You've thought of everything." He'd already made sure everything was taken care of. He'd taken the responsibility off my plate. Why'd it hit me like a lead weight in my stomach? Maybe for a second I thought he'd get so wrapped up in the moment that he'd forget. That he was feeling some of the same things I was, but he was still in it for the prize, even if it was one he was foisting on me. The need to win was driving him now, not the need for me.

"Learning all about those plans from you, and it shows on the leaderboard."

He swiped across his screen. His half of our entry picture inched ahead and the two of us together were finally at the top. The picture of us seconds away from biting each other's heads off in front of the balloon heart set above all others.

Cole was ages ahead of even me with this grand public display a hundred miles away from campus.

Turning, I flung my arms around him nearly toppling us both over. Those muscles and quick reflexes came in handy and he kept us upright. "We did it."

He squeezed me back. Those thick arms locking me in close. "I'm giving it to you."

I jerked back, setting my voice to stern. "Not this again. We talked about it. When we win, you get it."

"I never agreed to that." He brought his face closer to mine.

Wedging my arms between us, I tried to push him back. "Cole, be serious."

"I am." His gaze intensified, even in the low light. His certainty was unwavering. "I agreed that if I won, I got to choose. And I'll choose Paris for you."

My heart raced. I pushed against his chest and he let me go. "We had a deal."

"I'm not going back on the deal." Amusement rang in his words like this was a joke or not important to him.

If he wanted to play smug, so could I. "Fine, if I win, then I choose. I'll choose you."

"Then, I guess you'd better go big because it's going to take a lot to top this." He waved his arm up and down the window at the message and heart flashing in the Pittsburgh night sky.

Instead of the spiky thorns of anger or annoyance, concern sent panic rolling through me. "Cole, please don't do this. I know how much this trip with your dad means to you."

"And I'm wondering if it should matter at all."

He didn't want to get his hopes up, maybe hopes he'd been hanging on to for decades. But he'd always wonder, if he didn't find out, even if it shattered the last of his illusions about who his father was.

Being the person who deprived him of his one shot to hash things out wasn't who I wanted to be in his head. Between my bookstore job, styling clients, and class, I'd have to figure out a way to beat him at his own game.

He deserved to win, and I'd have to show him how much I believed he did.

20

KENNEDY

Pittsburgh blurred the lines even more between Cole and I, even more than the sex. Go figure a guy picking out and buying clothes for me would be a bigger deal than phenomenal sex. And that sex had been the best I'd ever had.

On the drive back, I curled up in my seat and watched him, this guy who I'd sworn I'd never let near me, who had turned my world upside down.

He brushed his fingers across my cheek before I nodded off. Instead of dropping me at my place, he'd parked at his place. It was closer to campus, right? But after our first night together, I had to admit to myself that I liked sleeping next to Cole. I loved how he went full octopus, wrapped around me like he wanted me as close as possible.

Stolen moments, hand holding, and kisses came much easier, which meant I had to work even harder to win, and picked up extra shifts at the bookstore to take Hannah to Paris.

I smoothed a Post-it note into place at the bottom half of my creation. The library this close to the Commons was usually empty and this afternoon was no exception. I grabbed the last stack of pink sticky notes. The recalled crate of them in the storeroom at the bookstore had been perfect for my idea.

"Damnit, Kennedy." Ashley sucked on her finger, waving it in the air. "Cole had better appreciate this."

"He will." I was sweaty and tired, but we were almost done. The ten by ten pink heart with his name at the center in blue Post-its had taken longer than I expected, but we were almost finished.

"He'd better," she grumbled. "The guys are grilling this weekend."

"Grilling? There's a foot of snow on the ground."

"Means you don't have to use a cooler for the beers." She ran her hands over the last of the pile she'd stuck to the glass.

"We're going to freeze our asses off."

"Your new boyfriend won't let you freeze. He'll sit you on his lap, so you don't have to freeze on a cold chair, and feed you burgers, hot dogs, and chicken breasts courtesy of Ezra's catering hookup."

I laughed and shook my head. "I'm not sitting on anyone's lap. And is that what you think having a boyfriend is? Him feeding me."

"You mean he hasn't?"

I stalled mid-stick. "Well, he has." Shaking my head, I went back to completing the reverse image picture on the window.

"You act like you know what it's like to have a boyfriend anyway." Ashley waved a stack of notes at me. "Weren't you the one always griping about girls dating guys and just totally losing their minds?"

"I haven't—" I looked up and she leaned against our

creation, running her hand down our sticky-note picture like a showcase model.

"It's for a reason." My cheeks heated. "Not for the hell of it."

"Uh-huh." Her smug grin rankled my nerves.

"What about you? You and Josh were pretty cozy last time I saw you together." I finished my sticking and stepped back. The symmetry of the heart was perfect with only the backward "Cole" breaking it up. Once the lights came on, it would glow across the courtyard in front of the Commons.

"Too bad he's hung up on you." She dumped her stack of notes into the nearly empty box with a thud.

I huffed. "Less hung up on me, more offended he got the brush-off. He doesn't care about me. He just wanted to do a little territory marking. It's not even like—" I swallowed the words of denial as to why Josh didn't need to be jealous in the first place.

"Not even like what?"

"If you're interested in him, don't let the little pissing match knock him out of the running. He looked into you at the party." He had when he wasn't trying to square off with Cole. If Cole and I hadn't been wrapped up in our own show at the party, I'd probably have tried to steer them toward each other after the looks they were giving when they thought the other wasn't looking.

She shot up straight. "Really?"

"Really. He's not after me, trust me."

"He'd be the only one, although now that you and Cole are official, I guess they'll all have to cry themselves to sleep that they never got a shot with you."

I picked up the now empty box and broke it down. "The tears would fill a thimble."

"More like the Poe Pond." Her lips twitched.

"True."

Her laugh filled the silent floor. "Will the librarians take this down before he gets to see it?"

"Nope, I cleared it with them. They said they'd let maintenance know to leave it up as long as I come back to take it down."

Ashley held up her naked wrist and tapped it with her finger. "Wow, can't believe it, but I'll be totally booked at that time."

"I didn't tell you when it would be."

"When will it be?"

"Tomorr—"

"Totally booked." She sucked in a long breath through her teeth. "Sorry, I wish I was free."

I smacked her ass with the folded cardboard. "Some friend."

"I helped with this, didn't I?"

Dropping my arm around her shoulder, I tugged her closer. "You did. Thanks, Ashley."

She nudged her head into the side of mine. "Don't worry about it. I see how happy Cole makes you. A few paper cuts are worth you both figuring this all out."

Fuck, I had the best friends. We couldn't ever tell them how this started. Whatever happened between Cole and I once the contest was over, I didn't want them to know I'd lied. They'd be hurt I just flat out lied to their faces repeatedly and probably made them feel like they were going a little crazy with our whiplash relationship announcement. Plus, I didn't even think I was lying anymore. No, I *knew* I wasn't lying anymore.

Outside, Ashley tucked her scarf into her coat. "You coming to our place? Leona scored a mountain of cookies from some event at her dad's office, so we're planning on slipping into a sugar coma along with hot chocolate."

"I'd love to come, but I'm working, and my ass doesn't need any more cookies. Save me some and I'll come by after work."

She smacked my ass. "That ass can have all the cookies it wants."

The best friends. "See you after my shift."

"I'll see if I can wrestle some away from Leona and Taylor."

"You're up for the challenge."

She laughed, puffs of breath escaping into clouds in front of her face.

My cheeks were already on fire by the time I made it to the bookstore for my shift.

New merchandise arrivals to the storeroom meant I spent half my shift in there wrestling cardboard with a dull box cutter. The plus side was I didn't have to deal with customers or folding clothes.

"Kennedy, there's a new box of lecture packets up on the second floor to be unpacked and shelved," Gretchen called to me with a cart stacked high with all the products I'd unboxed.

"On it." I shoved a forkful of wilted iceberg lettuce into my mouth. Grumbling, I dumped the last of my nearly expired salad I'd gotten on sale and headed back to work three minutes after my break officially ended. Couldn't professors order all their shit at the beginning of the semester and plan ahead like normal people?

The second my foot hit the bottom stair to the second floor the overhead announcement mic came on. A voice traveled through the speakers and I turned to tell Gretchen someone had gotten to one of the phones.

But she was standing at one of them with a speaker held up to it, swaying with a megawatt smile.

That's when the familiar melody hit me, and an even more familiar voice.

Sitting at the top of the stairs, Cole stared at me all doe-eyed, lip syncing about how I was just too good to be true.

One of the tour groups who was inside picking out swag whipped out their phones to record this in all its glory. I glanced around at the pockets of onlookers gathering. Outside the three sets of double doors at the back of the store leading to the food court, coffee shops, and study tables, people stopped and looked. Laptops were closed and they moved to get a better look at where the music was coming from.

At the first hit of brass, I clutched my chest and my heart hit the back of my teeth. Both sets of escalators had been set to down and at least half the marching band rolled down still playing in perfect time.

He'd even gotten a fake security guard to chase him all over the much narrower staircase complete with Cole riding partially down the escalator before flinging himself back onto the stairs for the last of his descent and landed in front of me with his best Heath Ledger impersonation.

"She's the best girlfriend in the world, everyone. Vote for Cole and Kennedy on the STFU Puppy Love site to show us both how much you loved this."

Swooning, fawning, clicking.

His stock had to have risen by at least a hundred points with this. He waved to the crowd like he was on the football field then spun me around and planted a kiss on me.

Breathless, I had no words, completely caught off guard.

He tossed the mic to Gretchen who beamed at his display.

My stupid sticky-note heart had to look like the dumbest low-effort reveal after all this. Defeat was a prickly pill to swallow. I was irritatingly impressed by Cole getting all this together, embarrassment be damned. "A little over-the-top, weren't you?"

"You didn't like it?" His hands locked around the small of my back. A smile in place, but the question in his eyes.

How could I lie? Because even though we were still in the contest, he'd done this for me. And like Pittsburgh, it didn't feel like it was only for the contest. "You know I did."

"Then what's the problem?"

Turning, I hugged him back. "You know why."

"And nothing you can do will change my mind. I love to win."

Out-romancing him wasn't nearly as easy as I'd thought it would be, especially when I didn't have his resources and connections.

People bent over backward to do him the smallest favor, and although he didn't think he had a romantic bone in his body, he'd done a hell of a job with the wooing. But now the new prize was the big win for totally different reasons. A way to not have to face the fear of what a real conversation with his dad might actually be, and I couldn't let him run from it. I couldn't let him keep it lingering in the back of his mind, filling him with more and more regret.

Crackles and pops escaped the ring of rocks and bricks. Tiny embers floated in the air, giving off extra heat.

The makeshift fire pit kept me warmer outside than I'd expected.

But my butt was still freezing. Half turns every few

minutes warmed it up enough, along with Cole's body heat whenever he was nearby.

The Friday night barbecue at The Zoo wasn't what I'd expected.

Griff and Hollis argued over the grill. The five-foot circle around them was the only spot where the snow had melted and exposed the dead grass.

Ezra sat in a chair with an untouched beer balanced on the arm of it and strummed his guitar like he wasn't even aware we were all here. His fingers had to be freezing, but he kept playing the same melody like he was trying to figure something out.

Waist-high snow mounds had been formed along the fence line and were studded with bottles and cans of beer and cider.

Reid's massive stack of paper plates was weighed down by bottles of ketchup, mustard, and barbecue sauce.

Cole stepped out of the kitchen and jogged down the two concrete steps leading to the back yard with a steaming mug wearing nothing but a thermal, headed straight for me. "I put extra mini-marshmallows in there for you." He presented the drink with a slight bow.

"My hero." Just when I thought the fall had already been hard enough. "Thanks."

"Of course." He kissed me right at the temple in what seemed like a reflex. "And Bailey's."

My heart triple beat, and I tried to keep myself upright. It was so easy, too easy to get comfortable with him.

He grabbed a beer from the slush pile and cracked it open on the arm of one of the folding chairs.

"Aren't you freezing?"

"That's what the beer's for. It'll warm me up."

"Or I can." I looped an arm around his waist and hugged

him closer, looking forward to getting him alone. I squeezed my thighs together. Was this the female equivalent of what Cole went through our first disastrous night? Because I was seconds from pulling him into the nearest closet to take the edge off.

His arm slipped around my shoulder and we stood together, heating each other up.

Hollis clacked his metal tongs together. "Food is done, but the buns might be frozen. Just a heads up."

Griff held the edges of the flimsy aluminum tray that bent under the weight of the meat piled inside. "This stuff is hot." He dropped it on the table and shook his hands before rushing to the snow pile and cooling them on a beer.

Reid walked out of the house with his arm around Leona's shoulder and the preheated tray of catering chicken from the oven balanced on one towel-covered hand. "Don't fuck up your hands, man. We've got practice tomorrow."

All five guys, even Ezra, groaned. So he *was* listening.

"How many more do we have this spring?" Reid squeezed mustard onto two hot dogs.

Griff took a bite of his hot dog, making more than half of it disappear. "Two."

Hollis shaped his fingers into a gun and mimed blowing himself away. "He's beating the shit out of us this off-season. It'll take all summer to recover." He picked up his can from the edge of the folding table and gulped it down.

Cole's muscles tensed.

Maybe the guys could help Cole. Help him figure out a way to connect with his dad. The thought of Cole spending more than a required minute with him twisted my stomach, but he deserved to at least know more about the man who'd been such an all-encompassing part of his life. They were the ones who spent the most time with him, although not under ideal circumstances.

Reid put one of the hot dogs on another plate and handed it to Leona. "I don't get how he's such a colossal asshole and made it to the top. You'd have thought someone would've pushed him down a flight of stadium stairs before he made it to a head coach position. Maybe he wasn't always this much of a dick?"

"Did you want a burger or a hot dog?" Cole dropped his arm from around my shoulder.

He was shutting down, pulling away from not just me, but the guys.

"A burger."

"Cheese?"

I nodded. There was a stiffness in Cole, every muscle rigid.

He needed to know he could rely on the guys. "Anyone know anything about the Coach outside of football?"

Cole's head snapped up and the fork he'd been using to spear the grill-marked patty slipped out of his hand.

Griff cleaned the ketchup and mustard off his thumb and picked up another bun. "Why would we want to know anything about him outside of football?"

Reid cheersed his hot dog against Leona's and took a bite. "Hell, we don't even want to know him *in* football."

Cole glared at me. The vein in the side of his neck straining. Not the reaction I hoped for. New tactic.

"He's pretty horrible, Kennedy. He and my dad have had run-ins over the years." Leona shuddered. "He's got a one-track mind and anything that gets in his way is run straight over."

I decided to pivot away from playing getting-to-know-you with the coach and move on to something that might show Cole how the guys stuck together. "But the team stood up to him for you guys, right?" If he could at least let his friends know, maybe the burden wouldn't feel so heavy—so lonely. I never wanted Cole to believe the only person he had in this world was a father who hadn't even acknowledged him.

Reid and Leona got dreamy looks in their eyes, staring at one another. She nodded. "They did. I still can't believe it, but it's not all sunshine and rainbows."

Reid wiped at his mouth with the back of his hand. "We're all paying the price for the act of solidarity. Sorry about that, guys."

Ezra stood and set his guitar down in the chair. "Don't apologize for him being human garbage. Some people just are and there's nothing you can do to change it." He patted Reid's shoulder and walked over to the food, loading up his plate with meat.

Cole marched back over to me and shoved the plate in my direction. His eyes burned holes in the side of my face. "Don't," he rasped.

Cole trying to control what I said pissed me off. These gripe sessions were standard, no one was going to randomly make the leap that my questions had anything to do with him. His secret had been locked inside him for years and clouded his judgment.

"Is there anyone who gets along with him?" I took a sip of my drink, pointedly ignoring Cole as much as he was dead set on making his scrutiny obvious.

Griff inhaled another hot dog. "No wife or kids."

My sharp inhale sent the hot chocolate down the wrong pipe.

"He probably doesn't even get along with his own mother," Griff continued.

Chest-racking coughs and gasps were the only sounds flooding my ears.

"Let me take her inside." Cole plucked the plate and drink from my hand and thumped me on the back, while guiding me inside.

He filled a cup with water from the tap and waited for my eyes to stop watering.

A paper towel was thrust in front of me.

My cheeks burned from the shift in temperature and my windpipe ached from the chocolate bath. My sternum felt like it had been compressed and I finally straightened.

I wiped at my choking tears and came face to face with a furious Cole. My heart raced for reasons other than sugar overload and the near asphyxiation.

Cole clenched his hands at his sides. "What the fuck?"

21

COLE

My blood boiled. Skin bubbled like someone had chucked me into the fire pit and poured the lighter fluid on.

She stared at me. Her hand, clutched around the paper towel, dropped to her side. "What's wrong?"

Air felt like it evaporated before it hit my lungs. I clenched and unclenched my hands, trying to crank the boiling inside to a simmer. "You think I don't know what you're doing."

"What do you think I'm doing?" Her hands flailed and she shook her head like I was being unreasonable.

My nostrils flared and I sucked in a steaming breath. "Trying to get me to say something about Mikelson. It's no one's business."

She pointed to the closed kitchen door. "They're your best friends."

"And I'd like it to stay that way." Finding out our number one torturer was my father? How would they look at me after they found out? Worse, how would they treat me? How would the whole team treat me?

"All I was trying to do was find out what they knew about him. What you've all learned about him after three years playing for him." Her tone was placating and she made gentle hand motions like she was smoothing out fur on an agitated stray.

"What does it matter?" It stung I didn't know much more about him than the rest of the guys outside of my existence and his relationship with my mom. Oh, and him using my mom to steal plays to stomp his way to the top. Pretty screwed up.

"You're the one who wants to go on a trip with him with the sole purpose of getting to know him. I'd think it was essential information."

"I told you I'm not taking it." I'd figure out a different way to keep the promise to my mom. Maybe tie him to a tackling dummy and withhold food and water until he gave in. At this point that felt just as reasonable as my original plan.

She crossed her arms over her chest and her gaze narrowed. "Just because you show up at my job with a marching band doesn't mean I can't still win."

A bitter laugh escaped my lips, and I folded my arms across my chest. "We've got a little over a week left, Kennedy. There's nothing you can pull off that I can't top."

She pressed two fists against her forehead. "Why can't you admit you're scared?"

My body jolted. I caught myself on the counter. "I'm not scared. When can you admit you've always got to be the one in control? I should've never told you. I'm not your little sister, Kennedy. I don't need you consoling me about my shitty parents."

She jerked like I'd taken a swing at her. "Is that what you think I'm doing?"

"I don't need you to fix me or this situation. I can handle it."

"Which is why you were desperate enough to get into a fake relationship with me on a wish and a prayer that you might have a shot at the golf weekend. To bribe him into spending time with you off the field." She tossed the paper towel and marched over to me, patting my shoulder. "Doing a real bang-up job of handling it, Cole."

A gust of freezer-cold air crackled against the heated skin at the back of my neck. The rage rolled off me in waves. My body vibrated with it.

Outside the laughter and low music felt like needles inside my head.

Tomorrow, I'd have to face him again. Another day of scrutiny and never measuring up. Another day of busting my ass for his approval that would never come.

He has a good heart. My mom's words echoed in my ears, charred their path to my brain. I'd made the promise to her, but every passing day, each new interaction felt like it would be the last one to her and the one I'd have to break.

Panicked breaths clawed their icicle path down my throat. Gripping the counter, I sucked in air and forced it out, trying to calm myself. My arm shook and I released the chipping linoleum and shoved myself toward the back door.

Maybe the freezing temperatures would calm me, like shoveling snow on top of a barrel fire. I stumbled down the two back steps. Ezra wasn't in his chair, his guitar wrapped in his coat while he stood at the table beside Kennedy, making another burger.

Reid and Leona were sharing a chair with his arms wrapped around her and the pair sipping from a cup of hot chocolate.

Griff and Hollis fought over the last grilled chicken breast.

Kennedy squeezed ketchup onto her cheeseburger and laughed. "But he can't be all that bad, can he?"

The gentle cooking cranked up, so fast the back of my head throbbed. "Kennedy, enough! No one wants to talk about this shit. Just fucking stop it."

Everyone froze. They stared at me with open mouths and confusion-clouded expressions.

Kennedy's breath shot out in chopping pants. Her wide-eyed gaze flooded before she straightened herself and shoved her plate at me. "Screw you."

The mess of ketchup and mustard smeared all over the front of my shirt.

I grabbed it, letting the condiment mix spill over my hands.

She didn't bother going through the house, instead walking around the side. The gate slammed behind her.

Leona disentangled herself from Reid's hold and rushed after her.

The tinny music from the speaker perched on the windowsill amplified the silence around me. It blanketed the space with an unbearable force.

"Dick move to snap at her like that." Ezra glared at me, snatched up his guitar, and marched back inside.

Steam felt like it was escaping from beneath my coat collar. I tossed the plate down and grabbed a stack of napkins, wiping at my coat. "I told her we didn't want to talk about Mikelson."

Griff cleared his throat. "She was asking about my snoring on the team bus."

The ground shifted under my feet.

Reid shoved out of his seat. "What's the deal? That was some old Kennedy-Cole animosity."

I raked my hand through my hair. "I...I just didn't want her making everyone tense up about how shitty tomorrow's going to be."

Hollis poked a finger at the center of his chest. "*I* brought up practice. All she was doing was asking questions. You know like someone might do, if they're interested in the thing that takes up a shit ton of our lives."

A cavern opened beneath me and I was flailing at the air. "Fuck! I screwed up, okay. Will everyone get off my ass about it?"

Leona walked around the side of the house. "She wouldn't let me drive her home. She got on the shuttle." Her gaze bored into mine.

"I'll go talk to her." I flung the napkins down onto the table, smearing even more mess on the dented plastic, and turned to leave.

Leona stepped in front of me, holding her hand up like a stop sign. "Maybe you need to cool down a little more."

"What makes you think I'm not calm?" My pulse throbbed in my hands. I glanced down and slowly uncurled them.

Reid brushed past me and pulled Leona in close like she needed protecting—protecting from me. "The way you just snapped at my girlfriend. You need to figure out what the hell is going on with you before you go talk to Kennedy or she's going to slam that door right in your face and no one will blame her."

Spinning on my heel, I stormed inside. Remorse set in, churning my stomach.

Ezra's playing paused while I walked past the living room and up the stairs.

I slammed my door so hard my bedroom windows rattled. Pacing and scrubbing my hands over my face, I tried to hold the threads together. The ones that had been fraying for as long as I remembered. Only what they were holding together felt more threadbare than ever. Almost see-through. My hope clouded by my fear of what had been right in front of me for ages.

Kennedy's shocked face replayed in my head.

I squeezed my eyes shut and knocked my hands against the sides of my head, trying to dislodge the image.

Walking to my closet, I knocked the lid off the box I'd brought with me from Seattle.

Three leather-bound books. One gray. One yellow. One maroon. I'd committed every scribble, every line to memory.

The pen and pencil strokes were harsh and jagged like their creator. But tucked inside the yellow book was the note I'd read and reread more times than I could remember.

"Thanks for keeping these safe for me, Brandy. I'll be back in a few weeks and I'll take Cole for a pizza."

He never had, not once in his life, unless he counted ordering pizza and keeping me busy with a new movie while he went to my mother's room.

I flung the books back into the box and shoved the lid on, crumpling the sides. At this point, I didn't even know what I was trying to prove—what I was trying to accomplish. Everything was muddled, threads intersecting and intertwining into what might just be a giant ball of chaos.

Needing sound other than my labored breaths, I stripped down and darted across the hall into the bathroom. My shower ran until the water beat against my back like ice blocks. I pulled my forehead off the tile and lurched forward, wrenching off the water.

In my room, the cold wouldn't leave. I stared at my

phone, at the darkened screen reflecting my face back at me. The words didn't come. Opening our chat, I typed out one message, then another, erasing them before hitting send.

Frustration hissed through me. I tossed my phone across the room. Instead of a satisfying thunk or crunch, there was a muted landing onto the stacked and folded clothes sitting in the laundry basket outside my closet door.

I shoved off the bed, picked up the basket, and chucked it across the room.

Kennedy's second-guessing. Her prodding. Her meddling. This was none of her business. She wanted to bring me closure and we weren't even in a real relationship.

I didn't have to apologize. I didn't have to care. I didn't have to feel this way about her.

I was choosing not to care, ignoring the little crack that widened in my chest making it hard to breathe. A hammer had been taken to my heart and I knew exactly who to blame.

22

COLE

I tugged out my mouthguard and spit into a trash can on the sidelines. A swirl of red was mixed in. I brushed my hand over the side of my mouth and it came away smeared with blood. The last hit I'd been late on the pivot and paid for it.

Last night's sleep sucked, if it could even be considered sleep. A bit before sunrise, I'd passed out only to have to wake up less than a couple hours later to gear up.

Kennedy's eyes were all I saw when I closed mine. My pillow was probably still flat from how much I punched it trying to get comfortable, but no matter what I did, I couldn't drift off.

Between practice dread and the Kennedy blowup, I was lucky my eyes had been closed for more than a blink.

The post and drag drills were murder on my thighs, which felt shredded. My tank was empty, but I dug deep for reserves. We had to be over the two hours allowed for spring practices, but that had never stopped Mikelson before.

"Hauser," Mikelson sneered. "You can get your ass off this field if you're going to take all day. Let's set up the play."

Everything ached, but I used his taunt to motivate me. Biting hard on my mouthguard, I pushed up and got back into position.

Dropping into my snap stance, I positioned the ball against the ground with my fingers wrapped around the laces.

Hollis stood a few feet behind me, ready for the snap.

In a practiced motion repeated hundreds of times between us, I shot the ball behind me to hit him hip height.

The line held and we clashed shoulders, petering out after a few runs. It wasn't a full on 7-on-7 game, only drills. Repeating the moves until walking upright felt less natural.

"The snap needs to be faster. Like breathing. Don't hand your QB that shit."

"Sorry, Coach!" My whole body shook with the force of my bellow. The frostbitten grass smushed under my gloved fingers pressed into the soil. Most teams practiced indoors in weather like this. Most teams weren't helmed by Mikelson.

Reid, wearing full pads, glanced over at me. Steam rose off him. We couldn't let him break us. It was the same for all of us, overheated and tired, but we wanted to win. For once, we wanted to win the whole damn thing.

Behind me, Hollis got into position. The suction noise of his cleats in the frosty, soggy ground sent my pulse pounding.

My other hand tightened around the ball and, exhaling, I shot it behind me and darted into position.

We finished the play and there was no whistle. Panting and standing shoulder to shoulder we waited.

Three shrill whistle blasts. "Hit the showers."

Everyone sagged. Relief so sweet, it tasted like a gallon of Gatorade. It reminded me of Kennedy's lips.

The fist-tight clench of my stomach that had just loosened tightened again with each step off the field.

Maybe the fight with Kennedy wasn't as bad as the guys made it out to be.

"Anyone going to The Library tonight?" I dropped my pads. The hidden on-campus bar where football players and rarely-invited guests could hang out and not have word get back to Mikelson had been kept secret since long before we arrived to STFU. When we didn't feel like cleaning up after a party at our place it was where we headed. And it was a minor miracle the place hadn't been shut down.

Ezra tugged his hat down low and marched past me.

Hollis and Griff stared disapprovingly.

Reid wrapped a towel around himself. "You talked to Kennedy yet?"

"Why's that any of anyone's business?"

Hollis kicked off his cleats. They thudded against the padded bench. "Because you're not that guy. You're not an asshole." He ducked his head and glanced toward the Coaching Hallway.

Bile rushed for my throat.

"And we'd have called Reid on the same thing with Leona."

Grumbling, I whipped off my T-shirt. "Since when do girlfriends get the royal treatment?"

"When you show us they mean something to you. You've been the biggest one about not being locked into anything, so she's got to be special if you're literally shouting from rooftops about how much she means to you."

Shot myself in the foot there. Now their misplaced loyalty meant they wouldn't let up until I made things right with her. And the ache in the center of my chest wouldn't let up either. It hadn't even been twelve hours and I was being driven crazy knowing she was out there angry with me, but knowing there was hurt in there, too, made it harder.

Without another word, I hit the showers. Mikelson hasn't summoned me, so what should've felt like a great end to practice felt like a size-ten boot pounded into my chest.

Inside my car, with my hair frozen down to the root, I picked up my phone. Maybe she'd cooled down by now. My stomach knotted, twisting like I'd been sent to run drills all over again.

A deep breath and I sent the message.

Me: *Can I come over?*

The reply took a while. I drummed my fingers against the wheel and turned my car on. Not waiting for her message, I drove in the direction of her apartment. The phone rumbled in my cup holder. I glanced at the screen.

Kennedy: *No need.*

I slammed on the brakes at a red light, snatched the phone up, and tapped out my reply, teetering on the edge of relief. Everyone else could suck it. She wasn't even phased, and we'd keep going like we had been before.

Me: *So we're good?*

Maybe it had all been in my head. She felt silly for running off. I felt like a dick for snapping and we got over this little bump with no issues.

Kennedy: *No, we're over.*

My heart punched at the back of my throat and my phone tumbled out of my hand into the passenger-side footwell. Cutting across a lane of traffic, I pulled over and tugged the floor mat toward me. The screen lit up again.

Kennedy: *I mean, it's over.*

My fingers felt numb and I punched at the screen with my finger.

Me: *What the hell? I'll be there in 3 minutes.*

Kennedy: Now's not a great time.

Absolute wrong answer to get me to not come over. She'd abandoned the plan over what? Some bullshit hurt feelings because I yelled. It wasn't a big deal.

Jerking the wheel, I slammed on the gas on the last stretch to her apartment.

Someone else was leaving the building when I showed up, so Kennedy didn't have to buzz me in.

Not waiting for the geriatric elevator, I charged up the stairs taking them two at a time.

The chipped paint on the metal door scratched at my knuckles as I pounded on it to get her to open up.

Stepping back, I rocked before bracing both hands on the door jamb listening. Nothing and I knocked again. The sharp, hollow sound echoed in the hallway.

The door opened. I took a deep breath to launch into the speech I hadn't had a chance to practice in my head, but I stumbled back like I'd been tackled.

It wasn't Kennedy. It wasn't Melody. It was a guy.

A guy in boxers.

"Are you Melody's boyfriend?" A sound escaped my throat.

"No, I'm here with Kennedy." His drawn-together eyebrows and forehead wrinkles smoothed out and he pointed a finger at me. "You're Cole Hauser. STFU center."

I shouldered past him. "Where's Kennedy?" My head rumbled like it had been shoved into an active volcano.

"She's in the bedroom." He glanced between the now empty doorway and me before letting the door close. "Does she know you're coming?"

"Who are you?" Anger built, pouring down my back as each muscle tightened and locked.

"Hey, Felix, here are your pants..." Kennedy walked into

the room with his pants in her hands. The belt jingled and her eyes were spotlight wide.

At my sides, I clenched and unclenched my fists.

A hiss built behind her pinched tight lips. "I told you now wasn't a good time, Cole."

"That's all you have to say to me." My molars felt like they were turning to dust.

"Should I—" Felix gestured to the front door.

"I thought you didn't do sleepovers." I stepped toward her.

Her gaze narrowed into razor-blade slits. "What I do is none of your business."

"The hell—"

"Hey, Kennedy, can I have my pants back?"

She jerked, looking over at Felix like she'd forgotten he was there. *Good.*

Turning away from me, she held out the pants. "I got the stain out and the length will work well with the black shoes you showed me. Throw in your grandfather's pocket square and you'll be all set."

"Thanks." His gaze darted to mine and back to Kennedy. "You good?"

She folded her arms across her chest and gave him a sharp nod.

An audible sigh of relief. He yanked his backpack off the floor by the door and left, pants still in hand.

She spun around and walked back toward her bedroom.

"You have nothing to say to me," I called after her.

In response, she raised her middle finger.

I jogged after her. "What was that about?"

She walked into her bedroom, sat on her bed with her legs folded, and grabbed her phone.

"You're going to ignore me?"

Her fingers moved over the screen.

The lava wasn't flowing now, but spewing up into the air. Charred heated ash billowing into the air. I marched over and grabbed the phone from her grasp.

She shot up off the bed. "What do you want, Cole?"

"I came over here to apologize and you've got some guy in your apartment with no pants on."

"At six p.m. on a Wednesday."

"So?"

"So." She snatched her phone back. "I don't owe you an explanation."

"Like hell you don't. You freak out yesterday and walk off after I told you to stop what you were doing. Then you take some guy home after you've decided we're broken up without even talking to me and I'm in the wrong." My chest felt like a furnace ready to explode. If she'd slept with another guy, then she was right, we were over.

"Lower your voice. And you couldn't be more wrong." She tossed the phone onto her bed. "Just to clear the air, I didn't storm out because you told me to stop doing something. I walked out because you screamed at me in front of my friends and yours. You embarrassed me, thinking I was talking about your dad."

I flinched. The word felt like a curse thrown in my face.

"Which I wasn't doing. You said to drop it and I did. But I told you not to scream at me. It's a no-go for me. It's a line that doesn't get crossed.

"And that guy you said I took home is one of the people I shopped for in Pittsburgh. Felix is proposing to his girlfriend over spring break and wanted to look good. He's a bit of a slob most of the time and wanted to surprise her. So no, I didn't go pick some guy up in the less than twenty-four hours since I left your house and bring him home to screw him, but screw you for thinking that. Even if I did, it would be none of your damn business."

The strangling silence stretched between us, punctuated only by my ragged breaths. Relief and panic were now clambering for a starting position. She hadn't cheated. Would it even have been cheating? But she still wanted us to be over.

"What about our deal? What about our plan?" Fear set in that she was ready to so easily pull the plug.

"You're not taking the trip anyway, and at this point, it's the only reason I was doing this, so it's fine." She dusted her hands off one another. "I'm done." The words hammered nails in our relationship coffin.

Trying to keep calm, I went for another angle. "Can you be reasonable?"

"Like you were yesterday?" Venom filled her voice.

I squeezed my jaw. "You don't get why I was mad? You can't understand why I'd want to keep this to myself?"

"Because you're used to secrets. You keep them well. You've kept this one for as long as you can remember. That doesn't mean it's how it always has to be. It doesn't mean your friends wouldn't want the chance to support you."

"I don't want their support." At least I didn't want to *need* their support. What if she was wrong? What if it came out and then I was alone, sloughing through my final year before being shoved out into adulthood completely cut off from them and the rest of the team.

"Not telling them doesn't make it go away."

"It makes it less real. If I tell them and they know, they'll hate him even more. It'll affect how they play. It'll change how they see me. They'll be so fucking pissed, they might do something stupid that would jeopardize their futures, and I can't lay that on them." I leaned against the wall and covered my head with my hands.

Her muted steps drew closer. Her tentative hand brushed against my shoulder. Her comforting presence cooled the churning lava between my ears. "Cole, you're carrying a lot with you. Too much."

"I don't know any other way to be." Lifting my head, I stared into her eyes. Losing her scared me. I'd always been preparing myself for someone to leave or for me to leave them, but there hadn't been any Kennedy prep.

"I get that, but..." She licked her lips. "Fake relationship or not, I—I can't have you shouting at me."

"Sorry." Some of the tightness in my chest loosened at the hard edge leaving her gaze. I hadn't ruined this completely. The window was opened a crack. The final nail hadn't been driven into our relationship, if that's what we had. "It was a shitty thing for me to jump on you about, especially when you weren't even talking about him."

"It wasn't about you being mad or even being wrong." Her chest rose and fell. "When you yell. When you shout. You screaming at me..." She squeezed her eyes shut and opened them with a pleading edge that sliced at my soul. "That's not okay. I've listened to my parents scream at each other for years. I've felt what it does to me—how it makes it hard for me to focus. My heart races. My hands tingle. My vision tunnels. My whole body shakes."

I reached for her and crushed her to my chest. "Sorry, I —I didn't even think." The call with her sister. The way she'd jumped up the second the screaming started and tried to coach her sister through it. The way her hands trembled. I brushed my hands down the back of her head.

"It's half the reason I don't even like going to football games. Maybe I won't always be this way, but you yelling at me is nonnegotiable." She lifted my chin and tried to put some space between us.

Misery engulfed me. "I'm sorry, Kennedy. I know I fucked up and there's no excuse. I'll never speak to you like that again."

"It's a firm rule for me with anyone I've dated." The words were whispered, almost lost to the pounding of my heart in my ears.

A shining light of possibility glowed in my chest despite my screw up. "I thought you didn't date."

"Exactly why."

The leap felt huge. The chasm she'd placed between her and every other guy, and she'd just thrown out a bridge. Set the planks on the edge for me to cross it. And I wanted to prove I could be that guy to her. To myself. That I could treat her exactly how she deserved to be treated. "Let me prove to you I can do it the right way. The real way."

Her head tilted, skepticism written in her drawn-together eyebrows. "For real? Not pretending anymore? You want to be together?"

I dragged the backs of my fingertips along her chin. "I don't want to be apart. Pretending with you has been better than any real relationship I've ever even come close to."

The creases smoothed and she stared into my eyes. With a dip of her chin, she seemed to make a decision. "I believe you."

"I want to try this on for real and let you know what happened before won't happen again." Tension tightened in my chest, stretching on as she once again weighed my words.

"I trust you." It shone brightly in her eyes, the trust she had for me, and it tore me up knowing I'd hurt her. That I'd put her through the feelings she was trying to shield her own sister from.

I wouldn't hurt her again. The vow was silent and instant, never again.

How could I when she had my still-beating heart in the palm of her hand?

23

KENNEDY

Those fears of falling straight into the situation I'd hated for as long as I could remember always loomed overhead whenever the opposite sex was involved.

It was a slippery slope into patterns so well-worn, I wasn't sure I'd be able to escape them. But when Cole stared into my eyes with the kind of look that made me light-headed, I couldn't push him away.

"Does this mean I get to call you my girlfriend now?"

"Weren't you before?"

"Sure." His arms locked around me, fingers running over the curve of my ass. "But now, it'll be for real."

"Who knew you were so hard up for a girlfriend?"

"Speaking of ha—"

He ground himself against me. His stiff length nudged against the front of my thigh.

My body tingled and a throb set in between my legs. It had only been yesterday morning he'd been inside me and I wanted him there again.

But jumping straight into bed after a fight wasn't the best idea.

I batted at his chest. My hand colliding with that body that had been keeping me warm only a couple nights ago. "At the risk of killing the peace between us. How was practice?"

His hands on my butt went from teasing to tempting. "More of the same." Rocking against me, he dropped kisses along the curve of my neck. "The usual back breaking and ball busting I've gotten used to."

The tingles were zaps, electric desire pulsing through my body.

"No injuries." I tugged at the hem of his shirt. What had I been saying about holding off on sex?

"Not anything worse than the usual." One hand stayed on my ass and the other delved under my shirt.

"Are you sure?" I dropped my head back, giving him even more access to my throat. "Maybe I should check you out."

His shirt was up and over his head in less than a blink and tossed to the far side of the room. "I'm all yours to explore."

"A little eager."

"For your hands, always." He dragged my shirt up and over my head. Behind me, his fingers worked their magic and I was braless. It dropped to the floor.

"Then let me get to work." I yanked his belt free from his jeans. The metal jingled.

"Me first." He cupped my breasts and brought his mouth to them, teasing the tips. "I've missed these." The perfected ministrations using his lips, tongue, and teeth spelled the end of my panties even having a chance of staying dry.

"It's been less than a day." I dragged my fingers through his hair, clutching him to my chest.

He shouldn't be this good at this. Every time he touched me he was unhurried like he wanted to cherish that part of me forever.

"Too long."

"You went twenty-two years without knowing anything about them."

"But now that I've experienced them, there's no going back." He sank to his knees in front of me.

I braced my hands on his shoulders. "Wasn't I supposed to be checking you over?"

"You can check me over once I'm finished with you." His fingers popped open the buttons of my jeans with excruciatingly slow precision. "This might take a while."

A shuddering breath rocked my chest.

The cool backs of his fingers brushed against the triangle of hair above my pussy and I bit back a groan.

My legs were bare and I stepped out of my now inside-out pants. Goosebumps rose all over my skin, tightening my nipples even more. Every brush of his skin against mine and the fabric along my flesh added more kindling to the fire. Fire building into a chaotic storm of craving.

"Beautiful." He stared up at me like he'd come to worship.

A tremble raced through me because every touch of his felt like a devotion.

I licked my lips, ready to feel him on me again —inside me.

A gentle knock at the front door burst through the haze of desire blanketing me.

"They'll go away." He growled, and tugged me closer,

setting my thigh over his shoulder and opening me to him completely.

The knock got louder.

"I'll get rid of them!" He jumped up and rushed out of the room.

My body hummed, eager for the full complement of his attention. "Put a shirt on." I grabbed his shirt to toss it to him, but he'd already opened the front door.

"Hey, Kennedy's boyfriend." An ice bucket of shock poured over the lust bomb Cole had lit the fuse on. My stomach plunged. The familiar voice. A voice that shouldn't be here.

I scrambled to put my clothes back on and turned my shirt right side out. Forgetting the bra, I yanked it on, threw on my pants, and burst into the hallway.

Cole looked to me with panic-filled eyes.

"Hey, Kenny. What's up?"

"Hannah, what are you doing here?" I flew across the room and hugged her, glancing behind her. Oh god, that's the last thing I needed right now. An impromptu family visit. Checking out in the hallway, there were no bickering parents at the elevator.

"It's spring break and I wanted a taste of college life." She dropped her stuffed backpack beside the kitchen walkway.

"Where are Mom and Dad?" I propped my arms under my chest, which blared my bra-lessness.

She plopped down onto the couch and rested her arms along the back of it. "At home, probably."

Shock gripped me and my heart pounded like heels on pavement. "Then how are you here?"

"A giant metal bird flew through the sky and transported

me here." Her unhelpful reply came complete with a hand airplane landing on the coffee table.

I thumped down on the table and grabbed her shoulders. "Hannah, I'm being serious."

She rolled her eyes like it was no big deal she was a four-hour flight and airport shuttle away from home. Shaking off my hold, she leaned back and crossed her arms and legs. "I booked the ticket."

"How?" My bewildered headshaking didn't seem to phase her.

"With a credit card," she mumbled while inspecting her chipped purple nail polish.

"Whose credit card?"

"Dad's." She shrugged and avoided my gaze. Her eyes landing on a shirtless Cole, she jumped up. "Hey, Kennedy's boyfriend, Cole." With her arm looped through his, she tilted her head and looked up at him. "Loved what you did in Pittsburgh. So romantic!"

"Hi, Hannah." He looked to me with abject terror swimming in his gaze.

"Cole, why don't you go get a shirt and I'll deal with this one."

After disentangling himself from her, he flew out of the room like a wide receiver going for a touchdown pass. See, some of that football stuff was rubbing off on me. Taylor would be so proud.

Hannah crouched down and opened her bag like her arrival was no big deal and arranged ahead of time.

"Hannah."

"Yeah." She continued her rummaging, plucking out a shirt and laying it across her chest. "I stink after all the time it took to get here. I need to change. What do you think of this?"

"Do Mom and Dad know you're here?"

"Yeah."

I marched over, snatched the shirt off her, and shoved it into her bag. "Hannah!"

"Don't yell at me." She glared.

Taking long, deep breaths, I got on my knees beside her. "Hannah, do Mom and Dad know you're here?"

Her face scrunched up like she'd smelled month-old take out. "Not exactly."

"You ran away from home?" Our parents would go nuclear. The mushroom cloud would be visible from here.

"Not like I didn't plan on going back."

"Anything could've happened to you." I shuddered, trying not to picture the worst.

"But it didn't, and it isn't like I won't be on my own when I graduate anyway. It's a trial run." She sniffed her pits and recoiled. "I'm rank."

"Would you be serious?"

"Would you be less?" She tilted her head and shot me a what-the-hell look.

That helped calm me some. She was here, she was safe, and she wasn't wrong.

Cole walked back in with his shirt on.

A thump of sadness at all his glory being covered was tempered by his look of complete uneasiness and the realization that we wouldn't be finishing what we started in my bedroom until after Hannah left. Another reason to be annoyed as hell.

"She ran away. Can you keep her company for a second while I make sure our parents haven't launched a statewide manhunt for her?"

"Sure." He nodded and shoved his hands into his pockets, rocking back and forth on his heels.

I marched toward my room.

"Might want to put your pants right side out and maybe grab a bra," Hannah called out after me. "Sorry for interrupting your grown-up time."

My eyes slammed shut and I stopped short of my bedroom door, cringing at the tease in her voice. Not how I wanted Cole and Hannah meeting to go. Inside my room, I grabbed my phone off the bed and tapped on my mom's name.

She picked up on the second ring. "Hello." Her tone was completely casual.

"She's okay."

"Who's okay?"

"Hannah."

"Why wouldn't Hannah be okay?"

Frustration and disappointment crashed into me with an anger chaser. They didn't even know. "Because she's sitting in my living room after flying here all by herself."

"What?" Her screech pierced my ear drum. "Richard! Did you know Hannah was visiting Kennedy? I swear that man never tells me anything, the least he could've done—"

Dad's voice boomed in the background. "She's where? Why didn't you tell me she was going to visit Kennedy?"

The tips of my fingers felt like they'd been charged with static electricity.

"Why would I be asking if you knew if she was visiting if *I* knew she was visiting?" The bickering continued.

"I never know what you're doing. And who paid for this? Who said she could—"

"Why is this automatically my fault? It's all—"

Their voices escalated. Overlapping retorts riddled with barbs.

My arms trembled and I gripped the phone tighter and

cut in. "She's here for the week. I'll text you with her flight number so you two can pick her up."

"Wait—"

I ended the call and waited for the callback. Five seconds passed and there wasn't one, which meant they were volleying their own shouting match, completely forgetting their sixteen-year-old had just hopped on a flight to escape them.

Righting my clothes, I went back into the living room. Cole stood in the kitchen slapping a slice of bread over meat and cheese on top of another. He chopped off the crusts and slid it to her.

"You can stay."

Their heads turned toward me. She jumped down and flung her arms around me. "Thank you! Thank you! I swear, you won't even notice I'm here."

"I highly doubt that." I hugged her back and mouthed "thank you" to Cole over her shoulder.

He waved away my thanks.

She let me go, went back to her seat.

"There's one for you too." He finished up the grilled chicken and cheese sandwich. "Crusts or without?"

"I'm not six, I can eat my crusts." I took the plate he held out, ignoring the glare from Hannah.

He put everything in the sink and turned on the water.

"You don't have to clean up, Cole."

"No problem. You ladies talk and I'll be out of here in a couple minutes."

Hannah turned to me and mouthed, "Oh my god, he's so hot."

I kicked her and snapped forward at her yelp.

Cole glanced over his shoulder and smiled. "Right, I'll

hit the road and leave you two to catch up." He extended his hand. "Nice to meet you in person, Hannah."

She blushed and took another bite of her sandwich while meeting his hand and shaking it. "You too, Cole."

"And you." He walked over to my seat. "I'll see you tomorrow." A gentle, chaste kiss on the lips compared to where we'd left things off in my bedroom.

It still stole my breath and notched up the heat in the seconds our skin touched. "Tomorrow."

The door slammed shut and Hannah nearly shoved me off the stool.

"He's even hotter in person, are you kidding me? You're the luckiest person in the world." She stared at the closed door while ripping another bite out of her sandwich like she wished it was Cole.

"Maybe you could say it a little bit louder, I don't think Mom and Dad heard you back home."

"Like they could hear me over their own shouting."

Touché. "I can't believe you made it here all by yourself."

"Why not? I'm an independent badass, right? Learned it from my big sister." She rested her head on my shoulder and looked up into my eyes.

I palmed her face and playfully shoved her away. "Nut."

"You know you love me."

"You know I do." I took a bite out of the sandwich Cole made. It had no business being this good.

"Your boyfriend's magic. I swear."

Right now, I couldn't dispute that one bit. He was magic and I hoped the spell didn't wear off anytime soon. That I wasn't fooling myself into believing we could work.

24

COLE

Hollis raised his bottle overhead. "To a week before we have to see Mikelson again."

My stomach lurched like I'd dropped a snap. I choked down a gulp of beer to wash the moisture from my mouth. A week wouldn't be long enough. Spring break would be over too soon.

"Hell yeah," Griff shouted over the floor-rumbling music, and clinked his bottle to mine.

The rest of the guys followed along. We were crowded into the kitchen, away from the rest of the party. Normally, we had no issue leading the best damn parties on campus, but right now, I didn't feel like entertaining.

This was the longest Kennedy and I had been apart since we'd started this whole thing. Which made me feel like a colossal asshole since her sister was here. But the minutes crawled by knowing I'd get to see her tonight.

"Stop sulking." Ezra tapped me with his elbow. "People are going to think you're doing an impression of me."

I half laughed, not having it in me, which was the epitome of Ezra, although not lately. "I'm not even sulking."

Anymore. I could barely stand still and kept looking out the windows at the front of the house.

"Fair enough." He followed my gaze toward the front of the house.

That's when it hit me. I ripped my drink away from my lips. Beer dribbled down my chin. "Where the hell's your hat?"

His hand shot to his head, rubbing his hands over his close-cropped hair. "Nowhere."

"Well, it's not on your head." I glanced around at the floor like it might've fallen off. Then another crash inside my head. "Does this have anything to do with your new girlfriend?"

He shot back so quickly beer spilled out of the bottle, all over his shirt. "How'd you—" He straightened and brushed at the liquid dotted on his chest. "I don't know what you're talking about."

I patted his shoulder and took a sip of my drink. "Real smooth. No one will know you've got a secret girlfriend with those stealthy, secret-spy tactics."

With a glare, he reached for the brim of his missing hat, grasping at the air.

My laugh cost me another eye-singeing look. "Don't worry. I'll keep your secret."

He clamped one hand onto my arm and took a drink of his beer with the other. "Same as I'll keep yours."

Beer erupted out of *my* mouth this time, and out my nose. Using the hem of my shirt, I wiped at my face. My stomach clenched. "What secret?" Did he know about Coach? How I'd been the reason for the last two torturous seasons?

"Don't like it when the shoe's on the other foot, huh?" The corner of his mouth twitched.

"I don't—"

"Please. You and Kennedy? I saw that from the beginning." His half laugh was as close as Ezra got to full-on laughter.

The knot loosened and I felt like the beer wasn't trying to make a reappearance. "But—"

"No, I know you two are good now. I can see the way you look at her and the way she looks at you. It's not fake anymore." He glanced over at me.

My hand dropped to my side and I stared at him slack-jawed.

"I'm not just a pretty face." He gave my cheek a double smack and wandered off into the packed living room, leaving me unable to form words.

Had we been that transparent? Crazy how I hadn't even thought of Kennedy as being the secret. What we had together felt more than real and had for longer than any relationship I'd had before, if it could even be called that, but had Ezra said this to the rest of the guys?

More people filled their cups from the kegs and the drum of jungle juice. We probably spent more on booze than food in the off-season and right now it felt like a waste. I didn't want these people here. I wanted Kennedy here. And I was whining again. Minutes. She was minutes away. Get a damn grip, Cole.

I rushed after him.

Dodging bodies, I caught up to him and tugged him onto the stairs, below the line forming for the bathroom. "Have you told anyone else about this?"

"Nah, man. However you guys started I'm glad you've figured your shit out." He waved his hand in the air like he was swatting a fly.

I sagged, relief unlocking every muscle, and leaned in. "What about you? Who's the girl who's got you hatless?"

He ran his hand over his head and glanced over at the party carrying on without us in the living room. "Remember the Pittsburgh game last year?"

I nodded. The one where Reid had been pretending he didn't know Leona and there had been a big fight in the stands behind us. A big fight where a girl had been knocked down a few rows of seats and landed on Ezra. He'd whisked her out to First Aid.

His tight nod confirmed it.

"Does that mean she's here?" I scanned the crowd at the party.

"She doesn't go here." From his tone, I couldn't tell if that was a good or bad thing. "She was visiting friends that week."

"Where does she go? CMU or Pitt?"

"No." His jaw set like he was preparing himself for a hit. "Fulton U."

I sucked in a breath that chilled my molars. Cracking my neck to each side, I shook it off. "Okay, not the worst thing in the world."

"Her brother plays for them."

Damn. "Hockey? Beach volleyball?"

"They don't have a—"

"I know, but I was trying to give the benefit of the doubt. He plays for their football team, doesn't he?"

A grimmer nod.

"Shit."

He clinked the neck of his bottle to mine. "You said it."

"Maybe it's not that bad. I mean, how bad could it be?"

He leveled his gaze at me.

"You're right, that's pretty screwed up."

He reached for his not-there hat again and let out a frustrated growl.

"So why does she like you with no hat?"

His chin dipped. "Said she likes to see my eyes."

"And you're doing it even though she's not here to know? Why don't you get your hat?"

A soft flicker lit up his eyes. "Promised her I'd try going without it every so often."

Was our house fumigated with some kind of relationship pheromone before we moved in? Ezra was the last of any of us I'd expected to fall for someone. He barely talked enough to carry on a conversation let alone a relationship, but it couldn't be denied. And I was happy for him. "She must mean a lot to you for you to try even when she's not here."

"She means everything." He dropped his half-finished beer in the trash below the staircase and took off up the steps.

Griff walked toward me and slung his arm around my shoulder, dragging me back down into the party. "What did you do to piss Ezra off?"

I shrugged his arm off. "Hey, asshat. His whole life doesn't revolve around me."

"No, but yours revolves around Kennedy." His knowing smirk was punchably smug.

I opened my mouth to shoot back a denial, but it stalled. It had been days without her and everything felt more annoying, like my balm had been taken away and hidden, making everything else feel coarser and more uncomfortable.

"And football."

"Foregone conclusion." He laughed and wandered off with a beer in his hand, watching the whole party.

A couple hours later, still no Kennedy.

Ezra found me again. "We're out of jungle juice."

Maybe because he knew I wasn't in full party mode, I'd be the perfect assistant.

"You get the handles. Meet me on the back porch." Ezra took off toward the kitchen.

I walked toward the basement stairs.

The basement door banged open, nearly cracking me in the face. Reid and Leona came out, both of their hair sticking up in all directions and Reid's shirt was inside out.

Leona's cheeks were flushed and she dragged her fingers through her hair. "Sorry, we were looking for the garbage bags."

Reid waved a thick stack of black plastic. "Found them."

"We don't have any in the kitchen?" I waved toward the sink where a few of them peeked out of the door under the sink that didn't close properly. "You know you two don't need an excuse to make out, right?" I couldn't say I wasn't a little jealous it wasn't me and Kennedy right now.

"You've gotta admit sneaking around does make things even hotter." Reid grinned with his arm over Leona's shoulder. Their first few months had been behind everyone's back, so maybe old habits died hard, whereas Kennedy and I had been flaunting ourselves from the beginning, even when we didn't want to admit how hard it was to keep our hands off each other.

"Well do it somewhere else. I've got to get more booze from downstairs for jungle juice."

I scooted past the two of them and jogged down the stairs.

"Be careful of the—"

My head solidly hit the beam running across the stairs that was way too low for nearly all of us. I rubbed the spot like that would stop the slowly growing pain now radiating through my skull.

"Ceiling." Reid's voice was drowned out by the music from the party.

Grumbling, I grabbed three handles of Everclear and one of vodka from the stockpile subsidized by the rest of the guys on the team. Keeping my head low, I walked back up the stairs and met Ezra in the kitchen.

"Still no Kennedy?" He cracked open the last of an over-sized can of fruit juice and poured it into the lined trash can used solely for party punch. The bottles crashed and clanked when we added them to the growing stack piled up in the non-punch trash can.

"When do you get to see your girl again?"

Someone shot a nearly empty can toward it and missed, wetting Ezra's jeans. "What the fuck? If you can't make the throw then don't try it."

A muted "sorry" came from the crowd. Whoever it was didn't want to be identified and from how Ezra scowled, I couldn't blame them.

He dipped a cup into the brew and took a sip. A look of consideration and his head tilted before he picked up a jug of orange juice taken from the dining hall and added more. "She's not my girl."

"Are you sure about that?"

"Why wouldn't I be?" He grabbed a ladle and stirred the ungodly concoction. Overly bright colors and mystery chunks of fruit swirled around in the vortex he created.

"Seems you're making a lot of changes for someone who isn't yours."

"It's a hat, man. Not like she's asking me to get her name tattooed on my ass."

I leaned back and peered behind him.

He snapped up straight and punched my arm before scooting around to the other side of the can. "Asshole. Add more booze."

Laughing, I dumped the last of the handle of Everclear into the already too strong punch. "Any more and we'll be cleaning up more than spilled drinks in the morning."

The bottles rattled in the trash, like a dinner bell being rung as partygoers wandered over to have their cups refilled. Out the open front door, a familiar head popped up over the lip of the porch.

I pushed past the crowd and jumped out the front door, meeting Kennedy at the top step. "Hey."

Kennedy stared at me with chill-reddened cheeks and a bright smile. Her hat covered half her ears with small studs dotted in them. "Hey."

"For the love of god, get in here, Kennedy." Hollis shouldered into me and dragged her over the threshold.

"Don't mind me, I'll just hang out here in the cold." Hannah tugged off her gloves.

My throat tightened and I turned to her. "Sorry, come in. How are you guys? How's the campus tour been going?" I locked my gaze onto Hannah, giving her my almost undivided attention.

"It's been great, so cool. This is where I want to go. And Kennedy got me this from the bookstore." Hannah unzipped her coat, flashing an STFU Bulldog hoodie underneath.

"You fit right in."

The party droned on behind me, but the most important people here were right in front of me.

She beamed with the kind of joy only a high schooler looking for acceptance could.

"Thought we'd stop by." Kennedy looked at me with her chest rising and falling.

It wasn't until I caught Griff's smirk over her shoulder that I noticed mine was moving with the same anticipatory excitement. "I'm glad you did."

Hannah and Kennedy had a lot to go over and she didn't need me hanging around like a lovesick puppy vying for her attention. The word lingered in my mind. Lovesick. Was that what this was?

"Hey, Leona!" Hannah shoved between me and her sister and flung her arms around Leona's neck.

"Hey, Hannah. Want to help me do something extra exciting and change the garbage bags?"

"Sure."

Leona guided Hannah into the kitchen, and I swear, I owed her a case of cookies.

Kennedy glanced in their direction and back at me.

I looked at the guys over her shoulder with their smirks and grabbed her hand. "We'll be right back."

Charging up the stairs past the people waiting for the bathroom, I ignored the flat tire Kennedy gave me, happy she was as excited for a moment alone as I was.

Unlocking my bedroom, I pulled her inside and closed the door. Bracing her against the surface, I kissed her. Needy, hungry, insatiable.

She grabbed my sleeves and tugged me closer. Her lips matched mine in ferocity, like she'd been starving for me just as much. Breaking apart, her deep breathing was even harder. She licked her rosy, swollen lips. "Did you miss me?" Her nails raked across my scalp and my cock stiffened against her.

"You have no idea."

She tugged at my hair and kissed me again. "Me too.

Only three more days and I'll take her back to the airport and we can finally get some time alone."

A voice shouted from the bottom of the stairs over the din of the music, laughter, and singing. "Kennedy, stop making out with your boyfriend! We're going to miss the movie."

"Want to come with us?" She nodded toward the closed door.

"That seems like we're playing with fire."

"You can come on one condition." She dragged her finger along the center of my chest. "Don't keep your hands to yourself." Her laughter was lyrically beautiful, like a song I never wanted to end.

"That I could definitely do." I palmed her ass, giving it a squeeze and coaxing a yelp out of her.

An insistent knock rattled the door.

"Enough making out. You said we'd go to the midnight showing. We're going to be late and miss the previews. We only have two minutes left." Hannah's voice came from the edge of the door like her lips were pushed up against the crack.

"Let's go before she starts singing songs from Frozen." Kennedy held my hand and opened the door. "Then you'll be happy to know, Cole's coming, so he'll give us a ride and we won't miss any of the movie."

I grabbed my coat off my chair.

"Just make sure your making out doesn't get too loud for me to hear the movie."

We marched down the stairs with Hannah mock glaring at us like we were two teenagers caught making out by our parents.

"I'm headed to the movies with Kennedy and Hannah."

Hollis came out of the kitchen with beers in his hands. "You sure? I got you a beer." He held it out to me.

"When I'm back."

We walked outside. The second the door closed behind me a scream came from the other side. "You're it!"

Scrambling and rumbling shook the windows and I peered through the glass.

Kennedy looked up at me from the bottom of the stairs. "What was that about?"

"You saved me."

Her head tilted. "From what?"

"A fate worse than death." She'd shown up at the perfect time. In fact, it felt like she'd come into my life when I needed her. Thrown together for an impossible ploy that felt more and more like an excuse I'd used to get closer to her even if I hadn't known it at the time.

After opening the car doors for both of them, the front door to the house flew open. Reid and Leona bolted across the street.

Griff shouted from the porch. "You'll have to come back sometime."

His gaze swung in my direction. I scrambled into the car and threw it into drive.

"You going to fill me in on whatever that's about?"

"Later." I wanted her to be around for every insane game of tag from here until the end.

25

KENNEDY

Waves lapped in the distance and seagulls squawked.

Beside me, Hannah's chair rattled. "This is the best spring break I've ever been to!"

"It's the only spring break you've ever been to. You're too easy to impress." I adjusted my sunglasses and leaned back into my folding chair. A trickle of sweat rolled down my cleavage.

"Come on, Kenny. This is amazing." She jumped up, feet flinging sand onto my legs. Her arms outstretched toward STFU South Beach.

"Not exactly a tropical vacation."

The beeping of a truck splintered our lazy Friday afternoon, complete with exhaust fumes billowing over us. People scrambled to get their chairs out of the way. Those who hadn't been fast enough to grab their shower shoes hopped from foot to foot on the freezing asphalt.

"It's better!" Her excitement about being on campus helped me remember how much I'd wanted to leave home and how magical this place felt when I first arrived. Fashion connections be damned, I was free.

This was the STFU version of South Beach. The south parking lot was transformed over spring break for all the students stuck on campus. The Student Government took pity on us and trucked in a couple tons of sand, some giant heaters that pumped out a blanket of warmth to keep us from freezing, and an above-ground pool heated with a janky setup that melted part of the lining. It might be why no one was in the water. Or that could be because of the pictures STFU Dirt had posted last year of a couple having sex in one of the STFU South Beach pools. No one wanted to take chances.

If you put on some sunglasses and a bathing suit, you could squint and imagine taking a plane ride to an exotic beach resort, even though that hadn't been in the cards or the bank account.

Some built sandcastles or buried their friends in the sand, careful not to go too deep to where they'd end up on the cold concrete. Others lounged like me and Hannah, packed under the limited radius of the heaters, which helped boost body heat.

The bathing suit might've been a little too much, but I couldn't help myself in pretending to soak up the way too northerly rays.

Hannah's head still whipped back and forth, not wanting to miss one weird campus quirk. "Can I borrow an ounce of your confidence?"

"You've got it and more, Hannah." I dropped my sunglasses and faced her.

"No freaking way. I feel like I'm ready to throw up and I'm in a one-piece with shorts that touch my knees and a towel around my shoulders." She pulled the edges of the towel across her chest.

Every bit of her insecurities needled my heart. I'd been there. I'd felt that. Somehow I'd hoped she might've weathered them better than me. "Here's something I learned. Most people are a lot more worried about themselves than they are about you. Sure, some assholes will pick at you to make themselves feel better, but that says more about them than it does about you."

Hannah sunk down deeper in her chair and glanced around. "When I feel like people are looking at me, it makes me want to run and hide."

"Weren't you the one trying out for the musical? Finally ready to leave the shadows and shine?"

"That was for a role. That wasn't as me."

"What do you think I do to hype myself up? Play the role until the role becomes you. No one knows you here. You're the mysterious transfer student. You'll never have to see any of them ever again."

She gnawed on her bottom lip. "What if I decide to go here?"

"What if you don't get in?"

Her gasp of outrage was enough to lessen some of her fear. "You suck! Of course I'll get in."

"I know you will. Your grades are way better than mine." I tugged at her towel. "No one will remember nearly as much as you think. If I need to, I'll make a big enough scene to out-silly however you're feeling, so it'll feel not so big."

Her fingers tightened around the towel like she was thinking it over. Then her head tilted. "I think that guy's checking you out." Her excited whisper was cute.

"The bikini top makes me hard to miss." I peered over my sunglasses. A cute guy, maybe a senior, with longish hair that ended just over his pale eyes, raised a beer in my direction.

I picked up my thermos of margarita and waved it at him. "I'm good."

"Why don't you and your friend come hang out with us?"

"Thanks for the offer, but I've got a boyfriend."

He nodded. "I had to shoot my shot." And sat back down.

"That's the third guy who's asked you out since I've been here." She stared at me, her voice filled with awe.

I scoffed. "He wasn't asking me to go out to dinner with him, just hang out and hook up."

"Do you want to know how many guys have asked me out?"

"Trust me, they'll get braver or you will."

"How—"

Cole landed face first in the sand right at my feet.

"What happened?" I yelped and lunged forward to help him. An adrenaline spike sent my heart rate soaring. "What's going on?"

He rolled over, eyes scanning my legs and glazing over a bit.

The stomach flutters made it worth the sidelong gusts of wind that overpowered the heaters every so often.

"Fuck, Kennedy." He glanced at Hannah. "Sorry, Hannah."

"Don't worry. I've heard all those words before." She laughed and stared at us like her new favorite TV show.

"When you said you were coming down here, you didn't say it was going to be in this." His hands were on my knees, massaging them with heated intention.

The heater beside me was nothing compared to the warm flush rushing through me at that look in his eyes.

"When you said you'd stop by, I didn't think it would be diving at my feet." I leaned in and whispered in his ear. "Not that I mind you on your knees between my legs."

His fingers tightened. "Now's not the time." His voice filled with a teasing warning. "Ezra's It and he's over there."

I sat up straighter and followed his gaze.

Ezra scanned the space, moving like a sprinkler head, sweeping back and forth.

"What do you mean he's It?"

He peered around me and jerked back down, putting my body between Ezra and him. "The game of tag, remember?"

There was a vague memory of him mentioning it right after Valentine's Day. "You weren't lying."

"Nope." He glanced around me.

"Having fun?"

"Loads." He got his feet under him, while still staying in a crouch.

"When's it over?"

"At the end of the week."

"What happens if you're It at the end of the week?"

"You've got to set up before any parties we throw and clean up after."

I sucked my teeth adding just enough extra drama to it. "That's a lot of cleaning up."

"One hundred percent. It sucks."

"Then what are you doing here? Shouldn't you be hiding in the woods wearing a gilly suit or camouflaging yourself against some rocks in the park?"

"I wanted to see you." He hopped up and planted a toe-curling kiss on me. "And Hannah, since I know you're leaving tomorrow."

"Do I get one of those?"

He laughed and leaned over and pecked her cheek.

She clutched her hands to her chest and let out a trilling sigh. "I'll never wash this cheek again."

"Smart ass." I punched her shoulder, but loved how the two of them got along so well. The two most important people to me laughing and joking together hadn't been something I realized I was missing.

If she came here, Cole would definitely want to be as embarrassing as possible on move-in day. And she'd love every second of it.

He brushed his fingers over my knuckles. "You're going to have to wear that bikini again, preferably somewhere warmer like my bedroom." He tugged me forward. His lips brushed against my ear. "Where I can peel it off you with my teeth."

"I heard that," Hannah chimed in beside me.

Cole smiled. "I don't know what you're talking about." He shuffled around my chair.

"I'm going to take Hannah to the Equine Department to check out the horses later, want to come? Might help you dodge being tagged." Plus, it never hurt to get some time with him.

He shuddered. "I'd rather have Ezra tackle me on the cold parking lot asphalt than be around those animals."

"Not a horse fan?" Hannah propped her chin on her hand.

"They're demon spawn that are just biding their time before they take us all out."

Hannah and I laughed. Of all the things for Cole to hate, horses wouldn't have made the top five on my list.

Ezra walked alongside the pool, rounding the closest corner.

His hatted head swept back and forth across the people sprawled out in their various beach setups. Then his gaze landed on me, a flicker of a smirk. Not a second later, he was in motion. Shit, he'd spotted Cole.

"Gotta go." Cole's lips glanced off the top of my head and he took off.

Ezra got closer, walking like a horror movie villain.

"Hey, Ez."

His head whipped around.

I slipped my hand into his pocket and snagged his phone, tossing it toward Hannah before wrapping my arms around him, and leaned into my momentum. Catching him off guard was the only reason I was able to move him. We both plunged into the four-foot-deep inflatable pool with Ezra on top of me. A shock of cold invaded my nostrils.

Forgot about those Baltic temperatures. So much for that heater.

Ezra flailed, flattening me for a second. A heavy body part whacked into me.

I shot up out of the water, pretty sure my face was melting down to my chin right now.

Laughter and clapping accompanied our pool splashes along with crowd commentary.

"That's what I call relationship dedication," a deep voice shouted, like he was cheering at a game.

"Badass. I haven't seen Ezra take a tackle like that since Berk from Fulton U." The speaker sounded impressed.

"She gets my vote in Puppy Love!"

Hannah stared at me with her mouth hanging open.

I was still in shock that I'd done that. What had I been saying before about no one looking at you half as much as you thought they were? Well, everyone was looking right now. The cold water had me high-beaming everyone through my bikini top. Own it, Kennedy. I cracked a smile and tried not to let my teeth chatter.

Ezra leaned against the edge of the inflatable pool, which sagged under his weight. He fished for his hat bobbing in the water and put it back on, showering himself all over again. "Seriously?"

I winced. Pin pricks of freezing water stabbed at my body. "I had to help him out."

"We've got girlfriends taking people out. Leona's playing now. Can't catch a break." He shoved up from the ground, grumbling. Water flooded the beach from his first step onto the sand.

My lips already felt like they were made of icicles. We were beyond goosebumps to turkey lumps at this point. "Sorry, Ezra."

He turned, newly placed hat shielding his eyes, and held out his hand to help me.

"At least you saved my phone."

I stepped out of the pool, shivering.

"And I'm taking your towel."

"Fair." My fingers were numb and I marched closer to the heater, holding out my hands.

He retrieved my towel from my seat and got his phone from Hannah.

One gruff swipe of the pink towel across his face and he held it out to me. "As much as I want to be an asshole, you're freezing."

My teeth chattering rattled my brain. "I'm fine."

"Take it."

"You're wet and cold too. You need it."

"I—"

Hannah stepped forward and draped her towel around my shoulders. "It's okay. She can have mine."

I smiled at her—at least I thought I did. I couldn't feel my lips anymore.

She glanced around a few times before standing straighter.

"Told you I'd make a big enough splash that no one would be watching you."

"I didn't think it would be literal." She laughed.

Ezra's lips looked like they were turning blue.

"I'm super sorry, Ezra. I didn't exactly think this through."

"Don't worry about it." He peeled off his soaked sweat-shirt and T-shirt along with it, revealing that football-conditioned physique.

Hannah leaned in and whispered, "This is definitely where I'm coming."

Ezra lifted his chin. "Come on, I'll take you two home."

A shudder rolled through me. "You don't have to."

"I know, but I can't go hunt your boyfriend down knowing you're here getting hypothermia."

"Fair enough."

We gathered up our things and walked to his car, which wasn't far with most of campus empty.

He cranked up the heat and I guided him to my apartment. Hannah hopped out of the back seat and I climbed out, leaning through the window he'd rolled down.

"Thanks, Ezra, and again, I'm sorry." I was sorry he'd gotten soaked, but also happy Cole had made his escape.

My toes squished inside my boots.

"Don't worry about it." The corner of his mouth twitched. "But if you really want to make it up to me, that chicken pot pie would help."

"Deal." I shoved my hand through the open window.

He shook it. "You're good together."

"Thanks." My throat tightened and heart raced, having nothing to do with trying to get blood to my extremities. "I think so too."

"Next time, you won't get the drop on me though."

"I barely thought it was a possibility this time. It was pure instinct and raw power." I curled my nonexistent bicep, still amazed I'd pulled it off.

"Maybe I'm getting too soft."

"Maybe." I stood and took a step back. "Bye, Ezra."

The window rolled up and he pulled away.

Our friends thought we were good together. Ezra had been the first to get everyone else on board at our first appearance and with what he said today, I didn't want to lose that.

Faking it had gotten more real than I could've imagined. How crazy was it that my first real relationship had started out that way? It was fitting. I'd told Hannah to fake it until you make it. All that lovey-dovey, over-the-top stuff happened around all the quiet moments no one else saw. The moments I couldn't get enough of. The moments I loved.

I stopped right inside the doorway to the apartment where Hannah stared at me like she'd kill me if I didn't get inside right now.

I loved him.

26

COLE

S weat streamed off the tip of my nose. I grabbed my towel and mopped at my face, which felt like it had sprung up a whole new set of leaks. The metallic and rubber scents hung so heavy in the air it coated my tongue along with the stinging salt of sweat.

"Everyone, wrap up your programs soon. Some of us have homes to get to." David Henley, one of the assistant coaches, smacked his hand against his tablet.

The gym was almost empty. Only a few guys left. Most were more than happy to blaze through their workouts during the spring.

But keeping in peak condition meant that scaling up to the next level didn't require as much work once the new season started. I wasn't looking for two steps forward and one step back. I wanted three steps forward for August.

"You staying for much longer?" Freshly showered, Reid walked up to me with his duffel slung over his shoulder.

"Just a few more sets, then I'm out of here."

"Don't push too hard. This is the off-season, remember?" He tossed my water bottle to me and walked outside.

I pushed through the circuits again, until my muscles failed. Normally, I'd have cut out earlier, still longer than most others, but not this long.

At least working out kept my mind off Kennedy. Since when had I become this damn needy? Was this how my mom had felt? A thump drilled into my chest.

Kennedy and I were nothing like my mom and Mikelson. Hell, it had been two damn days since the beach, and I knew where she was. I knew what she was doing, and we'd been texting. It was nothing like the weeks or months of radio silence he'd subjected her to—that she'd put up with.

I set the weights back on the rack and reached for the next higher matching pair. My hamstring locked up and I stumbled forward, catching myself on the dumbbells.

"Hauser." Coach Henley called to me and nodded toward the PT room. He was a new assistant coach, who'd replaced Coach Belton. Still feeling his way out in a team this big, he'd been a lot calmer than Mikelson, although that wasn't hard to achieve.

"Yes, Coach." With a grimace, I gingerly put my foot down, walking toward the other room. Slowly, the knot lessened, but was still painful.

A former pro-player-turned-coach was a similar story for a lot of guys. Better than the alternative of going bankrupt and exploding once they were no longer living in the limelight. The possibility had entered my mind, but I sucked at coaching. The doing was my strong suit, not creating the plays and knowing how far to push a player to make them better. Not that I'd had the best role model when it came to how to be the best coach. Winning, sure, but I wasn't willing to pull half the shit Mikelson did to win.

Rubbing a new towel over my head, I followed him into the more brightly lit recovery and physiotherapy room.

Padded tables, ice baths, whirlpools, it was as high-end as it came.

"Yes, Coach?"

"Burning the candle a little low, aren't you?" He patted the table and I slid onto it, clenching my teeth.

"Trying to be in better shape for next season."

"Better shape will be hard to do, if you injure yourself." His coaching focused more on the defense during the season, so this was our first conversation, but so far there hadn't been any whispers in the locker room or out about him following in Mikelson's footsteps.

"Leg up." He tapped the padding.

Knowing better than to argue with a coach, I kicked off my shoe and slung my leg up onto the table. "I know my limits."

He made a sound halfway between a laugh and a snort. "That's what all you young kids think." He grabbed my calf and pressed my toes up toward the ceiling.

I slammed my eyes shut at the rubber band stretch of my muscle that flowed into pain, but the good kind.

"One day you'll realize you don't know shit."

I hissed. "That go for you too, Coach?"

A true laugh. "Of course."

"Signing Day will be here and there'll be a new crop of freshman looking to prove themselves." I'd been one of them. Showed up to campus with stars in my eyes ready to finally get some recognition from my father, play for a team, and be carried off the field in a showering of confetti. A third of that had come true.

All I'd wanted was for all my work to finally pay off. It felt stupid to be disappointed that all I might walk away with was a pro contract when that hadn't been why I'd started in the first place.

"You think one of these incoming freshmen will be gunning for your spot?"

"They're the top players from all over the country. They're not used to riding the bench. Of course they'll want my spot. It's how I felt at Signing Day."

"I've heard about Signing Day. Must've been a big moment for you. Getting to hold up your jersey for all those photographers and screaming students."

"It felt good." Even after making first string, there was still a twist of guilt at how I'd ended up there in the first place. The blackmail I didn't know I was wielding. But once I'd made it to Signing Day, I'd made the team my life.

I wanted to shake that kid I'd been. Scream in his face and tell him to wake up. Go somewhere else. To any number of the other schools trying to recruit me, but I'd had no idea the shit storm I'd been wading into.

"Anyone ever not get signed on that day?" He pressed against the base of my foot, while keeping my knee only at a slight bend. The sharpness of the pain was gone, it was more of a dull throb now.

I gripped the edges of the padded table. "No, not that I know of. Even guys who've gone out and gotten blitzed the night before and showed up hungover as hell get their jersey and spot on the team. Whether they play once they're here is up to how much work they're willing to put in to satisfy Coach." The STFU signing day was out of step with most other national deadlines. It came later, which meant waiting to sign with STFU meant you'd given up your shot at signing anywhere else.

"No matter how much work they're willing to put in, you've got to know when calling it quits is quitting and when it just makes sense. Your body will thank you for knowing the difference. Don't keep chasing after a brass ring you're never going to pull. It'll lead to you getting hurt, and we need you out there next season." He pressed against the ball of my foot, pushing my toes toward my chest. Slow, methodical torture.

I clenched my fists and stifled my yelp. At least one of the coaches saw what I could bring to the team. Too bad it wasn't the one I'd been vying for since I was little. "How will I know how far I can get if I don't try?"

"There's pushing yourself a little more, then there's shooting into stupid territory. It'll come with time, knowing your limits or at least testing them in a safer way."

"Safe isn't what gets any of us here."

"But safe is what'll keep you in the game a little longer. I can't tell you how many guys I knew who got injured by not knowing their limits and then their careers were just over." He snapped with the hand *not* trying to rip my calf muscle from the bone. "Don't be the one who does it to yourself."

"Hauser." This time my name was barked. The gruff, unmistakable dig of Mikelson's head into my brain. "My office."

"Coach, he's dead on his feet. Can it wait?" Coach Henley called over his shoulder.

Stunned silence filled the air. I don't know who was more shocked, me or Mikelson.

Coach Henley turned and faced him.

Too bad he was a good guy but he wouldn't be here that much longer, if Mikelson's look was any indication.

"No, it can't wait. Get your ass in my office, Hauser." He was gone just as quickly as he appeared.

Coach Henley's jaw clenched and he picked up my shoe, handing it over to me. "Shower, then home as soon as you're done. Heat then ice that muscle and don't come back to the gym for at least a week."

A week. I nodded at him.

I'd try.

He was only looking out for me. It was weird to have a coach looking out for me. Being able to move better was a blessing and a curse; it meant I was outside the office I'd been in far too many times over the past three years way too soon. My body hummed in anticipation of walking into the lion's den.

He closed the door before I got there, forcing me to knock after putting my shoe back on.

"Get in here."

A barrel of fucking sunshine. What in the hell could anyone...I stopped myself, biting my tongue until it throbbed like my aching muscles. There had to have been a different side to him, one that wasn't saturated in piss and vinegar.

Standing with my hands behind my back, I wanted him to acknowledge me.

"Thinking the extra time in the gym will save you from the bench?"

Inside, I flinched, but kept myself statue still. Don't let him see me sweat. "It has so far."

"You're not the only center out there. New recruits show up every year."

He hadn't gotten more inventive in his threats ever since he'd been forced to start me last year, but the nausea still built that my own father would treat me this way. "Freshmen and transfers who don't have my skill and trust of the QB."

"Would they still trust you, if they knew how you ended up here?"

My pulse pounded in my neck, thumping along the bottom of my jaw. "I made it by being one of the top recruits in my class. I was there on Signing Day just like everyone else."

"Should've gotten what I wanted from you before then. Then I wouldn't have had to deal with your bullshit for the past three seasons."

The air whooshed out of my lungs like he'd landed a roundhouse kick straight to my sternum.

He wanted a reaction. He wanted me to lose it. He wanted me gone.

There's good in him.

The words rang hollower and hollower with every interaction. They shoveled fuel onto the fire consuming everything inside of me. The fires of rage at two people who'd worked together to destroy each other and any chances I'd ever had at a normal life.

"Is there something you needed to talk to me about?"

He stared at me over steepled fingers. "No. Leave." His gaze dropped down to papers on his desk and I was dismissed.

Leaving, I searched for why I'd ever thought there was chance he'd ever been anything different than he was. I went back to the locker room and grabbed my stuff without showering.

The burn inside my chest made me want to find an open field and scream until my throat was shredded. To think that any part of me was shared with Mikelson was enough to coat the back of my throat with bile.

Weathering the storm was all I needed to do. Ride out the last of the spring practices and next season—with Kennedy up in the stands. My pulse slowed and I pictured it all less bleak than it had been a second ago. I missed her.

At the house, Ezra was cleaning and setting up for the next party and had roped in a few underclassmen to help.

"How'd you swing that?"

"They get the keg tap return fee."

"Doesn't that mean they also have to return the keg?" A ping sounded from my pocket.

Kennedy: Headed to the airport with Hannah. On the bus now

Her name on my screen was an immediate mood enhancer. Eagerness washed away all the shitty feelings of my run-in with Mikelson.

Waiting to see her was like hearing the ice cream truck when you were stuck inside. Hannah's visit had made Kennedy so happy and I wouldn't have wanted her to miss a minute with her sister, but selfishly, I was happy Hannah was heading home because it meant I got to have Kennedy back to myself.

Me: How are you doing?

"Exactly. They can lug it back." Ezra gathered up a trash bag that clanked and crunched.

"Smooth."

He handed off a full bag of trash. "Hey, Rookie, change that water and grab more bleach from the basement."

The kid saluted and rushed off to do his bidding.

I grabbed bags of ice and dumped them into the plastic kiddie pools, thankful we got discounts on most of this stuff.

Ezra wiped at the beer stains on the wall. "Animals. There's a tarp for keg stands. This shit is ridiculous."

Kennedy: Okay. I know she'll be all right. Just sucks

Me: You should've let me come with you

If I hadn't gone to team workout, I could've. I should've skipped it. She had to be upset about Hannah leaving.

Kennedy: Not if it meant you missed your workout, plus it gave us extra time to talk

Me: Haven't you been doing that for a week already

Kennedy: Haven't you learned? We're sisters! There's never not anything to talk about

They'd definitely found ways to stretch even the slimmest of topics into hours of talking. It was great they were so close.

Me: You want me to come to you once you're back?

Leaving the party would be easy. No second thoughts. I could leave now and be parked outside her apartment door ready to hug her when she got back. Or I could grab some food for her.

Kennedy: No, I'll come to you

Me: We're having a party tonight

Which I wasn't in the mood to have, but the rest of the guys were serious about maintaining our party reputation— mainly Griff and Hollis at this point. Reid was content to be in a five-foot radius of Leona, and Ezra had been cagey lately. Not that I couldn't be accused of both of those things too.

Kennedy: Again?

Me: Our place is called The Zoo

Kennedy: How do you guys even afford that much booze?

Me: Under the table discounts, free player tickets and other guys chip in

Kennedy: Booze over food?

Yeah, it was stupid and felt less wise the older we got. The partying hadn't been something I thought could ever wear thin, but being surrounded by crowds of people only interested in drinking my booze and hanging out in our house for the association lost its shine quickly when Kennedy was in my life.

Me: Only in the off-season

Kennedy: I'm going to try to get some sleep on the ride back. Sorry if I have nap breath when I see you.

I'd love to join her for that nap. Maybe roll it into more than a nap when she woke. I needed to crash, myself, or I'd be bleary-eyed by the time she got back.

Me: I love your breath, no matter what

Kennedy: You've never kissed me after a half loaf of garlic bread

Me: We can add that to the list

Kennedy: Yes, the most romantic of declarations! Garlic breath kisses

Me: Tell Hannah I said bye and get some rest

Kennedy: See you soon.

Messages from Kennedy shaved the edges off the tension gripping my muscles after leaving the gym. And once she was in my arms it would all melt away into a distant memory.

She had that effect on me to the point it was almost scary. When she was around, there wasn't a mountain I couldn't conquer. My future snapped into sharp focus, always with her beside me.

I didn't feel alone with her and knew the loneliness would pierce that much sharper if she was gone. It's why I'd do whatever it took to prove myself to her and that there was no trace of my father in me. I wasn't like him. I could never be like him.

I'd never let her doubt how much she meant to me, what our future would look like, and I'd never hurt her.

27

KENNEDY

Bus brakes squealed and luggage in the compartment below shifted under our feet. The bus parked under the red-steel and frosted-glass awning to shield us from the rain.

The sliding doors of the Pittsburgh Airport slid open and closed as passengers dragged their suitcases toward checkout counters.

Beside me, Hannah sighed and traced her finger along the condensation on the glass. "This was a great week." She glanced over at me and offered up a wobbly smile.

I smiled back, each beat of my heart raised a welt, throbbing and stinging.

She needed me to be strong.

I squeezed her hand. "I'm glad you came."

"Not mad at me anymore?" Her attempt at a laugh was low and sad, not like the ones I'd heard throughout the week. It was as if she was conserving energy for going back to normal life. I got it. It was the same for me when I went back to visit, but at least I had seeing Hannah to temper the feelings. She didn't.

The bus cleared out with other passengers eager to get to their next destination.

The driver climbed the steps and sat back in their seat. "I'll be riding back. I booked a return ticket. I need to drop my sister off."

"I've got a timetable to keep. You've got..." He checked his watch. "Three minutes."

Outside, we got her carry-on from the undercarriage storage. The last piece left.

"Dad said he'll meet you at the airport."

"Just Dad?"

I nodded, not needing to know why she asked. "Mom's on a business trip for the next few days."

The sag of relief made me want to have her stay with me forever.

"At least a few days of quiet."

"Ease you back into things."

She popped the handle on her suitcase.

"You've got your ticket and ID."

"I don't need you to baby me, Kennedy. I made it here all on my own, remember?" She had. She was getting older. No longer the little kid I'd shared my headphones with under the covers to distract her, but still my little sister. Soon she'd be out there in the world living her own life and hopefully not making the same mistakes I'd made along the way. I wanted her to be better than me.

"A dangerous risk to take. Don't do that again, unless everyone knows where you are."

She rolled her eyes. "I know. I know. You'd better hop back on before he leaves you."

The bus driver sat with the door still open staring at me with poison-tipped daggers.

"Sorry, I'll be right there."

"I'll miss you." I wrapped my arms around her and held her close.

She squeezed me. The printout of her ticket I'd made her, in case her phone died, crinkled against my back. "Me too."

"And remember this summer. Paris. We don't even have to tell Mom and Dad." Day after day the decision to take the trip with her felt better, especially after this week together. We'd wander the streets eating too may croissants and pressing our noses up against windows for stores we could never shop in. Chocolate, cocktails, clothes. What could be better than that?

She laughed and her arms loosened. "I could be gone for a whole month and they wouldn't even notice."

"They would."

Her head tilted and eyebrow lifted.

"Maybe after a couple weeks."

"If I was lucky."

A sharp rap of the horn. Irritation grated on me, but also the tiny bit of dread that this was the official end to the week.

"Coming," I called over my shoulder, and backed up toward the curb.

"Love you, Kennedy!"

"Love you too, Pickle."

"Of course you had to get one in before I left."

I stood on the bottom step of the bus. "What kind of sister would I be, if I didn't?" Kissing the center of my palm, I blinked back my tears and flung my arm, sending her an air kiss.

She repeated the motion as the door closed in my face.

I found a seat and texted her throughout her whole

check-in and boarding. Seamless, easy, uncomplicated, but the knot in my chest was still there.

Paris would happen, no matter what. I was still determined to give the win to Cole. Needing a break was different than what he was dealing with.

Now that Hannah was gone, I wanted to see him. I wanted more than a quick kiss or sneaky make out before taking Hannah sightseeing or going to work. I wanted Cole.

That ever-present electric spark that could build into a buzzing bliss, I only found in his arms.

A couple hours later I was back on campus and didn't stop at my place to change. I went straight to The Zoo, where an Old School party was already in full swing.

I entered the house along with other partygoers who'd wandered from the house next door to make a pit stop for a beer before moving on to the next one.

The ice luge might make them stay a bit longer.

Griff held a bottle of Jaeger up high and poured it down the makeshift ice creation into the mouth of the next person.

I shuddered to think about being the hundredth person to put my mouth on that thing.

Shaking off my coat, I draped it across the banister with the stack of other coats all one Jenga move away from falling on the floor.

Leona and Reid marched over like the official party hosts. Reid held out a cup for me. Leona turned, waving their joined hands in the air, and cupped one hand around her mouth. "Cole, she's here, you can stop sulking now."

Cole shot up, nearly nailing a guy in the jaw with his head, and scanned through the people between us until his eyes landed on me.

My heart beat so fast it felt like my whole body was vibrating.

The smile. The way his arms wrapped around me. The way everything seemed to sparkle when he was close.

Smiling, excitement radiated off him and he raced across the room like he'd been tugged forward by an invisible rope.

It was me. I was the pull, and the flutter of butterflies made me feel seconds from knocking my head into the ceiling.

Did he feel half of what I felt for him? When he looked at me like that, it made me believe it might be true.

The front door banged open and Hollis rushed in. With two hands, he planted them on Cole's shoulders from behind. "You're it." He jerked his arm down in front of him. "Finally, I've been waiting for you to get here, I knew he'd be distracted for long enough. Thanks, Kennedy." He nodded toward me. "I can finally enjoy the party." With another pat on Cole's shoulder and a *woo* to the crowd that responded in the same way, he marched off.

"Sorry."

"Don't be, it was worth it." Without a glance at Hollis or the next person he could tag, he kissed me, fingers tickling along the buttons on my shirt.

The shooting sparks under my skin were spiking, leaving me wanting more than a kiss.

"Just one sec." He lunged toward Reid and Leona who both bolted, running in opposite directions.

Apparently, his peripheral vision was better than I thought and now that he'd had his kiss he could focus on their game.

The next thirty minutes the guys and Leona raced and rushed through the house, skidding on the floors and in and out of the doors.

Ashley, Taylor, and I jumped out of the way when they passed by and Cole always stopped for a kiss. The game was less cute when it was between me and Cole disappearing up into his bedroom for the first bit of alone time in a week. I refilled my cup from the drum of jungle juice.

A familiar body pressed against mine and lips traced over the back of my neck. "I missed you."

Goosebumps raised all over my body. I brought my arms up and clutched the back of his head. "I've been here. Are you finally no longer It?"

"Griff's It. He's chasing Reid and Leona down the street."

"If you take me upstairs right now, will you be at risk of getting tagged again on your bare ass?"

He laughed. "Even if I was, I'd take that risk, but the game officially ends in—" He raised his phone.

Leona jumped by the doorway and looked directly at us. "Ten."

She wove between two people doing double keg stands.

"Eight." Cole maneuvered me between him and the doorway.

"You're going to sacrifice me like this."

His lips tickled the side of my neck. "I'll make it worth it."

A tremble rocked my knees and I spread my arms wide across the kitchen blocking Leona.

"Come on, Kennedy." Leona tried to get around me. "I'll give you anything."

"Definitely not what he can."

"Two."

She let out a frustrated growl.

"One!" Cole's arms wrapped around me from behind, hustling me toward the stairs. "I'm sure Reid will help you out with the cleaning duty," he called over his shoulder.

We were past the bathroom line and in his room with the door locked before I could get my feet under me.

Instead of tugging me toward him, he lifted me. His hands cupped my ass and hefted me off the floor.

"Cole—" I yelped and held on to him. Attempts at picking me up had always ended in disaster.

I clung to him. The walk from the door stretched out to what felt like eternity. "What good would all this working out be, if I couldn't pick up my girl?" He set me on the edge of his desk. The whole thing rattled, but my moment of panic was over now that I wasn't hanging on to Cole. His girl.

"Have I told you I love it when you say that?" I wrapped my legs around his trim waist.

"Have I told you how much I love saying it." His fingers traced along my side, tickling me along the way.

My breath caught as I fidgeted and squirmed. He'd used the word. The same one I'd been thinking only a little while ago.

"I think—" He shook his head and stared into my eyes. They were nakedly vulnerable. His fingers traced along the neckline of my shirt, teasing and skimming my skin.

"I know I'm falling for you, Kennedy. Not falling, fell—hard. I love you."

My heart pounded so loudly, I could hear it in my ears. The feelings I'd been trying to deny came rushing forward and I rubbed my fingers against his chin.

He leaned into my touch.

"Me too."

His grin was blinding. The kind that exuded pure happiness and I knew matched my own. He grabbed me again and carried me over to the bed.

We were both out of our clothes in seconds.

His hips nestled between my spread thighs. His fingers teased my clit and sank into me. The wet sounds from my pussy were drowned out by the needy ones from my lips.

"Your fingers are magic."

"You're magic."

"You're already going to get laid, no need to lay it on that thick." A moan stripped my attempted laugh.

"That's not me laying it on thick, but you know what is?" He rubbed his cock through my folds and dragged it along my clit. His fingers worked me closer to a frenzy with the sounds sloppier than before.

My moan became a gasp. "Remind me to tease you more often."

He rocked his hips in a maddeningly slow speed.

I gripped the sheets beneath me. "Cole, I need you." My whole body felt like it was humming, being primed past of the point of survival.

"That's all you had to say."

The heavy weight of him let up for a second before returning covered in latex. A slow, spine-tingling advance of his body blanketing mine. His jaw clenched and his eyes were squeezed shut.

"Is it too much?" I brushed my hands against his chest.

His eyes snapped open and he shook his head. "It's always too much when I'm with you."

The high from the way he looked at me hadn't worn off. A rush of power flowed through me. I shifted my hips and his eyes rolled back in his head.

"It's too good, Kennedy."

Shifting again, I gasped, clenching around him.

"Fuck me, you're trying to end this too soon."

"It's your fault for getting me so worked up."

His hands raised my legs and settled each on top of his

shoulders with a kiss to my calf. The clenching increased with each rock of his body and rub of my clit. A shudder ripped through me. I teetered on the edge and falling over felt too soon and too far away all at once.

With both legs raised up, he sank even deeper. The tops of his muscular thighs smacked against my ass. His finger snaked around one thigh and toyed with my clit. Between the deeper penetration and the ministrations of his fingers, I bucked, nearly toppling us both off the bed.

Fireworks exploded in my chest. A cascade of colors so blinding they made it hard to see him. But I felt him. Grinding and still playing with my overly sensitive bundle of nerves. I gasped and screamed and clawed at the bed beneath me.

He groaned and stiffened over me, spilling into the condom.

Covered in a fine sheen of sweat, I tried to catch my breath, especially with my knees rammed against my chest. "Cole, babe, you're a little heavy."

His head popped up. The lazy, sex-dazed smile sent a shiver through my already humming body. "That's the first time you've called me a nickname."

My tired laugh became a groan when he raised up, freeing my knees from their sex prison. "I've called you plenty of nicknames before."

"But this time it was for real." He kissed me.

That stilled me for a second. It had just come out. I hadn't been thinking at all. "Do you not like it?"

"I loved it." Another kiss and Cole got out of bed to take care of the condom. He threw on his clothes and ran to the bathroom.

A couple people shouted in the hallway. House privileges.

I stretched, feeling like a cat ready for a nap after that workout. I rummaged around for something to wear and pulled on one of his T-shirts. I wasn't swimming in it. It was tight across my chest, but at least it covered all the important parts—barely. I didn't feel like getting back into my long bus ride clothes.

The music from downstairs vibrated the floor. At least most people hadn't heard our reunion sex.

He slipped back in the room with a towel and washcloth in hand and stopped in front of the door.

I tugged at the hem of the T-shirt. "What?"

My answer came in the unmistakable form of a tent in his boxers. I couldn't stifle my grin. It looked like my effect on him was still solid.

Deciding to make this even harder on him, I slid out of the bed and turned, knowing the shirt barely covered my ass. Before I made it all the way back around, he was on me again.

My hips pinned between him and the bed.

He must've had some magic of his own because he slid his latex covered length inside me with one hard thrust, nearly lifting my feet off the floor. "Fuck, Kennedy. You don't know how hot you look in my shirt."

"Not worried I'll stretch it out?" I panted, grasping at the opposite edge of the extra-long double bed for leverage.

"More worried about how every time I wear it after this, I'll get hard."

The comedown I thought I'd experienced wasn't all the way there yet and I was rushing right back toward the edge.

"You're making me crazy." His chest flattened against my back, leaving me with little else to be able to do but enjoy the ride. Full of power and passion, his new angle tapped into every pleasure button missed last time. Not a single one would go unfulfilled by the end of tonight.

Not one to miss the biggest of all, he slipped his hand between me and the bed to stroke my clit with the all-consuming tease that skipped me straight to the plunge.

I gasped and buried my head in the blankets, screaming my appreciation for all the body-shattering orgasmic bliss.

His moans over my head heightened mine to dizzying, frantic gasps.

Shaking and unsure I could even stand, I smiled into the bed and held on for dear life.

Panting, Cole dropped kisses against my back. "This is what you do to me."

"At least Reid and Leona had the decency to do it in the closet!" A shout came from behind us.

I whipped my head around.

Cole fell back on top of me, spreading out even more to cover me.

Griff had his hands over his eyes and grasped for the doorknob, finally snagging it and slamming it shut. The lock clicked with a decisive clink.

Embarrassment swamped me and I buried my face in the bed for totally different reasons. The giggles overtook me and tears soaked into the sheets.

Cole shifted off me and draped a blanket over my back, taking me by the shoulders and turning me over.

I wiped at my cheeks and covered my face with my hands, trying to get my giggles under control.

He cupped my cheeks. "You okay? Sorry about that, I forgot to lock it."

Dropping my hands, I burst into another fit of laughter. "I wish I could've seen his face."

Cole's face was drawn with strong lines of concern that slowly melted away into relief, then a smile.

"I'm glad you weren't facing the other way, then he and anyone else in the hall would've gotten a full view of these." The backs of his hands skimmed down my neck, brushing against my collarbones and down my chest until they skimmed over my nipples.

"Wouldn't have wanted that, now would we?" I let the sheet fall from around my body and raised my chin. "We've got some catching up to do."

He flew across the room, locking the latch and tackling me to the bed. His hot, hungry lips on mine again.

"I love you, Cole."

"I love you more."

28

COLE

She rested her head on my shoulder. Her hair tickled my jaw and neck.

I skimmed my fingers along her arm, loving the goosebumps raised along it. Inhaling deeply, I let her scent flood over me.

"Maybe I should stay away from you more often." She laughed and brushed her finger over my nipple.

I shivered and stilled her teasing hand. "Not if we'd both like to be able to walk for the majority of the semester."

Her leg settled over mine closest to her. The heat of her pussy rubbed against my thigh. Painfully tempting. "Speak for yourself. I'm happy to crawl to class."

I laughed, rocking her against my chest. "I'll keep it in mind."

She got quiet, tracing her fingertips along the thatch of hair at the center of my chest.

"Worried about Hannah?"

She nodded, keeping her head against me.

I kissed the top of her head. I hated seeing her sad. But the love she had for her sister only made me love her more.

She worried about Hannah like she worried about everyone who was important to her. Hannah was lucky to have an older sibling like Kennedy looking after her. A part of me couldn't help but be envious that I hadn't had someone like Kennedy watching over me—protecting me when I was younger. "She's resilient. Strong like you, she'll be okay."

"I wish she didn't have to be." She burrowed in deeper, and as much as I hated her worrying, I didn't hate how she looked to me for comfort.

"Don't we all. In a couple years, she'll get to leave and follow in her big sister's footsteps." I squeezed her against me and was rewarded with a contented sigh.

"I wish I could do more for her now."

"You will with your trip to Paris. She'll love it."

Her head lifted and I dropped my fingers across her lips. "The trip I'll be paying for with the money I've been working for and saving."

I sighed and shook my head. "Let's not argue about it tonight."

She zipped her lips and raised her arm to throw away the key.

I caught it and plucked the imaginary object from her grasp. "I'd like to use those lips tonight, let's not throw away the key just yet." Brushing my fingers along the seam of her lips, I unzipped them.

She scooted closer until she was laying on top of me.

With my hands wrapped around her, I spread my legs so hers fell in between and locked them against her.

"Now that you have me, Mr. Hauser, what will you do with me?" She rested her elbows against the sides of my neck and held her face just out of kissing distance.

"Instead of telling you, why don't I show you?"

She laughed and I rocked her forward using my legs, already very happy I'd kept her from zipping those lips.

The music downstairs died down by the time Kennedy threw a flag on the evening's activities. Sweaty, happy, and blissed out, we finally collapsed in the bed.

Kennedy's eyes fluttered closed. After getting us cleaned up in the now empty bathroom that had already been cleaned, I got back into bed with her.

"I love you, Kennedy." There wasn't a second of hesitation about letting her know.

She'd cracked open my chest, not with a punch or a hammer, but with her sweet smile, serious and silly sides to her that were all mine now.

Her lips curled in a sleepy smile. "I love you too. Now scoot closer, I'm getting cold." Who was I to argue?

Kennedy sat on my bed with her legs crisscrossed with stacks of notecards in front of her and my favorite pillow behind her back.

"How can you sit like that? Your legs haven't fallen asleep."

Another of my T-shirts was stretched across her chest. At this rate, I'd have only two or three in my closet that didn't conjure dangerous visions of her. She'd stayed at my place for the two nights since Hannah left.

"My legs are fine, stop stalling." She tapped her note-cards against her chin and stared at me expectantly.

I'd always expected a girlfriend to feel stifling, like I'd need my space and get tired of having another person around me all the time. With Kennedy, it was the opposite, I hated when she left to go to class or work. I hated leaving her when I went to the gym or to class or study hall.

The guys didn't care, and she whipped up some pretty spectacular meals that went beyond steamed broccoli and grilled chicken. During the season, we'd all be barely able to drag our asses across the field, but right now, the comfort of her food was exactly what I needed.

Beside me was a plate that had been piled high with a mound of her mac and cheese and was now scraped clean.

"Sports Marketing Mix?" Kennedy leaned forward tapping the top index card on my stack, giving me a spectacular view down her shirt. I loved that light purple lace-top bra. Now, my dick was jammed up against my zipper.

Focus, Cole. Although it was hard when she looked so damn good in my bed. "I'm playing football, why do I need to know this?"

"You're the one majoring in business. You'd also like to pass, so give me the answers."

I dredged my mind to the journal article that had been assigned weeks ago and was drawing a blank. "You know we're in second place again."

Her eyes squinted and her fingers tightened on the pen frozen above the white card. "I know." She wrote out another word in her flowy, loopy handwriting. "But we're not talking about the contest now. You need to study." With added flair, she handed over the card.

I scanned the card of "P" words that should be easy to remember, but right now, I couldn't give a crap about marketing principles.

"I can think of something better to do."

"Or I can go, if you're too distracted."

Gripping the blanket, I tugged her toward me.

She flailed, but caught herself and shook her head.

"None of that until we finish with this. If you're not going to be serious, I'll leave. I can't have you failing on my conscience." With a wave of the stack of white and blue cards, she cleared her throat and straightened her back.

"Give me three of the main actors in the e-commerce ecosystem?"

A sound of disgust shot from my throat. "Who the hell is making these questions?" I reached for the card to read it.

She played keep away, tucking it behind her back. "I've gone through the last eight years of exams from your professor and compiled the most frequent ones."

"That must've been so much work." The ache in the center of my chest grew. Was it possible to love someone too much?

"It was, but you're worth it. Let me choose another question, 'Name the marketing principles that use the acronym, C.O.C.'" Her plaintive and eyelash-batting look was way too inviting. "K."

I tackled her to the bed, trying to grab the notecard, but really enjoying being on top of her. "It doesn't say that. That doesn't exist."

Her laughter washed over me. "Yes, it does."

Attempting to keep the evidence away from me, she tried to roll, but I pinned my legs to the outside of hers.

Her pout and narrowed gaze were a playful look of defiance.

"Don't mind if I do." I plucked the card from her and barked out a laugh. "Name the three Cs of strategic marketing and provide examples?" I tapped the card against her chin. "Not exactly the same."

"I must've misread it." She squirmed beneath me. "Now hop off, I'm hungry since someone ate all the mac and cheese."

"All this squirming isn't incentive for me to get off you in the least bit." My cock stiffened with her beneath me.

"How about a nail file to the ass?"

"Point taken." Reluctantly, I climbed off her and checked the time. "Want to see something?"

Her smile was spine-tinglingly tempting. "I can see it all right." She reached for my zipper.

My exhale was a low drawn-out rasp. Clenching my jaw, I stepped back. "Not that. Later, but not right now."

She propped her elbow on her bent knee. "Then what?"

"Get dressed and I'll show you. We'll get some food."

She squinted without suspicion, more curiosity. "Is this an out-out type of place or are you looking to get adventurous in the back seat of your car again? I still can't believe you convinced me to do that."

A choked laugh escaped me, tweaking my throat. "Not that either. Although, I'd also be up for it later."

"So there will be other people?"

"Yes."

"What's the ETA on leaving?"

"We don't have to leave for at least forty minutes. Why?"

She let out a noise of mock annoyance. "Come on, man. I've got to get ready. Level of dress?"

"House-party level."

Her thumb dragged across her bottom lip. She marched over to my dresser and rummaged through her drawer before walking over to the closet and flicking through the hangers. "This'll work. The shoes won't go 100%, but I'll have to deal."

"The horror. They might not even let you in with those shoes and that outfit." I was buzzing with excitement like arriving to a favorite stadium.

Watching her face when she finally saw it would be worth the wait and the teasing.

She stuck out her tongue and walked over to my desk. Her assortment of makeup essentials were tucked into the corner along with a mirror.

"Should I be jealous of every guy who's going to be staring at you tonight?" I picked up a football and tossed it from hand to hand. Even before she'd put anything on she was the most beautiful woman I'd ever seen. But watching her get ready was always mesmerizing. So effortless, but thoughtful at the same time.

"Probably."

I laughed again and laid down on my bed, which still smelled like her.

In front of the mirror, her reflection had her total concentration. She picked up different bottles and compacts of various colors, shades, and liquidity. Brushes, sponges, and other tools I couldn't name were pressed against her skin or lashes.

"How'd you learn to do all that?"

She glanced at me through the mirror and tugged on the corner of her eye, drawing a faint line along the lid. "Trial and error. My mom wasn't big into it, but in the plays, I had lots of willing and sometimes unwilling participants. Online tutorials too. And hanging out at the makeup store near my house."

"I swear, I'm not saying this to be an asshole." It was her armor, her barrier against the world. I got that, but I didn't want her to think she needed it. To doubt for one second whether it had any impact on her and me.

She put down the pencil and draped one arm over the back of the chair with an expectant look. "This should be good."

"You know, you look beautiful without it."

Her head tilted. "As any boyfriend should think. But it's also a good thing I'm not wearing it for you. I'm wearing it for me." She swung back around and went back to the array of tools in front of her. "It's like my clothes. They make me feel a certain way. Sometimes I'm in fuzzy socks, pajamas and don't give a crap. Sometimes I want to spend the time putting all this on because I can or sometimes I need it." She shrugged.

"You look hot no matter what."

She peered at me through the mirror. "So do you. And just so you know, I'd love you even without all those rippling, sinewy muscles."

Every time she said it, it gave me shades of that first time. From the way she eyed my arms, I wasn't sure she meant it and I wouldn't find out, but I didn't doubt she believed it. I flexed, gripping the ball with one hand. "These are functional."

"So is all this." She waved her hands at her face and the rest of her.

I laughed and wrapped my arms around her, resting my chin on her shoulder. "I'll remember that when I'm stepping over drooling tongues all night."

She rubbed her hand along my cheek. "Still not going to tell me where we're going? You love a good secret, don't you?" Her eyes widened.

Jerking back, I caught myself and tried to keep my face neutral. The slipped reminder to my past and current situation had soured the mood some. "I do have a lot of them, don't I?" The words sounded as light as a lead balloon.

"I didn't mean..." She took my hands. "I didn't mean that in a bad way. I like your surprises and you have your own reasons for keeping secrets." Her eyes fell at the last bit.

"Even if you don't like it that I do." She'd made her stance known and even if I didn't agree, I didn't want it to ruin tonight. I took another calming breath. I wouldn't let Mikelson invade every part of my life.

Her thumbs brushed along the sides of my hands and along the webbing between my thumbs and fingers. "I don't like you feeling like you have to. I don't like that they weigh you down. I don't like that they make you feel like you're alone."

"I don't feel like I'm alone with you."

She sighed and brushed her thumb along my bottom lip with a glint of sadness in her eyes. "You should get ready. I can't wait to see what surprise you've got for me." Kennedy backed up and finished getting ready. She also didn't want to sour our evening. There were too many chances for things to get screwed up, no sense in us doing it to ourselves.

"Watching you get dressed is almost as big of a tease as watching you get naked." I buckled my belt and pictured her face when we arrived. Would that excitement spill back over into our night once we got back here?

She lifted her foot to slip on a heel. "I know." Her wink was a bullseye killer.

I felt like the luckiest guy on the planet walking out of the house holding her hand, opening her door and driving off to the old side of campus. The building that had been there since the university's founding in the 1930s.

The secrets didn't feel half as heavy when she knew them, but tonight's was one I couldn't wait to share with her. Truly a test of how real all this had become.

29

KENNEDY

My feet slid on the slick grass. "Where are we going?" The parking lot we'd parked in and walked across was mostly empty.

Cole steadied me. "You'll see." His fingers were twined in mine, keeping them warm, but my face was prickled by the cold.

"Isn't it March? Why the hell is it still cold?"

"You've been here for three years and you're just now figuring out spring doesn't show up until May."

This part of campus was desolate. Not that anyone in their right mind would be out here after dark where there was nothing going on.

"Maybe it's just wishful thinking that we'd have a warm snap at some point."

"Then I'd be deprived of all your winter looks." He tugged on the edges of my gray, silk-lined hat I'd stashed at Cole's.

"Wait until you see my spring outfits."

"Trust me, I've seen them. I'll need to constantly walk

around with a clipboard in front of me once the leaves show up."

It still tripped me up with how open he was about how hot he found me. Not that I needed his confirmation to feel good about myself, but—screw it. It felt good knowing I was so hot he couldn't wait to get his hands on me, and a spontaneous boner might be the outcome.

"No hints about where we're going?"

"Nope."

"Cryptic as ever, just like Pittsburgh."

"You like a little mystery yourself. I had no idea we were going to Case Clothes."

"It was in broad daylight. I should know better than to follow a guy into dark deserted spaces in the dead of night."

He tipped my chin toward him.

The spark grew with each touch. A finger-sized inferno. "You like my surprises. You'll love this one." He squeezed my hand and pulled me along.

Excitement radiated off him like a kid headed toward the fastest rollercoaster in a theme park.

Across the grass, a building from the older part of campus loomed. A small box of light appeared at eye level, illuminating a guy standing in front of a wall. It snapped closed and then the wall opened. No, not a wall. A door.

The guy disappeared and the door shadowed by the huge building above it vanished from view from our distance.

"Is that where we're going?"

He nodded. "We're almost late."

"Late to what?"

"A couple more minutes and you'll know." He vibrated with eagerness. Five-year-olds getting their first piece of birthday cake were less animated than he was right now.

Another couple showed up at the door and I could make out now that we were closer. The tiny window of light opened and closed again. But this time there wasn't a flood of light and the two walked away, shoulders slumped.

The pair disappeared through the stone archway leading to the front of the building when we made it to the door that melded in with the wall. Cole tapped out a beat with his fist and the small door opened.

"Guest—Kennedy Finch."

The eye staring back at us through the grate widened. "One second."

It slammed shut. The creaky metallic sound reverberating the air around us.

"Please tell me this isn't some weird campus sex cult or illuminati initiation where I'm going to have to drink my blood or something."

"If it were, would I tell you?" His teasing tone darkened, but it was tempered by his grin.

I eyed him, trying to figure out what was going on behind the totally-not-creepy door. Then the distant rumbling of rumors from campus about the football team struck me. "Is this the secret bar?"

"Maybe."

A flush of excitement rushed through me. Now, I was ready to beat down the door. "I thought only players got invites."

"Not just players, Leona's been inside."

"What?" She's been holding out on me. There was a splinter of offense that she hadn't spilled to any of us as far as I knew, but that was softened by the whole relationship origin Cole and I had been holding out on her. Everyone had their secrets. Now I'd be in on this one.

"It's kind of a secret thing. She's kept it well."

The door opened and we were let inside. "Which is probably the reason you're being let in."

He extended his arm.

Another guy stood to the other side of me. He was a hulk of a guy and if he'd told us we weren't coming in, I'd have definitely run off like the other two.

"Thanks."

"Have fun, Kennedy. Cole." He nodded to Cole and we began our descent down the ramp walkway. Lights hung on the walls, not sconces or anything refined, but more like something that would be found in a mine. I don't know what I'd expected, but this wasn't it. Maybe a small room, kind of like a walk-in closet. It sounded like we were walking to a bar complete with clinking glasses and music.

The bass of music grew louder with each echoing step down the ramp that ended in a doorway.

I peered through the opening in the wall and soaked it all in.

TVs were on the walls and there was a large one in the corner where some guys were playing video games. I wasn't the only woman, but we were certainly outnumbered. All the women were with other guys.

I snapped. "Damn, I was secretly hoping for the illuminati orgy."

Cole laughed and draped his arm over my shoulder. "I'll keep that in mind for our next visit."

Inside, there was long bench seating as well as a few round tables. A bar with bottles lined up on wooden shelves behind it and taps. Actual taps.

"Everyone..."

"Hi, Kennedy." The whole room chorused in various baritone and basses.

I grabbed onto Cole. "How do they know who I am?"

"It takes a vote for us to let in a non-teammate," he whispered, his voice brimming with pride.

Scanning the room, I let that sink in. "It does?"

He squeezed his arms around me. "Yup."

My heart skipped a beat, chasing the tingle flooding me at his touch. "That's unexpected." In the room were a couple guys I'd made out with. Nope, not awkward at all being here with my new boyfriend, but from their nods there didn't seem to be any issues. Had they voted against letting me in?

"Why would it be? You've been proving how much you're into me for the past five weeks. Of course, they'd want you to be here with me."

A pinch of sadness at the deception and circumstances that started all this dimmed that glowing feeling a little. It felt like they'd let me in under false pretenses.

"Drinks?" A stocky guy in a bow tie with a T-shirt walked up to us.

I tilted my head and looked back at Cole.

"All the freshmen have to do a week or so of bartending duty. It's tradition." He rattled off our drink orders, which were handed right back and we found an empty end of the table.

"What was this place? How have you all managed to keep the location quiet for this long?" The stone walls and concrete floor were covered over with posters, carpets, tables, and chairs. Lights from the ceiling were installed, not patched together.

I drank some of my rum and coke.

"Alumni get to come back here to remember their glory days, which means they're also open to donating to keep things entertaining. It was a storage area. Let's say the building and grounds offices don't mind us using this space as long as we don't fuck things up and cause an infestation problem or a fire."

He hadn't been exaggerating when he said there wasn't anything die-hard fans wouldn't do for STFU football and, by extension, its players. "They let you take this place over and hang out here."

"I'm pretty sure we took it over before anyone else long ago."

I kept soaking the place up and finished my drink.

Another couple walked through a doorway opposite the one we'd walked in from.

Leona and Reid. Familiar faces were welcome.

Her grin widened the second she saw me and she rushed over. "I knew they'd vote for you."

"You've been holding out on us. How did we not know this place was here?" I propped my hands up on my hips.

Her gaze dropped.

"She was sworn to secrecy." Reid jumped to her defense as he should.

"It's not like I could invite you, and I didn't want to brag about it or anything. I'm glad you're finally here, though." She hugged my arm. "We should play skeeball."

"There's skeeball?"

She pointed to the corner with mini basketball, skeeball, and pinball games.

"How'd you even get those down here?"

"Not us, those have been down here forever. The only new additions this year are this TV." Reid gestured to the one on a stand with two guys standing in front of it, pounding away at game controllers trying to block each other's view of the seventy-inch screen.

All four of us walked over to the bar. "The VR game

system and..." he raised his hand and the underclassmen slid the two bottles of not-beer toward us.

I checked the label.

Leona clinked the neck of her bottle against mine. "Hard lemonade. Just when you think this place can't get any better."

A guy called out to Reid and Cole who left us at the bar before promising they'd be back.

"Not like we'll get lost in the crowd here." I took a sip of the sugary sweet drink that packed a vodka punch. "That goes down too easily."

"These guys pretend to be tough, but there's a two-lemonade limit."

"I don't blame them. How could you not love these?" A gulp later and the bottle was half empty. "These are dangerous."

"Tell me about it." She drained the last of hers. "I'm so happy you're here. The guys get territorial about this place. Only those they can trust are let in here."

The trust bomb knotted my stomach. How would they feel if they found out we'd both been faking? "That's important to them."

"Totally important, especially with people ready to blab about anything and STFU Dirt sneaking around. It's one of the few places Reid and I feel like we can go to where I'm not going to end up plastered on their posts."

I hated she felt like she was living under a microscope. "Fuck those people, whoever they are." Although their posts about us had probably helped us gain rankings. And their posts about other competitors forgetting they were supposed to be in love had gotten at least two other couples kicked out of the competition. Now we just needed to make sure the same didn't happen to us.

"Totally."

We wandered over to the skeeball games. Two were side-by-side with glowing red lights displaying the high scores at the top. It had been forever since I'd played one of these. The smell of the wooden balls trapped in their holding place until the game started permeated the rest of the food, drink, and dude smells from the room. My fingers itched to get my hands on one of them again. "Do we need coins?"

She winked and punched the red blinking button in front of me. "Nope."

The wooden balls dropped down into position to my right.

"Are you any good?" She held a ball.

I picked one up and tossed it to my other hand. "I'm alright." Drawing my arm back, I focused on my target and swung through, releasing the ball. It rolled down the red runway and popped up flying through the air and falling short of my target, dropping into the ten-point ring.

"I suck at this thing too, but I figure I have a better shot at conquering it over the pinball machine." She rolled hers and it plopped into the twenty-point ring.

"It's been a while since I played on one of these." Normally, they were at carnivals or other places where I'd rather spend my cash on food or drinks, not the machine that'll spit out five tickets for prizes that start at a thousand. "How often do you guys come here?"

"Maybe once a week. During the off-season, the guys are normally partying at their house, so there's no need to come here."

I shot another and it dropped into the fifty-point ring. Damn. I chalked that up to another warm-up shot and not me losing my touch. "During the season it's probably a cool place to hang out without everyone crawling all over them."

"That and they're banned from a few places from August to January. I don't know if it's for their own good or not."

"Probably a mixture of both. This place feels like one where they can relax. Loser buys the next round." My next ball finally cooperated and went straight into the hundred-point spot in the top left corner. Elation streaked through me.

Leona yelped and stared at me wide-eyed. "You're a ringer."

I grabbed another ball and breathed on it before rubbing it against my shirt. "I know my way around a carnival game or two." Summers, I'd ridden my bike to them to escape the house for a few hours and spent hours scouring the lots or field where they were set up, looking for loose change to play. The next seven thunked into the hundred-point ring. The scoreboard blinked triumphantly and tickets poured out of the slot below the Start button. I felt like a kid again racking up another high score.

"Tickets!" I grabbed them and folded them. "They have tickets? I love this place!"

Leona and I finished three more games before we called it quits and I followed her over to the bar where the prizes sat along the wall.

"Five hundred tickets for a starfish bouncy ball. What a rip off!"

"Would it feel like the true experience if it weren't?"

I laughed and finished my drink, and squinted at the bottom shelf. "Pink ring, I'm coming back for you." I pocketed my tickets, excited to come back soon. It was surreal this place existed and even more so that Cole had brought me here and the entire place had voted to let me in. The final acceptance. I was never happier that we'd decided to make this real. Hanging out here next year would beat fighting for a spot at the bars to order a drink, plus we wouldn't be overrun by enthusiastic fans during the season.

We sat down on opposite benches.

"You ready for the dance-a-thon?"

I tipped my head back and slammed my eyes shut. "Don't remind me."

"Twelve hours on your feet, dancing?"

"Exactly. Like the bookstore shift from hell. The only thing I'm excited about is the clothes."

She chuckled. "Of course. But make it through that and you guys can take the crown."

"We can." I squeezed my fingers under the table. Cole was ahead of me in the individual scores, but with the clothes I could pull ahead.

"You two are going to be the epic story we tell after graduation. Do you know which trip you're going to take? You don't seem like a golf fan and Cole's not exactly high fashion. What made you guys want to enter in the first place?"

My throat tightened. I glanced around and took a sip of my drink. "Where'd the guys go?"

"No idea." She leaned back, trying to get a good look past the guys in front of the TV.

A player burst into the room in a block-striped gray, cream, and black sweater. Cole and Reid followed behind him. "Come on, guys. Why wouldn't you let Siobhan in?"

A guy in front of the TV paused the game and stood. "How many times has she cheated on you, man?"

"We all make mistakes." Sweater Guy's arms flapped at his sides like he was ready to take flight.

"Seven times isn't a mistake," another guy in a thermal called out. "No unanimous vote for her, man. Pick someone who isn't trash for you and we'll see."

Someone from the crowd chuckled.

I leaned forward, shocked. "There has to be a *unanimous* vote for us to get in?" My shocked whisper drew a furrowed-browed look from Leona.

She nodded. "Of the guys present." She swept over the room filled with at least fifty people.

"And they *all* voted for me?" I scanned the room, holding my past hookups in even higher regard now. No hard feelings at all. I was even more comfortable here than I'd been before.

"They did." She lowered her voice. "Pretty awesome, right?"

"Yeah." I turned back toward Cole and stared at him, stunned. The depths of my feelings for him and the ones he returned wrapped me up like a warm blanket. What exactly had he said to get them all to approve of me being here?

Cole shot me a helpless look and the two of them walked Sweater Guy over to the bar and ordered him a drink.

I was halfway through the drink when arms wrapped around me from behind. My heart skipped at the spark of anticipation. Cole slipped a leg on either side of me and hugged me tight, mainly so he didn't fall off the bench.

"My ass is bigger than it appears. There is no way you are fitting on this thing with me."

His body enveloped me even more. "Maybe I like being this close to you," he whispered against my ear, tickling my skin.

I laughed. "You're trying to figure out a graceful exit, aren't you?"

"Maybe a little."

I shook my head and looked over at Reid and Leona who weren't trying to cover their laughter. "What can I say? He can't keep his hands off me." Scooting forward, I gave him back enough leverage to swing a leg off and sit beside me.

"Kennedy's a skeeball ringer. Just to give everyone a heads up."

Under the table, I kicked Leona.

"Really?" Cole gulped from his beer.

"No idea what she's talking about." I stared at him and sipped my drink.

His gaze narrowed with a playfulness reserved for cartoon characters. "I'm not too bad myself."

"Oh, that must be good for you."

An outraged laugh erupted from his lips. "Head to head, me and you." He hopped out of his seat and held out his hand.

I loved how even when he battled with me, he didn't lose this side of himself. But that didn't mean I was going to take it easy on him.

"Your funeral."

"Don't think I'm above playing dirty."

I brushed across the front of him, letting my fingers trail across the zipper of his jeans.

He jolted.

"Same."

Amob of voices and footsteps rumbled around us in our quiet corner. A curtain hung to the left of the cinderblock wall in front of me.

Kennedy's back was to me with both hands against the wall. "Harder. I can take it."

I wanted to kiss the back of her neck, but there wasn't time for that.

I pressed in close behind her. My chest brushed against her shoulder.

She groaned, bit her lipstick covered lip, her eyes screwed shut.

My fingers tightened around her ankle and pushed the heel of her foot closer to her ass. "These hamstrings are going to lock up after the first couple of hours."

"It's why I'm wearing the flats. The outfits would look better with heels, but I don't want to have to amputate a toe when this is all over."

I released her foot and worked on the other leg. "How long do you think we have to last?"

"The whole way." She glanced over her shoulder with

her teeth clenched together. "How the hell do you do this after every practice?"

"Just used to it at this point."

"Then you're tougher than you look."

I let the other leg down and plastered my face with mock outrage. "Hey, what's that supposed to mean?"

"I never said you didn't look tough, just now I know you're tougher." She spun on her toes and pecked me on the lips.

"Five minutes," a voice boomed over the mic.

Kennedy picked up another adhesive hook and stuck it to the wall. "This is the last costume. You shouldn't have any issues getting into it, but let me know if you do." She slid on the rhinestone-studded headband with a red feather attached to the side. It matched her red-and-black fringe dress. The fringe brushed her knees, but the top of the dress was more structured with a black beaded design on lace over the red fabric beneath it. When she'd found the dress online, she nearly leapt across the room to show it to me. It hugged her body perfectly.

"I can handle dressing myself." I tugged up the suspenders that had been hanging at my side and snapped them onto my shoulders. Wincing, I rubbed the sore spots where they'd landed.

"Three minutes. Can we get our four couples ready behind the curtain?"

She walked over to me with a not-so-subtle laugh and handed over my newsboy cap. "I can see that."

Taking it, I slipped it on and circling her wrist with my hand, tugged her forward.

A yelp and louder laugh burst through her lips. "Save it for the stage. If we can't outlast everyone else, we'll at least have a leg up with the costume vote." Her fingers traveled along the suspenders pressing on my shoulders. She straightened them where they were twisted. "It's why I left it all in your capable hands and your job is to make sure I don't pass out."

"We've got enough carbs and sports drinks to get the whole team through a practice, you'll be fine. The whole thing will be more mental than physical, which means you've got everyone else out here beat."

"Says the guy who can bench press a couple hundred pounds." She squeezed my bicep for extra emphasis.

"I don't think that'll come in handy out there." My throat thickened, saliva was a distant memory. Nervousness shot through me like a firehouse to the face. I'd put this whole part of the competition to the back of my mind, locked it in a safe and had chucked it to the bottom of my subconscious. Dancing was one thing, but dancing in front of a hundred or so people up on stage was another.

"You're saying that now, but wait until you've got to drag me out of here."

Music on the other side of the curtain lowered and a mic turned on. Three rhythmic taps. Being in front of a crowd on the field was a lot different than up on stage. My stomach rumbled and roiled.

The dynamic host duo entered through the curtain. Chelsea swayed onto the stage with her arm linked with Mark's. "Thank you everyone for coming tonight. We're raising lots of money for charity and also having some fun. Our four finalist couples are also ready to treat you to their dance moves and costumes, so be sure to vote for your favorite couple over on the Puppy Love site by five a.m. The winner will be whoever is still standing at the end of the night—literally with the most votes. And votes for the whole contest wrap up at the end of the weekend."

A stage crew member flipped a switch and the curtains parted, temporarily blinding us with the lights pointed directly at our eyeballs. The stadium lights were way less harsh than they were up here. I wiped my soggy palms on my pants.

Wolf whistles and cheering rose from the shadows, attendees slowly coming into focus as I regained portions of my eyesight.

"Our couples have all chosen four time periods to dress up as. Your votes can be cast after the two hours." Chelsea's mic was raised above the music. "There will be a ten-minute break every two hours, and those of you who make it to five a.m. will get a delicious breakfast. If you stop moving, you're out and the charity loses an hour's worth of donations, so don't start doing the Charleston in the first five minutes." She walked to the edge of the stage with her hand shielding her eyes. "I'm talking to you two. How long do you honestly think you can keep that up?" She let out an exasperated sigh.

Our game plan was slow, steady movements with various arm positions to help resting. Other than the outfit changes, it wasn't that different than prepping for a game. Stretching, warming up and refueling throughout.

"Both participants must be moving for an entire three of the four fifteen-minute chunks for that to count toward your hours, but for our couples up here, they've got to be moving the whole time. Sudden death if they stop, and they're out."

It wouldn't be us.

Kennedy stared back at me, her eyes glinting with the same determination. "They'll have to shove our still wriggling bodies off the stage, if they think we're giving up."

"There's that cutthroat attitude I love." I kissed her and didn't want to let her down.

"Remember, we have spotters out there and if you don't make it until the end you won't be in the running for our incredibly generous prizes that, of course, as coordinators we're not eligible for. There are a few weekend trips to New York, Washington DC and Philadelphia as well as other way-too-nice-for—"

Mark took the mic from her. "Let's get started and raise some serious cash for charity. DJ, turn it up!" He swooped his hand over his head in a circle and the first song began.

Kennedy squeezed my hand and we walked forward to our taped off box closer to the front of the stage. "We've got this."

"Loving your confidence." Being beside Kennedy helped with the nervous gut that might've otherwise sent me off the stage. Focused on her, I didn't have to think about the dozens of people watching us and even more on the live stream ready to laugh. But we'd give them a show and I'd use every trick I had to keep Kennedy laughing and make this our crowning achievement.

"It's what I do best." She extended her hand and I took it, kissing the back of it.

The music was cranked up so loudly it rumbled under our feet and we danced, keeping to a low-energy version of the caricature 1920s dancing people expected. She glittered and shined in her sparkly outfit. "Have I told you how great you look?"

Her smile brightened. "Yes, but it's never too early to remind me." She batted her eyelashes dramatically.

Keeping inside our box, I pulled her into my arms swaying back and forth as one song melded into another.

"How are your feet?"

"Happy I decided to sacrifice time-period accuracy for

comfort. Heels would've been a terrible idea." She jerked her chin while staring over my shoulder.

Spinning her, I winced at one of the other couples who'd chosen platform heels and bell bottoms for their first outfit. "That's got to hurt."

They hobbled, barely moving and rested heavily on each other.

"You didn't see her trip about twenty minutes ago. I swear her ankles must be made of playdoh. That would've taken out lesser mortals."

I sucked in a breath through clenched teeth. Joint injuries were no joke. At least there wasn't a team of opposing players bearing down on her. Only her dance partner who was using her like a crutch.

"Glad my sneakers are firmly on the ground."

The mic flicked back on. "That's two hours finished. Everyone take a break. Couples, we'll see you back here in ten."

Grabbing Kennedy's hand, I tugged her back toward the edge of the curtain and flung it back, making sure it didn't hit her. That hadn't sucked as much as it could've. Nothing ached yet.

"How you feeling so far?"

"Not too bad." She smiled, so that was a good sign.

In our corner, I twisted the lid off a drink, handed it to her, and ran my gaze over her.

She dropped into the chair opposite mine and gulped it down while reaching for the clothes on the first hook. "It'll take you two minutes tops to change," she panted with a ring of red drink above her top lip. Taking another swig, she kicked off her shoes, which bounced against the wall.

I unwrapped a granola bar and handed it to her. I

grabbed my own bottle and wolfed down my own bar. "What about you?"

She held up one finger and finished drinking before tossing the empty bottle into the trash can. "Three minutes."

"Let's get you changed first." I shrugged off my coat and looked for a spot to hold it up to cover her.

"Don't worry about it. I'm wearing a body suit under here. After years of changing backstage, I don't really give a shit if anyone sees me," she mumbled through her mouthful of granola and ran her tongue along her teeth to clear away the stray bits of chocolate. "Unzip me and we're good to go."

I wasn't thrilled about her stripping down in front of everyone else, but if she didn't have an issue with it, I'd deal.

After unzipping her, Kennedy pulled the other dress over her head as the other one hit the floor. Watching it slip over the curves of her body was absolute torture. She stepped into the shoes while buttoning the last couple buttons at the top of her new outfit.

Ten more hours left, although I doubted we'd have the energy for more than sleeping once this was over. As disappointing as that was, I had no doubts we'd make it up to each other once we got some rest.

Hand in hand, she tugged me forward, laughing, and I realized I'd follow her anywhere. Anywhere she was, I wanted to be. Right now, that was on this stage to win her the prize she so deserved. The countdown ticked by and my heart rate jumped.

We made it back to our spot with seconds to spare. Renewed determination ran through me.

Kennedy and I traded off on close dancing to conserve energy, and putting a little more distance between us when the sweaty palms were too slippery.

"I never want to dance again," she groaned with her head on my shoulder.

I laughed, jostling her, trying to keep her upright. "You're going to let me lead, finally?"

Her head popped up and she shot me a playful glare, straightening a little, her moves less stilted. Much like practice, half the battle was mental. Lighting the fire for her would pull her through this next hour, and teasing her took my mind off the slow fatigue setting in.

In the middle of hour six a couple danced up to the front of the stage. I rubbed my eyes to make sure the contest hadn't taken an even bigger toll on me than I'd thought. In suit jackets I'd seen through every booster and press event, Hollis and Griff looked up at us. These goofballs.

Kennedy laughed. "Who's leading?"

"It's a standoff right now." Hollis switched his handhold with Griff. "You do know I'm your captain, right?"

"Only on the field." Griff let go to reverse the hold, but Hollis kept his grip.

"What are you two doing here?"

"Moral support," they replied in unison.

Griff leaned closer. "Plus, the spread is exceptional. Freshman year they had rock-hard cookies and watered-down Hawaiian Punch. They've skipped things up a lot this year."

I spun Kennedy and looped my arm around her, so her back rested against my chest. "Apparently, the couple sponsoring it this year's got money to burn."

"They can burn it on food like this all they want." Griff pulled a chicken finger out of his pocket.

Hollis jerked back. "Where did you get that from?"

"My pocket," Griff mumbled through a full mouth.

"Gross, man." I massaged Kennedy's shoulder as she shook her head.

"Learned it from Ezra." He chomped down devouring the strip.

"That's it!" A voice blared behind us. Ah, the unmistakable sound of someone losing their shit. I was wondering when it would happen. I'm surprised we made it this far before it happened.

Kennedy tensed and glanced over my shoulder. Maintaining our almost sway, we turned.

"I'm going to have to have my toes amputated if you keep this up!"

The couple behind us were in plaid bell bottoms. Hers were part of a jumpsuit and his were paired with an orange-and-yellow patterned shirt.

Kennedy's fingers tightened on my bicep.

"I told you we needed to practice, but no, you swore you had the moves to make it through with no problem." She made air quotes around "moves." Her blue eyes seemed even bigger matched with the blue eye shadow. Her partner kept trying to keep her from the edge of their box since technically they were both still moving.

I held on to Kennedy who swallowed loud enough for me to hear it over the music. I smoothed my hands over the sides of her face, semi-covering her ears, but also letting her know I was here. If we weren't trapped in this spot, I'd have gotten her out of here.

Her gaze flicked up to mine and she offered up a half smile, releasing her grip and smoothing her hands down my arms. "I'm okay."

"You think I want to spend another second with you. Screw this, I'm done!" She stepped out of the box, stomping with both feet before storming off the stage.

The three other couples all exchanged looks as the mic turned off. Mark stepped up to the podium. "Couple three has taken themselves out of the running." A light under their picture up on the wall was turned out in overly dramatic fashion with music to go along with it.

After hour seven Reid and Leona showed up decked out and dancing, trying to keep our minds off the aches and pains.

Taylor and Ashley came up toward the end of hour eight and cheered us on even louder.

"And we're at the end of our eighth hour, which means our couples will be back with new costumes. If you were waiting to vote, don't miss what they have coming up next."

Kennedy took off.

I leaned over the edge of the stage. "Smuggle us some of that food."

They both nodded and took off toward the buffet set up along the side wall.

Rushing after Kennedy, I got to the chairs as she uncapped another bottle and grabbed our clothes.

"I asked the guys to get us food."

"Is that allowed?" She wriggled out of her pants, trying to kill me with how good her bare legs looked. But my show was cut short.

A hair flip later and she changed in a flash, jumping into her T-shirt and overalls combo with only one side done up, complete with colorful lens glasses with a condom taped to one.

Down to my boxers, I grabbed the clothes bundle Kennedy had set up for me. "That was a lucky break, we're out one more couple."

She nodded. "We are. I can't believe she freaked out at him like that though."

"He wasn't exactly light on his toes. Probably hurt to get crunched." At least I hadn't done that and now I probably jinxed myself.

"Still, she didn't have to scream at him like that—especially not in front of everyone."

I chugged my sports drink and bit into the dry granola bar. "I promise when you step on my toes, I won't react that way."

"I didn't think you would." She tossed her bottle. "I just felt bad, that's all."

Griff and Hollis came back and slid the last few steps to us with plates piled high with food. Sliders, chicken fingers, meat on skewers.

"Ask and ye shall receive." Hollis stole a meat stick.

I took one and handed it to Kennedy.

She inhaled the smells wafting from the plate before diving in. "You two are my favorite people in the whole world."

"Hey," I called out around the cheeseburger slider I inhaled.

A head tilt from her.

"You're right. I can't compete."

"One-minute warning." The call came from the stage. The fatigue settled in deeper now. Like the last few feet before the toilet, when you'd been holding it no problem all through practice. I refused to buckle now.

Kennedy took another bite then shoved the plate toward Hollis. I got up and groaned the second my feet took my full weight. Football practice had nothing on this.

Kennedy stood looking out through the gap in the curtain with her hand sticking out behind her.

I took it and she bolted out onto the stage, pulling me

behind her. In shoes nowhere near as comfortable as mine, I didn't know how she did it.

We faced each other and I laughed. The weight of everything lightened around her.

"What?" The smear of ketchup smudged on the corner of her mouth.

I wiped it off with my finger and showed her before wiping it on my pants.

"Oh, thanks." She draped her arms over my shoulders and yawned. Her tiredness was the only reason I'd gotten away with the ketchup swipe. Under normal circumstances she'd have been horrified by treating clothes that way. Her sleepy, determined gaze lit up the second the music started.

Another thing I loved about her.

Kennedy never failed at anything. If things didn't turn out the way she wanted, she'd find another way and make it work. There wasn't anything she couldn't do, and I felt lucky to be standing up on stage with my arm around her.

"Four hours left." She yawned, never missing a beat.

"Let's show them what we've got."

31

KENNEDY

My eyes fluttered closed, but I kept my feet moving.

Right now, Cole was my rock.

Even in flats, being on my feet like this was worse than my first shift at the fast food place near home when I was sixteen. I'd woken up in the middle of the night with shooting pains in my stomach fearing I had appendicitis. Instead, it had been a severe lack of core muscles that had never been worked for eight hours continuously standing before.

But this was worse, much worse.

"Kennedy." Cole shook me and my eyes popped open.

"What's up?" My cottony mouth and bleary eyes were sluggish.

"You were snoring."

I yawned. "No, I wasn't."

"Over the music." His whole body shook with sleepy laughter.

Gathering up the energy for a scowl was impossible at this point. "You're lucky I'm too tired to prove you wrong."

"Fifteen minutes left. Rest your head on my shoulder."

"It's okay." I yawned again. "I can make it."

"I know you can, but you don't need to do it all by yourself."

Normally, I'd snap a comeback and stand even straighter just to prove a point, but I was too tired, and Cole was too warm and cuddly. To combat the heat of the room, they'd cranked the AC and dropped the temperature to the point where my corset top, belly chain and hip hugging jeans provided almost no warmth.

But Cole did. With his arms around me, I was ready to melt. Here with him, in the circle of his arms, I could drift off to sleep. To know he was here for me, not because he thought I couldn't handle it on my own, but because he didn't think I should have to. It was nice to have someone want to do that for me.

The shocks from our touches had lessened and now there was just a warm glow at the center of my chest whenever he looked into my eyes. The kind that made me feel like my heart was expanding with each breath.

"How are your feet?" I smacked one cheek and fought to keep my eyes open.

He shuffled back and forth doing most of the heavy lifting at this point. "Not too bad."

The room was quieter. Driving music had been replaced with slower melodies primed to make people pass out.

"Chelsea and Mark are totally trying to snag some of these prizes for themselves, aren't they?"

His arms tightened around me, shifting me closer. "Probably. There aren't too many people left."

"No idea why those two thought it would be a good idea to wear matching mascot uniforms last hour."

"They were going for the costume win."

"They would've won it, if they'd lasted. But now they've lost the chance, which means we might actually close the gap to the top." That fueled me, sending extra energy to my sluggish limbs. "Do you think we can do it? They were pretty far ahead of us."

"If we make it to the end and come in first for costumes, we can eek out first place."

I covered his mouth with my hands. "Don't jinx it."

A squeal from the mic drew groans from the crowd of shuffling zombies on the dance floor. "Thank you to everyone here, and we've raised over triple the donations we raised last year." Chelsea's voice was way too chipper for this late or early in the morning. She was nowhere near the zombie levels of the rest of us, but her words slowly registered. "It's the final dance, so let's go out strong."

Subdued cheers and a smattering of applause rose from the people continuing to rock from side to side in the final moments.

I stared into Cole's eyes, elation sending even more blood flowing to my arms and legs. "We're almost there."

"We've got this." His hand tightened around my waist.

Mark took the mic from her. "We're going to end this with a bang, so everyone get ready to jump around!"

The music blasted, a shock from the sleepy-time versions of songs that had been playing for the past hour.

"How do we party this late normally, but right now, I can barely keep my eyes open?" I used my fingers to pry my lids apart and grinned at Cole like a demented date, curling my top lip above my teeth. "Would you still love me if I looked like this?" A final burst of energy rushed through me and I jumped on beat with the song. The aches in my feet and body zipped away and I'd pay for it later, but I wanted to enjoy my last dance with Cole.

He laughed, made his own hideously hilarious face with his tongue hanging out of his mouth and jumped along with me. "Sure, I'd make my face like this so everyone would look at me instead of you."

"How chivalrous."

The song hit its peak and wound down, so did we. The fatigue roaring back after the final burst of energy.

"And that's time!" Over the mic the pair, who looked refreshed and only a little tired called out together. "Everyone currently standing, you did it! Someone will be around to give you your winning tickets, which you can use to claim your not-in-any-way-undeserved donated gifts. Thank you all for making this a success and to our two couples left, that's a tie. You'll both get an extra one hundred points added to your totals." My throbbing feet were no match for my unbridled excitement and final burst of energy.

I glanced over at the other couple who looked in rougher shape than we were.

Her kitten heels hadn't done her any favors with the red, rubbed raw spot on the back of her foot.

"You did it!" Her guy swept her up in his arms. They had been a cute quiet couple of the pack. A part of me felt bad that they were truly in this for the love spreading, not the prize hunting.

She nodded and clung to her boyfriend. "I won't be able to walk for a week."

"Have him carry you." I nodded to her boyfriend, who had over one hundred pounds on her and was at least eight inches taller.

"Tell Cole to do the same." She smiled and yelped when her guy actually swung her up into his arms.

Cole reached for me and I swatted his hands away.

"Don't even think about it."

"Why does he get to?"

"Because he could carry her in a freaking Baby Bjorn on his chest. She's about as big as a Pomeranian."

A blast from overhead wrenched gasps from everyone and nearly sent me diving for the floor. Cole steadied me and the room was filled with celebratory glittering confetti falling from above.

"Could that thing have been any louder?" I gripped at my chest feeling my heart punching at my ribs trying to break free. My legs were barely solid, and I plopped down on the floor.

"Those things are loud on the sidelines, no idea why they thought it would be a good idea to set one off in here." Cole groaned and stretched out beside me.

I closed my hand around some shiny confetti twirling in the air and collapsed onto my back. My chest heaved and fell, exhaustion settling into each muscle. I couldn't have made it without Cole helping me along and, in some cases, holding me up. "This is new for me. But this must be old and boring for you."

"It's all new and exciting when you're involved." He scooted closer until we were side by side and pushed up, skimming one hand along my cheek and dipped his head for a kiss. The gentle, demanding, exploring kiss he'd given me a hundred times now that only made me crave the next one that much more.

"And—" The mic cut in over the chaos of people laying on the floor being covered in shiny bits of floating confetti. "We have a new couple at the top of Puppy Love!"

My head whipped toward the screen that had been displaying the countdown timer, now with our picture at the top of the pack. Cole's line a little higher than mine. Cut the confetti cannon in my head. Bombs of bliss exploded in my chest. We'd done it!

"I won." His fingers interlocked with mine and he stood, dragging me with him.

With throbbing feet, I gave up on the shoes immediately. Who cared what was on this stage, I needed my toes to breathe. "No need to rub it in." My scowl didn't last long when he looked at me with such heated amusement, now against the warmth shining so brightly inside of me, it felt like it was flowing from my fingertips.

"I didn't mean the contest. I mean here with you. This was the prize I didn't even know I wanted and am so happy I stumbled into the greatest one that there ever was."

Had I thought I'd been steeled against sappiness? Not when it was delivered so earnestly and openly. It almost felt too clear, too vulnerable. Too scary to be real. Looping my arms around his neck, I tugged him in close and planted another kiss on him. "You always know the perfect thing to say."

He picked a piece of confetti from my forehead. "Tell that to Kennedy from five weeks ago. I'm just telling you what you deserve to hear."

My throat tightened. For so long I'd been so afraid of letting anyone close to me. I'd been afraid of falling into well-worn patterns. I'd been afraid of ending up like my parents. I'd been afraid to take a chance.

While I backed into this one in an unconventional way, being with Cole felt like a dream. A dream I hadn't thought possible. Too happy. The kind I was afraid could be snatched away from me or all a mirage. Breaking our gaze, I patted his chest. "Who could've known you were such a cinnamon roll?"

"I hide it well." He held on to my arm and guided me

toward our stuff that was now strewn all over our backstage area.

The co-hosts stepped up behind us. "Cole and Kennedy, can we get some pictures?"

"We're—" Cole stepped forward.

"Of course." I patted his arm. "I'm good, if you are. We need to commemorate our win. Do you care if I leave the shoes off?"

"Voting ends tomorrow night, but it'll be impossible for anyone else to catch up with this win, so congratulations to you both."

"Thanks!" I winced and squeezed the tightening muscle on the back of my leg,

"Have you decided on which trip you're going to take?"

Cole opened his mouth, and I pressed my finger against his parted lips. "We're still deciding."

After a molten look from Cole and way too many pictures, we hobbled to clean up our gear to find it had already been packed away.

Taylor, Ashley, and Josh sat on our chairs with our space cleaned up. Spotting us, they thumped the tables and cheered. Josh stuck his two fingers in his mouth and ripped an ear-piercing whistle through the backstage area.

Ashley uncovered her ears and hopped off Josh's lap. "The triumphant heroes have returned from their dangerous journey."

I attempted a smile, but I could feel that it was closer to a grimace.

"You might need these." Taylor flopped down my pair of slippers and I almost kissed her.

For Cole, she dropped some flip flops and a new pair of socks. "Taylor, I love you."

The two of us changed our shoes and hobbled to the

breakfast with an afterglow of satisfaction washing away the aches and pains at least while the adrenaline was in high gear.

Inside the dining hall, opened early for us, we followed the trio to a table with the rest of the guys.

I dropped into the chair so hard, I expected it to plummet to the center of the earth. There wasn't a single bit of energy left in me.

Cole rested his cheek against his palm on his propped-up arm. "Protein and carb loading after the night we just had and passing out for three days is my kind of plan." With one arm, he swept my legs up onto his lap and ran his hands over my calves. I groaned at the pressure release from the exhaustion-induced throbbing in my whole lower half.

I rubbed his shoulder. "Me too. Your place or mine?"

"Whatever's closer. I'd sleep here if they'd let me." His adorable sleepy grin faltered and his eyes drifted shut.

"We'll get food for you guys." Ashley kissed the tip of Josh's nose and left what seemed to be her new favorite seat on his lap. "Josh, I'll get some for you too."

The table was empty except for a snoring Cole, me, and Josh. I massaged Cole's shoulder, rubbing it after how long he'd been supporting my arms for half our time dancing.

Josh glanced over at me with a sheepish look. He opened his mouth and closed it. A deep breath. "Sorry about before." He rushed through the sentence, so it sounded like one long word.

My eyes snapped wide, no longer letting sleep try to drag me under. "What do you mean?" I yawned and buried my face in my elbow.

"You know, at the party. When you two first let everyone know you were dating. I was being a territorial asshole for no reason." He ducked his head.

Relief that I'd been right about him and hadn't encouraged Ashley to go out with a dick were swiftly swept up with his heartfelt apology. "I mean, I get it. I'm pretty awesome, I'd be mad if I couldn't date me too."

He laughed. "You are pretty awesome, but I think I've found someone I click with even more." Staring over his shoulder, he followed Ashley's every move through the breakfast line.

I was glad Ashley took my advice and had taken a chance on him. And that their one bad night hadn't colored the possibility of them finding happiness together.

"I'm glad you did and got over yourself quickly enough to not screw things up with her."

A sharp breath escaped his lips. "Me too. And about the whole you two faking things..."

Alertness rocketed through me. My hand stilled at Cole's neck. Us faking it didn't even feel relevant anymore. We'd both come so far from where we began.

"Sorry for trying to insinuate you two weren't the real deal. I can see—hell, everyone can see—how into each other you both are."

"We are." I brushed Cole's hair at the side of his head and he scooted closer.

The table was alive again with everyone pouring back in and stacking pancakes, French toast, bacon, and sausages in front of us. Glasses of juice and water as well as pastries stacked one on top of the other.

Everyone laughed and ate, recapping everything we'd missed while just trying to keep upright.

I waved bacon under Cole's nose to finally drag him from sleep.

He ate with one hand and massaged my legs with the

other. In his lap, the bulge of his erection brushed against my calf.

Shocked, I stared at him. "Aren't you tired?"

"I am, but he's not. Don't worry. I need to regain the use of my legs before we can think about that, so you've got about forty-eight hours before I need to make good on everything your body was promising me after twelve hours of rubbing against me all night."

"Lucky me." In that moment, with throbbing feet, screaming muscles, and a weariness settled around my shoulders like a blanket, I meant every bit of it.

Cole felt like a dream I'd thought could only ever live in my head. A creation that could never measure up to what I'd hoped might be possible for me and, if he was, I never wanted to wake up.

32

COLE

Out on the field it was usually easy to block everything else out.

The ball in my hands. The grass beneath my cleats. The game.

But today was different. The past loomed over today, waiting to haul me back to old memories whether I wanted to go there or not.

I'd only regained the ability to walk without a limp after the dance-a-thon less than six hours ago, so a brutal practice might kill me.

"Why do they make us come?" Griff tossed a ball from hand to hand. We stood around the thirty-yard line waiting for the media blitz to be over inside the press room.

"Photo ops." Ezra stretched his neck.

"Are they bringing cameras out here?" Griff dropped the ball.

Reid scooped it up and shoved it into his stomach. "Camera shy?"

"No, just don't feel like smiling for the cameras today."

Reid raised his arm overhead and grabbed his elbow,

stretching his tricep. "Or any day. No endorsement deals for you then?"

Hollis jogged out toward us from the flow of coaching staff and media pouring out into the stands.

"Who'd want a picture of this on their razors or cologne?" Griff gestured to his face.

Hollis tilted his head and squinted, shielding his eyes from the sun. "You're not hideous."

I checked the stands. Kennedy walked in with Taylor, both in their STFU jerseys. "A ringing endorsement, if I've ever heard one."

My heart hummed at her wearing my number. The clouds that were seconds from blanketing the whole field in a fog I couldn't see through were split by her ray of sunshine.

Waving my arm overhead, I tried to get her attention.

She found me immediately and threw a kiss across the field. The over-the-top gestures...it was hard to know how all this would've gone if we hadn't struck our deal from the beginning.

Well, we'd have still been at each other's throats. So as much as I didn't like the layer of untruth plastered all over our relationship, I couldn't hate it, not if it meant I had her.

Plus, lies had always been part of my life. They were ingrained, probably cemented to my DNA.

My fingers tightened around the raised texture of the ball and I exhaled, trying to focus.

Mikelson marched onto the field, flanked by reporters with phones and microphones held out to him as he spewed garbage, which was what he did best.

Get through today and Signing Day tomorrow. I turned to join Hollis in our formation.

Reid picked up a ball from the mesh bag handed down

the line by one of the equipment handlers. "Looks like he's playing nice because the media are here."

Hollis cracked his knuckles, shaking his head. "Like they don't remember him getting ejected from two games last year and the fine for throwing a chair at that reporter after the Fulton U loss."

"Hauser." Coach waved me over.

My spine stiffened, each vertebra locking corkscrew tight. I pivoted to run back over to him. My feet almost slipped out from under me, not sure what to expect. Berating me in front of everyone else didn't seem to be the MO for today, which made it even harder to trust whatever he had planned.

"Everyone to your positions." Mikelson called out in the least yell-like version of raising his voice.

Each stride closer was tendon tight. Standing beside him, I braced myself.

"Our newest recruits have a lot to learn from the starting lineup that'll serve up a phenomenal final season." Mikelson folded his arms over his chest like that was the end of any doubts about how we'd play starting in September.

"You have confidence that you'll be able to deliver next year after three seasons of bowl game wins, but disappointing finishes for the national championship?" The new soon-to-be-barbecued reporter held up his phone to get a response.

The vein we knew all too well that accompanied his blowups pulsed in Mikelson's neck. Instead of taking the bait and ripping the reporter's head off, Mikelson laughed. Each attempt at a chuckle sounded like broken glass and splinters.

"We've worked through a lot the last few seasons and

have finally got a motivated group that'll push through the pain and weakness to clinch the win next season." He grabbed my shoulder in a vise grip, shaking me like I'd been the one to ask the question.

Everyone looked to me.

Mikelson's hold on my shoulder tightened and I cleared my throat. "Of course we'll perform next season. The win's always what we're going for and we don't want to let Coach down." The coil in my stomach tightened.

"I'm proud of this team and know they'll deliver." He looked at me and I almost thought he cared. "They're good kids."

A wave of shock nearly rocked me off my feet. The words raced in my mind until they whirred into a blur.

He'd looked at me when he said those words. Was this because he remembered what today was? His attempt at making me feel better? At taking my mind off this horrible day in my personal history—a shared history he'd denied, or making up for not being there?

A glimmer of optimism in what had been a marred, messy, muddied past that we'd never been able to escape.

The new recruits stared at me with hopeful eyes, like I was holding a championship trophy over my head.

"Get out there, Hauser. Show the potential rookies what they have to stack up to."

I jogged back onto the field still stunned and glanced over my shoulder, soaring even higher when my gaze landed on the stands.

Kennedy stood at the railing to the bleachers. Her face creased with concern.

I shrugged and waved for her to sit back down. Maybe last night Mikelson had been visited by the Ghost of Christmas Past although we were well into spring, but whatever it was, it was hard not to be thrown off by his attitude.

I took my place beside Hollis, who stared at me like I'd started tackling the line of coaching staff. "What happened there? I didn't hear any yelling or screaming."

"He...he complimented the team. Complimented me." The words felt like the cashmere sweater Kennedy had me try on. I'd expected an itchy monstrosity, but it hadn't been prickly and uncomfortable. Still, I overheated quickly and had to take it off. An unexpected fit that I'd hoped I could've tried on again. Maybe after a while I'd get used to it. If he let me.

We went through a few different drills. The sharp bursts of whistle signals directed at various squads kept us on our toes, but I still felt off balance after my sideline encounter with Mikelson. And the fact that he hadn't pushed anyone to the point of puking.

I'd gotten used to how things went between us, but this had been different, and I didn't know why. It felt like I was being set up. A taste of the thing I'd wished for. I prepared myself to have it snatched away.

Coach Henley walked up to me and cupped his hands to call to the sidelines. "Mason!"

The kid jogged forward looking like he'd been handed a golden ticket. He had been. Being invited to this weekend on campus was the biggest step toward the pros. Signing Day was tomorrow, when all the prospects got to sign their names in front of a jam-packed room full of journalists and cameras, hold up their jerseys, and stand in front of the cheering STFU crowds that would scream their name for the seasons to come.

"Hauser. You want to run some drills with our newest recruit, Silas Mason."

"Nice to meet you." I extended my hand. "Cole Hauser."

"I know who you are." He shook my hand like he was ready to yank it out of the socket. Up and down like he couldn't contain his excitement.

Laughing, I squeezed his hand to snap him back to the fact that I needed this arm.

"Sorry." He dry swallowed. "I didn't think I'd get to meet you this weekend." He and I were built similarly, although he was definitely a high schooler. Not scrawny by any means, but still at the initial stages of testosterone pumping to enhance the weight training.

"We're always scoping out the new recruits. Gotta see who's gunning for our spots."

His eyes widened and he whipped his head back and forth. "No, I'd never—"

"Don't worry about it, Silas. I'm just kidding." I tossed the ball to him.

He double arm caught it and slammed it against his chest.

"Don't hurt yourself. You weren't here during the fall recruiting trip."

"No, I wasn't. The offer to come here came through last minute and I jumped at it. My mom's been my biggest cheer-leader. She probably called the coaching staff at least twenty times a day until they gave in."

A lump lodged in my throat. "That's great she's so relent-less for you."

"She's the best. She'll be here for Signing Day. She might be more excited than I am." The kid's energy ticked up another notch, which I hadn't thought possible. It was good there were people in his corner.

"You seem pretty excited to me." My signing day had been a broken promise of what I'd thought was to come, alongside a reminder of what I'd lost. There wasn't anyone cheering for me in those stands. Not even my own father.

"For as long as I can remember, I've always wanted to play for this team." The kid bounced on his toes like a current ran through the field.

"Me too." A sour knot wrenched in my stomach. The reasons I'd wanted to play here had been misplaced and misguided, although Mikelson's sideline praise didn't tighten the tension as much as usual. No matter what, without deciding to come here, I wouldn't have the guys. I looked up at the stands where Kennedy had her head pushed together with Taylor.

I wouldn't have Kennedy.

"Enough of the introductions." Henley stepped in. "Why don't you two head over and do some drills? Show him some pointers, Hauser."

"Yes, Coach."

We spent the next hour aware that cameras, watchful eyes, and STFU's most die-hard fans who'd been up since pre-dawn hours to get in line were up in the stands watching us.

"Is it always this intense?" Silas gulped from his water bottle and cast a quick glance over his shoulder.

"Things aren't this crazy at your school?" I downed my water, happy to see he was a bit more winded than me. At least they wouldn't be looking to replace me immediately.

"They are, but there aren't nearly as many—" His gaze lingered on the field and he ducked his head closer to mine. "As many girls who care about football at my school."

I grinned. "There are a lot of diehard fans here of all kinds."

"Are—is it easier to talk to them when you're on the team?" Every bit of his eighteen-year-old insecurity came pouring out. I empathized with the overwhelming anxiety that came from so many changes at once. He wasn't dealing with all I had been, but it didn't make it any less terrifying.

I patted his shoulder. "It can be, but you still need to know what you're looking for or it's easy to let it all go to your head." Newly arrived on campus, more than a few guys let things get away from them and the wash-out reports from STFU Dirt had highlighted those that were cut before the first game.

"Is your girlfriend up there or hookup or whatever?" He shook his head like he was kicking himself for saying anything.

"My girlfriend's up there." I loved the way it rolled off my tongue. How natural it felt. I pointed to Taylor and Kennedy. "But she hates football. Hate is a strong word. She's not big into it, but she shows up to support me."

He nodded and looked at me like a guy with all the answers. If only. "That's cool."

Mikelson's sharp triple whistle called an end to the open day.

"Great workout, Silas."

"Thanks, Cole. It was...I can't believe I actually got to play with you."

I grabbed his hand and pulled him forward, tapping chests and thumping my other hand against his back. "Have fun tomorrow."

"Will you be there?"

"Yeah, the whole starting lineup will be there. Get some sleep tonight, so you're not dragging ass and hungover for all the interviews tomorrow."

"Nah, I wouldn't do that."

I shot him a knowing look.

The tips of his ears darkened. "Okay, maybe *now* I won't do that."

Laughing, I waved to him again. He joined the other players and jogged toward the locker rooms.

Kennedy stood at the first row of seats.

Taking a running start, I jumped up and grabbed onto the rail, hauling myself up.

"Don't you dare hurt yourself!" Taylor shouted from behind Kennedy, who grinned at me like I was the biggest goof in history.

"It'd be worth it." Beckoning her forward, she licked her lips and laughed. Balancing my stomach against the cold metal railing, I grabbed both sides of her face and kissed her.

The crowd *woo*ed and clapped. Someone was probably taking pictures of this or recording us, but I didn't care.

Her lips were soft, but fierce, meeting my yearning with equal desire. She tasted like sunshine and sweetness. Her fingers tugged at the center of my jersey as she breathed against my mouth. "You're lucky I like sweaty guys."

"You do?"

"Maybe just you."

"Better be." I kissed her again and hopped down.

The locker room had emptied by the time I got inside. In the silence, the storm of earlier today brewed on the horizon. After my shower, I tugged my shirt on and hustled outside to be near Kennedy. I needed more of her to help me ward it off.

Outside the doors, she stood with her back to me, talking on the phone. "How could they not love it? Accept the praise. You deserve it."

She kicked a bit of gravel. "Waiting for Cole." With a glance over her shoulder, she straightened and smiled.

"He's here." Her smile brightened. "I will. Love you too, Pickle." She ended the call and stuck her phone in her bag.

"Hannah says hi."

"Hi, Hannah." I draped my arm around her shoulder and tugged her close, kissing her temple and inhaling her.

Did she know how much I loved her smell? How it lingered on my sheets and pillows and I never wanted it to go away?

"You looked good out there."

I looked over at her loving how much she tried to pretend she had any idea what was happening out there for my sake.

Her shoulders inched up and red splotches appeared on her neck. "Fine, Taylor said you looked good today."

"Thanks for sticking through it."

"I like watching you out there, even if I don't understand most of what's happening. How was it today?"

"Good." I stood straighter and opened the car door for her.

"What about the talk with Mikelson? You didn't seem pissed when you walked away." She gripped the top of the door like she was prepared to rush back into the locker rooms and knock him out.

"He was...nice."

Her head tilted to the side and her gaze narrowed. "Nice?"

I nodded.

"Mikelson?"

"Do you think he got hit in the head with a football or something?"

"Maybe."

We went back to her place and fell over onto the couch watching TV. My head in her lap and her fingers brushing through my hair. Each nail scrape against my scalp shot shocks down my spine. I filled her in on everything that had happened on the field.

"That's adorable that you're so excited for another player." She fed me some popcorn.

"He does play my position."

"You're not worried about him taking your spot?"

I laughed. "Not yet. He needs to bulk up a little more and increase his snap speeds, but he's damn close." Now I could see a bit more why coaches liked watching someone grow. Maybe now that my spot felt more secure, never totally with Mikelson at the helm, but more than before, I didn't see the younger guys as threats. At least not yet. Watch Silas put on forty pounds of muscle in the off-season and maybe I'd be spending a shitload more time in the gym and running my drills even harder.

"Good thing you only have one season left, right?"

"Hell yeah. If I was a sophomore, I'd be in the gym and out on the practice field even longer than I am right now."

"Not possible."

My throat tightened in this perfect moment. Suddenly, I didn't want her to be here to ward off the clouds, I wanted her to stand in the rain with me. To be there, so I didn't feel so alone, and the storm didn't feel like it raged nearly as hard.

"Today's the day my mom died."

Her fingers stilled and her whole body tensed. Eyes overflowing with concern stared down at mine. "Why didn't you say something?"

I shrugged. "What's there to say?"

"I don't know. I would've..." She swung her legs from under her, putting her feet flat on the floor.

My fingers tightened around her hand. "There's nothing

you could do. There's nothing I wanted you to do. I just wanted you to know. And I wanted to be here with you."

Her body sagged and her hand cupped my cheek. "If that's what you need, then of course you have it. I love you, Cole." She bent, nuzzling her nose against mine and gently kissing my lips.

She was my whole world where I no longer felt alone.

33

COLE

Cameras were all pointed at the fourteen guys sitting and standing in their suits looking ready to come out of their skin.

I'd been there along with thirteen other recruits on my big day. Even with everything that had happened since I started at STFU, I couldn't help but smile at the unbounded feelings of hope and pride each one of them were overflowing with. I put myself back in that moment and how for a few hours, it felt like everything was going my way.

It had hit me hard in the moments after the cheering died down that my mom hadn't been there to see it, but the sadness had been contained knowing my father was there. That he'd seen it happen and I'd be playing for him.

What a joke that was. But while it all went down, none of that had touched me yet. The hope for the future was so bright it had been blinding.

Soaking up a taste—even for a few seconds—was hard to miss out on, especially with the new group. They were good kids, especially Silas. He wasn't cocky or a prima donna. Every instruction the coaching staff had given him, he committed it to memory and tried to execute on it as perfectly as he could the next time out.

The campus broadcast team beamed the whole thing to the big screens in the auditorium rumbling with screaming STFU students and recruits' families waiting for their chance to welcome the new STFU players and grab the first batch of jerseys.

They'd take the stage after signing their recruiting papers over there to autograph the first run of jerseys.

All the first-string players for next season were lined up along one wall right beside me. Almost every one of us, tugging at our ties and pulling at cuffs. Not me though, Kennedy had worked her magic and mine fit now. It felt good. Made me feel like a pro player who could afford a tailor to make sure I wasn't swimming in my suit.

Beside me, Ezra's collar and tie looked like they were trying to strangle him. But with a neck like that, there was no picking up shirts from the shelves of a store. "Next season will be our year."

"Our first and second string will be unstoppable."

Kennedy was to the side of the stage with her manager and the boxes of STFU jerseys for the players. She wore jeans and a black shirt with an eyelet overlay around the buttons and collar. To other people, that might be too nice to wear to work, since she was technically on the clock right now, but the lacy or other patterned shirts were so the nametag didn't poke holes in one of her good shirts as she called them, which even referred to polos and T-shirts.

All eyes and cameras were on the stage and the new recruits, but mine were on her and thinking about a repeat of last night once I got her home.

"What do you think of our newest center? Will he take over for you after next year?"

From the table, Silas nodded in my direction.

I nodded back. "If he avoids injury. He's good kid. He'll put in the work and probably be better than me."

The 7-on-7 recruits were the freshmen who could have a real impact on the team from day one; good thing I only had one season left or Silas would be gunning for my spot.

"High praise."

"He deserves it. I see a lot of the same drive I have. Maybe even more."

Ezra nodded and went back to tugging at his tie knot.

Kennedy crept down the line of players until she got to me. "We have a little problem." Her eyes were panic-wide. "We only have orders for thirteen jerseys." She glanced over her shoulder to the table where the fourteen players were smiling and talking to each other, while we waited for Mikelson to arrive.

"What? There should be fourteen." I walked with her toward the coaching staff who was here already and headed for Coach Henley.

"That's what we thought. But we triple checked the order form and they only requested thirteen hundred jerseys. A hundred of each of the thirteen." She clutched the order form in her hand and held it up to me.

I scanned the names. Silas's was missing.

Bile heaved in my stomach and saliva flooded my mouth. I rushed over to Henley.

"Coach, we have a problem."

"What's up, Cole?" His attention snapped to us.

Kennedy explained it all and he grabbed his phone.

Just as he raised it to his ear, the door to the left of the stage opened and Mikelson walked in.

The press kicked up a notch, calling out his name.

Henley strode over to him and the two of us followed.

His head bowed and he spoke to Mikelson who cut him off and marched past. The rubber band was stretched, confusion and the simmer of anger tightening between my ribs.

Stepping in front of him, I held up my hand not letting him pass.

"There are only thirteen jerseys." I shook the paper in front of his face, hoping, praying he wasn't pulling some shit right now.

"I know." He tried to walk past me and I grabbed his arm. The rubber band was almost to the failing point. The anger cranked higher to fury with pops of rage like splattering oil in a heated pan.

My heartbeat throbbed in the back of my throat like it was trying to choke me. "Don't do whatever sick shit you're trying to do." I hated the pleading edge in my voice. My eyes bored into his, unable to believe that there was a shred of decency left in him. My mother's voice reverberated in my ears, rattling my heart. "All he wants to do is play for this team."

"Too bad he's not good enough." Spittle dropped onto the deep, dry grooves of his lips.

My stomach twisted. "How the hell can you say that? I've seen him out there. Everyone has. He's one of the top recruits in the country. The signing deadlines for all the other schools have passed."

"What you see and what I see is why I'm the coach, and he's not good enough." He tried to yank his arm back, but I held on to it, tightening my grip. My fingers tingled and the side of my neck throbbed.

Flashes went off in my periphery, the spots lingering in my gaze. Kennedy stepped forward, entering the corner of my vision.

"He's here. You invited him." My barbed words didn't

seem to faze him. Not a flinch, not an eyelash batted. Like nothing could touch him. The fury was nearly blinding.

"His mother's doing. Shouldn't have said yes, but who knows what the kid would've done if I hadn't. Maybe something crazy like you."

His mother. What did this kid's mother... The elastic snapped.

"He's one of the top fifty draft picks in his rising class." Why would he invite this kid here only to humiliate him? Silence engulfed me. No pulse. No breath. No thoughts.

"I don't want top fifty. I want number ones."

He plowed ahead like my silence was an invitation for more acid poured straight down my throat. My brain short-circuited. The neurons attempting to fire, but misconnecting like they were trying to protect me.

"Maybe one of these days, I'll have a kid who won't be a waste of talent." He patted my shoulder like he was imparting a piece of sage advice.

The shield broke and the wave hit me. This time it swept my feet out from under me. I swayed, gripping the wall to keep myself upright.

He was his. Silas was Mikelson's kid.

Cleat spikes ripped through my chest. His kid. Another kid. Another one out there with another mother hoping for his return.

Silas was me. The desperate need for recognition. His drive. His hope.

An ugly reminder of everything I thought possible and the charred remains of my last familial relationship standing in front me sneering.

Over his shoulder, Silas looked at the two of us with shocked concern. And for a second he was me. I was him. His leg bounced up and down, nervous energy making it hard to sit still. His heart raced like he'd just gotten off running sprints and he stared at Mikelson hoping against hope that he'd finally measure up in his eyes.

"Cole, not here." Kennedy's voice was like a bottle of water trying to douse a volcano. But the rage built, fed by years of neglect and mistreatment. There was no cooling this, there was no false alarm, there was only the explosion I'd been trying to rein in since the day I found out the real reason he'd accepted me here. Not because I was his son. Not out of a promise to my mother. For nothing other than protecting his reputation.

"Leave, Kennedy."

"Cole—"

He was me. All those same feelings had felt like bees buzzing in my head with my fingers clenched to cover the shaking. Bile raced to the back of my throat, singeing my tongue with its acrid bitterness. Flashes went off from phones and cameras alike. The students and press stood ready to cover the newest recruits to one of the best DI schools in the country. They'd all be there to witness his embarrassment. His destruction.

The flashes intensified. The attention was no longer on the kids at the table. Good.

Mikelson tried to shrug me off, but I wouldn't let up. I couldn't break the grip I had on him, even if I'd wanted to. My blood pounded so hard in my veins it felt like it was trying to pulverize me from the inside out.

"Stop—" Her words felt like sizzling moisture evaporating the second they touched my ear drums.

"I said leave." I didn't want her to see this. She'd been trying to push me to this point. To have a conversation with him, well here it was.

"Nothing I ever did was going to be good enough for

you, was it?" I let go, but got right in his face. Blood hammered against my skull, drowning everything else out.

His punch-worthy smirk was another blow. "Nothing you ever did *was* good enough. You don't have it in you." He jammed his finger into the center of my chest.

A roar inside my head was so loud my ears rang. But a hand at my back pierced through the rage veil before it slammed shut.

"She loved you. She loved you more than anything. She loved you more than me." My voice cracked through the fury building behind my eyes so keenly, I could barely see.

His gaze swept up and down me. "How could she not?"

I grabbed his shirt, jerking it up by his ears. "You're a bastard. You didn't give a shit about her. How many others were there? How many other kids you're going to jerk around and destroy?"

Hands were on me now, not the gentle ones from before, but heavy arms, tugging at me. Griff's fingers gripping me tight.

"Cole—" Her voice could normally bring me back, but this was so much bigger than anything I could hope to hold my sanity through.

"Do you know what I did for you? For the fucking hope of finally seeing what she saw in you?"

Now my spittle was flying.

"I pretended to have a girlfriend just to have a chance at some kind of connection with you—any kind. I went after the last person in the freaking world who I even wanted to be around and faked it—lied to everyone I care about, to everyone for the shot at a fucking trip I thought you might like, so I could find out who you really were. Turns out I knew all along." Flames felt like they were being stoked behind my eyes. I wanted to rip him apart. I wanted to smash his face in.

An arm tightened around my neck, the bone pressing into my throat, but I refused to let go.

He looked at me like I was pathetic.

Maybe I was.

"All I wanted was a chance." My blood was like acid in my veins, burning up any hope I'd had left.

"Cole—" This was what she wanted. I hope it was as perfect as she imagined.

"No!" I screamed and shook off the hold on me, staring her in the eyes. "No, get the fuck away from me! How many times do I have to say it? I don't want or need your goddamn help!" I screamed so loudly my throat stung.

Her gasp and stumble barely registered before I shot back to Mikelson.

"All I ever wanted to do was have you treat me like someone you loved, hell, I'd have even taken someone you liked, but now I see I was just as delusional as she was. You're a poison to everyone around you. All you care about is yourself and winning." My body shook, teeth-chattering tremors rocked me.

"You try to pretend you're not the same," Mikelson sneered and threw in a mocking laugh to spray more lighter fluid on the flames of my fury. "You could've cashed in your chips for your little friend at the end of the season, but you kept your ace in the hole for yourself. For what you wanted to win and left him out to dry. Sure, it was nice the whole team got behind him, but if they hadn't, would you have given it up?"

"It's not the same."

"I never made promises to your mother."

My vision tunneled, clouding out everything other than

his face. The one that had been much younger back then. "You said you'd be back."

"Of course, she was a good lay—"

Red, boiling rage ripped me from my locked-in position to diving for him. My fist connected.

His head whipped to the side and I went for another hit. But my arm wouldn't move. Spinning, Kennedy held on to me, stopping me from destroying this fucker who'd talked about my mother like she was nothing,

"Cole, don't. It's not you." Kennedy's voice was like icicles to my molten brain, stabbing and sharp, nowhere near enough to smother the live-wire sparks shooting through me.

Lies. It was all lies. My whole life was a lie. The people who were supposed to love me had fucked me over. Did I even deserve love? If my parents couldn't do it, how could anyone else? "How the hell would you know? I told you to leave." My voice boomed. "You don't know a single fucking thing about me. What? Because we were pretending to be together. Because we've fucked a few times. You don't know a single thing about me. It's over. The joke is played out. Now leave."

Her fingers fell away from my arm like they were lead bricks. She stared at me wide-eyed with tears brimming in them and it was a slice to the Achilles of the raging bull inside my chest. Turning, she fled, shoving her way past the legions of press and team members in the room.

Mikelson's slow clap cranked the lava burning in my brain back up to eruption levels. "And there you fucking go."

I turned to him and lurched forward, driving one fist into my open palm to keep them away from his face. "You don't know a single thing about me."

"Neither does she and she was fucking you. Good thing

that's not a prerequisite for learning about you. But I can see all I needed to see. The fact that you want my approval tells me you'll never get it. You don't deserve it. You're the same kind of needy your mother was. Get over it, Cole. I'm never going to be that guy. I've never even pretended to be that guy and maybe you aren't either. Maybe we've got a hell of a lot more in common than you think."

I jerked like he'd punched me.

Hands tightened on my arms, the guys still holding me back. "I could never be like you!" I spat back.

"Didn't come through for a friend you say is as close as a brother. Burned your little girlfriend. Seems to me you know exactly what I know. No one's going to look out for you other than you."

A voice on the mic filled the room.

Mikelson and I both turned. Coach Henley was at one of the mics between two recruits, who stared at the two of us on the far side of the room. "We'll be canceling the signing portion of the event for today. Sorry for the interruption. Everyone can now head to the auditorium."

Everyone stared.

Ezra.

Hollis.

Griff.

Reid.

Silas. He'd heard everything Mikelson had said. He knew.

Everyone knew.

The eyes that had stared back at me crushed. What hurt more were the eyes not on me. Kennedy.

A barb drilled deeper into my chest. Horror washed over me at everything said. Heated by my rage, I'd finally erupted, unleashing all the secrets I'd been holding in.

Everyone I'd cared about had been in the path of the incineration.

The room emptied.

So did my soul, like every bit of me was being siphoned off. Drained. Destroyed.

The guys looking back at me like they were seeing me with new eyes as they were corralled out by the rest of the coaching staff. Silas stared at me. I'd just blown that kid's life apart.

Double doors swung shut behind them and we were left in the eardrum-splitting silence.

"Now, if you try to pull a stunt with those playbooks it'll be the disgruntled word of a player against mine."

I whipped around and stared at him, bile racing for my throat at the blindness and belief that there was a shred of decency in him.

He wiped away a smear of blood from his lip with the back of his hand.

At my side, I clenched and unclenched my fists, shaking with a fury begging to be unleashed. "One day soon, you'll realize how many people you've hurt. How many lives you've destroyed, and for what? Another trophy? A fucking parade?"

"Don't hate me for having my eye on the prize."

"I don't. I hate you for shitting on everyone along the way and leaving nothing but a wake of destruction. The world will be a better place once you're gone." My chest felt like it was caving in. The image I'd built up in my mind of possibility cracked. Splintered. Shattered.

Leaving him behind, I ducked through the locker room. Each breath was laced with broken glass and hot embers. Every muscle quaking so badly it was almost impossible to stay standing. Outside, the no longer crisp air felt like flames shoved down my throat.

My forehead dropped against the brick and I released everything I'd been holding in, screaming so loudly I expected the concrete to split beneath my feet. I pounded my fists against the wall and grasped at what I had left. Empty air.

I tried to breathe and didn't bother blinking back the tears. In the distance, the fanfare from Signing Day broke through the thundering in my ears. And I was here feeling like I'd been hollowed out after holding in everything for so long. All the secrets. All the lies. All alone.

A husk.

34

KENNEDY

I'd never been punched, but I couldn't imagine it hurting more than wind leaving my body and my chest feeling like it would cave in. Tears stung my cheeks. Even in late March with how fast I was walking, the tears burned against my skin, leaving a salty trail.

The scene replayed every time I closed my eyes.

I dropped to my haunches and clapped my hands over my ears.

A few people walked past, but no one stopped. I could feel their eyes on me. Did they recognize me? I could feel their scrutiny. Ridicule. Pity.

I sucked deep, shuddering breaths into my lungs, my head above the crashing waves trying to drag me under. Sweeping me down into the depths of the churning sea of pain to never let me resurface.

In front of everyone, he'd broadcast just how little I meant to him.

My whole body trembled, buzzing with the drive to escape. To run, to hide, to disappear. A buzzing filled my ears and prickled my skin, nothing like it had when Cole had touched me. Instead, it felt like I was being hooked up to an electric charge. Tested to be broken.

"Kennedy!"

Ezra pulled up beside me.

I brushed at my face, wincing at the burn on my skin and kept walking.

"Kennedy."

My lead-heavy feet lightened to escape another witness to my humiliation.

Cole's relationship with his father was toxic, poisonous, ruinous, but I couldn't let myself get swallowed up by it. I couldn't fall into the trap my parents had, the one they let destroy the two of them as they tried to take Hannah and I down with them.

"Kennedy, let me give you a ride." He rolled along the curb, following at a pace that kept his window level with me.

Sniffling and puffy faced, I raised my head and marched toward the shuttle stop. That would be a wonderful ride as the sobbing girl who'd just been broken up with by her pretend boyfriend at the most well-covered event at STFU.

"I know you can hear me."

"So what, Ezra? I can hear you, but I don't want to. I just want you to leave me alone." It was the closest I'd come to a scream, my voice cracked.

I charged forward, not wanting to stop moving. If I stopped moving everything might come crashing down on me and I'd be rooted where I fell.

Ezra's car jumped the curb and blocked my path, tearing up the grass and coming within inches of the building to my right.

I yelped and jumped back, smashing my hands onto the hood. "What are you doing?"

He flung his door open and marched around the back of his car.

"Are you crazy? You could've killed me and wrecked your car!"

"It's just a thing." He stood in front of me without the hat that was usually welded to his head except when he was in uniform.

"Just go, Ezra." Anger burned hotter, singeing my skin.

He was the enemy. He was on Cole's side.

His head tilted. His eyes, which were usually hidden, glistened with unshed tears. "Kennedy." Staring at me with eyes so soft like he felt every ounce of my pain, reflecting, amplifying, wrecking me. He stepped closer and my nostrils flared, burning, but feeling like I'd been plunged headfirst into crashing waves all at the same time.

"Just go." My voice shook. I clung to the edge of my emotions, trying to keep the tattered edges together.

He opened his arms wide.

That broke me. As much as I thought I'd fallen apart, it didn't compare to the splintering when I fell into his arms.

He engulfed me, patting my back. "I'm sorry." The repeated phrase continued to undo me until I was a snotting, tearing mess.

As comforting as his arms were, I didn't want Ezra holding me. I wanted Cole. I wanted Cole to not have done this. I wanted this horrible day to be a nightmare.

My sobs slowed to hiccupping sniffles and the flood of embarrassment hit me in a new heated wave. The evidence of my breakdown was smeared all over his shirt.

I jerked back, attempting to wipe it away.

"Let's get you home." He let go, but kept one arm around my shoulder, guiding me to his car. "What happened was fucked up." The clunky *thunk* of his passenger side door opening jarred me out of the haze of numbness I'd been trying to wrap myself in.

"Why are you being so nice to me?" I peered up at him.

"You mean a lot to Cole." It was so strange to be able to look him in the eye. Full on, no shadow hiding his eyes, and that's when it hit me.

His eyes must've always been like this. Perfect reflections of what others were feeling. So easily able to slice through the fronts we put up. It had to be a hazard. Who wanted their cover blown with a single look?

"After today, I don't know if I want that to be true." The heat of the humiliation felt like a newly blistering sunburn.

His nod was grim, his eyes shuttered, his body rigid.

I got into the car and let him drive me back toward my apartment. Hiding out there for the next, say, eighteen months seemed like a solid plan. I wanted a dark hoodie, baggy sweatpants and an invisibility cloak. There was no outfit to fix this. There weren't enough bright colors in the world to keep me from wanting to be swallowed up.

Maybe the anger would hit later, but right now the twin beats of mortification and desolation ravaged my heart.

My throat tightened. Each breath a little shallower, a little quicker, a little harder.

Ezra's hand squeezed mine, zapping me out of the cloud I'd been drifting into. "It'll be okay."

With one hand on the wheel and one eye on me, he navigated the Signing Day crowds swarming campus. They thinned closer to my building and he let go, like he was no longer afraid I'd jump from the moving car. He pulled up in front of the entrance.

I halfway expected him to mount the curb again.

"Get some rest, Kennedy."

I reached for the door handle before turning back to him. "Why did you do this for me?"

Those piercing eyes swung back to mine. "If I fucked up as big as Cole did today, I'd want someone to make sure my girl was okay."

"I'm not—"

"That's for you two to figure out when things aren't so raw, but until I've heard otherwise, you're one of us, Kennedy. So, sorry, you're going to have to deal with us getting a little protective." His almost-smile was dredged in sadness.

I cleared my throat. "Thanks, Ezra. And whatever happens between Cole and I, I'll always think of you as a friend."

The flood of his words washed over me again. Not least of all the secret Cole had been hiding for years from his best friends. "Try not to be too hard on him about the whole thing about his dad."

Ezra darted a half glance my way and his hands tightened on the wheel.

"He didn't know how to tell you guys."

"He could've."

"I know."

"You say it's over, but you're still trying to look after him," he said with a dry tease.

Stunned, tears welled in my eyes and I sniffled. "It's not about still wanting him. It's about being afraid that I still want him. I can't still want him after today."

"Gonna have to remind your heart about that."

"Don't worry, I will." I popped the latch on the door and the creak reverberated through my arm. "Thanks for the ride."

"Don't mention it."

I walked to the building.

All eyes were on me. Whispered gossip, sidelong glances, barely contained laughter.

I wrapped my arms tighter around myself and ducked my head lower.

Ezra didn't pull away until I got inside.

The rattling elevator bumped its way up to my floor.

Melody was at her boyfriend's this weekend. The apartment would be empty. Cold. Empty. Alone.

Sniffling, I stepped out of the elevator doors hoping my puffy eyes didn't give me away to anyone in the hallway.

No one was there and the deflation hit me with pinprick quickness. Curling turtle mode was seconds from being activated.

I opened the door and yelped.

I wasn't alone.

Melody walked forward with a pint of peanut butter brownie caramel swirl ice cream.

Leona held a half-empty plastic container of smiley cookies.

Ashley shook out my robe, ready for me to step into it.

Taylor tapped a bottle of my favorite nail polish against her palm.

My lips quivered and the burning set in between my nose and eyes, clouding my gaze with tears all over again.

Their arms enveloped me and guided me over to the couch. Noises of reassurance dragged even harsher sobs from my chest. Everyone was being so kind—too kind. It was the sharp reminder of why I felt like this. Why it felt like my insides had been scraped raw.

A box of tissues was set in my lap.

My fingers were wrapped around a cold spoon.

Comfy, flurry blankets were set on top of me.

All the fussing, and everyone settled down into their roles, taking care of me.

As much as I wanted to tell them I didn't need them, that I was fine and it was no big deal, I clung to Melody's arm and didn't mind Leona being wedged in beside me.

We were a renaissance painting of despair and sisterhood. "I love you guys."

"We love you too."

No one said anything. Taylor worked on my nails, like a French pedicure was all I needed to get back on the horse tomorrow and walk through campus not feeling like a fool. But worse than the embarrassment was mourning the trust I thought I could put in Cole.

My shoulders curved, caving my chest in deeper. Leona leaned her head against mine and rubbed my back.

"It'll be okay. I know it doesn't feel like it. And it's like a chestburster is trying to ram its way out of your body, but I swear, it'll be better."

"That's what I'm afraid of." For years, I'd promised myself after hearing the quote that if I was ever with someone and they showed me who they truly were that I'd believe them. No matter what happened, I needed to be strong. I couldn't fall into the well-worn grooves dug in my head by the adults I'd looked to in my life.

Melody brushed my hair back from my face and tucked it behind my ear, holding out a tissue taken from the almost empty box on my lap. "Do you want more ice cream?"

I shook my head and winced. "The sugar, plus the crying, plus the cold. My head's pounding. All I want to do is get some sleep."

They let me disentangle myself from our pile. "Thank you for being here." My throat squeezed tight. "It means a lot to know I'm not alone." I attempted a smile, but it felt tissue-paper thin. "But I need to sleep for a while."

Taylor got up, fixing her satin black-and-white polka dot pajama set. "We're staying the weekend, so don't worry about it. Crashing on the couch and the floor is no biggie."

"You don't have to." My eyes felt seconds from swelling shut.

"We know." She slipped me a cold eye mask and rubbed my shoulder.

The sniffles attempted a sneak attack. I nodded, not trusting I wouldn't burst into sobs if I tried to speak.

In my bedroom, I crawled into the bed that still smelled like Cole. I buried my face in the softness and inhaled, muffling my tears. I'd give myself tonight to fall apart. Maybe tomorrow.

I dragged the cool eye mask Taylor had handed to me with black and white elephants on it over my eyes and tried to drift off to sleep.

Sitting up, I pushed it onto my forehead. My hand shot out for the pillow, the one that carried his scent. I let myself have one more inhale, then shook the pillow out of the case and tossed it across the room. I'd have to be strong enough not to look back, not to let him in. No matter how much it felt like a piece of my soul had been shattered.

35

COLE

Every ounce of anger I'd directed at Mikelson had faded and I was left with the biting desolation. Kennedy's look of shock and hurt pierced the base of my skull. I flinched, wanting to hide from it, but slamming my eyes shut only brought her eyes into clearer focus. Cutting clarity.

Mikelson had another kid. Two other people he'd poisoned and ruined. Another set of dreams he'd tried to steal. Had stolen? I still didn't know what would happen to Silas. What would happen to me.

I'd screamed at the top of my lungs that Mikelson was my father. The father who didn't want me. I'd punched my coach in front of witnesses. I'd turned on Kennedy like a feral creature. The fuckups mounted, stacked so high they were bound to crush me.

Counting them was hard with how messy the pile had gotten over the years.

The house was lit up, but completely silent. Across campus illegal fireworks were being set off. People cheered and yelled, but no one stopped at our house. The few people who saw me on the sidewalk snapped their mouths shut and skirted around me like I might explode any second.

News of what happened at Signing Day had spread far and wide. Glances were made between me and their phones. It was probably splashed all over STFU Dirt. The news of my paternity and the loss of the competition.

I'd let Kennedy down. That hurt more. I'd more than let her down. I'd left her shattered.

She'd asked me to make one promise, and when she'd been trying to save me from myself, trying to keep me from toppling over the razor's edge, I'd sacrificed her to it instead.

I dropped my head, shame saddled around my neck and sagged my whole body.

My bloody knuckles ached and scraped against the inside of my pockets. My pulse pounded in my clenched fist. My eyes burned with unshed tears. I didn't deserve to cry.

I don't know how long I stood out there, but long enough that the front door opened and Ezra jerked his head calling me forward.

They hadn't tossed my stuff out. It could still be piled up inside the front door.

I climbed the steps. Alone. More alone than I'd ever felt before. This was worse than walking into Coach's office week after week, month after month. It was worse than standing graveside after my mom had been lowered. Before, I had at least the glimmer of hope for the future. Now I had nothing.

I cared about these guys. They were my family. Not a blood tie that felt like it should mean something, they'd proven to me time and time again how much they cared about me.

And I'd dragged them all into a punishment they'd never agreed to.

Because of my selfishness.

Because of my fear.

Ezra closed the door behind me and the guys were sprinkled around.

Reid sat on the stairs.

Hollis sat in a kitchen chair he'd dragged out to the open space in the living room. He rocked back with two legs off the floor and his hands braced behind his head.

Griff stood in front of the kitchen doorway, lit ominously with the coin he only brought out when he was really agitated, rolling it back and forth along the backs of his fingers.

Their gazes were leveled at me, bored into me.

I scrubbed hands over my face feeling like it had been rubbed raw already. "I lied to you all."

Blood pounded in my veins like it was trying to escape my body.

My head dropped. My shoulders felt like fifty-pound dumbbells pressed down on me. I cleared my throat, trying to make a sound. With more force, I shoved enough air behind my words. "Coach is my father. He's not my dad. I have half his DNA, but he's never been anything more to me than an absentee father at best, and holding out hope for any of that to change was stupid. I put you guys through hell for a pipe dream. I lied to you for the last three years, not just about Coach, but also about Kennedy, so I'm sorry."

Pin-drop silence rang out. Blood whooshed in my ears, amplifying each skip in my heartbeat. The stillness made me jumpy, ready to come out of my skin.

Their scrutiny sent my stomach plunging.

I kept my head down and stared at my scuffed sneakers.

My throat felt like I'd gargled with sand. "It'll take me a while to find another place to live. If you can give me until the end of the week, I'd appreciate that." Would I even be able to stay on campus? My scholarship was most likely up in smoke, like my football career.

Griff's feet appeared in the periphery of my downward gaze. "Why would we want to do that?"

My stomach churned with an acrid burning. It's what I'd known would happen. The loneliness closed in on all sides. "I can sleep in my car, if you don't want to give me that long."

Reid stood and leaned against the railing. "What he meant was why would we want to give you time to move out when you live here?"

My head shot up, heart drumming against the back of my throat.

Ezra patted my shoulder like I had done to him when we talked about his mystery girl. "You're not moving out."

"What? Why not?" I blinked hard to make sure I wasn't losing it.

Griff pocketed his coin. "Why do you want us to force you out?"

"Why would you want me to stay?"

Hollis's chair thumped to the floor. "Because you're our friend. And our teammate."

"Who lied to you."

Ezra propped one foot against the wall. "You had your reasons."

The buzzing is back. Where it felt like a swarm of bees had taken up residence in my skull.

"And you're just fine with that? You don't need an explanation? You don't want to know why I didn't bring this up at any point before today? Why I couldn't help stop the brutal workouts or practices? Or why I didn't use my connection to help Reid?" I flicked my gaze in his direction. Guilt gnawed at my stomach. The serrated teeth sliced through my flesh.

Ezra rubbed the brim of his hat. "Could you have?"

I nodded.

"Without hurting you?" Even under his shadowed gaze, I could feel the probing.

"That doesn't—"

Griff huffed. "Of course it matters. Was there anything you could've done that wouldn't have jeopardized your spot on the team or blew up whatever you'd been working on with Coach—your dad?" The word sounded choked out.

I flinched. "It should've mattered to me. I should've given him what he wanted to save you all."

The foghorn silence confirmed exactly what I'd known from the minute he demanded the playbooks—if they knew who I was to him, I'd be frozen out.

Ezra tugged his hat off and marched over to me.

I tensed, waiting for the onslaught.

Furious, he glowered at me. "Who was going to save *you*?"

My mental stumble tripped up my body and I lurched back. "What? We're not—"

"The hell we are." Reid jumped down from the stairs. "You had a good reason. I sure as hell know if Mikelson was my dad, sperm donor, whatever, I wouldn't be on the loud-speaker about it."

"But at the end of the season, when you got benched—"

"I made my choice. Leona and I made that choice. And I never expected any of you guys to do what you did for me. I was willing to take my lumps."

"I made you guys take them for me. He told me what he'd do. He told me he'd take it out on you, if I didn't give him what he wanted." I couldn't meet their gazes, not with the hate they had to be feeling for me right now. I'd hate me.

Griff folded his arms over his chest. "What? You don't think we can take it? You don't think what we've been through hasn't made us stronger?"

"That's not the point. I could've saved you guys from that." I whipped around, looking to each of them, trying to win them over to my side of how much of an asshole I'd been. Them being understanding almost made it harder. It made it feel like I didn't deserve them as my friends. That I deserved to be cast out and alone again.

Hollis dropped his hand onto my shoulder, right by my neck. "If what we went through is what we needed to go through to keep you on the team, then it is what it is." He shrugged like it was an extra lap after each practice.

"You guys have seen how he is."

Reid stepped in front of me. "Which is why we're not blaming you, man. Why do you want us to? Why do you want us to turn our backs on you and kick you out?"

I'd been waiting for the deep freeze of loneliness for so long. Bracing myself for being alone all over again.

The hours where my mom would drift off into her fantasies about a life that wasn't ours.

The nights I couldn't sleep from shivering so hard in my fort in the woods when I was supposed to have been picked up by him.

The months after my mom was gone and there was only me. "Because that's how it's always been."

Ezra braced both hands on top of my shoulders. "You think it'll be that easy to get rid of us?"

"I—" The words deadlocked in my throat, evaporated by hope.

Griff jostled Reid. "Is it time for the group hug yet? Let's stop stalling."

They all enveloped me, squeezing me so tightly I could barely breathe.

"I'm sorry." It came out as a ragged sob. My whole body shook, held up by the guys. My teammates. My friends. My brothers.

Their hold loosened once I got control of myself.

Using the hem of my shirt, I wiped at my face, which felt hot and barbed. The guys nodded and gave me some time to myself. I let it all settle in. They hadn't abandoned me. They didn't hate me.

Griff and Hollis started on dinner, chucking pieces of chicken breast into the oven.

One relationship mended, but another was still shattered. On the couch, I held my head in my hands. Kennedy...there were no words. In front of everyone, I'd broadcast that the only reason we'd gotten together was for the competition and shouted at her with anger behind it. Not just anger, rage.

Reid tapped my shoulder with a cold bottle of water before handing it over.

I gulped from it before rolling the cold plastic over my forehead.

Ezra sat beside me on the couch. "I drove Kennedy home."

A shard of relief was tugged out of my impaled heart. My swallow was louder than the blood thrumming in my ears. "How was she?"

He didn't say a word, just leveled his gaze at me.

"That bad."

"It wasn't pretty."

I dragged my fingers through my hair and shot up, no longer able to sit still. "She hates me."

Reid lifted his hands palm up. "Maybe—"

"It wasn't a question. I promised her I'd never yell at her like that. She—she's dealt with people losing their shit at each other and it was the one thing she made me promise after giving me a second chance."

"We all make mistakes. Look at me and Leona."

"That was different."

"How? We found a way through it. It wasn't easy." He braced his hand on my shoulder and stared into my eyes. "Do you love her?"

My chest tightened. The loss of it all slammed into me even harder than before. I squeezed my eyes shut, trying to get the hurt reflected in her eyes out of my mind. I'd done that to her. "With everything I've got. I've never loved anyone like I love her."

"Then you've got to try."

"Try what? She's got no reason to even hear me out, let alone give me a third chance." The pit in my stomach split back open into a yawning void. "I—I don't know if she'll want to see me. I don't know if I deserve it."

Reid gripped the back of my neck and stared, his eyes blazing with intensity. "I fucked up with Leona and you guys were there for me. You have to try or you'll always wonder, and if she loves you like you love her, then she'll wonder too. Don't let being afraid get in the way of proving that she's your forever."

The plunging feeling stopped, beat back by renewed determination. "You're right. And I think I know exactly what I need to do." Apprehension tightened my chest making it hard to breathe, but for Kennedy I'd do whatever I needed to do to prove to her I'd go to the ends of the earth to fix this and never make the same mistake again.

I looked around at the guys who'd been there for me when I hadn't even felt worthy of their backup.

"I'll need your help."

36

KENNEDY

My hours dragged. My shift crawled. My soul grieved.

From the moment Cole blew up our no-longer-fake relationship, everything slowed to the point I might as well have been watching the world go by from underwater. That had been days ago. A week ago?

The hours, days, and weeks ran together. I went to class, went to work, pulled myself together to style a few people, but the pity in their eyes stung. The disappointment of losing the contest barely registered over the swallowing sorrow since I'd last seen Cole.

I'd kept my head high walking across campus although all I wanted to do was curl up and cry. But I pulled out my new boots and spent an hour perfecting my armor before I left the apartment every day.

A few minutes ago, Taylor had run off to class after spending half my shift flipping through some T-shirts she wouldn't even sleep in, careful not to disturb the folding and stacking. Since the day I'd come home from Signing Day one of them had come to loiter by me under the guise of just hanging around or happening to be in the same place.

But it was about them not wanting me to have to weather the storm solo, and if I didn't love them already, I'd be professing my love from every balcony in the vicinity. Kind of like I'd been doing with Cole. The jagged lump in my throat stalled my breathing.

He hadn't contacted me. Not a call or a text.

After nearly a month of sweetness and spectacle, it had been easy to pretend it was how life would really be. Not even the fake love we were blasting all over campus, but the real one we'd stumbled into.

Even if we were still together, every few days wasn't going to be obnoxious gestures and ridiculous professions of love to everyone nearby.

The clank of metal in the large area that opened to the food court and coffee shop drew attention from the prospective student tour rolling through the bookstore. No stupid campus pranks or other disturbances.

I gently guided one family toward a display. I really needed them to pick up the end of the season sports T-shirts and swag, so I didn't have to inventory it all and mark it down for clearance. Although being cloistered in the back room for a week didn't sound like the worst thing right now.

More heads turned to locate the source of the heavy clunking and jangling.

Noise and commotion got closer. A couple of my coworkers rushed out to see what was headed our way.

Please not another mob of streakers like we'd had to deal with during Prank War a couple years ago.

Gretchen stood beside me, staring out at the still empty back entrance to the store. "Does anyone else hear hooves?"

Nothing looked out of place. The coffee shop. Large

windows with study tables in front of them, although the people stationed there with their textbooks and laptops turned to get a look as well.

Then the crowd emerged, walking backward with their phones up. Flashes, live streaming, rushing from all directions.

In the center of the mob, a shiny body was raised up high above everyone's heads. The person on top looked stiff, although it was probably hard to look relaxed in a full suit of armor. Who the hell even owned a full set of armor?

"Is that a knight?" Gretchen turned to me like I knew any more than she did.

A person walked beside the horse and held on to the reins of the horse marching it in our direction.

"Is that the Fulton U mascot?" Another person called from behind the register.

Was this some kind of prank having to do with the ongoing campus rivalries?

The rider ducked under the second set of open double doors, which were tall enough for even the basketball players to walk through, but the knight had to bend forward, leaning against the horse's neck. On top of his head, there was a yellow-and-navy tuft sticking straight into the air. Weren't those Fulton U colors?

Using his metal-glove-covered hand, the knight pushed up the face shield.

I gasped and stepped forward. "Cole?"

The horse shook its head, tugging against the reins and neighing.

A look of intense fear washed over Cole's face under the knight's helmet. He froze, looking more like a knight statue than a guy wearing a costume.

The horse handler made noises of reassurance and brushed their hand along the horse's neck.

With some fumbling, Cole swung one leg over the back of the horse and got down sounding like a bunch of empty cans tossed into a dryer.

A flow of people followed behind him and encircled us.

"What are you doing here?" My eyes were drying out from how wide they were. I was stunned silent.

Cole was in front of me. Dressed as a knight. And within a football field's distance of a horse. He'd ridden in here on a horse, aka hell beast or any other number of things he'd called—more like cursed—them.

He stepped forward and took my hands.

The cold metal of the costume pinched from how he gripped them.

"What are you doing here?" My gaze skimmed over the droves of people gathering behind him.

He took a deep breath, rumbling the metal across his chest. "Kennedy Finch, I came here to tell you and show you that I know I fucked up, beyond fucked up, but I wanted to prove to you how much you mean to me."

"Puppy Love is over, man!" A guy in the crowd shouted. The circle of onlookers around us grew. I ducked my head, not loving being at the center of yet another romantic display. Normally, the spotlight couldn't get bright enough, but I was happy to fade into the background now. Did everyone think I'd paid him to show up here or that we were trying to pull a different scam?

"You hate horses." Leaning in, I whispered for his ears only. "I thought you were terrified of them."

It snorted behind him and Cole jumped again, jangling his armor. "It felt appropriate to face one of my fears because if I didn't, I might have to face my new biggest one." He took both my hands.

"What's that?" I whispered.

"Living the rest of my life without you. I love you, Kennedy. I've never loved anyone before, but you're it for me."

A thrill rushed through me at a literal knight showing up for me. Even after all the fake stuff we'd pulled off over the last month, this certainly took the cake. But we still had our problem. The problem that led to Cole blowing up at me and me not wanting to repeat the mistakes I'd promised I never would. Being alone hurt when he was so close, but taking that risk was throwing away how careful I'd been to not stumble down a path of pain.

Suddenly, things felt claustrophobic. The twenty-foot ceilings closed in along with the crush of people.

It would be so easy to believe him. So easy to forget what happened.

Cole stood in front of me in a shiny costume, professing his love for me. It scared the shit out of me. Not him, but how easy it would be to give in. Was this how things started with my parents? Sorries and apologies until they were to the point they couldn't be in a room together.

"Cole..." I wanted to say yes. I wanted this to be enough to make it all better. Better than before, but how could I trust him again?

"I can't," I whispered. Tears welled, stinging my eyes. I sucked in a shaky breath, breaking my own heart this time. "I wish I could say yes in front of all these people, but I can't. I can't do that to me." Turning, I rushed toward the open door at the back of the store where I'd be safe from prying eyes for now. After this, there would be even more staring. I'd need to armor up myself.

But Cole's costume wasn't exactly stealthy. The clanking metal followed behind me in a shortened gait. It's probably the only reason I made it into the refuge of the storeroom before he was on me.

He gently grabbed my arm and spun me around. "Kennedy—" His whole body stilled at my blinding tears.

"Why don't you two take my office to talk?" Gretchen walked past us and gestured toward the open door to her right. Over her shoulder prying eyes with their cameras at the ready filmed the whole thing.

My stomach clenched and curdled, and I tried to push my fears of their thoughts from my mind.

Inside the office, Cole stood in front of me with a crestfallen expression.

"I can't. Please just understand me, I can't do this with you again, Cole." My voice cracked, my heart cracked, my soul cracked.

He was so close. All I had to do was say yes. It would be so easy to say yes. The easiest of my life, but then what? What happened the next time or the time after that?

"I know you have no reason to believe me. I know I fucked up, even after you gave me a second chance, but I also know I love you, Kennedy."

The tears were in full force now. They were blinding, stringing pain streaking down my cheeks. It was hard to catch my breath and I wanted to reach for him. I wanted to believe. "I love you too, Cole, but sometimes love isn't enough."

37

COLE

I set the helmet down on the desk covered with binders and invoices.

She stood behind the desk with her arms wrapped around herself like her own protection.

I hated that she felt she needed it around me. The lump in my throat burned like a ball of icy hot.

"But sometimes love isn't enough." Her words reverberated through my head like I was still wearing the helmet and a sledgehammer had been taken to it.

Hadn't my mom thought she was in love with Mikelson? Hadn't she painted it with a brush of acceptance for a taste of what she thought was love? Hadn't she been willing to put up with anything, with his neglect, mistreatment, betrayal?

"You're right." My head dropped, so heavy I could barely keep it up.

She inhaled. Sharp. Quick. Shocked. "You don't—"

"It's not enough to say the words. It's not enough to show up and ask for your forgiveness with nothing to back it up." The vein in my neck throbbed, not with anger, but the strain of keeping myself calm, of not throwing myself at her feet and begging for another chance. But it didn't mean I was above grasping for any chance I might have. I swallowed, gravel clogging my throat.

"What if we started over? For real this time. Without playing pretend and social media tracking. Just me and you. I can rebuild your trust."

"Cole—" The single word swam in a pool of misery. "I —" She shook her head and seemed rooted to her spot on the other side of the desk. "That wouldn't change anything." Her eyes reddened, nostrils flared, and her chin quivered.

My heart constricted in my chest like someone grinding their cleats into it. This wasn't going to work. "I blew my second-chance card, didn't I? Knew that I hurt you, and I was so blinded by my own pain I unleashed it on you when all you wanted to do was help me. To protect me."

Her lips parted and chest lurched with a swallowed sob. Her eyes glistened with unshed tears, which lashed at me even harder.

The cracks in my chest deepened to chasms. "I'm sorry I came."

"You wish you hadn't?" she whispered.

I squeezed my eyes shut. "I regret this big, public sideshow. Putting you on the spot. It felt like a good idea at the time." I shrugged, the metal on metal squeaking and grating. Maybe part of me had hoped she wouldn't be able to turn me down if I made it as over-the-top as I could, which now made me feel like an even bigger asshole for trying to pressure her.

"It's very fairy-tale. I always wanted a knight to show up and sweep me away." A wistfulness entered her tone voice.

"And now..."

"Now." Her breath hitched. "Now, I realize it's easy to get

swept up in all the emotions and not fix anything that was broken in the first place."

I was plunging headfirst into the deep dark chasm. "I get it. I love you, Kennedy."

She blinked back at me. Her mouth opened and closed, chin quivering. "Goodbye, Cole."

This whole outfit felt fucking moronic right now. Like an idiot's play at something big to erase how I'd made her feel, how I'd hurt her. I tugged at the neck, ramming into my chest just below my throat. It was harder to breathe than when I'd first gotten on the horse. "I'm sorry I brought all this to your doorstep." Inhaling a shattering breath, I tried to fill my lungs with air and form words, but they all failed. My heart beat sluggishly in my chest, like moving the blood was too much work under this strain. I walked to the door and turned the knob.

"Cole!"

The urgency in her voice sent my heart soaring. My spin was made even more awkward by the chainmail and metal plates. "Yeah?"

"Your helmet." She picked up the shiny metal helmet with a blue-and-gold plume on top and held it out to me.

My hopes plunged into a rocky, muddy field. Another jagged strike to my chest. "Thanks." The word felt like a twenty-pound dumbbell lodged in my throat.

I walked out of the room and toward the bright light of the bookstore. From here, I could see the people standing, waiting for the triumphant kiss in front of them.

Maybe part of me had hoped, if I'd done this, she'd have a harder time spelling out that we were through. Had I said I wasn't an asshole? Each step doubled the pressure until my knees were seconds from buckling.

"Did he steal that from Fulton U?" someone whispered beside me.

Walking out past the racks of clothes and shelves of branded knickknacks, I tried to keep my head high, but what was the point? I'd surrendered all pride when I'd put this costume on and gotten on a damn horse to ride in here. If I didn't have Kennedy it didn't matter. Hiding it wouldn't make any of it easier.

The phones were out recording my failure. My rejection. My pain.

It felt deserved. A place I'd been trying to avoid for so long only to end up slamming into the concrete wall.

The horse snorted, clomping toward the exit. Security herded it out like it was another unruly customer.

Looking around, I had no idea where I was going. There was no plan for what now. But I sure as hell wasn't getting back on that horse.

I peeled off the pieces of armor, letting them fall to the floor. Each metallic clank was a piece of my heart being left behind. Left behind with Kennedy.

I was left in chainmail and shorts.

At the front of the store, people continued to stare and record me. Once, I'd soaked up the attention that came with being on the STFU team, but right now, they were all witnesses to my final failure. The one that felt like the wound might never close.

The squeak of sneakers on the tile turned a few heads including mine. Reid and Leona rushed toward me with faces drawn like I was painful to look at. Was it that clear? As sharp as it felt between my ribs.

"Do you need a ride?" Reid gripped my shoulder.

My head dropped, too heavy for a true nod.

Leona looped her arm around mine. "It'll be okay. She probably needs some more time."

"That won't help. She gave me another chance already." The desolation was all-consuming. It hurt more than I thought possible. Dealing with my father had hurt, but this was different. That was mourning a past that had never been. Wishing for a relationship that could never exist, but with Kennedy it had been there. In my hands, in my arms, in my heart. I'd felt her love and being without it was like the air had been sucked out of my lungs.

Reid picked up the rattling pieces of the costume off the floor.

I'd betrayed that trust that had been so hard for her to give me. I'd seen how much it affected her and her sister to deal with their parents, but I hadn't been able to stop myself. Maybe I didn't deserve her.

"You're both dealing with a lot." Leona guided me out of the store and patted my arm. Her comfort hurt worse. As much as she was my friend, I didn't want her standing beside me. I didn't want Reid ushering me to his car. I wanted Kennedy. I wanted her with me.

38

KENNEDY

The stockroom door that had closed behind Cole, not with a slam, but the gentle hydraulic hiss of the closing spring, opened again.

"Kennedy?" Gretchen poked her head in from the storefront. "You okay?"

I nodded, not trusting my voice. Not trusting any part of me not to sprint out the door and after Cole.

"Why don't you take a seat?" With her hands on my shoulders, she walked me back into the office. "Sit down for a little while."

My blood pounded in my throat making it hard to breathe.

"I'll go get you some water."

I nodded. My hands were clammy and tingling like I'd been wearing too tight gloves.

Gretchen left and it took long minutes of looking at the closed door to register my phone buzzing in my pocket. There was a gap in the ringing and it started up again.

I took it out.

Hannah's name flashed on the screen.

Taking shaky breaths, I wiped at my face with the heels of my hands and cleared my throat. During my texts or voice messages with her since Signing Day, I'd managed to keep a tight rein on my emotions, not letting her know how I was really feeling or that Cole and I were over. After a deep breath in, I answered. "Hannah? Is everything okay?"

"Fine, why wouldn't it be?"

"You rapid-fire called me three times."

"Oh! That was me checking in on you. I saw the video. Cole showed up on a horse? That's insane. Hand him the phone, I need to know how he got over his horse fear for that one."

I closed my eyes against the incoming disappointment. This was exactly why I had to stay strong to show Hannah what was and wasn't okay. "He—he's not here."

"Why not? Did campus security come get him?"

"No, he left."

"Why would he leave? Why isn't he there with you?"

"Because I told him to go."

"Until your shift was over?" Confusion flowed through each word.

"No, for forever. I told him we couldn't be together."

"Why the hell would you do that?"

"Hannah." I squeezed the bridge of my nose. "Because I'm not going to end up like Mom and Dad. I refuse to turn into them and live like they live."

"You and Cole are nothing like Mom and Dad," she said, baffled, like I'd said I wanted to live my life as a mermaid off the coast of Greece.

"You don't get it."

"Do you mean because he freaked out at you during Signing Day?"

"I—" The words caught in my throat. "How do you know about that?"

"The live stream and replay videos."

"You saw that?" I'd hoped to let her know Cole and I weren't together at the same time I gave her the tickets to Paris as a distraction.

"Of course I did."

"I'm sorry you had to see that."

"Don't be. Listen, Kennedy. I know living with Mom and Dad has fucked with our heads."

"Hannah—"

"Don't Hannah me. I'm sixteen, you don't think I know what curse words are? Just because I'm younger than you doesn't mean I don't understand."

Frustration surged through me. I couldn't rehash this with her—not right now. "I never said you didn't."

"Then let me be the first to tell you you're being stupid. Cole and you aren't the same as Mom and Dad. I've seen you two together. I've hung out with the two of you. There's not thick sour tension that invades a room once you're both together. There's no tiptoeing around, so either of you doesn't get set off. I could tell he loved you from the first time I saw you together."

"How'd you know?" My whisper was filled with disbelief. It had taken the two of us longer than that to admit how we felt about each other.

"He always looked out for you."

"That was just for the contest." I hated to burst her bubble; the best relationship modeled for her was a damn sham. But at least she deserved the truth.

"Maybe it started out that way, but there were plenty of times there was no one else around and he went out of his way for you. Opening doors, walking on the outside of the curb, warming up your hands when you said you didn't have gloves that went along with your outfit."

Our whole relationship—the real and fake parts came flooding back. Not just what he did, but the way what he did made me feel. "My heart hurts, Pickle."

"I know. I'm not saying what he did was okay or right, but maybe it's something he can work past. I feel like he was dealing with a lot with his coach being his dad. Maybe it was only about that one thing. That was his big red glowing 'Do Not Touch' button. How's he dealing with his dad situation?"

I pressed my fist against my forehead. "I don't know." Every blowup had always been about his dad. Those were the times he snapped, where the tension there had been tightened over his whole life.

"You're always the strong, responsible, kick-ass one, Kennedy. It's got to be scary to maybe be a little vulnerable with him. Letting him in close means he can hurt you."

My heart was splintering all over again. "And he did."

"Extenuating circumstances."

"What if it's not just about this one thing that he's keyed up about? What if this goes from arguing every so often, to every month to every week to every day?" There were gaps between the arguments for our parents once. Vaguely, I remember times when they laughed with one another before it became a marathon of screaming, shouting, and misery.

"People get upset. People get angry. It's a part of life. Do they sometimes yell, maybe shout a little? It happens. But that doesn't mean any time anyone raises their voice you have to hide under the blankets like we used to."

"How do I know if I'm making a mistake? If I'm becoming them?"

"I'll tell you."

"You're a kid." I wiped my nose with the back of my hand.

"A kid who's schooling your ass with some wisdom right now."

My laugh caught in my throat. "I don't know if I can *not* be afraid of what we might become."

"The only way you can prove it to yourself one way or another is to see where things go."

"But—"

"And if you don't trust yourself, trust me. I'd never let you turn into Mom or Dad. Just like you'd never let that happen to me. So we can make that promise right now. If one of us says the other is following in their footsteps, we warn each other and we believe each other. Deal?"

I released a shaky breath. "Deal."

"Now go get him. And tell him next time I see him, I'm expecting a huge gift."

A water-logged laugh escaped. "I will." Swallowing, I blinked back tears of love for the little girl who I'd take to the park for hours to be out of the house, who had turned into this person who was now there for me. "I love you, Hannah."

"I know you do. Stop stalling and go after your guy."

"I'm going."

"Love you, Kennedy." She ended the call.

I rushed out of the office and almost slammed into Gretchen.

Standing in front of me, she held up my coat and bag.

"What are you doing?"

"You thought I was going to miss the epic rush after your guy? Not in a million years."

"You knew I'd go after him?" I took my coat and scrambled to put it on, not worrying about the buttons.

"I had an inkling, at the very least, and if things didn't go that way, I thought you might want the rest of your shift off. But I'm glad to hear it was Option 1. Now go!" She shoved me toward the door.

"Everyone's so pushy all of a sudden."

"Shoe's on the other foot now."

I laughed and my chest loosened, no longer feeling like I'd been shoved into a corset that had been laced too tightly. Rushing out of the store, I didn't look at anyone else as I passed. There were bound to be people who'd seen Cole's knight act and his departure. But there was only one goal. Get to Cole.

Outside, I unlocked my bike from the rack. Then I was pedaling down the street. Wind whipped at my cheeks and stung my eyes. I pedaled faster, taking corners at high speed and nearly clipping a stop sign. Sweat gathered on my forehead and trailed down my neck.

I rode down a couple one-way streets then popped out on the long street that signaled the edge of campus. The street The Zoo was on. Three blocks from their house, I saw Reid's car pull into an empty spot steps from their porch.

Reid's lights turned off and he got out his side. Leona hopped out of the back, which must've meant Cole was in the front.

I pedaled faster with my coat flapping behind me.

The passenger side door opened and Cole stepped out, still in some of his knight gear.

He'd done that for me.

My heart swelled. "Cole, wait!"

His head whipped in my direction.

Ten feet from him, I ditched the bike and stumbled, nearly face-planting in front of him.

He was there. Arms around me, steadying me.

We stood, our breath mingling in the way-too-cold-for-spring air.

"What are you doing here?" He stared back at me with a hint of concern and a heaping helping of hope. Hope he put out there even if he'd be destroyed all over again.

People stopped on the sidewalk, but I didn't care about them. I focused on him. On his face. On his hands still holding on to me. On his eyes.

"What if we start over? What if we do this right this time? Take things slow. For real."

He was nodding before I finished the sentence. "A million times yes." His chin shook and he stared at me with moisture gathering in his eyes.

"You're not going to make fun of me for stealing your line?"

"You could steal everything I have, if it means I get to be with you." His hand cupped my cheeks and he kissed me.

I grabbed on to his chainmail and kissed him back. A heady kiss that left me unsteady on my feet. The kind that sent tingles tracing across my skin.

Panting, I stared at him. The tightness in my chest evaporated. "I love you, Cole."

"Sorry, who are you again? I don't think we've met before." He nuzzled my nose.

"How about we start over again tomorrow?"

"I'm game if you are."

Beside us, Reid walked by, pushing my bike. "Don't worry, I'll take care of this."

On the steps of the house, Leona jumped up and down punching her fists in the air.

I laughed and shook my head, shielding my eyes. A few people had stopped to watch with their phones out as always.

Turning to Cole, I looped my arm through his. "Too bad we weren't still in the competition. This would've definitely pushed us over the top."

His smile faltered. "I wanted you to have that trip." His sweetness made my teeth ache.

"And I told you, I'd figure it out. I did enough styling and have a few people signed up for spring interviewing that I'll be able to get Hannah and I there. Youth hostels and buses will be our friends, but I'm not going to complain, and I know she won't either."

We walked inside the house. Smells of meat wafted out into the living room from the kitchen.

After making it over the threshold, Griff rushed forward with long thudding strides and picked me up off the ground, squeezing me. "It worked!" He spun me around before setting me down and staring at me with full focus.

"Not really."

His head tilted like a confused St. Bernard. "It didn't?"

"I mean, it did, but that's not what made me choose him."

"What did?"

I took Cole's hands and hauled his arms up onto my shoulders. "I didn't want to spend the rest of my life afraid. I didn't want to be too afraid to let him love me like I deserve to be loved and how I want to love him."

Cole looked down at me with glistening eyes. "And I'll never take what you've given me for granted."

A blaring nose blow sliced through our tender moment.

Griff dabbed at his eyes with a roll of paper towels. "That

was beautiful." He clutched the crumpled up paper to his chest. "Just beautiful."

I rolled my eyes and laughed.

"Glad you're both here. The food will be finished soon."

"In that case..." Cole pressed his body against mine and moved one arm from my shoulder to my waist, walking me toward the stairs. "Call us when it's ready." He marched me backward up the stairs to his bedroom.

Both having the same idea, we frantically undressed each other. Chainmail dropped to the floor.

"Good thing you weren't still wearing the whole knight costume. That would've been a little harder to get off than this T-shirt."

"Another reason it was a terrible idea." His hands skimmed over my shoulders and down my arms. He backed up to the bed and sat, pulling me forward by the waistband of my underwear. "I love you, Kennedy." His arms settled at the small of my back and he looked up at me through the valley of my cleavage.

My heart swelled and fluttered, feeling like it was close to bursting with the warm, tingly sensation coursing through me. "I love you too. Thanks for letting me come back."

"You were never gone. Even if you hadn't come back to me, I'd always have a piece of you in here." He pressed my palm against his chest. "You're my heart, Kennedy."

EPILOGUE

KENNEDY

"What's this mean?" I waved Cole's phone in his face. My heart skipped in my chest. The email from the collegiate athletics board stirred hope in my chest. We were on his bed, getting ready for finals. Going to the library would've made more sense, but he did have a comfy bed. We also didn't have to gross everyone out with our excessive PDA.

Keeping our displays of affection smaller and just for us made them more special.

"It means they're leaving my punishment up to my program instead of banning me from playing next season."

The hope spark was doused just as quickly. "Meaning Mikelson would get to decide?" If there was ever a time I'd wanted to throat punch someone it was anytime his name was brought up.

"It would be, if Coach Henley hadn't been put in charge of player discipline."

"When did that happen?"

"A few days ago. The University Board met and the decision came down."

I flung my arms around his neck. "Seriously? Why didn't you tell me?"

"It didn't matter until the athletics board came back with their ruling. Coach Henley spoke on my behalf and apparently they're treating it as a family matter."

Mikelson was no one's fucking family.

"Do you know what punishment Henley will serve up? Do I need to go slash his tires?"

"Ruthless." He pecked me on the lips. "I'll probably have to sit out a few games. Maybe half the season."

I gasped.

He rubbed my thigh and squeezed it. "Henley will be fair. He made sure Silas got his spot and signed the offer letter. He won't be too brutal. Don't worry about me."

"Of course, I worry." I slumped back against his bedroom wall. "Taylor was so excited to shop for outfits for next season."

He lunged for me and I dissolved into a fit of laughter. Things had progressed a lot faster this time around.

It had been five weeks from Cole's big entrance at the bookstore and our relationship restart. A relationship on time lapse where the highlights were better the second time around.

"No freaking way!" Leona's shout rattled the floorboards.

I looked at Cole and lifted my legs off his, scrambling off the bed and out his bedroom door. "What happened?" I jogged down the stairs, Leona spun and charged up them nearly butting heads with me on the last step.

Ezra sat in the living room looking like Leona wasn't screeching at the top of her lungs, which meant it wasn't anything terrible or he'd be in fix-it mode.

"What is it?"

She thrust her phone at me. "I thought we weren't reading STFU Dirt anymore."

Leona looked up at me like I'd caught her sneaking out of her room. "I know. They suck, but they also have the scoop on a lot of stuff. Like this!" She waved her phone and wrapped my fingers around the case.

My eyes darted from the picture of a couple I recognized. "Did they get engaged?"

"No, the caption." She tapped her screen so hard the phone almost fell out of my grasp.

Holding on tight, I read the words, but my brain was a few seconds later with the processing.

Cole's steps creaked behind me.

"No freaking way!" I read and re-read the caption and that hummingbird hope in my chest took flight all over again.

"Everything okay?"

Ezra put down his guitar and stood, walking over to Leona's side.

Griff burst into the house sweaty and out of breath. "Did you guys see it?"

"What's going on?" Cole waved his arms in the air to try to get someone's attention.

I turned and held Leona's phone up.

"Hey, isn't that Mason Alcott?" Of course, he'd recognize the football player.

"The caption." Cole's gaze scanned the posting. "No freaking way." His legs gave out and he plopped down onto the bottom step. "Puppy Love benefactors revealed." He read it out loud.

"LA Lions Quarterback, Mason Alcott, and fashion designer fiancée, Amelia Darcy, have revealed their Puppy

Love connection and a special treat for the couple booted in final run up to the contest close. There's a video."

"There is?" I squeezed onto the step beside him.

Leona hung over the railing to get a better look.

Ezra being sensible, pulled out his own phone.

"What's everyone doing?" Hollis walked out with a handful of chicken tenders.

"Shh!" A collective sound from everyone around me.

Cole tapped on the play icon and the video started. The two of them had their faces smushed together to fit into the frame.

"First, we wanted to say thank you to all the Puppy Love participants and to the winners. Our time at STFU was some of the best of our lives and we loved seeing you showering campus in all your love for each other. It brought back so many great memories and we hope you all made some too."

"This message goes out to Cole and Kennedy." Mason took over. "We were rooting for you two the whole way through. Although it seems you two got into this for all the wrong reasons, we know you learned a lot and loved even more throughout it. It's hard to fake that kind of thing, we should know." The two of them shared a not-so secret look. "Because you pulled out all the stops, and may or may not have pulled off an epic prank against a certain rival, we thought it was only fair that you two have a shot at a consolation prize. Check your DMs and we'll see what we can do."

I popped up and nearly toppled down the stairs.

Cole caught me, giving me a shove in the direction of his room. Recovering, I darted into his room and swiped both our phones.

In my messages sat an unread one from Amelia. I tapped out a simple message.

Me: Hi

The message popped up in seconds.

I gasped and covered my mouth with my hand. "She's responding. Holy shit!"

I dropped Cole's phone into his lap and slumped against the wall.

"What does it say?" The six of them shouted at me.

"She's invited me to the summer and fall Paris Fashion Weeks and offered me an internship at her label." I repeated the words, my lips barely moving. Like if I said this too loudly all the messages would evaporate.

Cole hugged me and I buried my face in his chest. "See what Mason said." Tears burned in my eyes, turning my gaze watery.

My fingers trembled so hard, I had to retype my reply five times. I responded with all the thanks and a small ask I had no right to ask, but had do.

"And she said Hannah can come with me." I brushed away an escaped tear.

Leona flung herself at Cole and I, squashing the both of us. "That's amazing."

"That's not all," Kennedy mumbled beneath the Leona bear hug.

"It's not." Leona let go and sat on her haunches.

Reid grabbed the phone from Cole. He looked from the screen back to Cole and to the screen again. "He invited Cole to work out with him this summer and to attend training camp." His voice overflowed with awe.

I couldn't feel my arms or legs. Shock. One hundred percent shock had frozen every muscle.

Cole tackled me against the stairs, his full body weight on me with a hand behind my head protecting it from the hard wood.

I wrapped my legs around him and kissed him all over his face. My watery laughter mingled with his.

"This calls for a celebration." To my right, Leona marched out of the kitchen and handed Cole and I drinks through the banister railings.

Cole helped me up and held out his hand. We came downstairs and joined everyone in the living room.

Griff lifted his drink high above his head. "To Cole and Kennedy and to next season being the one where we finally get it done."

Everyone cheered and clinked their bottlenecks together. Cole wrapped his arms around me and tapped his bottle against mine.

On the TV, Predator played with no sound. Ezra mouthed the lines between pulls on his beer.

Leona sat on Reid's lap sharing a beer. She grimaced after each gulp.

"There's got to be another cider in the fridge. You can have mine if you want." I held out the bottle I hadn't yet taken a sip of.

"No." She shot up and screamed like I'd offered to set her hair on fire. With a face screwed up like she was drinking turpentine, she finished the beer they'd been sharing. "I don't need another drink, but I do have something for you." She walked over to me and put both her hands on my shoulders. "You're it." Spinning, she grabbed Reid's hand and bolted out through the kitchen. The back door slammed before anyone else moved.

Everyone around me checked the time. I turned, drink still in hand. "What the hell?"

Griff and Ezra turned their bottles upside down.

I whirled around.

Ezra dove for the front door. "I'm not getting stuck with clean up duty again."

Griff's footfalls right behind him shook the house.

"Am I really it?" I turned expecting a smoke plume where Cole had once been.

"Looks like you are." He grinned and leisurely sipped on his drink.

"You're not running?"

He stepped close and wrapped his arm around my waist, tugging me against him. "Not ever."

I walked over to him and rested my palms on his chest. "You're willing to take the hit for me?"

"Just like I did in paintball?" He brushed a curl back from my face.

Shock blazed through me. "You remembered?"

His full lips spread into an endearing smile that made my heart hum. "Of course I did, just like I remember how I felt that day you let me borrow your pen."

A gasp shot from my throat. "Why didn't you say something before?"

"And let you know I had a thing for you for years before I had the balls to go for it?"

"Who doesn't want to be wanted?" My mind whirred with this new information. "So you want to be it?"

"For you, I'm willing to be anything."

"Good thing I love you just as you are."

"Good thing." He kissed me. A kiss where time had no meaning, neither did the game or our pasts. Only the future together and the love he showed me every day.

～

Wow! Thank you for being here for Cole and Kennedy's story! Getting to know them and their struggles was so much fun throughout this story. I hope you enjoyed it as much as I enjoyed writing it. Grab another scene with these two, right here!

Ezra's story is up next! And our brooding football player, who you might know as Johannsen from the Fulton U books, is ready to meet you!

Want to meet their rivals?

The Perfect First - First Time/Mistaken Identity

The Third Best Thing - Secret Admirer

EPILOGUE

KENNEDY

"What's this mean?" I waved Cole's phone in his face. My heart skipped in my chest. The email from the collegiate athletics board stirred hope in my chest. We were on his bed, getting ready for finals. Going to the library would've made more sense, but he did have a comfy bed. We also didn't have to gross everyone out with our excessive PDA.

Keeping our displays of affection smaller and just for us made them more special.

"It means they're leaving my punishment up to my program instead of banning me from playing next season."

The hope spark was doused just as quickly. "Meaning Mikelson would get to decide?" If there was ever a time I'd wanted to throat punch someone it was anytime his name was brought up.

"It would be, if Coach Henley hadn't been put in charge of player discipline."

"When did that happen?"

"A few days ago. The University Board met and the decision came down."

I flung my arms around his neck. "Seriously? Why didn't you tell me?"

"It didn't matter until the athletics board came back with their ruling. Coach Henley spoke on my behalf and apparently they're treating it as a family matter."

Mikelson was no one's fucking family.

"Do you know what punishment Henley will serve up? Do I need to go slash his tires?"

"Ruthless." He pecked me on the lips. "I'll probably have to sit out a few games. Maybe half the season."

I gasped.

He rubbed my thigh and squeezed it. "Henley will be fair. He made sure Silas got his spot and signed the offer letter. He won't be too brutal. Don't worry about me."

"Of course, I worry." I slumped back against his bedroom wall. "Taylor was so excited to shop for outfits for next season."

He lunged for me and I dissolved into a fit of laughter. Things had progressed a lot faster this time around.

It had been five weeks from Cole's big entrance at the bookstore and our relationship restart. A relationship on time lapse where the highlights were better the second time around.

"No freaking way!" Leona's shout rattled the floorboards.

I looked at Cole and lifted my legs off his, scrambling off the bed and out his bedroom door. "What happened?" I jogged down the stairs, Leona spun and charged up them nearly butting heads with me on the last step.

Ezra sat in the living room looking like Leona wasn't screeching at the top of her lungs, which meant it wasn't anything terrible or he'd be in fix-it mode.

"What is it?"

She thrust her phone at me. "I thought we weren't reading STFU Dirt anymore."

Leona looked up at me like I'd caught her sneaking out of her room. "I know. They suck, but they also have the scoop on a lot of stuff. Like this!" She waved her phone and wrapped my fingers around the case.

My eyes darted from the picture of a couple I recognized. "Did they get engaged?"

"No, the caption." She tapped her screen so hard the phone almost fell out of my grasp.

Holding on tight, I read the words, but my brain was a few seconds later with the processing.

Cole's steps creaked behind me.

"No freaking way!" I read and re-read the caption and that hummingbird hope in my chest took flight all over again.

"Everything okay?"

Ezra put down his guitar and stood, walking over to Leona's side.

Griff burst into the house sweaty and out of breath. "Did you guys see it?"

"What's going on?" Cole waved his arms in the air to try to get someone's attention.

I turned and held Leona's phone up.

"Hey, isn't that Mason Alcott?" Of course, he'd recognize the football player.

"The caption." Cole's gaze scanned the posting. "No freaking way." His legs gave out and he plopped down onto the bottom step. "Puppy Love benefactors revealed." He read it out loud.

"LA Lions Quarterback, Mason Alcott, and fashion designer fiancée, Amelia Darcy, have revealed their Puppy

Love connection and a special treat for the couple booted in final run up to the contest close. There's a video."

"There is?" I squeezed onto the step beside him.

Leona hung over the railing to get a better look.

Ezra being sensible, pulled out his own phone.

"What's everyone doing?" Hollis walked out with a handful of chicken tenders.

"Shh!" A collective sound from everyone around me.

Cole tapped on the play icon and the video started. The two of them had their faces smushed together to fit into the frame.

"First, we wanted to say thank you to all the Puppy Love participants and to the winners. Our time at STFU was some of the best of our lives and we loved seeing you showering campus in all your love for each other. It brought back so many great memories and we hope you all made some too."

"This message goes out to Cole and Kennedy." Mason took over. "We were rooting for you two the whole way through. Although it seems you two got into this for all the wrong reasons, we know you learned a lot and loved even more throughout it. It's hard to fake that kind of thing, we should know." The two of them shared a not-so secret look. "Because you pulled out all the stops, and may or may not have pulled off an epic prank against a certain rival, we thought it was only fair that you two have a shot at a consolation prize. Check your DMs and we'll see what we can do."

I popped up and nearly toppled down the stairs.

Cole caught me, giving me a shove in the direction of his room. Recovering, I darted into his room and swiped both our phones.

In my messages sat an unread one from Amelia. I tapped out a simple message.

Me: Hi

The message popped up in seconds.

I gasped and covered my mouth with my hand. "She's responding. Holy shit!"

I dropped Cole's phone into his lap and slumped against the wall.

"What does it say?" The six of them shouted at me.

"She's invited me to the summer and fall Paris Fashion Weeks and offered me an internship at her label." I repeated the words, my lips barely moving. Like if I said this too loudly all the messages would evaporate.

Cole hugged me and I buried my face in his chest. "See what Mason said." Tears burned in my eyes, turning my gaze watery.

My fingers trembled so hard, I had to retype my reply five times. I responded with all the thanks and a small ask I had no right to ask, but had do.

"And she said Hannah can come with me." I brushed away an escaped tear.

Leona flung herself at Cole and I, squashing the both of us. "That's amazing."

"That's not all," Kennedy mumbled beneath the Leona bear hug.

"It's not." Leona let go and sat on her haunches.

Reid grabbed the phone from Cole. He looked from the screen back to Cole and to the screen again. "He invited Cole to work out with him this summer and to attend training camp." His voice overflowed with awe.

I couldn't feel my arms or legs. Shock. One hundred percent shock had frozen every muscle.

Cole tackled me against the stairs, his full body weight on me with a hand behind my head protecting it from the hard wood.

I wrapped my legs around him and kissed him all over his face. My watery laughter mingled with his.

"This calls for a celebration." To my right, Leona marched out of the kitchen and handed Cole and I drinks through the banister railings.

Cole helped me up and held out his hand. We came downstairs and joined everyone in the living room.

Griff lifted his drink high above his head. "To Cole and Kennedy and to next season being the one where we finally get it done."

Everyone cheered and clinked their bottlenecks together. Cole wrapped his arms around me and tapped his bottle against mine.

On the TV, Predator played with no sound. Ezra mouthed the lines between pulls on his beer.

Leona sat on Reid's lap sharing a beer. She grimaced after each gulp.

"There's got to be another cider in the fridge. You can have mine if you want." I held out the bottle I hadn't yet taken a sip of.

"No." She shot up and screamed like I'd offered to set her hair on fire. With a face screwed up like she was drinking turpentine, she finished the beer they'd been sharing. "I don't need another drink, but I do have something for you." She walked over to me and put both her hands on my shoulders. "You're it." Spinning, she grabbed Reid's hand and bolted out through the kitchen. The back door slammed before anyone else moved.

Everyone around me checked the time. I turned, drink still in hand. "What the hell?"

Griff and Ezra turned their bottles upside down.

I whirled around.

Ezra dove for the front door. "I'm not getting stuck with clean up duty again."

Griff's footfalls right behind him shook the house.

"Am I really it?" I turned expecting a smoke plume where Cole had once been.

"Looks like you are." He grinned and leisurely sipped on his drink.

"You're not running?"

He stepped close and wrapped his arm around my waist, tugging me against him. "Not ever."

I walked over to him and rested my palms on his chest. "You're willing to take the hit for me?"

"Just like I did in paintball?" He brushed a curl back from my face.

Shock blazed through me. "You remembered?"

His full lips spread into an endearing smile that made my heart hum. "Of course I did, just like I remember how I felt that day you let me borrow your pen."

A gasp shot from my throat. "Why didn't you say something before?"

"And let you know I had a thing for you for years before I had the balls to go for it?"

"Who doesn't want to be wanted?" My mind whirred with this new information. "So you want to be it?"

"For you, I'm willing to be anything."

"Good thing I love you just as you are."

"Good thing." He kissed me. A kiss where time had no meaning, neither did the game or our pasts. Only the future together and the love he showed me every day.

～

Wow! Thank you for being here for Cole and Kennedy's story! Getting to know them and their struggles was so much fun throughout this story. I hope you enjoyed it as much as I enjoyed writing it. Grab another scene with these two, right here (https://dl.bookfunnel.com/gxh99dk4f1)!

Ezra's story is up next! And our brooding football player, who you might know as Johannsen from the Fulton U books, is ready to meet you!

Want to meet their rivals?

The Perfect First - First Time/Mistaken Identity

The Third Best Thing - Secret Admirer

EXCERPT FROM THE PERFECT FIRST

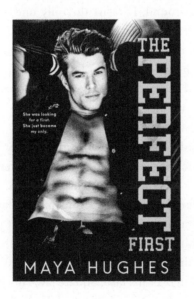

Seph - Project De-virginization

The jingle sounded again as the door to the coffee shop swung open. My head snapped up and my bouncing leg froze. The sun shone through the doorway and a figure stood there. He was tall, taller than anyone who'd come in before. His muscles were obvious even under his coat. He paused at the entrance, his head moving from side to side like he knew people would be looking back, like he was giving everyone a chance to soak in his presence. His jet black hair was tousled just right, like he'd been running his fingers through it on the walk over from wherever he'd come from. The jacket fit him perfectly, like it had been tailored just for his body.

I glanced around; I wasn't the only one who'd noticed him walk in. He seemed familiar, but I couldn't place him. He bent forward, and I thought he was going to tie his shoes, but instead he wiped a wet leaf off his pristine white sneaker. Heads turned as he crossed the floor toward me. Squeezing my fingers tighter around the notecards, I reminded myself to breathe.

He glanced around again and spotted me. The green in his eyes was clear even from across the coffee shop. Dark hair with eyes like that wasn't a usual combo. He froze and his lips squeezed together. With his hands shoved into his pockets, he stalked toward me with a *Let's get this over with* look. That didn't bode well. He stood beside the seat on the other side of the booth, staring at me expectantly.

My gaze ran over his face. Square jaw. Hint of stubble on his cheeks and chin. My skin flushed. He had beautiful lips. What would his feel like on my mouth? I ran my finger over my bottom lip. What would they feel like on other parts of me? My body responded and I thanked God I had on a bra, shirt, and blazer or I'd have been flashing him some serious high beams. This was a good sign.

He cleared his throat.

Jumping, I dropped my hand, and the heat in my cheeks turned into a flamethrower on my neck. "Sorry, have a seat." I half stood from my spot in the booth and extended my hand toward the other side across from me. The table dug into my thighs and I fell back into the soft seat.

Sliding in opposite me, he unzipped his coat and put his arm over the back of the shiny booth.

"Hi, very nice to meet you. I'm Seph." I shot my hand out across the table between us. The cuff of my blazer tightened as it rode up my arm.

His eyebrows scrunched together. "Seth?" He leaned in, his forearms resting on the edge of the table. He was nothing like the guys from the math department. They were quiet, sometimes obnoxious, and none of them made my stomach ricochet around inside me like it was trying to win a gold medal in gymnastics at the Olympics.

I tamped down a giggle. I did *not* giggle. The sound came out like a sharp snort, and I resisted the urge to slam my eyes shut and crawl under the table. *Be cool, Seph. Be cool.* "No—Seph. It's short for Persephone."

He lifted one eyebrow.

"Greek goddess of spring. Daughter of Demeter and Zeus. You know what, never mind. I'm glad you agreed to meet with me today."

"Not like I had much choice." He leaned back and ran his knuckles along the table top, rapping out a haphazard rhythm.

I licked my lips and parted them. Not like he had much choice? Had someone put him up to this? Had something in my post made him feel obligated to come? I hadn't been able to bring myself to go back and look at it after posting it.

Shaking my head, I stuck my hand out again. "Nice to meet you..."

He looked down at my hand and back up at me, letting out a bored breath. "Reece. Reece Michaels."

"Very nice to meet you, Reece. I'm Persephone Alexander. I have a few questions we can get started with, if you don't mind."

"The quicker we get started, the quicker we can finish." He looked around like he would have rather been anywhere but there.

Those giddy bubbles soured in my stomach. A server came by with the bottled waters I'd ordered. I arranged them in a neat pyramid at the end of the table.

"Would you like a water?" I held one out to him.

He eyed me like I was offering him an illicit substance, but then reached out. His fingers brushed against the backs of mine and shooting sparks of excitement rushed through me. Pulling the bottle out of my grasp, he cracked it open and took a gulp.

My cheeks heated and I glanced down at my cards, flipping the ones at the front to the back.

"I have a notecard with some information for you to fill out."

Sliding it across the table, I held out a pen for him. He took it from me, careful that our fingers didn't touch this time. I'd have been lying if I'd said I didn't want another touch, just to test whether or not that first one had been something more than static electricity. He filled out the biographical data on the card and handed it back to me.

I scanned it. He was twenty-one. Had a birthday coming up just after the New Year. Good height-to-weight ratio. Grabbing my pen, I scanned over the questions I'd prepared for my meetings.

"Let's get started." *Just rip the Band-Aid off.* Clearing my throat, I tapped the cards on the table. A few heads turned in our direction at the sharp, rapping sound. "When were you last tested for sexually transmitted diseases?"

Setting the bottle down on the table, he stared at me like I was an equation he was suddenly interested in figuring out. And then it was gone. "At the beginning of the season. Clean bill of health." He looked over his shoulder, the boredom back, leaking from every pore. *Wow.* I'd thought guys were all over this whole sex thing, but he looked like he was sitting in the waiting room of a dentist's office.

"When did you last have sexual intercourse?"

His head snapped back to me, eyes bugged out. "What?" I had his full attention now.

"Sex? When did you last have sex?" I tapped my pen against the notecard.

He sputtered and stared back at me. His eyes narrowed and he rested his elbows on the table.

I scooted my neatly lain out cards back toward me, away from him.

"No comment."

"Given the circumstances, it's an appropriate question."

The muscles in his neck tightened and his lips crumpled together. "Fine, at the beginning of the season."

"What season?" I looked up from my pen. That was an odd way to put it. "Like, the beginning of fall?"

"Like football season."

The pieces fit together—the body, the looks from other people around the coffee house. "You play football." That made sense, and he seemed like the perfect all-American person for the job.

"Yes, I play football."

"When did the season start?"

He shook his head like he was trying to clear away a fog and stared back at me like I'd started speaking a different language. "September."

"And..." I ran my hand along the back of my neck. "How long would you say it lasted?"

His eyebrows dipped. "It didn't last. It was a one-night thing. I don't do relationships."

Of course not. He was playing the field. Sowing his oats. Banging his way through as many co-eds as possible. Experienced. Excellent.

I cleared my throat. "No, I didn't mean how long did you date the woman. I meant, how long was the sex?"

The steady drumming on the table stopped. "Are you serious?"

I licked my Sahara-dry lips. "It's a reasonable question. How long did it last?"

"I didn't exactly set a timer, but let's just say we both got our reward."

"Interesting." I made another note on the card.

"These are the types of questions I'm going to be asked for the draft?" He took the lid off the bottled water.

The draft? Pushing ahead, I went to the next line one my card and cringed a bit. "Okay, this might seem a little invasive." I cleared my throat again. "But how big is your penis? Length is fine. I don't need to know the circumference, you know—the girth."

A fine spray of water from his mouth washed over me. "What the hell kind of question is that? I know you're trying to throw me off my game, but holy shit, lady."

～

Persephone Alexander. Math genius. Lover of blazers. The only girl I know who can make Heidi braids look sexy as hell. And she's on a mission. Lose her virginity by the end of the semester.

I walked in on her interview session for potential candidates (who even does that?) and saw straight through her brave front. She's got a list of Firsts to accomplish like she's only got months to live. I've decided to be her guide for all her firsts except one. Someone's got to keep her out of trouble. I have one rule, no sex. We even shook on it.

I'll help her find the right guy for the job. Someone like her doesn't need someone like me and my massive...baggage for her first time.

Drinking at a bar. Check.

Partying all night. Double check.

Skinny dipping. Triple check.

She's unlike anyone I've ever met. The walls I'd put up around my heart are slowly crumbling with each touch that sets fire to my soul.

I'm the first to bend the rules. One electrifying kiss changes everything and suddenly I don't want to be her first, I want to be her only. But her plan was written before I came onto the scene and now I'm determined to get her to rewrite her future with me.

Grab your copy of The Perfect First or read it for FREE in Kindle Unlimited at https://amzn.to/2ZqEMzl

ALSO BY MAYA HUGHES

Fulton U

The Second We Met - Enemies to Lovers Romance

The Third Best Thing - Secret Admirer Romance

The Fourth Time Charm

The Fulton U Falling Trilogy

The Art of Falling for You

The Sin of Kissing You

The Hate of Loving You

Kings of Rittenhouse

Kings of Rittenhouse - FREE

Shameless King - Enemies to Lovers

Reckless King - Off Limits Lover

Ruthless King - Second Chance Romance

SWANK

The Proposal

The Sweetest Thing

CONNECT WITH MAYA

Sign up for my newsletter to get exclusive bonus content, ARC opportunities, sneak peeks, new release alerts and to find out just what I'm books are coming up next.

Join my reader group for teasers, giveaways and more!

Follow my Amazon author page for new release alerts!

Follow me on Instagram, where I try and fail to take pretty pictures!

Follow me on Twitter, just because :)

I'd love to hear from you! Drop me a line anytime :)
https://www.mayahughes.com/
maya@mayahughes.com

Made in the USA
Monee, IL
20 June 2023

36427504R00246